# RISE OF THE DRAGON RIDERS

*Dragon Tongue*

*Dragon Scales*

*Dragon Fire*

*Dragon Plague*

*Dragon Crystals*

*Dragon Wars*

# DRAGON CRYSTALS

## RISE OF THE DRAGON RIDERS : BOOK FIVE

## AVA RICHARDSON

# BLURB

*A girl and her dragon must conquer an ancient evil, before it's too late...*

Dragon rider Cora, her dragon Alaric, and their allies have shielded the dragon rider school from the vicious Blight... for now. But the deadly plague is still a threat, and if the sinister forces who control it find the Heart of Tenegard, there will be no stopping it.

Cora soon discovers that the Blight is even more dangerous than imagined, spawning deadly beasts that can't be killed. As war looms on the horizon, time is running out to banish this supernatural evil.

Cora's enemies have forged new alliances, and grow more dangerous by the day. Her best hope to defeat them is an arrogant dragon rider with secrets of his own. Trusting the wrong person has already led to one disaster. Doing it again could lead to utter catastrophe...

This could be her only chance to save Tenegard. But if she fails, everything Cora knows and loves will perish...

# MAILING LIST

**Thank you for purchasing *Dragon Crystals*
(Rise of the Dragon Riders Book Five)**

If you would like to hear more about what I am up to, or continue to follow the stories set in this world with these characters—then please take a look at:

AvaRichardsonBooks.com

You can also find me on me on
www.facebook.com/AvaRichardsonBooks

Or sign up to my mailing list:
AvaRichardsonBooks.com/mailing-list

# CONTENTS

# CHAPTER 1

## CORA

The shield surrounding the school was only visible on sunny days. If Cora tilted her head at the right moment and waited for the clouds to pass, the sun would catch in the web of magic, briefly sending a kaleidoscope of shimmering color waving over the entire school like a ripple over water.

For a moment, there were hues of pink and purple, blues a shade lighter than the sky itself, and greens as lush as the woods after a rainstorm. Sometimes, if she squinted, there were oranges to match the helenium flowers she'd picked at the base of the mountains in Barcroft as a little girl and bursts of yellow that reminded her of flying blindly into the sunrise on the back of her great, winged dragon, Alaric.

As beautiful as it all was, Cora would never forget the battle that had necessitated the shield in the first place or the comfort it now brought the dragon riders to be surrounded by its protective charms. The school, bathed in the warmth of a new day, had finally started to feel like home again after so many days of panic and uncertainty. Trainees moved across the campus with their dragons by their sides, attending lessons and lifting in flight, practicing aerial skills.

The routine was familiar to Cora, and she was glad for this one part of her day that felt normal, but an anxious beat had pulsed in the back of her mind this past week. She needed to resume her search for the Heart of Tenegard, the source the subterranean crystal river flowed to, the source of Tenegardian magic. She had to return to her mission.

"It's quite the sight," Elaine marveled. "No matter how many times I witness it, I don't think I'll ever grow accustomed to seeing a dragon rider take to the sky."

Cora turned to the healer who had joined her for this morning's walk. "There were days when I didn't think I'd ever get to see the trainees and their dragons up there again."

"Those days are behind us now," Elaine said with a measure of certainty and confidence that Cora wished she possessed.

Elaine had come into Cora's life when Cora's partner Faron had enlisted Elaine's help in the war against Onyx, the tyrannical king they had defeated more than ten months ago. Elaine had remained after the war and fallen in love with Cora's father. They'd married not long ago, the day of the wedding so serene, so perfect. How quickly everything had gone downhill since then.

Cora paused between the school buildings to watch a team of dragon riders soar past in a complex battle formation, letting herself pretend for a moment that the trouble of the previous weeks had never occurred. When some of the dragon riders mysteriously fell ill with what they had then coined the sleeping sickness, Cora had put out a call for help, and Melusine had been among those who turned up. Cora had truly believed the young healer was there to help the school, but it had all been a ruse. Melusine had invited the Blight into their midst, a strange and powerful creature of unknown origin, to feed off the magical bonds between dragons and dragon riders.

The thought of the betrayal filled Cora's chest with a raging heat. Her fists curled so tightly her nails bit against her palms.

Elaine, noticing, took her hand.

Though they had banished Melusine and the Blight from the school, the trainees and dragons who had been affected by the creature did not wake. Their magical wounds no longer seeped, but they remained trapped in endless sleep. Even Cora had been touched by the Blight's evil and her bond with her dragon had been damaged enough that their ability to communicate continued to suffer greatly.

And all for what?

Cora didn't know what Melusine's ultimate endgame was. The healer had led Cora and her friends into the mountains under the guise of helping them find a cure. And though they had located a magical subterranean river that would supposedly lead to what they determined was the Heart of Tenegard, Melusine had only wanted access to the wellspring for nefarious purposes. She'd intended to feed the Blight from the wellspring, destroying all of Tenegard's magic in the process. Cora had never figured out why Melusine was so determined to destroy it, nor who she might have been working for, but now she saw the sorceress for what she truly was: the enemy. That's why reconvening her search for the river was so important. Melusine, in the wake of her failure at the school, was likely doing the same.

Cora's thoughts turned to Faron suddenly. He'd been attacked by the Blight in the mountains, immediately falling unconscious. Though he was well cared for by Elaine and the other healers, his body remained in the infirmary, caught somewhere between life and death. He was part of the reason she'd lingered after Melusine's attack instead of immediately resuming her search for the river and the heart. Of course, she'd wanted to ensure that Melusine wouldn't try to mount another strike against the school, and she'd also wanted to be sure that the shield held, but she'd hoped Faron would wake up, that he would be by her side once again, and she could stop feeling guilty.

"I wish I possessed even half of your certainty that those days are truly behind us," Cora told Elaine.

The healer looped their arms together. "I have to be certain. I refuse to even give recognition to the thought that we will lose any more of the victims."

"And how are they faring?" Cora asked. This question had become part of a regular update that Elaine provided her.

The healer hesitated a moment. "There has been no change."

Cora nodded. She'd learned recently that sometimes no change was good news, though she could hear a *but* in Elaine's tone.

She stopped suddenly, pulling Elaine to a halt. They were in sight of the infirmary. From where they stood, Cora could make out the roof of the converted dorm that now housed the victims. "There's something you're not saying. Are the dragon scales not working anymore?"

After a long battle of wits with the council in Kaerlin, the school had finally received the remaining stockpile of dragon scales from the capital. They were able to use them to bolster the sick dragons and their trainees, but even the scales had not woken the victims.

"It's not the scales," Elaine assured her. "They are working as well as we can expect. But I've conferred with my colleagues. And though we all agree that the Blight's hold on the victims has been broken and they are no longer losing magic to the creature, there is still concern."

Cora swallowed hard. "Go on."

"The longer the victims remain unconscious, the more work they will have to do to regain their strength once they awake."

There it was. The thought that kept Cora up at night. She sighed as they began walking again.

"They're sustained on their remaining magic and what little broth we can get into them," Elaine continued, "but the reality is that they're weak. And they will feel it most when they wake."

The hopeful look on Elaine's face remained in place despite her words, and though Cora was trying to be positive, she couldn't help her mind from drifting to the thought that it wasn't *when* the victims awoke but *if.*

"The victims will be in no shape for dragon riding," Elaine said. "Not for a while."

"Or perhaps ever," Cora muttered. "We have no clue what shape their bonds will be in."

Elaine didn't argue that point. If Cora and Alaric were any indication, it could very well be possible that even if the victims regained consciousness, their bonds might be too damaged to sustain the dragon rider relationship.

"If I only knew *how* to wake them," Cora said. The shield shimmered above them, but whatever beauty it held had been eclipsed by the nagging worry that the remaining victims of the Blight's attacks might die upon their cots. The truth was that they didn't fully understand the enemy they were facing or the ramifications to come. What was worse, other than Melusine, they still had no idea who they were dealing with because there was no way she was working alone.

That's why Cora needed to wake the victims now, and to do that, she had to start tracking the river again to reach the heart. The anxious beat in the back of her mind worsened. Elaine was right. The longer the sickness lingered, the more uncertainty there would be surrounding the victims' recovery.

"You'll find a way," Elaine said, oozing more of that certainty Cora wished she could bottle and harness. "The trainees are lucky to have you fighting for them. *Faron* is lucky to have you."

They reached the infirmary and Cora hesitated at the door. The burden of being without answers dragged at her, and Cora wasn't sure she could face the other healers, never mind the gaunt, unconscious faces of the trainees.

"Come along, then." Elaine's tone was brisk, as if she would have none of Cora's uncertainty. "Your presence is a balm to him. His color is always better after you've visited." She steered Cora by the shoulders, ushering her inside. Cora took a deep breath, steeling herself against the nagging thoughts of failure that plagued her every time she walked through this door, certain Elaine was only telling her what she wanted to hear.

Inside, she braced for the sight of all the bodies. Among the rows and rows of cots, Faron's form drew her gaze instantly, as if some magnet pulled her to him. She'd spent so much time at his side in the weeks since the battle with Melusine had ended, that a stool had been permanently set at his cot for her.

Elaine squeezed her hand, then sent Cora in Faron's direction. She stepped gingerly between the cots, mindful of limbs that had slipped from beneath sheets and long strands of hair that had pulled from braids.

Cora touched her own braid, wondering when she'd last fixed her hair or eaten a regular meal or even brushed her teeth. Every moment of the day had been consumed with one goal: fix this. Fix them.

*Fix him.*

Cora paused at the end of Faron's cot. A pair of healers hovered at his bedside. One held a bowl of broth in her hand. The other crouched next to him, sending waves of that cold healer magic through his limbs to keep his muscles and joints mobile. Atrophy was a word Cora wouldn't have known had there not been a bevy of healers at the school keeping the victims from losing what little strength remained in their muscles. But the fact that they did this every day—with the same meticulous care with which someone would tend a garden or paint a portrait—reminded Cora just how long Faron might be lying on this cot.

*What if there is no cure*, a voice inside her head whispered. *What if this is forever?*

The thought sent a shiver through her. What if? Would the victims survive an entire lifetime like this, or would they eventually fade away? She imagined Faron on the cot, older, his face marred by wrinkles, his hair thinner, grayer. She imagined spending decades of her life waiting for him to wake, knowing very well he never would. And, in her mind's eye, she imagined the moment his paper-thin skin turned to ash, his body finally wasting away.

Would it be relief he found then?

Was he in pain now?

This last was a thought she'd yet to verbalize. Instead she held it close, hidden in the dark recesses of her mind because Cora didn't know what to do if she learned that the victims were hurting.

She didn't think she could bear it.

One of the healers looked up at her. It was Nadia. She was the school's private healer, so she'd been here since the beginning. She gave Cora a soft smile, and Cora did her best to wipe the worry from her face, to hide her concerns in the friendly twist of her lips.

"We were expecting you," Nadia said.

Though Cora's presence had, at one point, been a point of contention for some of the healers, they had grown used to her visits now. It probably helped that she no longer hounded them for information and answers. Before Cora had uncovered Melusine's plot, she'd spent numerous hours watching and waiting for the healers to make some sort of miraculous revelation.

Though there was still no tangible cure, now that the healers knew what enemy they were fighting, some of the tension in the infirmary had abated. They no longer racked their brains and pushed their magic to discover the cause, but instead spent their efforts testing for cures.

Cora had stopped expecting they would find one. Melusine might have betrayed them, but Cora truly believed that she'd been right about the heart. It had to contain the cure needed to wake the dragon riders. That was another reason Cora needed to resume her hunt as soon as possible. Beating Melusine to the heart not only meant saving Tenegard's magic, but Faron and all the unconscious dragon riders.

"How is he?" Cora asked when Nadia tilted her head in concern.

"He is keeping his strength." She eased a small spoonful of broth into Faron's mouth. "But how are you? You look as if you haven't slept in days."

"I'm fine." Cora brushed her off. How anyone could expect her to get a good night's sleep right now was beyond her. She was running herself ragged looking after the trainees and teaching classes, all while preparing to leave the school, so she'd be ready to go when she figured out the best moment.

"You could rest here if you like," Nadia said. "I'm sure we could find an extra cot, and you could close your eyes for a bit. It must be so taxing trying to maintain appearances out there."

Cora shook her head, grateful for the healer's suggestion, but far too busy to even consider it. "I just want to sit with him for a while."

"Of course. I'm sure he'd love that." Nadia and the other healer excused themselves, moving on to minister to the next victim.

Cora took her usual seat next to Faron, searching beneath the sheet for his hand. His skin wasn't cool to the touch but neither was it warm. He was somewhere in between.

"It's me," Cora said softly, giving his hand a squeeze. "Sorry I'm late. I was on my way over when I bumped into Elaine and we started talking. You know how your aunt likes to talk."

It was Elaine who had originally suggested that Cora continue to talk to Faron. She had said there might be benefits to the conversation. If Faron could somehow hear them or sense their presence, it might ease his mind to know he wasn't alone.

Cora wanted Faron to know that she hadn't given up on him, so she'd made it a priority.

"Strida's running her class on battle strategy again," Cora told him, a smirk twisting her lips. "Guess who turned up to watch that? Emmett, of course."

The two of them, Emmett and Strida, had been at odds ever since he'd relocated to the school to act as the council's liaison. His time there hadn't been easy. Even Cora had reached her limits with the man at times. But they'd found a new understanding following the battle with Melusine. Emmett had stood by them, even offering his magical help. So, despite getting off to a rocky start, Cora had made her peace with his random visits and sometimes critical nature. Strida, their fellow dragon rider and one of Cora's very good friends, had not quite come to terms with what she considered to be Emmett's continued interference, and the two of them often bickered to the amusement of everyone else.

9

"You should have seen them today," she continued, knowing Faron would have laughed if he'd been there. "I thought Strida was going to throttle him. Emmett might have deserved some of it, though. I swear he goes out of his way just to bother her."

Cora looked down, tracing the lines of Faron's palm. She released a heavy sigh.

"It's not all fun and games out there, you know. There's been some talk again from the trainees. Whispered worries about what happens if Melusine comes back."

Cora pictured the horde of crystals that powered the shield around the school. Every day they had to top the crystals up with magical energy to keep the shield in place, adding to the never-ending list of duties she needed to stay on top of. Though it was an ingenious design, and Cora was glad that the crystals had proved helpful in the end, it was a lot of work to maintain.

"We can't keep the trainees locked up here forever. Some of them are already talking about going home and seeing their friends and families. Sometimes I think we gave Melusine exactly what she wanted. The Blight may have failed to drain the rest of the school of magic, but we effectively locked ourselves away. If there's a threat to Tenegard right now, we're useless cowering behind our shield." Cora dropped her voice so no one would overhear, imagining that Faron would bend close to listen better. "We both know something more must be done."

She finally looked at his pale face, reaching out to brush the hair from his forehead. "I hate seeing you like this, especially when it's my fault. I let Melusine infiltrate our group. I dismissed your concerns about her. I know you would tell me to stop blaming myself, but I can't. Not until I wake you and all the others."

Cora returned to her earlier thoughts about the source of Tenegard's magic. "It's time that I finish what we started and find the source of the river. The heart." She could almost hear Faron protesting. *Wasn't this just another one of Melusine's lies?*

"Melusine lied about her reasons for wanting to find the Heart of Tenegard. It wasn't altruism. She didn't really want to help us," Cora said. "We still don't really know her reasons for wanting the wellspring, other than wanting the Blight to destroy the magic contained there, but I think she's right about the Heart of Tenegard. We all felt how powerful it was. Powerful enough to reverse the sleeping sickness. And I know you would tell me not to go, not to risk it, that you're not worth it. But *you* are. All the victims are."

He would've been silent at this point, the way he always was when he was uncertain. When he was thinking deeply.

"I have to go alone," she said, threading her fingers between his. "It's the only way now. I'm the only one who can really sense the river through the rocks in the mountains. And I need the rest of the riders here to bolster the magic in the crystals. I need them to keep the shield intact."

Cora knew he would be angry about her plan, but she'd already wasted so much time. Melusine hadn't returned to the school and Faron wasn't waking on his own. He would hate that she was going alone, and, of course, she hated to leave him, but at least this way she wasn't risking anyone else's life.

"I know you don't think this is the right decision." She sighed, studying the pale, veiny lids of his closed eyes. She imagined the deep blue that lay beneath and almost thought he might say something. That he might protest her leaving somehow. But, of course, he couldn't.

"I do love you, Faron. And I intend to keep my promise. I will wake you and all the others." She lifted his hand to her lips and pressed a firm kiss to his fingers.

She left his side before the tears behind her eyes could fall. Outside, she gasped in a breath of fresh air, blinking to clear the unshed tears. Alaric was waiting for her, his blue scales dazzling under the sun. She went straight to him, throwing her arms around him and leaning against his side. He curled his body around her, the closest thing to a hug she would ever get from a dragon, and despite the frayed bond, she knew he understood.

"Decided?" he asked.

She nodded against him. It still tugged at her heartstrings, the damage that lingered between them. His simply worded question felt hollow compared to the way she was used to communicating with her dragon. Cora missed the sound of Alaric's voice in her head, the telepathic connection they shared. She missed having his counsel, his voice in her ear, his mind as a sounding-board.

She supposed she should be grateful. She could have ended up on a cot like all of the others. Swallowing her feelings, Cora straightened, standing before Alaric with what she hoped was a brave smile. She needed to be strong for everyone relying on her.

"Strida?" she said.

Alaric inclined his head, pointing her in the right direction. Cora nodded and the two of them set off for the training field. Strida was the final person she needed to tell about her decision, and with Faron unconscious, she was likely to be the biggest obstacle to Cora reconvening her hunt for the source of Tenegard's magic. Its heart.

# CHAPTER 2
## CORA

"Does this look like an appropriate place to land a dragon?" Strida crowed at a trainee as Cora and Alaric approached. "You had the entire training field, and you chose here of all places? Did you not see the other recruits?"

Both the trainee and his dragon hung their heads.

Alaric made a chuffing sound and Cora didn't need to be able to read his mind to know he found this all very amusing. Cora missed the days when her biggest concerns were the overbearing council in the capital and managing unruly dragon-riders-in-training.

"Stop laughing," Cora whispered at him. "You'll only encourage the trainees."

Alaric pulled his lips back, flashing his teeth and confirming that he'd understood the gist of what she'd said.

"It won't happen again," the trainee said quickly.

"I should hope not," Strida replied. "We've got enough students in the infirmary already. We don't need to be adding to the pile." She waved her hand. "You're dismissed."

The trainee and his dragon scurried off, passing by Cora so quickly she had to jump out of their way to avoid being stepped on.

Strida simply shook her head. "Unbelievable."

Cora chuckled. "Looks like things are going well."

"Looks more like things are getting sloppy," Strida muttered. "Ever since we've restarted classes, the focus isn't there."

"You think the students are distracted?"

Strida blew out a heavy breath that ruffled the black hairs against her forehead. "How could they not be?"

Cora hummed, looking over her shoulder to make sure the students were out of earshot. She walked with Strida, to an empty patch of grass on the training field. Alaric settled down beside them, his hulking figure guarding against any eavesdroppers.

"I hear whispers in the halls between classes and as I walk by the dorms," Strida said. "They all think the same thing we do."

"Which is?"

"That we won't be ready when Melusine returns. They want to prepare to fight. The next assault is likely to be magical as much as it is martial. I can't blame them for being fed up with performing the same basic aerial maneuvers that they could do in their sleep. They want to be tested. They want to learn more."

Cora hadn't wanted to teach the new recruits the way she'd taught the rebel army when they were preparing to go to war against Onyx. Back then she'd been rushed. The rebels needed fighters. She wanted the school to be something different. A place where the trainees could take their time, truly get to know their dragons, and develop their bonds. She wanted them to learn; she didn't want them to have to fight already.

"Emrys and I aren't as strong as we once were. The communication …" Strida huffed. "Well, it just isn't there like it used to be."

Cora reached out and placed a comforting hand on Strida's shoulder. She understood what that loss felt like.

"We're not communicating midair as smoothly as before. I feel like the damage has plateaued, but it's not improving. I thought it would get better. That the bond would repair itself."

"So did I," Cora said almost bitterly. She'd fought off the Blight, beaten Melusine at her own game, but her bond hadn't grown any stronger.

"I wish Faron were here," Strida said.

The absence of one of the three strongest dragon riders weighed heavier than it ever had. Cora and Strida were trying to make up for it, but there was only so much they could do. Only so many classes they could teach. Only so much magic they could expend into the crystals to maintain the shield. Only so many hours they could devote to fussing over their next steps.

"I miss him," Cora said. "Every day I walk into the infirmary thinking it'll be fine, and he'll be sitting up in bed, waiting for me. Only he never is. I can't keep doing that every morning. It's making me crazy, wishing and hoping that something changes. All I'm doing is more of the same, wasting time here, when I know what needs to be done. I have to fix this, Strida."

Strida frowned. "You want to go after the Heart of Tenegard again?"

Cora wasn't surprised that Strida had guessed her plan. The magical wellspring had been on both of their minds since having to abandon their mission to bring Faron back to the healers and defend the school. "I think it's our best shot."

Strida nodded and Cora felt a rush of gratitude fill her chest. Faron would have protested, and though Alaric was going along with the plan, their bond was too damaged for Cora to really assess what his thoughts were. But Strida agreed easily and wholeheartedly. Strida knew the danger and the risk, and she still thought it was the best option.

"It'll be harder with just the two of us," she said, "but we'll make it work if we—"

Cora took Strida's hand, silencing her. Strida's eyes widened, then narrowed, perhaps guessing at what Cora was going to say. "I have to do this on my own."

"You don't," Strida said. "I'm going with you."

Cora simply shook her head. "Not this time."

"You haven't thought this through properly."

"I have. We can't leave the school undefended, which is why I need you here. I need someone strong. Someone I can trust to keep everyone safe."

Strida swallowed hard. Cora could tell she didn't like the idea even before she spoke. "What if something happens to you in the mountains? What if you get hurt?" At least her questions indicated her softening to Cora's plan.

"I have Alaric. The two of us will look after each other." Half the danger they'd faced before was because Cora had unknowingly allowed their enemy to accompany their travel party to the mountains. Melusine had been the one to bring the Blight into their midst and allow it to feed off them while they were attempting to track the river to the wellspring. This time Cora wouldn't be so quick to trust another stranger.

Strida grumbled, turning away to scan the school. They both watched the recruits run to their classes, to their dorms, to the dining hall. "There's a lot to lose here," she said.

Cora nodded. "They need your leadership. And the crystals require constant magical recharging. I need someone experienced to take care of that." She caught the telltale glimmer above. "This shield is the only thing protecting us from Melusine. It cannot fall."

"I know," Strida said reluctantly. "It won't. But I'll only agree to stay on one condition."

"What?"

"That you make contact frequently."

"How is that poss—" Cora frowned, then caught on to what Strida was talking about. There *was* a way to communicate over long distances. She barked a laugh, and Alaric tilted his head curiously. "That would require Emmett handing over two of his magical anchors to us."

At the word Emmett, Alaric rolled his eyes. Though Emmett had been more tolerable lately, she wasn't sure he'd agree to parting with the tiny pieces of intricately carved and spelled bone that he used to communicate with the council in Kaerlin.

"And why wouldn't he?" Strida remarked, taking Cora by the hand and marching toward the wing of the school where Emmett had set up his office.

"Maybe because you're charging toward his office like a bull."

Strida didn't slow even for an instant, but she did release Cora's hand. "He said he wanted to remain at the school to help us. This would be how he does that."

Cora had to admit that having the anchors would be helpful. It was a neat little bit of Athelian magic, and though she didn't exactly understand the spellwork, she'd seen it in practice before. If a little piece of bone could allow her to stay in contact with Strida and the school, it would lessen the stress of being separated. It would also allow Cora to quickly call for aid. When and if she found the Heart of Tenegard, she was going to need help defending it in case Melusine showed up.

When they reached Emmett's office, Strida barged right in without knocking. The space was furnished with a large wooden desk and trinkets that had clearly accompanied Emmett from the palace in Kaerlin. Perhaps that's why he had so many bags when he'd first arrived, Cora thought. She wished she could relay that thought to Alaric privately. She knew he'd find it amusing.

Emmett scowled from behind a rather large stack of ledgers and receipts, and Cora could tell that they'd interrupted him in the middle of some complicated calculation. His pen scratched loudly across the paper he was marking.

"Can I help you?" he said, glaring at Strida.

"Don't look at me like that."

"You know, knocking is still considered a basic courtesy. Even out here in the wilderness."

Strida rolled her eyes. "What are you doing anyway?"

"What does it look like? I am trying to reconcile your accounts, as I have been for the past three days," he complained. "Do you know how disorganized they are?"

Cora tipped her head and pursed her lips. Admittedly, keeping track of the accounts was not one of her better skills.

Emmett pulled out a scroll of parchment, shaking it at them. "And some of this spending is most irregular. Do you know how much the school has spent on nails alone these past months?"

"This place is held together with wood and nails," Strida said. "Why would that be surprising?"

Emmett harrumphed. "It doesn't take a genius to see that the math is wrong."

Despite reconciling with Emmett, Cora still prickled at the insults about how the school was run. In fact, considering the struggles they had faced recently, his words frustrated her. They had bigger problems than whether the budgets were balanced. "I'm happy for you to take your complaints back to the council," she said flatly.

Emmett rustled through a stack of parchment, not meeting her eye, and sniffed, his nose shooting into the air the way it had when they first met, and he'd been unimpressed with the school and his accommodations. "It has been some time now since I've provided the council with such details."

*Oh*, Cora thought. She glanced over at Strida, whose brows were knotted in confusion. After the battle with Melusine, something had shifted in their relationship with Emmett, however minutely. Though he was still an intruder sent from the capital to provide regular updates, perhaps he had started to shelter the school from some of the council's more probing inquiries. Cora thought of Councilor Northwood, in particular, the commander of Tenegard's army and the metaphorical thorn in her side. Then again, perhaps there was something for Emmett to gain from his silence. If Cora's experience with Melusine had taught her anything, it was that she should be more wary of strangers, and despite his recent help, that's exactly what Emmett was.

"Why?" she asked, focused on the small shifts in his features. Lines appeared by his eyes and his lips puckered.

"Why what?"

"Why would you withhold information from the council?"

Emmett cleared his throat, once again becoming interested in the ledgers before him. "It is my belief that the council may be overstepping in some areas. I still offer up reports if requested, but they are far less detailed than they once were."

"Had a change of heart, have you?" Strida said, with a smirk.

Emmett snapped a ledger closed. "Any good public servant should balk at an attempt to undermine or—"

"Sounds as if you just like us better than Northwood."

Emmett huffed. "I was going to say that I should balk at any attempt to unduly influence an effective and vital public institution. But of course your simple mind cannot comprehend the gravity of such a statement."

Strida crossed her arms. "Translation: you told Northwood to keep his nose out of our business."

"That is not what I said."

"Sounds exactly like what you said."

Emmett muttered something unintelligible under his breath, and Strida grinned at him, sitting on the edge of his desk. They bickered like long-lost siblings, and if Cora didn't have to prepare for her departure, she might have taken the time to tease them.

"You should be glad that I'm here to put the mess that is your book-keeping to order," he told Cora. "In that area, you are certainly *not* effective. The council might be less prone to pry if they think someone on the faculty has basic math skills."

"Don't forget the school is still full of dragons that could eat you," Strida warned.

Emmett sat back in his chair, drumming his fingers on the armrests. "How can I be free of you two?"

"Glad you asked," Cora said. "There is something we need."

"What will it cost me?"

"We're not asking you to give up life or limb," Strida said.

"Then tell me what it is you want and let us be done. I still have dozens of files to sort through."

Strida leaned toward him. "We need your communication anchors."

"Is that all?" Emmett said.

To Cora's surprise, he stood without protest and retrieved the anchors from a shelf. Before handing them over to Strida, he said, "Please bear in mind that these are not easily replaceable. Do your best not to go losing or damaging them in the wilderness."

Cora couldn't believe her ears. She also couldn't believe how easily he'd handed them off to Strida.

He sat back down. "Am I to presume that you are once again going in search of the Heart of Tenegard?"

"Why?" Strida asked. "Is that the kind of information you'll put in a report?"

"After you dragged me all over the Therma Mountains looking for it, I do have a certain interest in the matter," he said testily.

Cora supposed that was true. He *had* accompanied them to the mountains, and after enduring the suspicion of the group for most of that time, he'd finally proven himself an ally by helping them return Faron to the school. "I will be going alone," she told him.

His eyes widened. "You?"

"What about it?" Strida asked.

"I find it foolish that the school's most valuable asset would be setting off on some risky expedition at a time like this. Melusine could return to attack at any moment."

"And for that reason, I will not leave the school unguarded," Cora confirmed. "Strida will remain here and in charge while I'm away. She will ensure the shield remains in place. And we will stay in contact using your anchors."

"Oh, goody," Emmett said in reference to Strida being in charge. "I will have to inform the council of your departure. This information is too important for me to sidestep. What would you have me tell them?"

"Whatever you like," Cora said. "I don't owe the council an explanation for my actions."

"Of course not." Emmett sighed. "When do you ever?"

For the first time, Cora considered the difficult position Emmett was in. He was both the council's lackey and an administrative aide to the school. It certainly wasn't an easy role to play, and for that reason alone, Cora remained suspicious of his motivations.

They left his office after Emmett muttered, *well, good luck, then.*

In the hall, Strida handed Cora one of the anchors. It was pale white bone, with small carvings etched into its surface. Cora imagined that each one was a spell that helped convert the anchor from bone to a communication device.

"You have to check in every night," Strida said. "No matter what."

Cora nodded and put the bone in her pocket. "I will."

"I honestly didn't think Emmett would give them up so easily," Strida said. "I was prepared to argue but I'm glad I didn't have to. He's trying to hide it, but I think he's had a bigger change of heart than he's letting on where Northwood is concerned."

"I don't know," Cora said, familiar worries nagging at the back of her mind. "He's kept secrets from us before."

"But never intentionally to hurt us. Just to protect himself. Maybe he has earned the right to a little bit of information. He might be a pompous toad, but he has supported us against Melusine and the council."

Cora lifted her shoulder.

"Does it seem like he's taken another step toward our side? Can we trust people who want to be our allies?"

Cora remembered the moment Melusine had defended her to the other healers. The exact moment she'd manipulated Cora into thinking they were friends. "After what happened with Melusine, I'm not willing to be duped again."

"Is this where you tell me to keep an eye on him?"

Cora nodded slowly. "Don't forget that Melusine is the reason neither of us have a strong telepathic bond with our dragons anymore." She was the reason for their lingering magical weakness. "I don't want to give anyone else an opportunity to hurt us like that ever again."

"It's nothing to be ashamed of, Cora. No one blames you for not being at your best."

"I'm not ashamed," she said. "I'm angry. And the bottom line, though Emmett is proving to be helpful in his own way, is that we don't know where his ultimate loyalties lie. Just keep your guard up around him, okay?"

Strida nodded. "Should be easy. I think he's secretly afraid of me."

# CHAPTER 3
## OCTAVIA

I*'ve never been so eager for a council session to be over*, Octavia told Raksha as she sat among the ring of chairs that occupied the cavernous hall. Abandoning the council chamber for the rest of the day would feel like a reward for all the arguments they were enduring this morning.

*We're certainly going in circles*, Raksha agreed, mindful of her tail as she paced behind the other council members, listening to the opposition list off their rebuttals to Octavia's latest argument.

As both a dragon rider and a councilor, Octavia took her role very seriously, but they'd yet to make it past the first point on the agenda: the best location for the dragon conservation area.

Now that human and dragon relationships had been reforged with the emergence of the new generation of dragon riders, the council's intention was to force the dragons onto a preselected piece of land. No matter which way the proponents of the plan framed it, there were no benefits to forcing the dragons to remain within a conservation area besides having control over them. Though the council sessions often devolved into a grueling battle of wits, there was a futility to this conversation. Octavia gripped the polished wooden armrests of her chair.

She would not concede.

And neither would Raksha.

*Keep your head,* Raksha warned her, eyeing Octavia's blanched knuckles. *Losing your temper will do little to convince the other councilors that we have anything worthwhile to say.*

*I know,* Octavia replied. *They will think I am some foolish, hot-headed princess.*

In the midst of the negotiations, Octavia was glad for the ability to speak to Raksha privately. Their telepathic connection was something she cherished now more than ever, especially after how the Blight had affected both Cora and Strida's bonds. And poor Faron. Just thinking about what it would be like to lose the ability to hear Raksha inside her head made Octavia tremble. As it was, Raksha was the only other being in existence who knew Octavia as well as she knew herself. The mind of a dragon was a miraculous thing, and Raksha spared a portion of it for Octavia every day, keeping her secrets and cradling her innermost thoughts with such understanding.

A figure brushed by her chair, knocking Octavia's shoulder and making her elbow slip from the wooden armrest. She turned to see wide-set shoulders draped with the finest garb Kaerlin had to offer. Octavia bit her lip to keep from spearing the man with a barb she'd regret. It was only Northwood, after all, and to be expected. As the commander of Tenegard's army, Northwood had made it his mission to be the opposition to each of Octavia's comments or suggestions. No matter the topic, no matter the point on the agenda, if Octavia and Raksha voted one way, it could be certain that Northwood and his followers would vote the other. He was particularly cautious when it came to the dragons. He no more wanted to give them power or governance over themselves than he wanted to hack off his own arm.

He paced between the chairs, nodding as one of his lackeys droned on, presenting their suggestion for the location of the conservation area.

Raksha didn't bite her tongue, however, and let loose a low, rumbling growl, the kind that would linger in the room long after their council session had ended.

Northwood spared a glance over his shoulder. At the sight of Raksha's teeth pulled back over her lips, he dipped his head. It wasn't an apology, but an acknowledgment, which Octavia had seen many times before. Growing up in the palace as the adopted heir to Onyx the Deathless, Octavia had grown used to the deference bestowed upon a princess. But she'd also learned that obedience did not always mean respect. Though she'd rejected Onyx and joined the rebels to bring him down, the weight of her past still lingered in these halls, and sometimes she wondered if the council only tolerated her because of what she once was and not because of who she was now.

There were days she worried that the council didn't trust her judgment. She'd certainly given them reason to question her in the past, but she thought they'd moved beyond that. Northwood wouldn't let his animosity go, however, still bitter that Octavia had managed to convince the council to release the remaining stockpiles of dragon scales in order to help the sick trainees at the dragon-rider school.

Considering Northwood was relying on the dragon riders to come to the aid of Tenegard should the need arise, he'd certainly gone out of his way to make enemies of them.

*Enemies?* Raksha said.

*Maybe not enemies,* Octavia conceded. *But you have to admit we certainly aren't his biggest fans. And I think it would take a great threat to Tenegard for Cora to even consider taking orders from the man on behalf of the dragon riders.*

Thoughts of the dragon riders filled her with longing, and she sighed. It was hard to be away from them so soon after the battle with Melusine, especially from Strida, but important matters continued to pass through the council, and if Octavia and Raksha weren't present to make sure the dragons had a voice, Northwood would ensure their needs and wants were thoughtlessly cast aside.

The presenter's voice filtered back to the forefront of her mind and suddenly Octavia was out of her chair.

"No," she said loudly. "Absolutely not."

The presenter, a boy really, hardly older than she was, stuttered to a stop. He'd proposed forcing the dragons into a forest on the outskirts of Kaerlin, a place Octavia knew was thick with swamplands.

"And what reason do you have to complain now?" Northwood asked her.

"The swamplands in that area will make it almost impossible for the dragons to prepare a nesting ground. Their eggs will not do well in that kind of damp environment."

Besides the problem for the hatchlings, keeping the conservation area so near Kaerlin meant only one thing: Northwood wanted the dragons close enough to monitor.

He chuckled, like she was a petulant child. "I don't think a little water will be the dragons' undoing," Northwood said. Others, his followers, filled the hall with laughter, but Octavia did not back down.

Other voices joined hers from the shadows. They were dragons that had been summoned by Raksha: historians and herd leaders and some of her oldest and dearest friends.

Though the council members only heard growls and snarls, Octavia had spent the better part of the morning translating for the dragons. They'd provided the council with irrefutable proof about which areas were best suited to dragon survival.

But Octavia and Raksha both knew this conversation was a great injustice, so they'd suggested multiple regional territories as potential locations in order to avoid disrupting the dragons' way of life. There were already herds in the mountains and deep in the timber woods. Their true purpose in suggesting these locations was to make it painfully obvious to the council that the dragons were already governing themselves and managing their herds without the council's interference.

"Is it really that funny to you?" Octavia said. Northwood and his followers grew silent, embarrassed perhaps at being called out before the rest of the council. Octavia had her own supporters, the old rebel leaders who often sided with her, but she truly had to convince those whose loyalties lay in between. "Do you not care about the life you seek to condemn them to?"

"That is the very reason for the conservation area," Northwood said, throwing his arms wide as if to welcome the others to his ideas. "Because we care. Because we want the dragons protected."

"To me it seems as though you only seek to control them. To make them an attraction for the people of Kaerlin."

Northwood's face darkened. "Do not make a mockery of our plans."

"Then do not make a mockery of the dragons!" Octavia retorted. "They are not pets to be bound up and played with when you see fit." She ground her teeth together. "Onyx already tried that once."

Mentioning Onyx's name was always a risky move, evident in the wide eyes that darted around the room and the muffled gasps and whispered words. So much struggle and turmoil still lingered because of him. Being accused of following in the footsteps of the tyrant king was a blow unlike any other. Octavia knew because she'd once been accused of being like him herself.

It had certainly knocked all the fight out of her when it had happened.

Northwood swallowed hard, his eyes on the floor.

"Maybe she is right," one of the councilors said. His name was Artex, and he was younger than most, not easily swayed to either side, but always a voice that asked practical questions and demanded evidence. "Isn't cooperation with the dragons what we want? Isn't that in our best interest?"

Several other council members murmured their agreements.

"How will forcing the dragons into conservation areas protect our relationship with them?" he continued.

Bellamy, one of the old rebel leaders, spoke up next. "I think we might have to revisit our initial vote on the conservation areas."

"It would certainly be easier to leave the dragons be," Craille barked. He was another of the former rebel leaders. "And cheaper."

At the mention of cost, the voices of agreement grew louder, and Octavia felt a weightlessness in her chest. She turned to Raksha.

*I think they're starting to come around.*

"Perhaps we should adjourn for today," Northwood announced suddenly. He was losing ground and he knew it. "We've argued this point long enough and we have still reached no decision."

"No," Octavia said.

"We grow weary of this conversation," Northwood continued. "Thanks to *certain participants* drawing it out longer than it needed to be."

"Call for refreshment then," Raksha suggested coolly, and Octavia translated every word. The dragon stepped into the center of the circle as she spoke, her dark scales sparkling in the firelight that flickered from the torches on every wall. She looked directly at Northwood. "I'm sure the council doesn't want to insult their most powerful allies by making uninformed, unilateral decisions about our future."

With the hulking figures of the visiting dragons surrounding them, the council grew quiet. Contemplative. They were used to Raksha's presence, but having multiple dragons in the room was a new experience. The fire cast monstrous shadows upon the walls, and they seemed to press in, awaiting a verdict.

"You mean to intimidate us with this show of strength?" Northwood said.

"Yes, it is a show of strength," Octavia said. "But it is not meant to intimidate. It is only meant to show what you stand to lose should you fail to cement your alliance with the dragons."

"The dragons are not your enemies," Raksha added for Octavia to translate. "We never have been." Her words lingered and perhaps there was even something unsaid. *But we could be.*

When no one spoke up, Octavia realized that perhaps Northwood was right. There would be no decision today, but not because they had grown weary of the conversation. "There is insufficient evidence to support your claims that a single conservation area would foster better community among the dragons or even that it would be easier to defend under the threat of an attack."

Some heads nodded along.

Northwood's mouth stretched into a thin line. "Is that so?"

Octavia nodded. "If you truly wish to maintain an amicable alliance with the dragons, perhaps you could do them the courtesy of producing such evidence to support your assertions."

The tone of Raksha's accompanying growl was as diplomatic as Octavia had ever heard it, but the thoughts inside her head had been lit by Dragon Fire. *It is a miracle I don't burn him to a crisp where he stands.*

Octavia shared her anger. There were days when she wanted to wipe that ignorant smirk off Northwood's face, but today most of all. If Tenegard truly wanted to maintain a working relationship with the dragons, the council was doing a terrible job of convincing them that any loyalty remained between humans and dragons outside of the dragon riders.

Octavia's gaze darted to the other dragons. She wondered what of this encounter they would take back to their herds. The council was leaving a terrible impression. Dragons shared their own telepathic bond, and she could only hope that Raksha would smooth it over.

"Very well." Northwood plastered on a friendly smile as he faced the rest of the council. "We will provide the requested evidence and reconvene in two days' time."

The councilors began to shuffle in their seats.

"We're not done here!" Octavia said suddenly. "That was only the first point on the agenda."

"Which took an entire morning to discuss," Northwood pointed out.

"We are not done," Octavia all but growled. She'd been in this position before. Left standing before Northwood as if she were nothing more than an ignorant child. He often dismissed her ideas or the things Raksha said. Octavia knew now that it came from fear. Northwood feared the power the dragons could hold, the sway they could invoke over the council, so he held tightly to every scrap of control.

Still, Octavia stared him down. She'd fought too hard to have this next topic included on the agenda today, and she would not be the first to resign. Octavia could feel Raksha at her back. Feel the burst of strength and resolve she sent through the bond. It all helped Octavia stand a little straighter. Some of the council members may have thought her just the rebel princess, but she was more than that. She was a dragon rider and she carried with her the hopes and fears of all the dragon riders that had come before.

Finally, Northwood relented, slumping into his chair and rolling his eyes for the group to see. "Very well. Let's get on with the discussion."

Drawing on some of the strength Raksha fed through the bond, Octavia looked to her fellow councilors. "There is another matter of equal importance to the dragon conservation areas that must be discussed."

Heads whipped back and forth, lips pursed, brows furrowed. Octavia didn't know how the councilors could be so far removed as to not see the problem that was brewing. But true to themselves, they were most concerned where Kaerlin and their livelihoods might be affected. The dragon-rider school was far enough away that it almost slipped their minds.

She cleared her throat. "As you well know, a sleeping sickness still lies over some of the trainees at the school. With so many dragon riders incapacitated, our struggle against our magical enemy has been badly hampered."

"I thought you said the dragon riders had successfully defended the school?" someone called.

"They did," Octavia confirmed, thinking back to the hideous specter of Melusine and the way she'd forced the Blight past the school's shield using an anchor in the dining hall. If not for Octavia's vision about using the crystals and the strength of Cora's character, they might not have a school to defend any longer. "But it was only that," she continued. "Defense. Cora managed to banish the enemy from our midst, but it was not struck down. We know Melusine will regroup and when she does, she will return to finish what she started."

Melusine would return to let the Blight feed on the remaining magic at the school, and it would be the end of the dragon riders as they knew it.

Northwood pretended not to care, more interested in the gaudy rings he wore on his fat fingers, but Octavia watched his eyes. She saw them dart to the dragons that still hovered in the corners of the room.

She knew he saw power there. The most powerful force in all of Tenegard. If the dragons should ride to his aid as commander of the army, he would be unstoppable. Despite Northwood's constant badgering, he did have a vested interest in the future of the dragon riders.

Octavia let her gaze linger on him. "You know it to be true," she said. "Emmett has informed you of as much."

As the liaison, Emmett reported directly to Northwood, and Octavia knew he'd sent a report following the battle.

"And what would you have us do?" Northwood countered. "Beat back this enemy for you?"

"We do not need the council to fight our battles," Octavia said, knowing very well that whatever force they mustered would never stand a chance against Melusine and the Blight. "But we do need you to wake the unconscious dragon riders."

"How exactly do you propose we do that?"

"Summon sorcerers from Athelia."

Northwood's jaw dropped and there was a resounding protest throughout the room.

Octavia scanned the appalled faces. She knew the reaction to her suggestion would be strong. The council was prejudiced against their neighboring nation, a remnant of the war Onyx had tried to provoke against the homeland he'd been cast out of centuries ago.

*Steady*, Raksha said.

"Out of the question," Northwood said as soon as he'd regained his composure.

"At least make the inquiries," Octavia said. "Whatever this Blight is that we are fighting, it does not respond to dragon magic. Perhaps not even to any magic blessed by the lands of Tenegard. The Athelian sorcerers might know of a way to cure the aftereffects of the Blight." The more Octavia thought about it, the more she was convinced that they could wake the trainees and determine a way to heal Cora and Strida's fractured bonds with their dragons.

Northwood rose to his feet. "Do you even know what you ask of us?"

Octavia made her voice firm. "I am asking you to cease your protests for once and help the dragon riders."

"It's absurd," one of Northwood's followers declared.

"Naive," someone else barked.

Octavia's cheeks flushed with heat but she pushed on. "We must exhaust all our resources, and we have reached our limits at the school. The healers have tried for weeks but there is no waking the afflicted. All they can do is try to keep their bodies alive. If I could be permitted to speak to Athelia—"

"Your resources do not include Athelia," Northwood growled. "Have you considered what such a request might convey? If we were to ask for their help, they would know we are at a disadvantage. They would know that our greatest asset has been struck down by a magic that we cannot yet control. What do you think they will do with that information?"

Here he was, warmongering again. Northwood thought of nothing else but of taking up arms against Athelia. Even with Onyx's defeat and peace between their borders, Northwood had not let go of the notion that their neighbor had the ability to raise arms against Tenegard, and indeed *had* raised arms in response to Onyx's provocations. He festered about it and every mention of Athelia was fraught with suspicion.

"They might very well help us," she said in answer to his question. "They might tell us how to wake those that sleep like the dead." There were loud protests from the group. Even the councilors Octavia could usually count on, the old rebel leaders, sat silent, their lips pursed. She could tell they were hesitant to support her suggestion.

Fear was like that.

It sucked all the courage from your bones.

"No," Northwood said simply. "They will consider Tenegard weak, and they will rise to strike us." He shook his head for all to see. "The council will not endorse your request."

Octavia's teeth ground together. He hadn't even put it to a vote. The anger inside her was so hot she thought steam might leak from her nose, the way it did from Raksha's when they conjured Dragon Fire.

But with Northwood's declaration, the council began to disperse, taking his announcement to mean the end of their debate.

Before leaving the circle of chairs, Northwood gave her an awkward bow, then fled from the room, his cloak billowing behind him.

Octavia wanted to shout after him, but it was no use. Her anger wouldn't be enough, because under the fury was worry.

"You tried your best," Raksha said, aiming to comfort her.

Octavia reached up to rest her hands along Raksha's snout. The scales there were warm from the heat of her breath. "It feels like we're abandoning Cora and Strida without support."

Though she and Strida had been at odds for some time, they'd reconciled after the battle with Melusine, and Octavia had done nothing but fret over the situation at the school since. What if the shield did not hold? What if the crystals failed? What if Melusine and the Blight returned while she was here, occupied by her role on the council? The only good she could do was try to win the dragon riders the support they needed from Kaerlin, but that had never been an easy task. And in the days that it took her to make headway with the obstinate councilors, terrible things might befall the school.

"I wish Strida could be here with us, safe from whatever Melusine might try next." She knew Strida would never abandon the school or the trainees. She would stand and fight, even in the face of defeat. Octavia's wish to keep Strida and the school safe was almost as futile as her standing against Northwood when it came to Athelia.

"I, too, wish my son could be here." Cora's dragon, Alaric, was Raksha's son, and Octavia knew she missed him while they were apart. "But they would never be happy here. In fact, I suspect they would find it quite maddening being unable to confront their enemies directly."

Octavia wrapped her arms around herself, tilting her head in thought. "They have the right idea. I've started to see the appeal of direct action."

There had to be something more tangible she could do to help their cause. But what?

# CHAPTER 4

## CORA

The chill in the air grew the closer Cora and Alaric got to the Therma Mountains. The wind pressed against her face, chapping her cheeks and her lips with its bitter touch. The scent of rain hung in the air, as tangy and sharp as the mountain peaks themselves.

Alaric swept across the sky, keeping a low altitude so they could retrace their journey from weeks ago. It almost felt as if it had been years since they'd begun tracing the crystal river in search of the Heart of Tenegard. So much had happened in such a short time. Cora certainly felt like a different person, a different dragon rider.

She was more cautious now, and certainly more vigilant. She carried the weight of Faron's injury, of Melusine's threat, and of the fractured bond with Alaric like physical loads. They burdened her mind and left her shoulders sagging. Now that Faron was among the afflicted, Cora had more at stake this time and she was determined not to lose sight of their goal.

The Heart of Tenegard.

The beating lifeblood.

The source of all Tenegardian magic.

The origin of dragon magic itself.

But would it be enough?

She pressed forward in her saddle, laying her hands on the warmth of Alaric's scales. Sometimes, when the communication was particularly bad, this was the best they could do. Cora would press her hands to his scales, hoping it spoke the volumes she couldn't.

They'd become somewhat adept at touch now.

Panicked, drumming beats when she was nervous or scared.

A long, steady hold when she was feeling particularly sentimental.

A soft brush for comfort.

Alaric reacted to her touch, snorting softly and drifting back and forth. He swayed gently, like a parent rocking a baby, and she knew he meant to give her that same comfort. That same reassurance.

*Everything will be okay*, he would whisper to her mind if he could. *We will find the Heart of Tenegard. We will wake Faron and the others. We* will *stop Melusine.*

Cora patted him gently in thanks.

Alaric's claws grazed over the rich canopy of greenery beneath them, ruffling the trees as they flew past. The leaves parted like waves, opening and closing with the tide of their flight.

Eventually the tree line thinned and the branches grew bare and the shadow of the mountain eclipsed them.

Alaric grumbled and Cora imagined it meant *hold on, rider* as he gave a mighty flap of his wings and soared upward along the base of the mountain. Tears formed in the corners of Cora's eyes, and she drew herself down, almost flat against Alaric's back. He climbed steadily through the air, cresting the first peak of the Therma Mountains.

They were suddenly cast in brilliant sunlight, and Cora felt the heat of the sun prickle against the chill that seemed to be permanently etched into her cheeks. The mountains were known for their extreme temperature shifts, raging hot one moment and bitterly cold the next.

Alaric slowed, but did not land. Instead he picked his way from peak to peak as they attempted to track their original path through the mountains. When Cora spotted familiar landmarks, she pointed and said "there" or "north" or "keep going."

Alaric pressed on and by the time the sun had climbed directly above them, they had reached the site of their confrontation with Melusine. Cora slid from the saddle and down Alaric's back. She swallowed hard. Though sturdy and unyielding, the rock bore memories of their time here like scars.

Cora could see the crack where she'd driven her tent peg into the ground. The place where Melusine had been bound by her surprise spell. A black smear of magic lingered on the rock like ash from when she'd broken free of Cora's spell.

Scraps of tent fabric fluttered in the wind, reminders of when they'd hastily tied the tarps together. She still couldn't believe they'd managed to make a sling large enough to transport Faron and his dragon Wyn back to the school after they'd been attacked by the Blight.

Her heart beat a little faster, noting the place where Faron's body had been laid after the attack. Because of the way the sickness affected them, it had been too painful for Cora and Strida to approach Faron, but Emmett had made sure he was still breathing and had covered him with blankets to keep the worst of the chill away.

They'd worked until dawn, only by the light of their fire. It had long burned out, leaving nothing but charcoal behind. Cora kicked at the burnt remains with the toe of her boot. The shock of Melusine's betrayal still hung potent in the air. At the school Cora could distract herself, could push the memory aside. But here, there were no lessons or letters from the council to occupy her. Here, all she could do was replay the sight of Melusine caught by the spell and the wicked sneer that had crossed her face when she realized that Cora had trapped her.

There was no fear, no remorse.

Just cold, bitter amusement.

Cora wished she could go back and do it all over again. She'd never have invited Melusine into the mountains. Never shared words of friendship with her. Never believed her to be something she wasn't.

Most of all, she wished she'd known better.

Alaric huffed, the sound vibrating up his throat. When she glanced at him, he tossed his head up and down, his scales glittering under the sun.

"Sorry," she said.

He blinked at her slowly, intentionally. *What's wrong, my rider?* he seemed to say.

Cora sighed, trying to find a way to put her thoughts into words he might understand. The trouble was breaking her worries down into simple terms. Worries were never simple, and it was almost impossible to convey how she truly felt, while still determined not to let Melusine win at everything.

"Melusine," she said.

Alaric nodded. That was simple enough to understand.

Cora lifted her arm, waving into the distance like she'd just tossed a ball. Alaric turned to follow the trajectory of the invisible ball she'd just thrown.

"Head start," Cora said then, frowning. She hated how much time Melusine had on them now. While waiting and hoping for Faron to wake, Cora had expected Melusine to return to the school, to at least attempt to mount a counterattack, but she hadn't. That told Cora she'd likely already fled to the mountains to resume her own hunt for the Heart of Tenegard.

If Melusine reached the heart first, she would allow the Blight to feed from the magic. Cora could guess how that would work, having seen Faron's magic drained from him.

If she was right, the Blight would consume and consume until all the magic was gone from its source. And if there was no magic left in the Heart of Tenegard, Cora had to assume that all magic that fed from that heart would cease to exist.

There would be no more dragon riders.

No more bonds.

No more magic to protect Tenegard.

It would be the end of their world as they knew it. And with no more dragon riders, Tenegard would be left defenseless.

But for whom?

Cora dropped to her knee, pressing her hands to the rocks beneath her. Tracking the river was going to be harder and slower than ever. Last time it took them over a week to get this far, and she'd had Strida and Faron to help her. They hadn't been able to track the river as easily, but they'd shared their magic with her to bolster her strength. Now it was just her and Alaric.

He inched closer to her, pressing his snout against her back.

Immediately, she felt the trickle of his magic join hers. It was slow, like a drying mud, and Cora wanted to swear. The damaged bond was impacting every facet of their lives. She pulled back from the ground, biting back the sob that raced up her throat.

She wouldn't cry here. She'd known that this would be difficult. She'd anticipated how hard it would be to find the river alone. She just hadn't expected the swell of emotion when she returned to this place.

"Melusine," Alaric said gently, prodding at her. Cora turned to look at him and he stepped back so he could gesture into the distance. "No dragon."

"No dragon?" Cora repeated.

Alaric shook his head. "No dragon," he said again.

What did he mean, *no dragon*? Of course Melusine didn't have a dragon. The Blight was bad enough, adding a dragon really would have been the end of them.

Alaric gestured in the same direction Cora had earlier when she'd worried about Melusine's head start.

"Oh," Cora said. *Of course*. Melusine didn't have a dragon. So maybe her head start wasn't as great as Cora was anticipating. How would she even begin to track the river without the magic of a bonded dragon pair to trace it? Even alone Cora didn't think she could do it. Alaric was the sole reason they'd gotten this far.

And Melusine didn't have Alaric.

Cora climbed to her feet and smiled. She could tell by the look on his face that Alaric was trying to convince himself as much as he was her, but she appreciated his vote of confidence all the same. Besides, he

43

was right. Melusine didn't have the benefit of dragon magic at all, so really, maybe they were still a step ahead.

Whatever she had to tell herself to strengthen her resolve, Cora would do it, because despite their damaged bond, they had to keep going. She pressed against his side, throwing her arms out in her best attempt at a hug. She brushed against the saddlebag strung over Alaric's back and something poked her in the ribs.

She dug her hand in the bag, retrieving the crystal she'd brought from the school. Turning it over in her hand, Cora remembered why she'd stuffed it in her bag when she'd been packing earlier.

The crystals acted like batteries at the school, holding extra magic to bolster the shield. She'd hoped she could use it in the same way. Fill it with her magic and use it to bolster their attempts at tracking the river when she was feeling particularly weakened.

They might not have the other dragons or dragon riders here to help them, but maybe this was a way they could help themselves.

Cora lifted the crystal into Alaric's sight line and shrugged. Could the crystal aid them in their journey? Could they keep it filled with enough surplus magic to support their tracking attempts? Or would it all be for nothing?

Cora pursed her lips as the questions continued to bubble to life in her mind, but Alaric must've come to the same conclusion she had, that using the crystal might help them, and he stomped on the ground to show his enthusiasm about the crystal.

Cora's knees buckled and she reached for the saddle to steady herself. "Whoa." She laughed. "Glad you think it's a good idea."

She was happy to have Alaric's support. At least she felt less ridiculous for bringing a crystal into the mountains. Cora placed the crystal on the ground, took a deep breath, then let a torrent of magic fill the stone. She could feel the trickle of Alaric's magic join hers, and soon the crystal glowed with that familiar light that now surrounded the school.

Cora picked the crystal up, cradling it in her hands. "Okay," she said. "We should try tracking." Cora pointed to the ground when Alaric tipped his head. "River."

He nodded as Cora crouched down, holding the crystal in one hand and pressing her other palm to a flat part of the mountain. She closed her eyes, focusing on her goal, and let her magic filter through the stone, deep into the mountain, looking for the torrent of unbridled magic rushing deep in the rocks.

Cora concentrated so hard that she held her breath. She gasped now, teeth gritted as she caught a glimpse of it, rushing off to a point high in the mountains. A flash distracted her, and she looked down at the crystal, her focus waning and the rush of the magic river fading further away.

"What?"

Alaric made a noise of inquiry.

"Look at this." Cora held up the crystal so they could both watch as the glow shifted from one end of the crystal to the other. As she stepped toward Alaric, the glow adjusted again, like the needle on a compass that always pointed north. "Did you see?"

The crystal grew impossibly heavy suddenly. Not expecting the weight, Cora's hand buckled, and the crystal slipped from her grasp.

# CHAPTER 5
## CORA

S taring down at the crystal, which landed at her feet, Cora watched as that glowing ball of magic within adjusted itself again.

"Strange," she said. She hadn't noticed the crystals at the school behave in such a way. "Have you seen anything like this before?" she asked Alaric.

He simply shook his head before nosing at the crystal on the ground. Cora picked the crystal up, this time prepared for the weight. She turned it over in her hands, keeping a solid grip as she studied the smooth facets. "I wonder..." Cora added a little more magic. The glow behaved the same way, and the ball of light adjusted its position in the crystal whenever she moved.

Cora paced with the crystal, her eyes trained on the glow.

As it shifted, Cora began to feel the weight tug her in the same direction each time. If she turned her back, the crystal wanted her to turn around. If she went left or right, the crystal pulled her back to the center.

It was an odd feeling, like the crystal was pointing her toward something, and Cora thought again of a needle on a compass. But there was also a lesser pull she could feel. Cora turned between them, noting that the glow was brighter when facing the stronger pull. Cora stared off in that direction. It pointed high in the mountains, which was the same direction she'd caught a glimpse of the magic river.

The lesser pull, which glowed more dimly, pointed to … what?

"Barcroft," Alaric said.

"What?"

He looked from the crystal to the sky.

"Barcroft," Cora repeated. "You're sure?"

He nodded.

"What's in Barcroft besides the … cave," Cora said suddenly. "The cave!"

If the lesser pull pointed to the crystal cave in Barcroft, what lay in the other direction? Cora turned again, watching the crystal burn brighter. If the crystals were magical deposits from the Heart of Tenegard itself, as Melusine had once told her, then maybe they still held a connection to the heart even when separated.

"I think the stronger pull is pointing the way to the Heart of Tenegard," she told Alaric, excitement rising in her voice like a thousand songbirds. She jumped up and down, practically squealing.

Alaric looked stunned and he opened his mouth as if to respond but nothing came out. No grumbling. No growl. No choppy words.

"This is how we find the source of the river!" Cora said again. She pointed from the glow to the spot high in the mountains. "Heart," she said slowly.

Alaric closed his mouth, a growl slipping between his teeth. It sounded like a question.

"I don't know how," Cora said. "But I think it's worth checking out."

She pointed once more to the cliff they could see in the distance. Then she climbed on Alaric's back, cradling the crystal in her hand. Alaric lifted off, flying toward the peak.

Her greatest fear was that she might be wrong, that they would travel all that way only to find a dead end.

It would be smart to confirm that the crystal and the river were indeed traveling in the same direction. She scanned the mountains for a smooth patch of stone. Enough space for Alaric to land.

"There," she said, tapping his scales to get his attention.

Alaric flapped his wings, halting in midair.

"Down," Cora said.

Alaric drifted into the rocky clearing. Cora set the crystal down and pressed her hand to the rock, searching for the rush of the river. She frowned when she didn't immediately find it, certain she'd been right about the glow in the crystal. Sighing, she got to her feet. She wandered across the clearing, wondering what the purpose of the crystal's glow was if not that.

When she reached a sheer wall of rock, she stopped, pressing her hand against it. For fun, she let her magic drift through it and pulled back suddenly as she felt the coarse churn of the magical river.

"It's here," she called over her shoulder to Alaric. He was still on the other side of the clearing. Her test proved it: the crystal's glow was following the path of the river. The river snaked and turned, but the glow was like following an arrow. It took them in a straight path, whereas the river flowed and spiraled.

When Alaric joined her, Cora's smile must have said a thousand words because he all but picked her up to throw her back in the saddle.

She laughed. "All right, I'm going." She settled herself down, pointed Alaric in the right direction based on the crystal's glow, and they took to the sky once more. Alaric glided between cliffs and peaks. They stopped occasionally to verify their direction against the flow of the river, and at each point, Cora's findings held true and soon they stopped less frequently.

They made more progress in an hour than they'd made in a week on foot. They flew deeper into the mountains, where mist clung to the cliffsides. Suddenly, the glow in the crystal shifted and the weight centralized on her lap. Cora could feel the downward tug.

"Here," Cora said to Alaric. "It's here."

Alaric circled briefly, neither of them able to see beyond the veil of fog. He descended slowly, careful not to crash into the jagged peaks of rock. The mountain range was sharper here, like the wind and rain had yet to batter its sides smooth.

As they dropped beneath the cover of fog, Cora spotted the dappled slopes of village houses. The closer they drew, the more she could see specks of movement below—the villagers. The people pointed as they spotted them in the sky, then darted for the old brickwork forming a wall around the village. Inside, in addition to small crofts, there were gardens of wildflowers and crop fields overflowing with produce.

Alaric set them down just outside the village, at the base of a steep slope. The mountains seemed to curve around them, but it was the carved stonework that drew her attention. Above them, etched into the side of the mountain, was a pillar of stone that had very clearly been topped with a fearsome looking dragon. Its stone wings stretched out across the mountainside, watching the village from above.

"That looks like a good sign," Cora said.

"Caleb, no!" a voice cried out.

Cora turned to see a small boy running from the village gate in their direction. His hair was shaggy, falling into his eyes. He pushed it back from his face, wearing a giant grin as he did so.

A man who looked to be not much older than Faron dashed out to catch him. He swept the boy up in his arms, stopping a fair distance from Cora and Alaric. "What did I tell you?"

"But Papa, she has a dragon!"

Other villagers had wandered out beyond their wall. Some looked intrigued. Others were wary.

"State your business," the man called, holding his son close. Alaric shifted behind Cora, lowering himself to the ground to appear less imposing.

"We don't mean to intrude," Cora said. "We have been looking for something and our search has led us here." She pointed to the carved dragon on the mountainside. "We mean you no harm or misfortune."

"We?" the man said.

"My dragon and I," she explained. "My name is Cora. This is Alaric."

"You're a bonded pair?"

Cora nodded.

He put his son down and the boy took a few careful steps in their direction before his father caught his arm. "We've only heard rumors of such things."

"The rumors are true," Cora said with a smile. "There's an entire school of dragon riders where humans learn Dragon Tongue and form bonds with dragons."

A murmur of surprise went through the crowd, though none of them approached Alaric.

Cora held up her crystal. "We've been following the magic in this crystal. It has pointed us here."

"We have crystals similar to those."

"You do?"

He nodded. "In the cave up there. We've never concerned ourselves much with them."

Cora glanced back at the carving.

The villagers didn't seem to comprehend the connection of the crystals to the Heart of Tenegard. There was clearly Tenegardian history here, but whatever remained of the old stories had been lost or become just that to these people: *stories*. She wanted to explain the power they held, but she hardly understood it herself. Perhaps the crystals were what kept their mountain gardens bountiful and their people healthy. Perhaps it was the crystals that had kept Barcroft strong despite living in the remoteness of the mountains. "I would like to see this cave, if you will allow it."

Another murmured whisper went through the crowd, and this time Cora knew it wasn't in surprise over a dragon bond. The villagers were suspicious, and she worried they might try to bar her and Alaric from entering the cave. The man before her turned, joining the crowd to whisper about her request. Cora glanced over at Alaric, swallowing her worry. If the villagers refused, she didn't know what they would do next. This was where the crystal had directed them. They needed access to that cave. Suddenly, the man turned to face her.

"You are welcome here, dragon rider," he said, his expression softening. "We hope your search is a fruitful one."

Cora inclined her head in thanks as relief flooded her. There'd been nothing to worry about after all. The villagers fled back to their homes and their jobs. Some lingered at the wall, watching her and Alaric. The boy complained to his father, wanting to meet Alaric.

Cora smiled at his interest. He would likely make a great dragon rider himself. Perhaps one day, she thought. But that was a concern for another time. Right now she and Alaric had a job to do.

Cora turned once more to the dragon that stood proudly above them. She followed its wingspan to a stone ramp that had been carved into the mountainside.

"Over there." She pointed. "That's how we get inside."

Alaric followed Cora up the slope to the carved pillar. Up close Cora could see just how intricate the carving really was. Someone had individually etched each dragon scale. Beneath one of the wings sat the entrance to the cave.

Looking back at Alaric, Cora gave him a smile before ducking inside.

It was just like the cave in Barcroft. Hundreds of crystals lined the walls and floor and roof of the cave. But unlike the crystals in Barcroft, these ones glowed faintly with their own light. They dazzled like a smattering of stars across a black sky. When Cora pressed her hands to one, the river's power was easy to sense through their magical roots. She pulled her hand away as if burned.

Alaric grumbled in concern.

"The magic is strong," she explained.

He nodded. He could certainly feel that himself. This wasn't the Heart of Tenegard, but they had taken a significant step closer to it. The crystal in Cora's hand no longer pulled in any direction, but pulsed with energy. She might not know where they went from here, but at least they'd shaved miles off their journey.

The flight they'd just taken would have taken weeks to do on foot. Maybe even months. That would be months of time she'd be away from the school.

As Cora examined the crystals again, she wondered about their glow. The ones in Barcroft didn't glow on their own, but was that because they were too far from the Heart of Tenegard? Or was it for some other reason?

Cora held the crystal in her hand up to the glowing crystal on the wall, wondering if she could siphon some of their power to recharge her own. She tried it, and a rush of energy filled her, making the crystal in her hand pulse stronger.

She could indeed siphon some of the power from these crystals into the one she'd been using as a lodestone. Though unexpected, Cora was glad to find another way to recharge her crystal. Relying on her and Alaric's magic alone had been worrisome.

Cora followed Alaric back outside. As they emerged from the cave, Cora was startled to find the crystal tugging in a new direction. It glowed brightly as she pointed it further into the mountains. When she turned in the direction they'd come from, the pull was weak, the glow dull.

"Do you think they call to each other?" she asked Alaric. "The crystals." She made a jumping motion with her hand, moving the crystal from one imaginary deposit to the next. So far they seemed to beckon to each other across great distances and the energy from each deposit seemed to be uniquely attuned to its own position along the flow of the river.

Alaric lifted his claw in the direction of the mountains. Cora could almost hear him say *there's only one way to find out.*

He was right.

If the crystal lodestone now led them to another deposit of crystals, they should be able to tap into the energy there to lead them to the next one.

For the first time in a long time, Cora felt something like hope bloom in her chest. Using the crystal as their guide, they would reach their goal even faster.

She scrambled onto Alaric's back and settled herself in the saddle. "Let's go!"

But the instant the words left her mouth, she heard the first scream.

# CHAPTER 6
## CORA

Alaric stumbled on the edge of the slope, his wings stopping mid-flap, as another scream ushered from the village. Cora grasped for the saddle, trying to keep herself from being thrown from Alaric's back while also holding onto the lodestone.

"Cora!" he growled, turning his long neck to shove her back in her seat.

"I'm okay," she said, letting the frantic beat of her heart calm. "What was that?"

Alaric looked back toward the village, his muscles rippling as he coiled tight, prepared to spring into the sky at the first sign of trouble. For a long beat Cora thought maybe she'd imagined the scream. Maybe it was just the wind, whipping through the narrowed peaks.

Alaric lifted his snout to the sky, inhaling sharply.

"What do you think?" Cora said.

Alaric shifted from foot to foot.

"The wind?" she said.

He made a soft hum of agreement.

Cora's gaze returned to the crystal in her hand. They'd just made an incredible discovery. They didn't have time to be distracted by the wind of all things.

Another sharp scream echoed through the air and this time Cora's eyes snapped up to scan the village. She knew she hadn't imagined it. Alaric's body tensed once more and a low growl rattled up his throat.

"There!" Cora said, patting Alaric's scales frantically. She pointed toward the stone wall that rose up around the village. People were flooding through gates and from secret tunnels, fleeing the village.

They ran, clutching only their children, shouting words Cora couldn't understand for how frantic they were.

A few of them drew toward Cora and Alaric. They pointed to the cave, hurrying up the sloped path at the base of the mountains.

More screaming ripped from the center of the village.

"What is it?" Cora demanded of the first villager to reach the point where she and Alaric stood, protecting the mouth of the crystal cave.

The teary-eye woman blubbered and gasped. "It's under attack," she said, lifting a shaky hand. "Our village. Something wants to destroy us."

"Under attack?" Cora said.

Alaric paced, eager for information. He couldn't understand non-riders and he couldn't glean the conversation from Cora's mind any longer. So Cora did the one thing she knew he would understand. She reached down into the saddlebag, feeling for a familiar leather sheath, and in one great sweep, pulled her sword free. Where the dull light bled down from the sky, the sword glistened, each of the inlaid crystals catching the light.

They were crystals similar to the lodestone she was using.

Crystals meant to protect the bearer of the sword.

The last time she'd drawn arms it had been against Melusine and the Blight. Now she had no idea who their enemy was, but she couldn't leave the village defenseless.

"Let's go!" She gave her heels a soft tap against Alaric's sides and he understood immediately, leaping from the mouth of the cave and diving into the air. Cora's gut did a flip as they fell, picking up speed, and at the last moment Alaric unfurled his wings, catching the wind and soaring straight for the village.

Adrenaline roared inside her, each flap of Alaric's mighty wings echoing the crash of her heart against her ribs. Within a few wing-beats, they were upon the village center. Screams and cries and shouts were carried off by the wind. Villagers darted in a dozen different directions, and it was impossible for Cora to find the source of the commotion. She could see nothing that was attacking the villagers.

What had them so scared?

She pointed with the tip of her sword to the base of a statue in the center of the village. It was another dragon, carved from polished white stone. Alaric circled and landed quickly, lacking his usual grace, and Cora was almost blasted from her seat. She managed to hang on with one hand, the other holding tight to her sword. She shuffled down Alaric's side, turning to face the screams head on.

The village reminded her of Barcroft, though there was more stonework. The roads were cobbled in places. The houses were inlaid with large boulders. The statue of the dragon that had seemed like a good rendezvous point now towered over her. Only when Alaric rose to his full height did she realize the statue had been carved to scale.

Clearly, this village had once known dragons as more than just stories. But Cora didn't have time to marvel at this mountain village or its secrets. Not until she saved it from whatever beast now hunted them.

Cora stepped to the side as a man bolted by her, cursing loudly. Cora turned in the direction he had just come and started to run. The ground shook beneath her feet, and even if she couldn't see his looming figure, she knew Alaric was right behind her.

They turned and the road narrowed, stalls and carts lining both sides of the street. Alaric bumped one and a line of dried fish snapped, scattering the salted remains across the cobblestones.

Cora pressed on, drawing her sword up with both hands as she maneuvered through the road. Shrieks seemed to echo from the alleys in every direction. The road dipped, dropping to a courtyard that was thick with carts and stalls. A market.

The screaming intensified as Cora scanned the space, and in the center of the chaos, she finally spotted the attackers.

It was a pair of hounds.

If she could even call them that. She hugged the shadows of the alleyway, making her way toward the creatures as some of the villagers attempted to fight them off. They threw stones and bricks and sharpened spears, defending the market square, but nothing deterred the hounds.

They were monstrous in their proportions, with sharp canines that jutted out in every direction from a shortened snout. Some teeth were curved, others filed to points. The creatures' bodies were bulky in places, fat muscle piled up randomly, like a child had crafted them from clay without care. Their front legs were longer than their back, with unkempt claws that scratched upon the cobbles. The sound was sharp, sending a shiver through Cora. But it was their eyes that troubled her most of all. They were unlike any animal or beast she'd ever seen.

Empty was a good word for them.

A gust of wind buffeted her from behind, and she whirled in time to see Alaric lift into the sky. He'd perched himself carefully among the rooftops, gazing down at their enemy from above.

The closer Cora got, the bigger the hounds looked.

They crashed through the market, reducing carts to splinters of wood, and upending displays of fruits and vegetables. The longer she watched them, the more she realized they weren't directly attacking the village or the villagers. They were simply responding to the violence of the villagers with their own violence as they tried to inch their way across the market.

Where were they trying to get to?

The air was ripe with the scent of citrus, but something cut through it. Something that smelled of rotting meat.

Cora held the back of her hand to her nose, swallowing the bile that rushed up her throat. As she crouched in the shadows, one of the hounds darted across the market, roaring as it went. It rammed a stall where a villager had been firing arrows from, sending the owner flying backward. Another villager helped him up before raging at the beast with a spear. The hound broke it as easily as one did kindling for a fire.

Cora scanned for the other hound.

There was no way she could take them both at the same time.

But perhaps if they stayed separated she would stand a chance. She bent down and picked up a loaf of bread that had spilled from a basket. She hurled it across the market and the sound drew the second hound further away as it went to investigate.

Cora lifted her sword then and sprang from the shadows into the sight line of the first beast. It rounded on her, abandoning the villagers, who used the distraction to scramble away to safety.

As Cora got a closer look, she could see that the masses of muscle she'd spotted from above were held together by leathery, mottled webs of skin. A patchwork of flesh that seemed at once both half-decayed and half-alive. It was like the maker of these beasts had abandoned their work at the halfway point. Never in her life had she seen such a creature.

The rotting stink of old flesh consumed her again and Cora could see that she'd just stepped between the hound and its exit. Whatever it wanted was behind her. The hound paced, eyeing up Cora, and she braced herself for it to strike.

Before it could, the other hound burst from between the stalls, sprinting right for her, the heavy tread of its paws cracking the cobbles beneath it. She readied herself for its attack, gripping her sword tightly, but as its muscles coiled to lunge at her, Alaric was there. He dove from the sky, flicking his massive tail like a whip. It caught the hound, sending it tumbling back through the debris of broken carts, finally colliding with the side of a building.

The collision alone should have shattered every bone in the hound's body, but it rose from the debris, unharmed, leaving a massive, crumbling dent in the wall. It didn't even stumble as it resumed its hunt.

The other hound leaped for her, but Cora rolled out of the way, behind a cart, leaving the path open. It sprinted hard but Alaric swept across the marketplace, claws out, snatching the hound from the ground.

It gave a vaguely dog-like howl, but it was tinny and unnatural.

Alaric tightened his hold, claws ripping into the creature, but it was surprisingly unbothered by the attack, instead twisting to nip and bite at Alaric. Forced to drop the hound, Alaric sent it crashing into the wall of another building. The structure trembled, roof tiles sliding free and smashing to the ground.

The hound sprang back to its feet.

"What are these beasts?" Cora cried. She struck out at the other hound as it drew near and she managed to hack off a bit of that mottled flesh. It fell with a sickening thump against the ground but the hound didn't even flinch at its loss. What kind of creature could be unbothered by the steel of her sword or the piercing grip of Alaric's claws?

The hound darted side to side, attempting to get past her. It swiped at her with one of its paws and Cora struck back, hacking the beast's entire leg off.

It stumbled then, unbalanced, smashing to the ground. Where Cora expected a puddle of blood, the hound simply writhed. As she drew near, she spotted the stump where she'd sliced the limb from the beast. It bore strings of that fleshy skin and beneath it grew a new limb. The hound was regenerating, impossibly fast.

"Alaric!" she called, making sure he was seeing this.

He snorted, the sound both an acknowledgment and mutter of confusion. How was this possible?

When the other hound lashed out at her, Alaric intercepted, shoving it away. They were keeping the hounds busy, giving the villagers time to flee. The market square was almost empty enough for Cora to consider other forms of defense. Steel hadn't worked. Dragon claws hadn't worked. But perhaps magic would.

Cora conjured a line of ice spears, sending them flying. Some of them struck the hounds, slicing through their meaty bodies without consequence. Other spears accidentally ricocheted off the ground. Cora lost control of them, and they slashed against buildings, gouging stone from walls, before becoming embedded in wooden doors.

Cora abandoned the ice and summoned her strength. She pulled at the earth with her magic, raising a wall of stone and debris around the creatures to pen them in. She funneled them toward her and Alaric, keeping them from escaping the market square or lashing out at the remaining villagers.

"Fire?" Alaric asked.

"Fire," she agreed, mustering the magic. She thought of the raging heat of Dragon Fire, and together they manipulated a stream of red flames that licked and crackled around the hounds like a great flowing tongue. Part of her was still glad they could manage this much magic together. It made her feel close to him, as if maybe there was hope yet for their fractured bond, even though maintaining the magic to conjure Dragon Fire was draining and she didn't think she had it in her to raise the flames for long.

When the flames cleared, the hounds stirred, unfazed by their attack.

"Impossible," Cora said.

"Look!" Alaric glared at one of the hounds. As it paced, stalking toward them, Cora spotted a place on the hound's haunch where the flesh had melted enough to reveal a glowing spark.

It was a familiar glow. The same glow she'd been following all morning.

"The crystals?" she said, tripping over a charred block of brick as she backed away, keeping distance between herself and the hounds.

Alaric tilted his head curiously.

The glow certainly shared a similar coloring.

Before the hound could pounce, Cora summoned her strength to raise another wall of earth, trapping the creatures from all sides. The hounds snarled from within their fabricated cage and after a moment began hammering at the walls.

Despite her magic, the earth wouldn't hold them for long, and Alaric pushed the remains of a cart against the walls to strengthen the cage. The hounds split up inside, battering at the barrier and looking for weak points. Cora and Alaric also had to separate, doing everything they could to keep the hounds pinned. Cora used her magic to drag the rubble of damaged homes toward the cage, making the walls taller. It was harder than usual to coordinate without their bond, and Cora had to shout over the vicious snarling sounds echoing from the hounds.

She missed that automatic awareness of what Alaric was doing.

She missed being able to sense him regardless of distance.

As one of the hounds broke free, Cora conjured another spear of ice, but the spell went wide and ricocheted off a building, shattering a window.

Perhaps she'd been too generous with her earlier thoughts about their magic. Certainly she was tired, but there was a strain there too. This was the most magic that Cora had used since the battle with Melusine. Since their time in the mountains. For the first time, she noticed how difficult it was to direct their offensive magic.

The surrounding buildings already bore the scars of their attempts. Cora didn't relish bringing any more destruction upon the village, but the hounds were determined to get past them, and Cora knew if she let them escape the market square, they would carry the destruction with them.

Cora groaned, sweating as she summoned more of the earth to strengthen the wall.

"This isn't sustainable," she said. Maybe Alaric didn't understand her, but he would be growing weary himself. The hounds were relentless. In a way, it reminded Cora of an inventor's mechanism. The kind that never grew tired as long as the gears were oiled and greased.

And while her muscles ached from the strain of maintaining her magic walls, the hounds snapped and snarled as if they would be able to do so forever.

The wall before her began to tremble and Cora jumped out of the way just as a hound came bursting through.

"What do you want?" Cora cried at the hound. It was after something. She and Alaric were just an obstacle. Just an unfortunate bump in the road.

Cora staggered, whipping her sword around as the hound dove at her. She struck its haunch where that still-glowing patch of skin was. Her sword sliced clean through the hound's flesh and that glowing hunk of fleshy mass dropped to the ground. Separated now from the crystal-like mass, the hound stumbled and collapsed. Unmoving.

Whatever that glowing mass was, it must have been what animated the creatures. Cora whipped around as the other hound broke from its magical prison, scattering wooden debris across the market square.

Cora bolted after it. She couldn't see any glowing spots among its rotted flesh.

"Alaric," she called, pointing at the beast. "Fire!"

It had worked before, melting enough of the flesh to see the glow. Perhaps it would work again. Cora dropped behind a crushed rock wall, diving into the rubble as she envisioned a stream of incendiary Dragon Fire. She heard the crackle as it poured from Alaric's throat, consuming the creature.

When the flames and the smoke cleared, Cora ducked out of her hiding spot. But as she finally spotted that animated glow, the creature was upon her. It sprang and Cora stumbled back, hitting the ground hard enough to lose her breath.

Alaric cried out, the growl ripping through the village. She heard as his wings unfurled.

Her sword had bounced from her hand, lying inches away and she scrambled after it, but the putrid stench of the creature was already upon her. Its coiled shadow hovered above, and Cora gritted her teeth, braced for pain as she stared into its soulless eyes. Alaric wouldn't be fast enough, she already knew that.

But then a figure dropped into her line of sight, brandishing a large weapon. The stranger hacked at the beast above her, separating that glowing source of power from the hound. The beast collapsed on her, like an unanimated puppet, and Cora groaned. She struggled out from under the weight of the hound and grabbed her sword, springing back to her feet.

When she raised her weapon, she came face-to-face with her savior, a young man who held his own sword at the ready. But what was even more astonishing was the serpentine-like dragon that flanked him.

# CHAPTER 7

## CORA

"W ho are you?" Cora demanded, still trying to catch her breath.

Maybe she'd hit her head when she'd fallen. Maybe this was all a dream. She was still trying to wrap her mind around the dragon that was towering above the young man. The feathery mane. The long snake-like body that coiled like a spring. The unusual iridescence that covered every scale. It looked like the opals she'd once seen when she was a young girl or like the colorful film that encircled a soap bubble in the sun. The creature looked nothing like Alaric and yet there was no mistaking it was a dragon.

"The normal reaction to someone saving your life is usually to say *thank you.*"

Cora blinked, startled by her curiosity about the odd dragon. She looked back at the young man, intrigued by the accent with which he spoke Tenegardian. Each word was measured and slow, as if he had to be sure to shape it correctly in his mouth, or like he'd not spoken the words for a very long time. Cora listened to the way his letters rolled and the sounds dipped. She'd never paid quite so much attention to her own tongue before.

It reminded her of the way some of the elders still spoke, a dialect passed down from the days before Onyx had usurped Tenegardian culture. That's why it sounded so peculiar to her ears.

"What is it?" he asked.

"Nothing," she said. "I was just listening to the way you speak Tenegardian."

"You seem to understand me well enough."

"It's not that," Cora said. "It's a dialect that's been lost. One you don't hear very often except from some old family lines."

The tension in his shoulders eased somewhat and the boy—man—straightened to his full height. He had to be at least Cora's eighteen years. Perhaps a little older. Early-twenties, maybe. His eyes were almost as dark as his hair, and he wore a roan-stained traveling cloak that complemented the golden-brown tones of his skin. His face was thin and his cheeks, ruddy from exertion, darkened as she stared.

"What?" he demanded again, refusing to drop the point of his sword.

Cora was no longer staring at him exactly, but instead studying the travel-worn garb beneath his cloak. It carried unfamiliar patches and insignia reminiscent of an army. She was certain one of them had to be a rank badge, but she only caught a quick glimpse before he was demanding answers from her again.

"Who are you?"

Cora frowned. Despite saving her life, he was clearly a stern, serious sort of person, and Cora wondered if he already regretted helping her. She sheathed her own sword. Exhaustion had won, and if he meant to harm her, certainly he would have done it already. "My name is Cora, and this is my dragon Alaric," she said instead, aiming for a cordial answer. "Thank you for saving me."

She lifted a shaky hand in greeting but he merely nodded, ignoring her hand completely, and strolled past her to prod at the fallen hound. Cora caught Alaric's eye as her cheeks flushed with heat—not from embarrassment, but irritation. Alaric wouldn't have to be able to read her mind to know that she'd taken offense to being blatantly ignored.

She twisted on her heels, staring at this stranger and his dragon. "The normal reaction to someone introducing themselves is to at least offer your name in return," she said, echoing his own words from earlier.

He turned his head a fraction, looking at her over his shoulder. She thought he might sneer at her, but when he turned away, she heard him mumble.

"What was that?"

"Lenire," he said as she came to stand next to him. "That is my name. And this is Yrsa."

Alaric tipped his head back and forth, clearly intrigued by the other dragon. He studied Yrsa the way Cora had Lenire, likely taking stock of the differences and similarities and weighing them as either an ally or an enemy. Cora wondered if Alaric's ability to communicate with other dragons extended to Yrsa. Clearly, wherever they'd come from, it wasn't anywhere near Tenegard because she'd never heard of these other dragons. Then again, maybe this was just another consequence of the spell Onyx had used to try to wipe dragons from the memories of the Tenegardian people. He might have just as easily hidden away more than the dragons of Tenegard, but those from other regions as well.

Cora sighed. Even if Alaric could communicate with Yrsa, it was little help to her now. Not when their bond was this broken.

Lenire had crouched beside the hound, pulling apart some of the rotten flesh with the end of his sword. He was obviously a man of few words.

Cora knelt down beside him, figuring it would be easier to glean information from him if she could at least see his face. Though he looked disgusted, he wasn't quite as alarmed as Cora had been when she'd first encountered the hounds. "What do you know of these creatures?" she asked. "What are they? Where did they come from?"

Lenire stood, wiping his blade on the bottom of his boot. His mouth stretched in a thin line. "That is none of your concern," he said grimly.

"None of my concern?" Cora started. "You did notice me in a battle for my life against these hounds, did you not? I think that would make this situation my concern."

Lenire ignored her protest. "Where is your superior officer?"

Alaric growled, clearly insulted by Lenire's dismissive and challenging manner toward Cora. "Yours?" he seemed to ask Lenire.

To Cora's surprise, Lenire looked right at Alaric as he spoke, responding to the half growl that she'd heard, almost as if he'd understood him.

"Save your impudence," he snapped.

Cora's jaw dropped. Lenire *could* understand Alaric. That meant whatever bond he shared with Yrsa was likely built off a similar Dragon Tongue magic. Cora's gaze flicked to Alaric briefly. They would have to be more careful with their words. Without their telepathic bond, there would be no way to hide their communications from Lenire.

Alaric growled back, or at least, that's all Cora heard in the moment. He was clearly defending them, but the words were snapped so quickly that Cora could only look between Alaric and Lenire for clues as to the content of Alaric's reply.

Lenire's entire face tensed, the muscles in one of his cheeks twitching. "Again, I will say that this is none of your concern," he said firmly. "You should hurry back to whatever squadron or patrol you are a part of while I handle this."

Cora scoffed. "I don't think so. We want answers just as badly as you do, so we're not going anywhere."

Yrsa, the serpent-like dragon, opened her mouth and a glittering range of teeth came into view. Her growls were softer than Alaric's, almost a hiss. "… depth …".

"Depth?" Cora repeated. She was surprised she could understand her at all, considering this dragon was not Tenegardian, but her theory of a common Dragon Tongue magic persisted.

"She said you're clearly out of your depth here and it would be safer for you to stand down." Lenire still hadn't sheathed his sword, and Cora watched his hand tighten around the hilt.

"I got that much," Cora said. "I was just surprised that I could understand Yrsa or that you could understand Alaric, considering neither of you are Tenegardian. That's all."

Lenire glanced at Yrsa, rolling his eyes. He sighed, muttering something irritable in a language Cora didn't understand. When he looked back at her, he was still frustrated, but regarded her the way one might a child that you had to repeatedly explain things to. Cora bristled at the assumption. "Regardless of where a dragon originates, Dragon Tongue isn't bound by the limitations of human language," he said. "That's part of the magic. You don't know this?"

"You're the first we've encountered from beyond Tenegard," Cora said, defending her ignorance.

"But you should still know better. And the fact that you don't doesn't bode well. You and your dragon have no business straying so far from a more experienced company."

"You know nothing about me or my level of experience. Alaric and I don't answer to anyone here. We are on a solo mission through the mountains. When the hounds attacked the village, we answered the call for help."

Lenire grimaced and Cora couldn't tell if he was shocked or appalled. "You are telling me that you willingly and knowingly took on two creatures animated by the Shagrukos with your weak magic and no one to back you up? That might be the most foolish thing I've ever heard."

"Shagrukos?" Cora looked at Alaric. Now they were finally getting somewhere.

"You must have a death wish." He laughed, though it was without humor, and even Yrsa shook her head in disbelief.

"What is a Shagrukos?" Cora demanded. "Is that what was controlling these creatures?"

"You can't be serious? How can you not know of the Shagrukos?" He groaned. "It moves as a black mist, feeding on magic, and can imitate the shapes of living things." Cora's jaw dropped and he rubbed his eyes with his fingers. "Even one as uneducated as you must have heard of it now that the creature has crossed into your lands."

Though his condescension stung, Cora couldn't help but feel anything else but shock. The creature he was describing sounded exactly like the Blight. "I do know of it," she said. "I have seen it. Fought it. But we don't call it Shagrukos. Here it is called the Blight."

"The Blight?" he scoffed. "What a stupid name. A blight is a disease of plants. This creature has nothing to do with plants. Trust me."

He brushed by her, headed to the remains of the other hound, but Cora caught the sleeve of his tunic. "What else do you know of the Blight? This Shagrukos. Tell me."

Lenire tried to shake her off, but Cora's fingers had seized around the starchy fabric of his coat.

"What does it have to do with the hounds that attacked this village?"

Lenire took a step forward and Cora was forced to back up, releasing him. "What do you know about it?" he countered. "You've seen it. You've fought it. Surely you must know something."

Cora considered lying. Alaric paced behind her, his steps impatient. He was as eager for the information as she was. The only way to get Lenire to confide in her would be to start earning his trust—not that he seemed like he trusted easily—and that had to start with telling the truth.

"I don't know much," Cora confessed. Lenire's eyes narrowed but before he could respond, she pressed on. "The creature is controlled by a sorcerer named Melusine. She is a young healer, but her magic seems to have some sort of sway over this Shagrukos, and it follows her. Doing her bidding. But in all the times I've watched the Blight shapeshift, I've never encountered it in creatures like this," she finished, glancing down at the putrid remains of the hounds. "Have you?"

Lenire seemed to hesitate, and Cora could tell he was weighing his words. Trying to decide if he could trust her enough to share what he knew. "I've also never known the Shagrukos to take such a shape. It almost looks like …"

"Like what?" she pressed.

"Like they were fashioned by somebody. But poorly."

Cora considered her original thought about the hounds. She'd thought they'd looked like a child had molded them together. "This has to be Melusine's handiwork," she muttered. "She must be coming up with new tricks."

"Or someone must be," Lenire said, though he didn't elaborate on who this someone might be.

Lenire had no idea who Melusine was or what she was capable of, but Cora knew Melusine was smart and devious. This would be exactly the type of thing she would craft.

Though how and for what reason, Cora couldn't be certain.

"This place isn't safe," Lenire said suddenly. "Yrsa and I will escort you and your dragon home."

"Absolutely not," Cora said, rejecting the offer. Alaric huffed behind her. "We have urgent business of our own that we must attend to."

"What urgent business?" he said, his eyes narrowing into slits.

"That is none of your concern."

"What are you really doing in these mountains?" he said.

"What are you really doing in Tenegard?" she countered. "Where do you come from anyway?"

Lenire briefly touched the patches on his chest. "We're dragon knights from Itharus, of course."

Cora crossed her arms, hugging her elbows. She felt like an idiot for constantly being startled by his revelations, and she could think of no suitable response to his statement. He'd said it so easily, so freely, like she should have known there was another land with dragon riders.

"Why do you act as if the existence of dragon knights is new information for you?"

Cora was still trying to wrap her head around the words *dragon knights*.

Lenire turned away, shaking his head. "What has happened to dragon riding in this country?"

It was a rhetorical question, but it still struck a nerve in Cora. "A tyrannical king expunged nearly all knowledge of dragons and dragon riding from Tenegardian memory, from all its recorded history. We have only lately recovered it." Cora could not keep the biting tone from her voice. "I am from the one remaining dragon-rider school." She strategically didn't mention that she also ran said school. Lenire had judged her enough. "But it has only recently been established, and we still struggle with knowing our own history, never mind that of the lands beyond Tenegard."

It was Lenire's turn to be shocked into silence. Yrsa made a sound that was at once curious and comforting. She blinked at them, her eyes like great black pools, and all at once Cora got the feeling that Yrsa was sorry for what they had lost.

Lenire exchanged a look with Yrsa. Cora recognized it from all the times she'd looked at Alaric in a similar way. They were communicating privately. From behind her, Alaric came and lowered his head to bump gently against her shoulder, offering what comfort he could. Explaining Tenegard's dark history to a stranger had exhausted her more than she'd expected. She lifted her hand, running it along the underside of Alaric's head. She could feel as a soft huff made its way up his throat.

Lenire turned back to her, dropped his head briefly, as if to let her know that his guard was down. It was still there, but he no longer wielded his words with the same bitterness. "I will start at the beginning, then, and fill in the knowledge that has been hidden from you." He cleared his throat. "Itharus is a country far to the north, days across the great sea as a dragon flies. It was once a friend to Tenegard.

Our dragon riders shared a common history, but then one day Tenegard's dragon riders fell silent."

"That must have been when Onyx took over," Cora said. Lenire nodded, as if everything made sense to him. "Did none of your riders think to check on Tenegard?"

"I'm sure they did. Multiple times. But the outbreak of civil war has kept Itharus occupied for a few generations now. The Shagrukos, in my enemies' hands, ravaged the place I called home before abruptly vanishing in response to a mysterious call that originated here. From the land of Tenegard. I have tracked the creature from my homeland, across the sea. I pursue the Shagrukos to find a way to destroy it." His tone shifted, once again taking on that same condescension. "This is why I urge you to return to the safety of your school."

Cora bit her tongue, refusing to reveal that the school wasn't exactly safe. That it had suffered its own attacks from the Blight.

"You are nowhere near strong enough to confront the creature alone."

"Thank you for your concern," Cora said icily. "But as I've said, I have already stood against both the Blight and its master. I will not be returning to the school until I have completed my mission."

"You do not understand how dangerous this could be for you and your dragon."

"We don't need your protection."

"Why are you so stubborn?"

Because she'd been through this before. Blindly trusted strangers offering help. "I appreciate the information you've provided, but there's no way for me to know if you're actually telling the truth or if you've just rattled off an outrageous story to deceive me. There's no way for me to actually know if you are who you say you are. For all I know, these hounds were your doing."

Lenire finally sheathed his sword, curling both fists. "Was saving your life from those monsters not enough proof for you?"

"Look, I'm not about to blindly trust every stranger who does me a favor." Melusine herself had pretended to protect Cora and her friends from the Blight, even as she was setting it upon them. "You clearly have unfinished business, so feel free to continue on your quest and we'll continue ours."

"Very well," he spat. "I shall happily continue on my quest. But I am not leaving without at least learning more about the hounds first." He pushed by her then, stepping carefully around the chunks of mottled flesh. "I was following the Shagrukos westward from the coast and first encountered the creatures coming from that direction."

"So you chased them toward the village?"

Lenire looked like he might spit fire. "I did no such thing! Yrsa and I tracked them for some distance. We couldn't be certain of their objective, but we knew they shouldn't be permitted to reach it."

"I don't think the village was their objective," Cora commented. During the fight, she'd repeatedly felt as if the hounds were trying to get past her. They reacted to her with violence, but only as a means to escape. She'd managed to keep them trapped, but where would they have gone had she stepped out of the way? "Whatever they were looking for, it's done now."

"You don't know that. There might be more of them out there."

Cora resisted the urge to roll her eyes. Though he'd saved her life, she was looking forward to the moment she could leave this unpleasant new acquaintance behind. She was certainly not about to lead him to the Heart of Tenegard—she'd already made that mistake once—but perhaps knowing more about the monsters would work to her benefit.

She didn't know what the next phase of her journey would bring, and if Lenire happened to be right and she encountered more of these creatures, then she wanted to be ready. Lifting her hand, she gestured to one of the corpses. *Go ahead*, she wanted to say.

Lenire crouched down by the creature, prodding with his bare hands instead of with his sword this time. Cora gritted her teeth and looked away. The creature had already smelled of rotting meat before, but now it reeked of decay.

Lenire shifted around the corpse. "Did you or Alaric see black mist leave the creature at all when it died?"

Cora had been fearing for her life so she wasn't exactly paying attention in the end, but when she'd slain the first hound, she hadn't noticed anything. She shook her head.

Lenire frowned, shifting to examine the creature from another angle. As Cora stepped over a hunk of flesh, she noticed an odd gleam from something buried inside it. She knelt down and slipped a dagger from her belt, carefully and quickly cutting away the flesh. This was the glow she'd seen coming from the hounds. The glow that when cut away had rendered the hounds dead.

This was what had been animating them.

It was a crystal, similar to the one Cora had been using as a lodestone. This must have been what had responded to her magic with that tell-tale glow. She pocketed the crystal.

Lenire had shucked off his jacket and was up to his arms in monster guts, digging through the creature's chest cavity, muttering something about finding the heart.

As he and Yrsa were busy, she scoured the ground for the severed limb of the other hound. Alaric growled softly and she turned, spying the limb he was nosing out of the rubble. Cora hurriedly cut through the limb, unearthing another crystal.

Her animation theory had to be right. This had to be the source of their life force.

Lenire was still occupied, and Cora slipped the second crystal into her pocket. Alaric snorted but Cora shook her head, glancing over at the others from the corner of her eye. She wasn't ready to reveal what she'd found to Lenire yet. She didn't know if she could trust him or Yrsa. Until she figured that out, she would keep the discovery between her and Alaric.

She didn't know what this meant for Lenire's mission, but Cora knew exactly what it meant for her: their enemy had figured out a way to use the crystals too.

# CHAPTER 8

## CORA

S weat beaded across Lenire's forehead like miniscule crystals, each one shiny and shaped like a dew drop. He wiped them away with the back of his hand, smearing red monster guts across his face. Bits of flesh caught in his eyebrows and in the wisps of hair at the front of his head.

Lenire didn't seem to mind the scent of rotted flesh that now covered him, but Cora had taken another step away from the carcasses, putting more distance between them. Even with the mountain fog hovering above the village, a late afternoon sun poked through occasionally, baking the remains. Cora breathed through her mouth to avoid losing her breakfast on the cobblestones.

"It's not nearly as bad as you're making it out to be," Lenire said, grunting and groaning as he continued to dig through what would have been the chest cavity of one of the hounds.

"It's putrid," Cora said. "I don't know how you can stand it."

Alaric snorted to show his agreement. His nostrils flared and his lips pulled back from his teeth in disgust. So did Yrsa's for that matter, but she remained dutifully behind Lenire, never taking her eyes off him or their fleshy prize.

Alaric hunted for his food. Cora assumed Yrsa did the same. An animal carcass wasn't an oddity in their world. But if even the dragons were saying that the flesh was beyond rotted, then Cora was inclined to believe them.

"Why are you looking for a heart anyway?" she asked.

"I'm trying to find what makes them tick," he said. "What keeps them alive. But there's nothing here." He sat back on the cobblestones with a huff, hanging his flesh-covered arms over his knees so as not to dirty his trousers.

Cora's hand fell to her pocket, feeling the crystals there. They were the power source that controlled the hounds; she was sure of it. Though she still wasn't ready to confide in Lenire, she found herself curious about his thoughts. "What's your theory?"

"I'm giving up on a heart," he said with a measure of certainty. "Whatever they were, the creatures were fashioned somehow from an undifferentiated mass of flesh, without a single organ or anything internally to keep them alive." He looked at his hands, then away as villagers began to return to the square. Now that the fighting had stopped, they had started to pick through the damaged carts and stalls and market goods. "Maybe it had something to do with that glowing patch," he said, getting to his feet. "I saw it before I struck the creature." His brow furrowed. "I wonder what it was."

His curious gaze turned to Cora and the crystals suddenly felt heavier in her pocket, weighed down by her guilt. Cora wasn't a liar by nature, but her experiences with Melusine had taught her better than to lay out all her secrets up front. Now that she knew enemies could hide in plain sight, that they could even be her friend, she couldn't risk inviting strangers into her inner circle or trusting them with her confidence. Even one that had saved her life. Maybe *especially* one that had saved her life. Melusine had also ridden to the aid of the school once. She'd followed them into the mountains and patched them up when they'd been injured by the Blight. She'd healed burns on Cora's skin and set Strida's ribs and cleared the abrasions on Faron's knuckles. She'd done all of that and she'd still betrayed them. By those standards, no one could be trusted.

"I'm not sure what you're talking about," Cora finally said.

"You didn't see it?" He touched a spot on his side. "It was about here. And shining like the reflection off water when the sun hits it just right."

Cora swallowed down her lie and shrugged. "I didn't see anything glowing."

"No," Lenire said, talking mostly to himself. He rubbed his jaw, smearing more of those monster guts around. "You were on the ground. Perhaps from that angle it wasn't visible."

Alaric growled gently, the sound like a hum in his throat. He looked from Cora's face to her pocket.

Cora moved her head, just a fraction, once again telling Alaric that they had to keep this quiet. He huffed and Cora realized he didn't agree. She wished she could talk to him. *Really* talk to him. Alaric would notice things about their new companions that she didn't. He could understand both Yrsa and Lenire better than she could at this point. She missed his voice in her head. Missed the conversations they would have. But now, more than ever, she missed having him to confide in.

Cora reached out and touched the side of his head, running her fingers over the warm scales along his jaw. *Please*, she tried to convey, hoping her eyes would speak for her.

Alaric nodded once and Cora knew he would keep her secret. There had never been any doubt. Fractured bond or not, Cora was still his rider. She knew he would protect her, even if there was nothing to protect her from.

"There's nothing more left to do here," Lenire said, pulling Cora from the moment with Alaric. "The creatures have told us all they will." He shifted the sheath of his sword onto his hip. "Will you accept my offer to escort you back to your school?"

Cora shook her head. "We've been over this."

"We have. I just thought some common sense might have gotten into you as you watched me dig through the remains of creatures that are apparently fueled by some sort of magic that neither of us can identify."

"I was doing fine before you showed up."

"Before I showed up that creature was about to slaughter you."

"I guess we'll never know if I would've succeeded or if it would've prevailed." Cora clenched her jaw and steeled herself for more arguments. She wasn't going to budge on her position. She wasn't returning to the school. Not now. Not when her quest might be possible.

Lenire turned, waving his hand as if to dismiss her from his sight. "I can't force you to accept my help. Just get on with it and leave if that's what you're so determined to do." He started across the square.

"Where are you going?" Cora called after him.

He turned, walking backward. "To check on the villagers. Some of them might actually appreciate my help."

Alaric hummed, the sound almost sad as he watched Lenire and Yrsa depart. It bothered her that she couldn't get a handle on the root of his sadness. If the bond were intact she would have been able to send him a burst of comfort, but now all she could do was guess at his thoughts.

"What is it?" Cora asked him. "You're sad?"

Alaric tipped his head and Cora wasn't sure if he'd understood her. Then he said, "Never seen ..." He gestured to his own body, mimicking the serpentine movements of Yrsa.

Cora sighed. It wasn't sadness that he felt then, it was regret. He was clearly interested in these newcomers, and the fact that he'd never seen a dragon like Yrsa before was all the more reason for him to wish their departure hadn't been so sudden. That perhaps Cora and Lenire had gotten off on a better foot. That an alliance had been forged between them, like the one their countries supposedly had once shared.

If anything, the opposite had happened. Cora knew it was the right thing to do, but she still felt bad for Alaric.

"Sorry," she said. Standing there, beside Alaric, surrounded by Lenire and Yrsa and a multitude of villagers, she'd never felt so lonely. Grief filled her and it was like someone had died.

Cora blinked away the tears that stung her eyes.

She had more important things to do than feel sorry for herself. For her bond. For the fact that her dragon perhaps preferred the company of others over her. She didn't blame him. How could she? They could hardly speak now and because of that, they'd drifted apart. Cora could deny it all she wanted, but the more time that went by, the more she kept to herself.

It was too difficult to share with him, so why bother trying?

Alaric nudged her, pressing against her shoulder. When she didn't look up, he pressed hard, before carefully grabbing the cloth of her tunic with his teeth. He tugged and she went with him to avoid ripping the fabric. "Mine," he said, bending down until one large black eye set its sight on her face. "My ... rider."

A sound curled its way up his throat, reminding Cora of a cat's purr. It eased something in her, and the loneliness and grief receded. Cora hugged him, throwing her arms around his neck as far as they would go. Alaric curled around her, and she knew then that they would be okay. Somehow, when Melusine was dispatched and the Blight was gone, Cora was going to fix what they'd lost. She was going to repair their bond.

Pulling away, Cora swiped at her eyes quickly, nodding to show Alaric that she was okay. She turned back to the decaying hounds, gesturing to their bodies. "Fire?"

Alaric grinned, took a mighty breath, and together they used a controlled stream of Dragon Fire to incinerate the remains of the hounds. If Melusine really had animated this flesh with a crystal, there was no reason to leave the corpses behind, giving her the opportunity to do it again. Once the flesh had been burned into flakes of ash, Cora and Alaric wandered through the market, helping the villagers right their belongings, but keeping their distance from Lenire and Yrsa.

They'd caused almost as much damage as the hounds in their effort to contain them. Earth had been pulled from the ground to cage in the beasts, leaving loose cobbles everywhere. Using the same elemental magic, Cora returned the earth to ground, packing it down until only the smooth market space remained.

Alaric used his strength to lift carts and move debris. He followed the villagers around, guessing at their gestures. He was good at it, considering he and Cora had been relying on a language of simple words and hand signs to communicate.

While he did that, Cora used her elemental magic where she could, repairing the homes and businesses that had borne the brunt of the

84

attack. More of the villagers trickled back through the marketplace. Some were wounded and Cora was surprised to find that Lenire had set up in the center of the marketplace healing injuries. He used a tipped cart as a table, calling each new person from a line that winded down a side street. He studied each wound with grave compassion before offering his talents to ease their pain.

Worry flared to life in her gut as she watched the line of injured villagers grow smaller and smaller. Lenire's resemblance to Melusine in that moment was uncanny—not just his skill as a healer but how quickly he seemed to endear himself to these strangers. Children gathered around him, watching him work his spells. Melusine had been the same. She'd mentioned her interest in Dragon Tongue, and Cora had immediately pulled her into her confidence. But then she reminded herself that Lenire had come from Itharus, a land Cora had not even known existed until today. Though his healing art could all be an act, just as it was for Melusine, Cora was fairly certain that the two had nothing to do with each other. If Lenire was meant to deceive her, it was not by Melusine's design.

Cora turned back to her work, securing a few loose cobblestones in the street.

"Thank you," a voice said. It was the same man who had greeted Cora outside the gates earlier in the day. The one who had told her about the cave. He now introduced himself as Pieter and reached for Cora's hand. "The stars must have aligned today, for it is fate that you and your companion," he gestured to Lenire in the distance, "should have stumbled upon our village in a time of great need."

Cora didn't know if the timing was fate or if it had been designed by Melusine, but either way she was glad she and Alaric had been there to stop the hounds. "We were happy to help. And we're sorry for all the damage."

"Please," he said. "You and your blessed dragon have spared so many lives today. I don't know if there is a way to thank you."

Pieter's son, Caleb, raced past him to greet Alaric, and with the threat of the hounds gone, Pieter didn't try to stop him this time. Caleb pushed the shaggy hair from his face as he peered up at Alaric, his eyes widening at the sheer size of him.

"Papa, he's even bigger than the horses!"

"He certainly is."

Alaric bent down, nosing gently at the boy and he laughed, throwing his arms around Alaric. There was no fear in him, no hesitation, and Cora knew the blood of a dragon rider surged through his body. Caleb scrambled up Alaric's leg, climbing into the saddle.

"Careful," Pieter said, hurrying to his side.

"It's okay," Cora said. "Alaric doesn't mind."

"How does he fly?" Caleb asked. "Are all dragons this color? What does he eat?" The boy cocked his head, a line appearing between his tiny eyes. He reminded her of Bodi. The eagerness. The obvious love of dragons. A pang caught Cora in her chest, like the tip of a blade. She rubbed at the spot, remembering the boy who had been lost to the Blight, the first of her students.

He was never far from her mind, but today he was here, his spirit with another.

"Well," Cora said. "Perhaps when you are a little older, you might travel to the dragon-rider school, and if you work especially hard, the dragons might be able to answer your questions themselves."

"You mean they'll talk to me!"

"Maybe," she said. Lenire had finished his healing and now leaned against a building, hidden among the shadow, but Cora knew he watched her. She could see the gleam of Yrsa's scales, even from this distance.

"Papa, did you hear that?" Caleb slid from the saddle on Alaric's back and into Pieter's arms.

"I did, my boy. But I think dragons only talk to those who finish all their chores."

Caleb looked to Cora for confirmation. "It's true," she said. "Only the hardest of workers get to be dragon riders."

With that, Caleb sprinted from the marketplace.

Pieter laughed. "He'll be halfway home already."

"I bet."

"Do you have somewhere to stay the night?"

Cora frowned at his question.

"My family, we run an inn just up the street there. It's a small place. Quiet. We don't get many travelers out this far. But the beds are soft and the meals are warm. If you don't plan to set off tonight, we would be happy to host you and your friend."

"Thank you," Cora said. "That's very kind."

Pieter nodded, then hurried off after Caleb.

Cora hadn't been thinking about food or a bed, but now that she was, now that she allowed the ache and the hunger to break free, she didn't think she could turn them down. It would be dark soon, anyhow. She turned to Alaric. "Stay?"

He nodded.

They wouldn't make good progress in the dark. It was best to stay put for the night. Cora looked back over her shoulder. She should probably extend the invitation to Lenire. It would be the courteous thing to do. Now that she'd had some time to dwell on the attack, she'd also become conscious of how alarmingly close she and Alaric had come to being defeated by this new weapon. The only way she was going to be able to get ahead of Melusine was with information. She needed to know more about the Blight and what it was capable of. And, unfortunately, there was no better person to give her that information than Lenire.

She made her way across the marketplace with ease now that the damage had been cleared and she stopped before him. He'd settled on the stoop of someone's home.

"Finished giving dragon rides to the locals?" he muttered.

"Those locals just offered us a place to stay at their inn for the night," Cora bit back.

"As thanks for all the handiwork you've done around the village today?"

Cora held her tongue, setting off for the inn. She hadn't come over to argue with Lenire, no matter how difficult he was. She was going to accept Pieter's offer of a place to stay for the night. Lenire could take his prickly and standoffish self into the mountains to sleep for all she cared. Still, something like satisfaction filled her when he fell in step next to her. "Look," she began, "I know I told you I didn't need your protection."

He glanced over at her, listening more closely.

"Which is still true," Cora continued. "But I do need your insight. You know more about the Blight than I do."

"Shagrukos."

"Blight. Shagrukos. Call it what you want. The fact is, I need to know everything I can about what the Blight is. What it's capable of. I need you to tell me."

Lenire shook his head dismissively. "Not interested."

"What do you mean you're not interested?"

"I'm staying for a bed and a hot meal. After that, you go your way. I go my way. That's what we agreed on. I'm not interested in filling your head with stories. My only interest is tracking down the Shagrukos and getting rid of it. That is all you need to know."

"I could help you," Cora said. Lenire didn't know anything about the Heart of Tenegard, but Cora knew that somehow Melusine was going to be with her every step of the way. She was going to encounter the Blight again, one way or another, which meant she and Lenire were destined to cross paths again. She might not trust him, but she was beginning to see that in teaming up against the Blight, they could both get what they wanted.

"And why would I need your help?" He snorted, eyeing her like one did the runt in a litter. "I don't think you or your riders will be of much use considering how weak your magic is."

"You know nothing about our magic," Cora said, the words racing up her throat as hot as Dragon Fire. She was angered by his assessment but could do little to set him straight. If she did, she would have to admit to the cause of her fracture bond with Alaric, and he would see it as more evidence that she was unprepared to handle the Blight. It would be another reason for him to dismiss her.

"You're right," Lenire said. "I don't. But if you'd seen the things I have, you wouldn't be running toward the Shagrukos, you'd be running away from it."

# CHAPTER 9

## CORA

The inn was cramped and small, just as Pieter had said, unused to accommodating dragon riders or dragon knights and the accompanying onlookers that filtered in and out just to lay eyes on Cora and Lenire. But it was also a homey place that immediately reminded Cora of Barcroft, framed by softwoods turned amber by the flickering glow from the hearth fire. A dozen square tables were squished into the front room, surrounded by mismatched chairs and stools. Most were occupied, the locals stopping in for ale and conversation after the harrowing afternoon they'd had. Some of them still bore the scars—healed now thanks to Lenire—and the dirt smears from earlier, making Cora wonder what she now looked like after fighting the hounds.

Lenire had rubbed the hound guts from his face, but that did nothing to dampen the smell. Cora breathed through her mouth, forced to share the last tiny table in the corner of the room with him.

Pieter had brought them both a bowl of steaming stew filled to the brim with potatoes and leeks and chunks of savory beef. Cora's mouth watered just looking at it. For the most part, Lenire ignored her, spying out the smudged window.

Cora could see the iridescent shimmer of Yrsa's scales through the glass. There was no way a dragon could have fit through the doorway, never mind in the front room of the inn, so Alaric and Yrsa had curled up outside, much to Caleb's enjoyment. He'd already spent a great deal of time running back and forth between Cora and Alaric to ask questions and relay answers, not that Alaric could understand a single word he was saying. The boy was fascinated. It wasn't until his mother emerged from the kitchen, calling him to bed, that Caleb marched back into the inn, whining in protest.

"You've bothered our company enough for one night," his mother said, shooing him up the stairs with a wave of her apron. "Go on. Your father will be up to say goodnight."

Caleb hung his head, muttering under his breath as he stomped on every step. Cora could hear his thundering footsteps across the ceiling as he found his way to his room. She turned and caught his mother's eye. The woman simply shook her head, exasperated, but there was a hint of a smile on her lips.

Cora knew Caleb would spend all night with the dragons if his parents let him. Even now, she suspected he was hanging out his window just for a glimpse of them. For a moment, she wondered what dragon lore still existed in this village. There were clear monuments to dragons all over the village. Even the inn had intricate carvings along the border of the ceiling: fire breathing dragons with great scaly wings; dragons soaring between mountain cliffs; dragon eggs surrounded by scales.

How had Onyx's memory spell affected these people? Or perhaps, like Nana Livi, some memory of the dragons had remained. Perhaps the crystals in the cave, with their soft glow, had kept the power of dragons alive for these people. It was fascinating, really, to think there were people so removed from Onyx's power that they didn't have to fight to return the memories that were rightfully theirs. They didn't have to struggle to remember the relationship that once existed between humans and dragons. They'd simply always known.

Cora's hand dropped to her pocket beneath the table, feeling the edge of the crystals she'd taken from the hounds. Perhaps the crystals were more powerful than anyone ever thought.

Cora caught a whiff of petrified flesh and pressed the back of her hand to her nose. Whether it was coming from Lenire's flesh-stained tunic or from herself, she couldn't be sure, but Lenire had spent more time digging through hound guts today.

"What is your problem?" Lenire asked, hovering over his stew. He refused to look up at her, shoving meat and potatoes into his mouth like he might never get a chance to eat again.

"You smell like death," Cora said, taking a tentative breath. If she leaned close enough to her bowl, the fragrant aroma of the stew drowned out the stench of decay.

"Well, excuse me for wanting answers," he muttered, unfazed by her telling him he stank. He probably knew it. He needed to soak both himself and his tunic in a bucket of boiling water to steam the smell from them. "I didn't see you offering to help. You stood there trying not to puke."

"Digging through hound guts wasn't going to accomplish anything," Cora said.

"And how do you know?" he snapped.

She knew because of the crystals in her pockets. She had answers he didn't. But Cora wanted to know more about the Blight. She thought about trading the crystals for information. Lenire could fill her in on everything he knew about the Blight, and she would help him figure out how the crystals powered the hounds. *If* they did.

It was still a theory but definitely the most promising one, especially since Lenire had confirmed the absence of organs needed for survival.

Cora glanced to the window, looking for any sign of Alaric. She knew he didn't necessarily agree with her decision to keep the crystals a secret. But something in her gut told her to hold the secret tighter, to keep the truth of the crystals to herself for now.

They were still strangers after all.

So Cora left the crystals in her pocket and picked up her spoon. She would just have to pester Lenire for the information. She looked around as the rest of the inn filled up around them, villagers pressing in on all sides.

At least he had nowhere to escape to.

"I'm sorry," she said, figuring it was best to start with a clean slate before she started demanding answers. "I didn't mean looking through the hounds' remains wasn't a good idea. I just know Melusine's tricks. She's usually pretty good at hiding things."

"The sorcerer you mentioned earlier?"

Cora nodded.

"You still think this is her doing?"

"I do," Cora said. Of that she was certain. If the hounds were products of the Blight, fueled by the crystals, who better to create such a concoction than Melusine? She controlled the Blight and, thanks to the battle at the school, she'd also seen how the crystals might be used to bolster magic. She was also the only one Cora knew with magic strong enough to experiment like this.

"If you know her so well, then what were the hounds after? Clearly it wasn't you or they would have ripped you limb from limb long before I showed up."

Cora was reluctant to tell him any more. She wasn't sure what the hounds were hunting, but she was almost certain Melusine was hunting the Heart of Tenegard. Maybe their purposes were one and the same. "Where did the Blight come from?" she asked instead of answering. "I know you've come from Itharus, but it had to have originated somewhere else. Right?"

Lenire did not answer her question either. "I'm here to destroy the Shagrukos. Keeping information from me is going to make my job harder."

"And what of the information you are keeping from me?"

"Where the Shagrukos originated from is not important. What matters is what must be done now."

Cora stuffed a spoonful of potato in her mouth, her teeth grinding through the vegetable. This conversation would continue going in circles until one of them started giving up information. She swallowed, having begrudgingly realized that it would have to be her. Lenire had no real reason to share with her. As far as he was concerned, he was going to ride off into the sunrise, sword drawn, and chase the Blight across Tenegard. He didn't care that what he knew might very well help Cora keep Melusine from reaching the heart.

"I don't know what the hounds are after," Cora finally said. "I could only guess at it. But I know what Melusine is after."

Lenire put his spoon down. "Go on."

"She is looking for the Heart of Tenegard. The origin of this land's magic. If she finds it, she'll use the Blight to drain it."

"Tenegard would become a land without magic. Without dragons." Lenire said, and it was the first time he seemed to be truly concerned over what might befall Cora.

"I don't know why she's determined to do this," Cora continued, "but my intention is to stop her. If I can reach our target first, then I can protect it." Cora spoke carefully, keeping the role and use of the crystals quiet for now. She needed him to trust her, but she didn't want to overshare.

"Though my people's enemy also used the Shagrukos to do their bidding, they had very different goals in mind," Lenire said.

"You mean the civil war you spoke of earlier?"

His shoulders fell, as if the burden of memory weighed him down, his entire body slumping against the table for a second. "Many years ago, the Shagrukos was summoned from its home dimension by my enemies—an Order of Itharusian sorcerers. They used the creature as a weapon against the Itharusian government and as a way to maintain control of the people. To punish them. To hurt them. War broke out as the Order attempted to seize power and rebuild Itharus according to their ideals. We've been fighting ever since. I didn't think we would ever be free of the Shagrukos, and then one day the Order lost control of it."

"What do you mean they lost control?"

Lenire shook his head. "It doesn't matter. Your sorcerer seems to be the one who summoned the Shagrukos away from my homeland, and when she called to it, the creature fled Itharus. I knew Tenegard would not be prepared to handle such a monster, so I followed." Though he didn't smile, his cheeks were pinched in something akin to amusement.

"What's so funny?" Cora asked.

"It's nothing, really. I was thinking about how some solitary mystery woman robbed my enemies of its direst weapon."

Lenire clearly drew some sort of bleak enjoyment from the image. Cora didn't find it funny. If anything, she found it alarming. It only spoke to the magnitude of Melusine's power if she'd managed to summon the Blight from the magical Order. They fell into silence, Lenire's eyes drifting from the table and back to the window, leaving Cora to wonder what he wasn't saying.

When his attention returned, more of that reluctant amusement colored his features. "Yrsa at least seems happy for Alaric's company," he said. "She sounds more like herself than she has in a long time."

Cora wondered what Alaric was telling Yrsa, hoping he hadn't revealed anything she would rather keep private. As quickly as the thought occurred to her, shame filled her. Never would Alaric be so careless.

"Er," Lenire said, somewhat awkwardly. "They're fascinated by each other, comparing notes on their time as hatchlings and their herds. Though Alaric is also anxious to reassure you. I thought you would like to know."

Having to hear this news from Lenire instead of directly through her dragon bond left a bitter taste in Cora's mouth. Anger and grief roiled in her gut, and she suddenly wished she hadn't eaten so much. The fact that Lenire was telling her this meant that he assumed she and Alaric were too new for the advanced communication that came from a dragon bond. Tears threatened to fall. Cora jumped to her feet before they could. "I'm going to see Alaric so he won't have to worry over me."

She hurried through the inn, shoving past the villagers, trying not to sob. Outside, the mountain air was clear and brisk. She inhaled deeply, letting the shadow of night and the cold eclipse her misery.

Alaric found her after a moment, almost prancing upon the cobblestones in his excitement. Despite Cora and Lenire's reluctance to share information, clearly Alaric and Yrsa were becoming fast friends. Cora reached up and brushed her hand along Alaric's snout. He rambled off a long string of thoughts, most of them sounding only like grunts and snarls to Cora's ears. She caught the occasional word —*lore, hatchling, herd*—assuming he was reporting the similarities and differences he'd found during their conversation.

Cora would have loved to hear his thoughts on Itharusian dragon lore. She might not exactly find Lenire the easiest person to talk to, but there was much to learn from the dragon lore of another country. Especially one that had been close allies with Tenegard in the past.

Yrsa joined them, dipping her head in Cora's direction. Her greeting was cordial, if reserved, and Cora wondered what Lenire had already shared with his dragon about their discussion. That she was weak? Magicless? Talentless? That she couldn't even speak to her own dragon?

The door to the inn opened and Lenire appeared, stopping next to Yrsa's shoulder, nodding silently to something she said. With Lenire's arrival, Alaric's stream of excitement ceased, and he made an urging sound in the back of his throat. But instead of looking at Cora, he was looking at Yrsa.

Cora narrowed her eyes just as Lenire said, "I don't think so."

"What?" she asked.

Lenire scoffed, looking from Yrsa to Alaric. "Our dragons think we need to team up."

Cora turned to Alaric, her gaze questioning.

"Please," he said.

Cora crossed her arms. She'd been trying to find common ground with Lenire all afternoon. With every step forward, they seemed to find another obstacle, and she was already tired of having to tiptoe around the conversation, careful not to let go of too many of her secrets. There was no way they could work together.

"We're leaving in the morning," she said, mostly to Alaric. His eyes narrowed and she couldn't tell if he disagreed with her or if he hadn't understood her. But then he growled, a real growl that would have raised the hair on her arms had she not been a dragon rider.

So he was disagreeing.

"We need to move on," she said.

Alaric shook his head vehemently. She turned to Lenire for help. Even he had to admit that a partnership would never work. But instead of support, she found that Yrsa and Lenire were engaged in a silent debate.

After a moment, Lenire looked to the night sky, his chest rising and falling with a heavy sigh. Then he leveled his gaze at Cora. "The dragons say we should strike a deal. Since I can't afford to let the Shagrukos feed in Tenegard and grow more powerful, and since you don't know how many more of those hound creatures are out there, we should work together to protect Tenegard's magic and destroy the Shagrukos."

"Are those your words or Yrsa's?" Cora asked.

"Does it matter?" he replied. "Are you really willing to leave Tenegard's magic undefended? What if there are more of those hounds on the loose?"

"I think they might have been after the village's crystal deposit," Cora said reluctantly. She pointed to the mountains. "It's up there in a cave.

I think the crystals will lead us to the Heart of Tenegard, but we have to hurry and find the next deposit."

Lenire studied her in the flickering darkness. The lamplight above the door to the inn highlighted his questioning gaze. "How do you know all that?"

"I told you. You're not the only one who has experience with the Blight."

After coming to a hesitant agreement, which delighted both of their dragons, Cora and Lenire retired to their respective rooms. Lenire was a good ally to have. Cora knew that. She would be foolish to continue letting her personal feelings put Tenegard's magic at risk. If she had to bite her tongue and play nice to protect the source of the magic that might be strong enough to wake the dragon riders, then she would do it.

Cora had waited for Lenire to push her for information or to bait her into another argument after what she said about the crystals, but he'd just nodded and said goodnight.

Maybe Yrsa had told him not to push or maybe he too had recognized some benefit to having a Tenegardian ally with a direct line to the source of power the Blight was hunting. If Lenire really wanted to find the Blight, he would do well to follow her and Alaric.

Once alone, Cora's thoughts drifted back to the school. To Faron and all the sleeping riders. To Elaine and the healers. To Strida. She retrieved the communication anchor from her pack and whispered Strida's name. Even though she'd expected it to work, she still jumped at Strida's voice.

"You're okay!" Strida said. "It was getting so late I was starting to worry."

"Alaric and I are fine," Cora assured her. "We just had a really long day."

Cora jumped into the events of the day, relaying how the crystal had acted like a lodestone and led her to the village and the new crystal cave. She also explained about the hound attack and the arrival of Lenire and Yrsa.

"Itharus?" Strida said. "I've never heard of it."

"Likely none of the dragon riders have. It would have been lost with Onyx's spell."

"And you're sure it's smart to align yourself with Lenire?" Strida asked, her tone cautious. "For someone who claims to have been an ally of Tenegard, he's awfully reluctant to share information with you."

Cora held the anchor closer. "What are you saying?"

Strida's voice was almost a whisper. "I'm just worried about what other secrets he's keeping."

# CHAPTER 10

## CORA

Cora startled from sleep, her pulse racing, certain that she'd heard a voice in her room. She glanced around, grappling at the bedsheets. She threw them off and stumbled out of bed, looking from one dark corner to the next. As she focused and the shadows took on the dim form of furniture in the room, Cora relaxed, the beat of her heart calming beneath her ribs.

At first she thought it might have been Pieter's wife, again asking her if she needed another blanket, or maybe even Lenire, telling her he'd changed his mind about the tentative alliance they had formed before retiring for the night, but her door was still closed tight, her sword draped across the handle in a way so that it would have crashed to the floor had someone opened it while she'd been asleep.

As far as Cora was concerned, she was alone.

So why were the fine hairs on her arms still standing on end?

Cora rubbed some life into her limbs, thinking maybe she'd just been chilled. She walked barefoot across the floor, the wooden beams creaking beneath her feet, her toes curling against a draft.

She paused at the window, the fine glass panes coated with condensation. Rubbing away the moisture, Cora peered out into the darkness below. She hadn't been asleep long, for the moon was high in the sky, dawn still treading far below the horizon. The same yellow lantern light glowed above the entrance to the inn, catching the reflection of misty puddles on the cobblestones and the flicker of dragon scales. Alaric appeared like a stretch of midnight sky where he slept, the shimmer in his scales winking like stars. Yrsa wasn't far from him, and Cora imagined the two had fallen asleep after another long conversation.

For a foolish, sleep-hazed moment, Cora had thought that it was Alaric who had woken her. She thought he'd called her through the bond, his words drawing her out of sleep, but as she looked at him now, unaware and dreaming down there on the cobblestones, she knew that thought had been ridiculous. Their bond was broken. She hadn't heard Alaric's voice inside her head in weeks.

As Cora turned back to the warmth of her abandoned bed, determined to get at least a few more hours of sleep, she froze, a chill dripping down her spine like water over river rocks. She'd heard something.

"Hello?" she rasped into the darkness.

She took another step, the floor creaked.

And then she heard it again: a faint, indistinct whisper. It rustled, like leaves moving across the ground in autumn. Cora stepped closer to the wall, and then to the door, tracing the sound. Was it coming from the next room? Cora dropped to the ground, peering through the crack beneath the door. There were no feet on the stairs, no lights in the hall. The inn was quiet, but for the crackle of the hearth in the front room. Cora jumped back to her feet, scanning her room.

Then she noticed a dim glow coming from the pocket of her pack. "By the stars?" she breathed. Cora snatched up her pack and reached inside, retrieving the two crystals she'd pulled from the hounds' corpses.

They glowed brightly against her palm, as if fueled by magical energy, only Cora hadn't made magical contact with these crystals since defeating the hounds. They should have been inert, drained. She lifted them almost to her nose, holding them close enough that she could study every smooth facet on their surfaces.

That rustling whisper started again and Cora startled, clutching the crystals in her palm as the rustling grew clearer, the whispers becoming actual words. Cora's heart raced. This was the voice that had drawn her from her sleep.

A man spoke urgently. "Cora, I am relieved I have finally made contact with you!"

Cora frowned, staring at the crystals, her mouth open. They were working almost like Emmett's communication anchors. Was that possible? Or was the voice some magical conjuration—a trick of whoever had controlled the hounds? "Who are you?" she asked warily, wondering how the man had learned her name. "What do you want?"

Walking to the door, Cora picked up her sword, the weight of it comforting in her hand. She didn't know what help it would be against a voice, but she felt better for having it.

"I reach out to you with a dire warning," the voice expressed.

Cora swallowed. Nothing about this moment made sense. Who was this stranger and how had they known where to reach her? "Go on then," she said. "What is your warning?"

"Lenire," the voice began, "the young man who killed the hound. Do you know of him?"

"Yes," Cora said through gritted teeth. "I am familiar with him. What is this about?"

"Then I urge you to keep your guard up in his company, for he is a thief and traitor to Itharus. But more concerning than all of that, he is a murderer."

"Murderer?" Cora stammered, almost dropping the crystals. She laid her sword down upon her bed, holding the crystals up to her mouth. "What do you mean?"

"I have said it as plainly as I can. That young man and his dragon are dangerous to be around. He is not to be trusted for any reason."

Feeling her forehead wrinkle, Cora said, "You are even more suspicious, using Tenegard's crystals in such a way. You speak of Itharus as if you know it, and yet you refuse to identify yourself."

The voice chuckled. It was a soft sound, unoffended by Cora's accusations. "You are wise to be cautious of strangers, and I applaud you for thinking in such ways. You are correct, I am from Itharus myself. I have been sent by my people to retrieve Lenire and his dragon, both dangerous criminals who fled across the sea to Tenegard after stealing a rare magical technology."

Cora thought again of the hounds, wondering about their creator. She'd put the blame on Melusine and her magical experiments, but if this man had reached her through these specific crystals, that tied him to those monsters too. "The hounds," Cora said, looking for confirmation. "Those were your doing?"

"Yes," the voice confessed. "They were indeed my own creation, but they were simply meant to pursue Lenire."

Cora scoffed. "They almost leveled an entire village. People were hurt. Homes destroyed. You're telling me that was all for one man?"

"And that I regret. I never intended for others to get in the way, though many more would come to danger should Lenire be left unchecked."

Something wasn't quite adding up. Cora had been certain that the hounds were merely reacting to her. That their goal lay beyond the village. Had it been Lenire they were chasing? If so, then he'd risked his life to fly to her aid.

"Why the crystals?" she asked.

"I simply used the materials I had at hand in Tenegard, though they have proven to have remarkable properties thus far. Giving life to dead flesh for example. Allowing us to communicate."

If the man could use the crystals in such a way, he must be a sorcerer or else a manipulator of magic. Cora and the dragon riders had just learned of the power of the crystals. How had this man arrived in Tenegard and immediately learned of their uses? For as warm and scholarly as he sounded, Cora remained unconvinced by this stranger. "If you will not identify yourself, I cannot blindly believe your story."

The voice remained soft spoken, understanding even. "I could hardly expect you to. This was the safest way I could think to make contact. And regardless of your feelings toward me, I felt obligated to share my warning to prevent you from getting entangled in a far-off war you do not understand."

Cora's thoughts jumped to the civil war Lenire had described. She had believed him when he'd spoken of his home, of the dangers he'd faced, of those in power who'd threatened his people with the Blight and then lost control of it. As stubborn as he was proving to be, she'd even felt a measure of sympathy for him. She knew a little of what it was like to fight a losing battle. But now all she could wonder was if he'd lied to her? Had his stories been intended to manipulate her sympathies, to escape the consequences of his actions, or was he truly on a crusade to bring down the Blight?

"If you need proof," the voice continued, "see if Lenire carries a disk with him. It will be unnaturally heavy, made of ice-like stone, and engraved with elaborate knotted designs that mislead the eye. He stole it from me and I intend to get it back."

With that final assurance, the crystals went dark and cold in Cora's hand. She listened for the rustling, but the room had grown quiet except for the creak of the floorboard beneath her feet. As Cora returned the crystals to the pocket of her pack, only now did she realize that she'd not even gotten the stranger's name.

When the sun came up, Cora might have been inclined to think the entire encounter was simply a dream, but she'd hardly been able to sleep after the crystals went dark. She was up and dressed the moment the sun peeked over the horizon.

She tightened the leather belt around her waist and slipped her sword into its sheath. Now that she knew something strange was going on with Lenire, she'd decided to keep her weapon close. She took her pack and left her room, running into Pieter's wife in the hall.

"Good morning," she said.

Cora smiled.

"I hope you found everything to be adequate," she said. "I know the rooms are small and the finishes are old but—"

Cora took her hand, silencing whatever she was about to say next. "It was more than adequate. Lenire and I are both very grateful for your hospitality. I hope we didn't put you out too much."

Judging by the sounds downstairs, the inn was full for breakfast.

"The opposite, in fact," she said. "I haven't been so busy at this time of the day in years. I suspect it has something to do with housing the two dragon riders who saved our village."

Cora smiled, though it was weak. She couldn't help but think that if neither she nor Lenire were here, the village might never have come under attack. Then again, the hounds might have run through the town with nothing to stop them but weak spears and dagger blades. Many lives might have been lost. "I'm glad everyone is safe."

With that, Cora took her leave, hurrying downstairs.

Caleb passed her on the landing, jostling Cora to the side as he raced outside to greet the dragons. Cora grinned after his antics before spotting Lenire. He was already seated at a table, his breakfast dishes empty, his pack resting on the floor beside him. He nursed the last of his drink, perhaps a coffee or tea, while scanning the street through the window.

Cora made her way across the room to him, slowly, weaving between the tables. She studied him in a way she hadn't before. She observed how he sat, how he spoke to passersby that wished him good morning, the way his eyes skittered about the room. Cora tried to determine if these were the habits of a murderer, if an unnamed accuser could be believed.

Before she could get any further into her observations, Pieter approached the table, wringing a cloth between his hands. "Please," he said, "if you have some time before you leave, I wondered if you might take a look at my family's foundered horse. I saw how you healed people yesterday, and though I do not know if your abilities extend to animals, I hoped you might try."

Lenire perked up at the request. "You've had a farrier look at the animal?"

Pieter nodded. "The condition has resisted all the farrier's efforts to cure it. We rely on the horse to transport provisions. Without it, I'm not sure what we will do."

To Cora's surprise, Lenire stood and laid his hand on Pieter's shoulder. "Of course, I'll be happy to take a look."

"Oh, thank you," Pieter said, escorting Lenire toward a back hallway that she suspected led to the stables. "You don't know what this means to my family."

"It's the least I can do," Lenire said, "for supplying us with such wonderful accommodations."

As they drew near, Lenire spotted her in the crowd. "I'll be right back," he said.

Cora merely nodded, carrying on toward the table where he'd eaten breakfast. She nudged the edge of Lenire's pack as she sat down and the voice from last night whispered in her mind. *If you need proof ...*

She eyed the pack. The voice had said Lenire carried some sort of magical disk with him. Her gaze drifted to the hallway where Lenire and Pieter had disappeared. This might be her only chance to confirm if the voice had been telling the truth. Was she sharing tables and joining forces with a murderer?

Cora snatched Lenire's pack from the ground and dragged it onto a chair. It was surprisingly heavy for its size. She yanked the top open and began rifling through the contents, knowing very well that Lenire might return from the stables at any moment. It hadn't taken him long to heal the villagers, so she suspected he would make quick work of the horse if he was able to help.

Cora shoved aside provisions and blankets, digging to the very bottom of the pack, and her hand seized around something cool and smooth. It felt almost like bone, but as Cora pulled the item free, she saw it was exactly what the voice had described: a disk of ice-like stone covered in elaborate knots. She tried to examine the designs but the longer she stared at them the more turned around she became. Shaking off the dizzying feeling, Cora stuffed the disk back into the bottom of the pack, shoving the provisions and blankets on top. She latched the pack and tossed it back on the floor where it had been before Lenire had left.

Cora took a deep breath, letting it out in a heavy sigh. Whatever the intentions of the voice she'd spoken to last night, she'd found the disk, just as he said she would. But she felt no closer to knowing if his other accusations were true. Could Lenire really be a thief and a traitor and a murderer? She couldn't afford to let anything derail her mission to find the heart—to save Faron. If Lenire meant her harm, then he was a threat to her entire plan. Her thoughts lingered on Faron, unconscious in the infirmary. She missed talking to him, confiding in him, and wondered how he would counsel her now.

Cora jumped as a plate was set on the table. She turned to find Caleb there, setting a pile of toasted bread in front of her. "Mother said I was to bring you breakfast."

"Thank you," Cora told him. "Did you see the dragons?"

He nodded, though it was sad. "Couldn't you stay a while?" he said. "There's room in the stables. Alaric would like it in there."

His words eased the tension brewing inside her, if only for a moment. "I'm sure he would like it. I bet you keep it nice and tidy for the other animals."

Caleb frowned. "We only have one horse in there right now and he's lame. The farrier can't fix him, and father said we might have to put him down if he can't pull the wagon."

Cora didn't quite know what to say, but was rescued by Lenire as he appeared, putting his hands on Caleb's shoulders. "I don't know," he said. "That horse was looking mighty strong when I was in the stables."

Caleb pulled back to look up at him. "He was? When?"

"Just now," Lenire said, gesturing down the hallway. "He looked about ready to gallop right down the road."

"I don't believe you," Caleb said, his lips puckering into a suspicious grin.

"It's the truth. Your father's out there right now, hitching the wagon."

Elation filled Caleb's eyes and he dashed away from them, hurrying out to the stables to go see for himself.

Lenire stared after the boy for a moment, then slumped into his seat.

"You managed to heal the horse, then?"

He nodded, finishing the rest of his now cold coffee.

"That was good of you to help this family."

He shrugged off her praise as if embarrassed. "It's no big thing. I've always been better with animals than people anyway."

"I've always had a fondness for animals too," she said.

Lenire confused her. He couldn't be everything that mysterious voice had accused him of and yet be so kind, so generous with his talents. He'd saved her life, she had to admit, and then he'd healed half the village. Now he'd just saved Pieter's family horse. Would a criminal on the run really give of himself in this way? It didn't make sense. Cora picked at her toast, wondering about him. "Well," she said, "I'm sure Pieter is very grateful."

"It's just a bit of magic," Lenire muttered. He reached for his pack and his expression changed. Or perhaps Cora would say it froze. His eyes moved across the table but didn't quite land on her.

"You know," he said casually, finally looking at her, "Itharusian magic is based on knots. I've been practicing them since I could speak."

Cora must have untied the pack's magical knot when she'd opened it. But she gave nothing away, taking a bite of her toast. Instead she casually asked, "Do you know of a magical knot that will bind someone to telling the truth?"

Lenire's eyes narrowed, only slightly, and he gave her a long, searching look before standing and shouldering his pack. "Why?" he said just as casually. "Is there a liar you're looking to catch?"

# CHAPTER 11

## OCTAVIA

T he draft from the windows nearly blew out all the lanterns in the palace meeting room, threatening to leave Octavia—and her guests—in darkness.

"My apologies," she said, hurrying from closing the shutters back to the small table she was using to host interviews. Octavia had spent the morning meeting with citizens of Kaerlin whose businesses would be impacted if relations between Tenegard and Athelia continued to sour. She hoped that by compiling the information into a report, she could sway the council into listening to her. If she proved that Athelia and Tenegard already relied on each other and had a beneficial trade relationship in place, perhaps she could convince the council to request an audience with Athelia's sorcerers. Then she could ask them about the sleeping sickness. A continued alliance was a good thing for Tenegard, and she wanted to push all thoughts of war from the minds of the councilors. "Please," she said, gesturing with a welcoming hand to the parchment she was using to take notes, "continue with what you were saying."

"Yes, princess," the man said. He was wringing his hat between his hands, clearly nervous.

"Just Octavia," she insisted. "The time of princesses is long gone now." She smiled gently at the man. He was of strong build, with flecks of gray in his hair and an even temperament. His name was Aldon and he was a merchant. His store was small, but profitable, selling fineries that were only made with materials that came from Athelia.

Aldon nodded. "As I was saying, if the border to Athelia should be stacked with any more soldiers, I fear the relations with my suppliers might be damaged beyond repair. Already they are suspicious of Tenegard's motives. I try to assure them that there is no talk of war among the people. But that doesn't mean whispers of it don't exist within the palace itself. If the supply chain were to break down, I would lose the entirety of my business." Aldon stopped wringing the hat in his hands and set it on the stool beside him. His eyes narrowed, his nerves steeling. "What do you hope this report will accomplish?"

"I hope to present it to the council. To show them that alliances already exist with Athelia and that it would be most beneficial to continue to foster those relationships." Octavia underlined the last sentence she had written. "I have spoken to many of your neighbors. Merchants, bakers, salespeople. They all rely on good relations with Athelia. Right now, there is no war among us. I hope to keep it that way."

"We watch Tenegardian soldiers march off in the night," Aldon said. "We can see their torches burning far into the distance. It is only small companies of soldiers. Sometimes no more than four. But there is nothing in that direction except for the border."

"Perhaps they are switching out the watch duty."

"That's what we thought," Aldon said.

"And what do you think now?"

"The people in Kaerlin are careful not to whisper things on the streets. We know better than that. Living under Onyx's rule for so long taught us how not to anger those in power. But that doesn't mean worry hasn't festered among us. We watch those torchlights bleed into the distance, my lady. But none ever return."

Octavia frowned, making a note on the parchment, her quill scratching sharply in the silence that followed. "And what do you think they are doing?"

Aldon hesitated. As far as he was concerned, Octavia was one of them. *The council.*

"I am trying to help," Octavia assured him. The complicated relationship with Athelia affected more than the dragon riders. She knew that. The council must know it too. She just needed the facts to support her point. It was harder for Northwood to dismiss her when she presented the research.

Aldon's gaze flickered to Raksha, curled up in the corner of the room, her eyes closed as if in sleep, though Octavia could sense that she had merely closed her eyes to ease the minds of the interviewees. She breathed easy and deep, yet her thoughts were quick and sharp, lashing out like whips with each new piece of information. Perhaps it was Raksha's presence that assured Aldon that Octavia was different from the others. She was a *dragon rider* after all. One of the riders who'd gone to war against Onyx. She'd already brought one tyrant down. She wasn't about to let the council become another.

"They're moving the troops into a better position, albeit slowly," Aldon said finally. "Slow enough that maybe they think no one will notice. But we have noticed. The council will never admit it, and they may not call it war, but they are readying Tenegard for a fight. One the people do not want."

Octavia swallowed hard, reaching for his hand. "It will not come to that," she promised.

"How can you be sure?"

Octavia glanced at Raksha and made sure Aldon saw her do so. He nodded in understanding—he'd gotten the message. She would not let a war ravage both their countries. She was determined to go to Athelia for help and to do that she had to cement their relationship. Athelia and Tenegard could be allies—*would* be allies. Even if it was the only thing she ever accomplished as a member of Tenegard's council, Octavia would see this through, both for the dragon riders and for the people. *Her* people.

Aldon's hand flinched beneath hers. "I have a family," he said. "Small children to care for. Losing the trade alliance I have with Athelia would crush my business, but war would kill us all. It would tear me from my children, and I might never return. If you truly are *for* the people," he said, looking her deep in the eyes, "you have to fix this. You have to keep us safe."

He pulled his hand free and stood, dismissing himself with a small bow. Aldon fled from the room, leaving Octavia's pulse racing. She herself had felt the looming threat of war hanging over her head like an ax poised to strike. Ever since Onyx's fall, Northwood had been chomping at the bit, looking for any excuse to rise up against Athelia, but this felt different. He was no longer talking: he was taking action.

Raksha stirred in the corner, rising to her feet. Shadows flickered about the room as she stretched in front of the lamps. Octavia wandered to the window, throwing open the shutters. She let the breeze crawl over her skin, washing away the flush of uncertainty. The sun was already setting. Where had the day gone?

"What plagues your mind?" Raksha said. It was an amusing question, considering Raksha could read her thoughts. Perhaps it was simply that Octavia's thoughts could not settle.

"Everything Aldon said," she began, turning from the window to face Raksha. "I hadn't realized there was such fear among the people." She truly thought they were free now—free of Onyx, free of their fear, free to live as they wanted. But could life really be that different if they were too terrified to even whisper it on the streets? "It's almost as if nothing has changed."

"Everything has changed," Raksha assured her. "Onyx is gone and the people are safe."

"Are they, though? Is Aldon right? Does Northwood march small companies of soldiers to the border? Is he stacking the army for battle?"

"I wouldn't put it past him," Raksha relented. "But that doesn't mean we are poised for war. Northwood wouldn't dare to declare war on Athelia without the council's backing. We still have time to change their minds."

Octavia sighed. Her main goal today had been to secure enough information in support of contacting Athelia on behalf of the dragon riders. Now she felt as if she carried the worries of all the people of Tenegard on her shoulders. "Fix this. Keep us safe. That is what Aldon said to me."

"And we will," Raksha said, shifting close enough to pin Octavia with her gaze. "You are not in this alone. I will be by your side through everything."

A flash of comforting warmth shot down the bond and Octavia smiled, leaning her head against Raksha's scales. "What do we do now?"

"We start as we intended, with your report."

"Is it enough?" Octavia said, glancing down at the stack of papers she'd collected over the course of the day. Looking at it, her work felt insignificant.

"Even something small can have a big impact," Raksha reminded her. "Remember when we met? A wisp of curiosity brought you to me, and your simple human words put in motion what would become our dragon bond. Look where we are now."

A surge of hope flowed through Octavia. This report might not be enough to convince them all, but it might just convince some. Raksha was right.

"I am often right," Raksha agreed.

Octavia chuckled and the pressure in her chest eased, her heart lighter. Raksha turned her head to the door suddenly.

"What is it?" Octavia asked. Then she heard the footsteps. She returned to her desk, rifling through her papers. There was no one left on her list. She'd seen all the interviewees for the day.

Raksha tilted her head curiously, but then a toothy dragon grin stretched across her face.

Strida appeared in the doorway a moment later and Octavia's heart soared. Joy filled her so quickly she thought she might burst as she scurried to the door and into Strida's arms.

"What a sight you are!" Octavia gushed, pulling back enough to look Strida in the eyes.

"A good sight, I hope."

"Of course," Octavia said. Strida's arrival had both surprised and delighted her. "It's so good to see you." She laughed. "It's almost as if you heard me wishing you were here and appeared." Then, like all the wind had been knocked out of her, Octavia withered, the happiness sucked straight out. "Though it's rare that a visit is accompanied by good news." Her fingers tightened around Strida's arms. "What's wrong? What happened?"

"I hate that an unexpected visit from me is a reason for worry instead of joy," Strida said.

"There was a moment of joy," Octavia assured her. "So much I thought I might burst." She hugged Strida once more, then pulled away. "Tell me the news," she said and listened while Strida filled her in on the school and Faron, but most of all, Cora's new mission.

"I do bring disturbing tidings," Strida continued. "Cora contacted me earlier using the communication anchors from Emmett. She reached a remote mountain village using the crystals, but it looks like our enemy had also learned to use the crystals."

"What do you mean?" Octavia asked.

"Cora said the village was attacked by hounds. Or something like it. They were odd. Like someone had created them. And when they were slain, she found crystals hidden inside their flesh." Strida continued, updating Octavia on Cora's journey, her encounter with the hounds, and with the foreign dragon knight, Lenire.

News of Itharus—another country with dragons—captured Octavia's attention, but what held it was the fact that Melusine had figured out how to use the crystals to her advantage so quickly. What else was the healer capable of?

"Killing Cora didn't seem to be the end goal for the hounds," Strida offered. "So that's something at least."

"Do you think it was only meant to be a distraction? Something to lower the guard at the school?"

"Cora is our best hope of finding the Heart of Tenegard and protecting it from Melusine. It makes sense that the healer would be trying to keep tabs on her. So far the school has been left alone, but that doesn't mean that couldn't change. The shield is still in place and with Cora gone, that has to be our priority. Now more than ever it's important to keep the shield as strong as possible." Strida took Octavia's hand. "That's why I'm here. Come back with me and help us. You're one of the stronger dragon riders. And we need all the power we can muster."

Octavia's first instinct was to say *yes*. Yes, she would go. Yes, she would answer Strida's call. But then she caught sight of the messy draft of her report sitting on the table. "My work is nowhere near complete," she began. "After the conversation I just had with one of the merchants, I can't abandon my place in the capital knowing the council might be gearing up for war." It felt like they were teetering on a precipice, and if Octavia and Raksha left, the council would fall at Northwood's feet. They would be conned and coerced and convinced, feeding a necessity for war that did not exist.

And if they went to war, there would be no way for Octavia to secure help from Athelia's sorcerers. Not only would Tenegard be fighting for survival but so would the dragon riders.

Octavia looked Strida in the eye, silently begging her to understand. "I want to. You know I do, but now is not the time to leave the council."

Strida's face fell, though she didn't immediately argue as Octavia had been expecting. They so often argued these days.

"Are you hungry?" Octavia asked, not knowing what else to say. "You had a long ride. I can have food brought up by someone if you'd like."

But instead of soothing or distracting her, the offer seemed to ignite the fire in Strida. She paced the length of the room before exploding.

"Is there even a point in fighting the council politically if you and Raksha are so outnumbered?"

"We have supporters. The old rebel leaders—"

"Are not enough to make a difference!" Strida snapped. "At least at the school you could actually do some good."

Octavia shook off the familiar wounds that festered. "This is my job," she said calmly. "All the people I spoke to today are counting on me to stop a war from breaking out between Tenegard and Athelia."

"And while you're here arguing with ignorant fools, Melusine could destroy the school or, stars forbid, magic itself. Losing the magic in Tenegard would hurt it more than a war ever would. You need to get your priorities straight."

Her words felt like a slap, and Octavia grew silent. She grappled for the right words. The right combination that would make Strida see that the dragon riders couldn't survive both Melusine and a war. "You're right, Cora is our best hope at finding the Heart of Tenegard, but I am the best at *this*. If anyone is going to broker peace between our two nations, it's me. I just wish you could believe that. Believe in me."

Something in Strida's manner softened, however minutely. "I'm sorry. Cora's absence has me on edge, especially knowing Melusine has such a dangerous new weapon. I shouldn't even have left to come here."

"It's okay," Octavia said, her voice barely above a whisper. It wasn't really okay. The argument festered between them still like a fire that would not be dampened.

"Of all the things to come out of this," Strida said, trying to lighten the mood. "The shift in Emmett's allegiance wasn't something I was anticipating. He said he's only sharing what's absolutely necessary with Northwood. Cora's not convinced of anything, but he even offered to help with the school's messy accounting."

"Oh," Octavia said, grateful for the change of subject. "I wonder if I could test his story by checking what Northwood last heard from the school."

"I'd be very interested to hear what he says."

Octavia nodded, shooting Strida a small, although weak smile. "You know, I'm fighting too. Just in my own way. Fighting to get the school more resources. Fighting to get access to Athelia's sorcerers. I think maybe they can help with the sleeping sickness where we can't."

Strida nodded wearily. "I know."

"It's not like I've forgotten you."

"I *know.*" There was more Strida wanted to say. Octavia could tell by the firm line that stretched her lips, but she held her tongue. "How about dinner then? Maybe we could share a meal and forget about all of this. At least for an hour or two."

Octavia was grateful for the suggestion, but just as before, her eyes strayed to the papers on the table. To the report yet to be written. The longer it took, the closer the threat of war loomed.

Strida let out a heavy sigh. "I'll be in my usual guest room overnight. If you decide you can spare a moment, come and find me." She turned on her heel then without even a *goodbye.*

Octavia felt hollow as she slumped into the chair at her desk, picked up her quill, and gripped it tight enough to keep the tears at bay. She wouldn't cry over her lovesick heart. There were real troubles in Tenegard that she needed to solve. People's livelihoods and families were counting on her.

"The report could wait an hour," Raksha said. "You also haven't eaten recently."

Octavia shook her head, returning to her work, swiping at the few tears that got away. The conversation haunted her as she strung the facts into a coherent report. Part of her couldn't help wondering if Strida was right, that she was wasting her time on the council. When had a report accomplished anything?

There was a new threat from Melusine and if Octavia really wanted to help, she couldn't sit around and wait for council votes. If she wanted to save her friends, she needed to exhaust all her options. That included finding out if the Athelians had a way to wake the sleepers. As Strida said, the school needed every magic user they could muster. Maybe it was time to take communication with Athelia into her own hands.

Contacting Athelia, however discreetly, without consulting the other councilors might be enough to get her accused of treason, but what other choice was there? And from where Octavia was sitting, saving the school and her friends and maybe even Tenegard itself was worth the risk.

# CHAPTER 12

## OCTAVIA

O ctavia tapped her foot against the polished stone floor, sending a *tck, tck, tck* across the room. A thread of impatience pulled at her leg, bouncing it faster and faster until it matched the hurried beat of her racing heart. She glanced over her shoulder through the open door of Northwood's office once again, studying it as if it was the man himself. The furniture was sparse and the room was clean, almost immaculately so, not a paper or quill in sight, and Octavia knew at once that this office was merely for show. It was the office he invited Tenegardian citizens to when they had concerns or complaints worth exploring. This wasn't the place where he regularly conducted business.

Northwood must have an office in another part of the palace. A secret room filled with private council communications, letters destined for the dragon-rider school, and military memorandums. That was where he did business with the council members. That was where he spoke with his confidants and afforded his colleagues meetings. But he clearly didn't consider Octavia a confidant nor a colleague, since his private secretary had directed her to this tiny mockery of an office when she'd requested this meeting yesterday.

The time for their meeting had already come and gone. Northwood was late, if one could even call it that now, but Octavia remained seated in the chair outside his office door despite the insistence of his secretary that they could simply reschedule. Even now Octavia could see the woman, Marija, counting the minutes until she could again ask her to leave.

While she waited, Octavia's thoughts strayed to Strida and their argument from the previous night. Like they so often did, their visit had gone poorly. Octavia had inquired after Strida first thing this morning, only to learn from one of the palace staff that she'd already departed for the school. Clearly, she hadn't felt like talking. The stress of their relationship only added to Octavia's agitation with Northwood and her foot bounced even faster.

A group of council members hurried by, chatting to each other. They inclined their heads when they spotted her, looking curiously from her to the office. When they'd gone, Marija jumped up from her desk and scurried to Octavia's side.

"Princess," she began.

Octavia stopped herself from rolling her eyes. She'd already asked Marija to call her by her name on multiple occasions.

"Please let me reschedule for another day," she said. "I'll send word to your chambers as soon as Councilor Northwood confirms."

"Why should I reschedule?" Octavia countered. She'd done her best to be pleasant and cordial despite Marija arranging this scam of a meeting for her. It was likely at Northwood's insistence, so she knew where her frustration needed to be directed, but she'd already watched Marija surreptitiously retrieve a small piece of bone from her pocket. It was a communication anchor, Octavia was sure of it, used to whisper updates to Northwood wherever he was hiding.

Marija's eyes narrowed. It was only by a fraction. If Octavia had blinked at the wrong moment she would have missed it, but it was enough to tell Octavia not to trust the farce of a smile on Marija's face. As much as she wanted to convince herself that Marija would never stoop to Northwood's level of lies and deceit, she also knew that only a certain type of person worked this closely with Northwood.

She thought of Emmett briefly. Although he'd come to his senses and grown to be somewhat of an ally to the school, Octavia still remembered when Emmett had run around after Northwood, practically groveling at his feet, looking down on anyone who dared contradict his boss. Marija had the same look about her now—shifty and condescending—as she implored Octavia to leave.

"I was on time," Octavia continued. "And Northwood sent no communication to me that our meeting today needed to be changed."

"Yes, I understand that," Marija said. "But things do come up. Last-minute things. Unavoidable things. It isn't often that he forgets an appointment—"

"Well, which is it?" Octavia asked, interrupting the woman's string of excuses. "Did something come up or did he forget?"

Marija's too-pleasant expression finally faltered, and she leveled Octavia with a pair of dagger eyes. "What is it that you want exactly?"

"I would like Councilor Northwood to keep his appointment times. We are all very busy, but none of the other councilors have trouble remembering a meeting that they have expressly agreed to attend."

"I may have misspoken when I said he'd *forgotten*," Marija said diplomatically. "Perhaps it was something of more urgency that pulled him away from his appointments. Commanding the military does take precedence as you can probably understand."

"Unless Kaerlin is burning down as we speak," Octavia said, glancing out the window and pointedly nodding to the blue skies that stretched over the capital, "there should be no such emergency to attend to."

The corners of Marija's mouth flickered. Octavia could tell she was trying hard to maintain a smooth, placid expression. Would it have been easier to reschedule? Perhaps. But Northwood would have likely just blown her off again, and every moment they wasted rearranging meetings was another moment the school and the dragon riders suffered with the sleeping sickness.

"Very well," Marija said. "I will let Councilor Northwood know you would like to keep your appointment today. But perhaps you would like to come back at a later time? We could arrange something after dinner. Or this evening. I'm sure you have other appointments to attend to."

"No," Octavia said, making a show of getting comfortable in her chair. "My schedule is clear. Besides, I've waited this long. I don't mind waiting a little longer."

Translation: Octavia was going to sit here as long as it took, even if she had to announce to all of Kaerlin that she was waiting on a meeting with Northwood. He could procrastinate as long as he wanted, but Octavia had been trained for this. Before she'd fled and been branded the rebel princess, she'd spent hours sitting in on Onyx's council sessions, just an unheard shadow in the corner. If Northwood wanted to play that game, she would win.

"Perhaps if you could speak to the urgency of your meeting," Marija said. "I could let Councilor Northwood know what exactly you hoped to discuss with him."

Octavia smiled this time, the way one did at a small child. How much of a fool did they take her for?

"I don't think that's any of your business," Octavia said. She was not unkind, but she was forceful. If she let Northwood's staff walk all over her, it would do nothing to legitimize her place as one of Tenegard's council members. They would always regard her simply as the runaway princess, lost and confused in her duties, left alone to ride dragons through the sky and nothing more. "Now, if you could please inform Northwood that I am *still* waiting and I intend to keep waiting, it would be much appreciated."

"Very well," Marija said again, the words forced out between her teeth. She begrudgingly returned to her desk and, from the corner of her eye, Octavia watched her whisper into the anchor. The woman grimaced. Clearly, whoever was on the other end of the anchor wasn't impressed.

Octavia could only assume it was Northwood, and she got a pleasant sort of satisfaction knowing he was storming through the palace somewhere on his way to meet her.

*Don't stoop to his level*, Raksha warned gently. She'd mostly stayed out of the way as Octavia argued with Marija, but she was always there, a warm presence in the back of Octavia's mind.

*For all the grief he puts us through*, Octavia said. *I thought I would enjoy his frustration, if only for a moment.*

*Just don't lose sight of what we are trying to accomplish here.* With those words, Raksha pulled Octavia's goal into focus. It had been a deliberate decision to keep the dragon away. There was a part of Northwood that was still unnerved by Raksha's presence, both within the palace and as a councilor herself. They thought this conversation might go over better without a dragon hanging over their heads.

*I won't*, Octavia promised. Today was about helping the school. She needed access to the communication anchors Northwood had in his possession. The ones that would likely be able to make contact with Athelia. She knew he would never agree if she outwardly told him that her intention was still to ask the Athelian sorcerers for help, but perhaps he would let her use them for something else. Something that he perceived as innocuous.

Footsteps thundered down the hall and Octavia braced herself.

Northwood swept into the room, his cloak billowing behind him. She watched as the frustration on his face melted away, masked by faux amusement.

"Octavia!" he said as if her presence had been unknown to him. "What a pleasant surprise."

*A surprise indeed*, she thought.

"Come, step into my office."

He took her by the shoulder as she stood, guiding her into his office and to the wooden chair before his desk. It was small and uncomfortable, immediately digging into her spine, and she suspected he used this tactic to hurry unwanted visitors from the room.

"Now, to what do I owe the pleasure of your company?" He sat, not behind his desk, but on the corner of it, hands folded in his lap, where he could tower over her like a school teacher did a student.

"I was just wondering if you'd found the school's expenditures to be within your expectations?"

"And why would that be any of your concern?"

Northwood loved to spar with her during council meetings, to shoot down her proposals, and question her decisions. But most of all, he loved to treat her like an idiot, to convince others that her place on the council was nothing more than a nicety granted due to the position she once held as Princess of Tenegard. Well, if that's the game he wanted to play, then so would she. She could be bashfully ignorant. She could let him believe that he knew better than her.

"Oh, I was just trying to help. I know the school has been working extra hard since Melusine's attack to make sure all the expenses are in order to ensure further funding from the council. I'm sure you can imagine that upkeeping the school is of vital importance, especially now."

"So far," he said rather brusquely. "Your little friends have managed to keep their accounting in order."

Octavia resisted the urge to smile. She knew well enough, thanks to Strida, that it was Emmett putting the school's finances in order. The fact that Northwood seemed oblivious to that fact might very well prove whose side Emmett was on. He could have easily outed them to Northwood, but instead he'd worked extra hard to ensure the council couldn't question their expenditures and withhold further funding.

"Though I am expecting another report shortly," Northwood said, rubbing at his jaw. His gaze grew distant, a smirk on his face, as if maybe he was hoping he would finally find a fault in the numbers that he could exploit.

"Of course," she said, preparing herself to shift the conversation. "I should probably touch base with the school to further discuss the latest spending." Octavia schooled her face, practicing a blank stare. "Perhaps you would allow me to use the council's communication anchor to contact Emmett. It would be so much more timely than a letter."

Northwood reacted as she'd expected, sputtering on his answer. He had no idea that Octavia or the school had learned of the magic of the communication anchors thanks to Emmett. Despite how much he tried, Northwood couldn't hide his surprise. It was evident from the way he'd jumped off his desk as soon as she'd finished her question to the way his face puckered, the lines across his forehead as deep as carriage tracks through the mud.

Thanks to the hours spent in the council chamber arguing, Octavia was well aware of the fact that she'd genuinely thrown him.

*Stay focused*, Raksha reminded her.

*It feels good to have the upper hand for once.*

His surprise also confirmed that Emmett hadn't mentioned the use of the anchors at the school or the fact Cora and Strida were now using them to communicate while Cora searched for the Heart of Tenegard.

Northwood flitted around behind his desk. "How did you come to know of the anchor?" he asked, doing his best to keep the question casual despite the pitch in his voice.

Octavia dodged his question with one of her own. "It's for the council's use, is it not?"

Northwood blinked at her, his mouth set in a firm line. His silence was her reward. She knew she had him. If he refused her, if he made a show of keeping the anchor private and secret, he knew she might very well take her questions to the rest of the council. And then his private little way of scrying information from the lands would be general knowledge. He would have to field a myriad of questions from the other councilors. Questions he likely didn't want to answer. As Octavia leveled him with her best, most innocent smile, she knew they'd reached an understanding.

"The use of an anchor is usually reserved for more important conversations," he began. They both knew that was a lie. "But I'll allow this once. The anchor here will connect you to Emmett at the school.

Seeing as he is my liaison, I should be present in case there are any important updates."

Octavia nodded, knowing it was best not to push him. She'd never really expected Northwood to leave her alone with the anchor anyway.

"Shall we?" He lifted his hand, gesturing to the door, and Octavia could tell Marija was surprised to see them leave together. Northwood led her down the hall and into a familiar stairwell. Octavia had used this passage to escape into the bowels of the palace when she was younger, hunting for old books once she'd finished those in Onyx's library.

Northwood emerged into a dim, dank passageway, torchlights leaving only a few feet of visibility before them. Octavia hurried to keep pace.

*Where are you?* Raksha asked.

Octavia shivered. *Somewhere deep, where no one else ventures, especially not the council members.*

Northwood slowed by a door. It was so old and worn it almost matched the stone of the surrounding walls. He pushed it and with a creak the door gave way, revealing a shadowy chamber. He took a torch from the wall and Octavia did the same, surprised by what she found.

The anchor she'd seen at the school had been small. A mere piece of carved bone. A trinket you could keep in your pocket. The anchor set up in this room was something else entirely. It appeared more like a sculpture, bone white, and curved into a set of elaborate arches that filled the room with an uncanny magical charge.

It pressed against Octavia like invisible waves, ebbing and flowing from the arches. A tingle shot down her arm and she could feel her own magic responding, getting caught up in the waves and tracing them back to their source. If she let herself go, she knew she could follow the charge to the other end and find who lingered there at the end of each arch. It was similar to the way Strida had described them tracing the river, pushing their magic along through the bedrock. Only there was no mountain here to impede Octavia. Speaking to someone would be as easy as pulling back a veil.

Clearly this room was meant to be a more permanent center of communication. Northwood, who had no magic as far as Octavia knew, had to activate the device by rearranging a few bone-like pieces secured to a specific arch into a particular pattern.

To Octavia's surprise, it wasn't a voice that emerged from the arch, but a ghostly image that appeared between the pillars.

"Emmett?" she said.

He jumped, looking up from the grainy image of a desk. "Octavia? What can I do for you?"

Octavia was well aware of Northwood, pacing in and out of the shadows, the eerie flicker of his face appearing between the other arches. He listened as they exchanged pleasantries, growing bored as she began to audit a list of very mundane details about the school.

"I've kept notes," Emmett was saying, rifling through the papers on his desk.

She almost laughed. Leave it to Emmett to be excited about discussing these scrupulous details at length. "I wanted to be sure the expenses for the dining hall repair were being tracked properly."

"So far the school's biggest expenditure has been nails if you can believe it."

Octavia did believe it, knowing the school was being held together with nails and cheap scraps of wood. When Melusine and the Blight had attacked, they had all but leveled the dining hall. "Has the glass been purchased to repair the windows?"

"Not as of yet," he said, reading off his notes. "But the brick has been ordered for the fireplace and new tables should be delivered. There was an attempt to repair the old ones, but that creature didn't leave much to work with."

Octavia caught the moment Northwood rolled his eyes. He carried his torch back across the room, slipping out the door just as she'd hoped he would. Once Northwood was gone, Octavia flitted to the door to ensure the hallway was clear. Then she turned and cleared her throat, interrupting Emmett in the middle of rambling on about some expensive fixture for the dining hall that Strida had insisted on.

Emmett quieted.

"I wondered," she said casually, "if you could recommend anyone in your line of work."

"A liaison?"

"A liaison," she said. "Or an aide. Cora noted the *wide range* of duties you are now performing, and I could use someone with similar *flexibility* to help me out."

Her purpose for contacting Emmett was two-fold. She needed an excuse to gain access to the anchor in order to try to make contact with Athelia, but after talking to the citizens yesterday to compile her report about the importance of alliances at the border, specifically Aldon, Octavia had realized that she needed more information about what was really going on in Kaerlin.

When Aldon had told her about soldiers marching toward the border, carrying out orders from Northwood under the cover of darkness, she knew she had to confirm Northwood's intentions for herself.

So, what she was really asking Emmett for was the name of someone loyal. Someone who would find her the answers that she needed without drawing attention to her. If she had any hope of combating Northwood's lies to the council about amassing troops at the border in preparation for war, then she needed someone in her corner. Hoping Emmett had truly made up his mind to support the school, and gambling on his trust, Octavia held her breath. If Emmett had understood what she was asking of him and he decided to work against her, she might have blown her cover.

"There are a select few I can think of," he said finally, and the tone of his voice suggested he'd caught on to her true intentions. "Who will be more than happy to aid you in whatever *endeavors* you have in mind. But my first suggestion would be Jeth Arenson."

"I do not know that name," Octavia said, trying to pinpoint a face in the capital.

"All the better," Emmett said. "That means he does his job well."

"Yes," Octavia agreed. This Jeth Arenson would be someone she could trust to gather intelligence on her behalf.

"If you are in agreement, I will be sure to let him know that you are looking for aid and that I have made a personal recommendation."

"Thank you, Emmett," Octavia said, feeling a strange kinship with him.

"I'm glad to have been of help," he said. And with that, she let the communication end, his hazy image fading from view.

Before she stepped away from the anchor system, Octavia set her magic loose, letting it sift through the charges that eclipsed the arches. She traced one that felt familiar but distinct, foreign—the unique energy of Athelian magic as she made contact with whoever was at the other end of the anchor. It was a risky move, blindly reaching out.

Octavia knew that it could backfire, putting her in touch with some Athelian spy network that was loyal only to Northwood, but this was her only avenue of communication and she had to try.

As Octavia let her message settle, she felt an answering twang in the magic, and she made it clear: she wanted to talk.

# CHAPTER 13

## CORA

The mountain wind whipped around Cora, snapping at her cheeks like icy hands. Alaric flew higher, trying to pull out of the cold front, but no matter how high they climbed or how low they swung, the frigid air followed them. Cora had wrapped herself tightly in her cloak, tucking it around her legs and the saddle to preserve what little warmth she could. When that wasn't enough, she blew hot air against her aching hands and stuffed them in her armpits. What she would give right now for a great big ball of Dragon Fire.

As she fought off another round of teeth chattering shivers, she thought about the blinding orange blaze. How ferociously it would burn. How the heat would bite at her skin if she stood too close. But there was no sign of Dragon Fire or warmth in their future because all Cora could see in the distance were more snow-capped peaks.

She'd never ventured this deep into the mountains before. Frankly, she was starting to wonder if *anyone* had. They'd left the sparse, rocky terrain of the last village behind yesterday and discovered tree-lined, snow-covered slopes where the air would freeze her lungs if she gulped too deep and the cliffs spoke back to them in creaks and cracks. She wondered if these could even be called the Therma Mountains anymore. Surely they had another name.

When they'd stopped for a break earlier, Lenire had been wary of the way the mountains echoed back at them. He'd warned the dragons about making too much noise as they set out to hunt, and when Cora had started snapping sticks to make a fire, he'd stilled her hands and pulled out his knife instead, shaving down some kindling.

"What are you worried about?" Cora had asked him. It was the most words they'd exchanged since they'd set out.

"I trained in mountains like these," he'd said, his eyes lifting to those snowy peaks. "When the mountain talks back it is getting ready to throw snow."

"Throw snow?" The idea of a mountain throwing anything sounded ridiculous.

Lenire had nodded. "The mountain will shift and cast entire ice fields down to the ground. It will trample everything in its path on the way down, swallowing you up in a wall of snow so terrible that even your dragon could not save you."

Cora's gaze had brushed the sky in search of Alaric.

"If we're not careful," Lenire had said, "we will be buried here among the trees."

They hadn't stayed long enough for Cora to truly worry, but she considered his words now as she shifted in her seat, trying to get the blood flowing to her feet. During their initial encounter, Lenire had told her that Itharus was to the north. Perhaps much of his land was covered in mountains and snow. He was certainly dressed for it. Because she was so cold, she'd taken notice of the way his cloak was fur-lined on the inside. She'd also noted the thick riding gloves he had clipped to his belt—marveling that he had yet to put them on—and the tufts of fur that peeked out over the tops of his boots.

Cora curled her toes in her own boots, all at once frustrated with herself for being ill prepared and jealous of Lenire's attire. To be fair, she hadn't known their journey would lead them this far into the mountains. When her journey had started, Cora figured she'd be poking around the rocks the way she'd done when they'd been tracking the river with Melusine. She'd never imagined she'd be surrounded by arctic snow. She would certainly know to pack for all contingencies the next time she set out on an uncharted journey.

Alaric swung right and then left in quick succession, avoiding a pair of jagged peaks that clawed at the sky. Cora's hands cramped around the saddle, using every ounce of strength she had left in her frozen muscles to hold herself in place. When they'd left the village early yesterday morning, Cora had been hopeful that they would quickly find another crystal deposit, but even guided by the lodestone, an entire day had passed since they'd taken to the sky without so much as a whisper of a cave or village.

Cora laid her hands on Alaric's back. His scales were cool to the touch, some of them even covered with a fine film of frost, and she almost recoiled from the feeling.

"Change?" Alaric asked as soon as he'd felt her touch. He wanted to know if their heading had shifted, if he needed to shift with it, but according to the crystal, they were still on the right path.

"Steady," she said, glancing at the crystal in her lap to be certain. "Hunt?" she asked him instead.

Alaric made a low grumble of agreement. Between the cold and the miles they were flying, the dragons were burning an incredible amount of energy and required food more frequently. Cora started looking for a good place to land.

"You do know where we're going right?" Lenire called out. He and Yrsa had followed at a distance for most of yesterday and today, close enough to keep tabs on Alaric's flight path, but not close enough to force awkward conversation between him and Cora.

Part of her was grateful for that. After discovering the disk hidden in his pack—the same disk the mysterious voice had said she would find —she worried that the rest of the stranger's accusations would turn out to be true. That would mean Cora hadn't just partnered up with a thief, but that she'd made an alliance with a murderer.

"Hey!" Lenire called again, his voice drawing nearer. Cora could feel him hovering over her shoulder and she turned to spy Yrsa flying close to Alaric's left flank. "You're not flying us in circles, are you?"

"We haven't flown in one circle since we set off and you very well know that." Cora frowned. What was he getting at?

"Do I?" Lenire challenged. "Easy to get turned around flying through mountains like these."

"I'm not lost if that's what you're worried about," she said, hardly paying attention to him as she scanned the ground. "But I do think we should stop again. The dragons need to hunt."

Lenire leaned over Yrsa's side, gazing down between the peaks. "Not here," he said.

"Why not?"

"Can you just trust me?"

Cora wanted to laugh in his face but somehow she managed to keep it to herself. "The sooner they hunt, the sooner we keep going."

"Not here!" he said again. Yrsa responded to a silent command and cut Alaric off as he started to descend.

Alaric flared back in the sky, leaving the two dragons not beside each other but facing off, their mighty wing beats sending waves of icy air whipping about them. Cora blinked away the cold tears that formed in her eyes. "What are you doing?"

"Listen!" Lenire shouted at her and though all she wanted to do was yell at him, she calmed. When the sound of her own heartbeat faded from her ears, she could hear the howl of the wind and the rough cracking noise that accompanied it. The cracking grew louder and louder until something finally snapped, the sound echoing through the valley of cliffs.

All at once a flurry of snow dust rose up beneath them. The mountain was throwing snow, Cora realized. Just like Lenire had told her it could. An entire slab of snow released from the peak, racing down the mountainside faster than Cora thought possible. If they'd been down there, if they'd landed like she'd intended them to, they would have all been swept away.

"By the stars," Cora said, wide-eyed. She'd never seen something so incredible. So terrible. She gasped in a breath of frigid air, wishing Faron were here to experience the sight with her. He'd never believe this.

"We should find somewhere else to land," Lenire said when the snow and the mountain had startled to settle. "The dragons do need to hunt, but preferably not where the snow has just released. There's no reason the mountain can't do it again."

Cora nodded. She didn't thank him or sputter about how he'd been right all along, but they both knew it. Lenire had saved her life, again, and though she didn't think she could trust him, she was starting to owe him.

They carried on and Yrsa took the lead this time so Lenire could scan for an appropriate landing site. It had only been a few minutes before

Cora noticed the weight in her lap shift. She looked down at the crystal that she'd almost forgotten about. She rapped on Alaric's scales excitedly.

"Down!" she said. "It's here."

Yrsa turned in the sky and Lenire leaned around her neck. "What is it?"

"The crystal deposit. It has to be here."

"How do you know?"

"I just do!" Cora called. She'd told Lenire about the crystal deposits, about using them as a sort of trail to the source of Tenegard's magic, but she hadn't told him about using a crystal as a lodestone to help them find each deposit. She knew she had to keep some things to herself, and she wasn't about to freely hand him both the lock and the key.

Alaric descended.

"Cora, wait!" Lenire called. "You don't know what's down there!"

But Cora knew. It was the next piece in her puzzle. One step closer to the heart. One step closer to having Faron back. As they rounded the side of a large cliff, plumes of white smoke filled the sky, puffing from the chimneys of another remote mountain settlement. How anyone could survive in such a place, she didn't know, but if she could find a pair of gloves to purchase here, she would.

As Alaric touched down on the outskirts, surrounded by a thick forest of fir trees, Cora noticed that each of the homes was built of stacked logs. Though there was no snow on the ground here, the earth was packed and hard, and she could hear the bleating of animals. Sheep maybe. Alaric had heard it too and his ears quirked.

"Don't even think about it," Cora told him.

Whether Alaric had understood her or not, he didn't pay much more notice to the sheep because Yrsa touched down beside him. Lenire slid from his saddle and Cora quickly pocketed the lodestone.

"The crystals are here?"

"Somewhere here," Cora said. "We just have to find them."

She started toward the houses. Alaric followed.

"Where are you going?" Lenire called.

"To ask somebody," Cora said. "No point wandering around like fools if they can tell us where it is." The last village had been carved against a mountain. The cave would have been obvious even if there had been no one to point it out. But this settlement was built beside the woods, far enough away from any peaks that might drop snow.

As Cora approached the settlement, she spotted a few surprised faces. Judging by the smoke plumes, she suspected most people were inside, keeping out of the cold. The side streets were dirt-packed and narrow. Alaric's tail left a groove in the earth and his scales rubbed off on piles of firewood.

Once they'd reached the main square, a few children appeared but the sight of Alaric skulking along behind Cora sent them running. Cora glanced over her shoulder to find Alaric grinning with all his teeth.

"Why?" She sighed.

Alaric's grin turned dangerous, accompanied by a menacing growl. Cora turned around to find a man with a spear. He'd appeared from one of the houses.

"Whoa!" Cora said, holding her hands up. "Hang on a second!"

Alaric snatched the back of her tunic, dragging her out of reach as another armed villager appeared.

"I wouldn't if I were you," Lenire said, stepping out of the shadows with Yrsa. He placed his hand on his sword but did not draw it from its sheath.

The villagers backed off, glancing at each other, and slowly lowered their weapons. Apparently, their bravery would hold up against one dragon but not two.

"We do not mean you any harm," Cora said, pulling herself free of Alaric's teeth.

"Then state your business!" the first man shouted, his hands tightening on the pole of his spear.

"My name is Cora, and this is my traveling partner, Lenire. We are dragons riders," she said. "And have come very far in search of something of great importance. Our quest has led us here."

More villagers had been drawn from their homes at the commotion. Children gawked at Alaric and Yrsa. Parents pointed, worried expressions filling their faces. Cora wondered if they'd ever seen a real dragon before. Were there dragon herds this deep in the mountains? Did they ever fly overhead?

The villagers murmured amongst themselves, but it was the man with the spear who answered.

"We are a simple people. We live off the land and our animals. What could you possibly want from us?"

Cora pulled the lodestone from her pocket to show him. "A deposit of crystals like this. Perhaps in a cave?"

The man took the crystal, running his thumb over the smooth edges. He handed it back. "I have lived here for all of my life, and I have never seen anything like that in our village."

A whisper of agreement sounded.

An old woman stepped forward, followed closely by a young girl. She couldn't be much older than twelve. Immediately they reminded Cora of herself and Nana Livi. The woman took the crystal from Cora, closing one eye to inspect it. "I have never seen anything like this in my lifetime," she said. "I can only recall legends of their likeness. Stories that have long been dismissed as tales for our children and grandchildren." She looked to the young girl, who spied over the woman's shoulder.

"Why is your village so leery of dragons?" Cora wondered.

# CHAPTER 14
## CORA

"Many of them have never seen a dragon," the old woman answered, a small smile curling her lips.

"But you have?"

"Once. When I was a girl. I was out trapping with my father and we came across the creature deep in the woods. I don't know what became of it, but we never saw it again. The only measure of dragon culture that remains within the village are the monuments our ancestors once built to honor the creatures." She lifted her hand, gesturing to a strange sculpture that sat in the corner of the square.

Though time and nature had not been kind to the stone, Cora could still see the likeness of a dragon. "Are there more of these?" she asked.

The women shrugged. "Several others scattered about the village. They were once said to show the way to a dragon's hoard of treasure. Now the children just play on them."

Yrsa made a noise. Alaric snorted a moment later and Cora suspected that Lenire and Yrsa had shared what the woman had said. Dragons might hoard dragon scales for their nests and hatchlings, but they certainly didn't hoard treasure. If the stories held any measure of truth, Cora wondered if this treasure was actually a crystal deposit.

"I presume this treasure was never found," Cora said.

The woman chuckled. "If it was, our houses would be made of gold, not wood."

"Would you mind if we stayed to have a look at these monuments?"

"You will find them more suitable for inspection under the morning light."

"Do you have an inn?" Lenire asked. Once the sun fell beneath the mountains, the light quickly disappeared. Only now did Cora notice all the lanterns and torches the villagers carried.

"Not exactly," the woman said, "but Harlan will take you in for the night. He has extra room." She pointed and a man stepped forward.

Cora watched as Lenire sized him up. Finally, after apparently determining that Harlan was not a threat, he nodded. "We would be very grateful."

"Then welcome Cora and Lenire," the old woman said. "You and your dragons are very welcome here."

Cora inclined her head in thanks. With that the woman turned and many of the villagers returned to their homes. Cora watched as doors popped open and small heads peeked out. Watching two massive dragons make their way through the village must have been a marvel to behold. Cora tried to imagine the way she would have felt if a pair of dragons and their riders had descended upon Barcroft when she was little.

Being equal parts terrified and exhilarated, she too would have probably watched them from the safety of her doorstep. The young girl, the one she understood to be the granddaughter of the old woman, lingered. There was no uncertainty as she darted around Yrsa, taking in the dragon from every angle.

Lenire walked up behind Cora, whispering for only her to hear. "There's no crystal deposit here."

"We don't know that for sure."

"Did you not hear what these people said? No treasure, no crystals, nothing."

"There's something to their stories," Cora said. "The history might have been lost, but their stories retain some of the clues. We just have to piece enough of them together."

"You think you're going to listen to bedtime stories and figure out where the crystal deposit is hidden?"

"If that's what it takes."

Lenire rolled his eyes. "Let me know how it goes. I'm going to bed."

Cora watched him and Yrsa follow after Harlan. Though no longer shivering, the cold had turned to exhaustion in her bones, and Cora yearned for a warm bed almost as much as she wanted to find the crystals. She turned around to find that even the young girl had disappeared for the evening. If Cora really wanted to talk to these people, she was going to have to wait until morning.

Cora was up with the sun.

She'd fallen asleep fully dressed last night, too exhausted to even shed her traveling cloak. Harlan had kept a fire burning in the hearth, and she'd not even noticed the cold until she stepped outside this morning. Cora rubbed at her forehead where a twinge of pain shot across her temple. She'd woken with a bit of a headache, and she was hoping the brisk air would help clear it.

Pulling her cloak tighter, and donning gloves she'd borrowed from their host, Cora hurried down the road to find Alaric. The dragons had been welcomed into the stables last night where they could curl up in the hay so long as they promised not to relieve the villagers of any of their livestock.

When she reached the stables, Alaric and Yrsa were still asleep, tucked up in the hay together. Cora grumbled. It wasn't often that Alaric slept past her waking, but as she regarded him and Yrsa, she couldn't help but be glad that at least *some* of them were getting along. She hadn't seen Lenire again last night after he'd marched off after Harlan. The door to his room had still been closed when she left this morning.

No matter. Cora didn't need his help. She left the stables quietly, letting the dragons sleep. They'd flown hard yesterday and could probably do with the extra rest. When she turned the corner, she startled, her hand unconsciously dropping to the sword on her hip.

But it was only the young girl from yesterday.

"You scared me," Cora said, her heart ramming against her ribs.

"Sorry," the girl said. "I didn't mean to. I was just—"

"Looking in on the dragons?"

The girl grinned.

"What's your name?" Cora asked.

"Alia," she said.

"Was that your grandmother that I was talking to last night?"

"Yes. She's the head of our village."

"I thought so," Cora said, setting off toward the main square where she'd spotted the monument. "She's very wise."

"That's what everyone says." Alia followed her. "Do dragons eat people?"

"Never."

"What do they eat?"

Cora grinned. "Sheep."

"But not our sheep. I counted this morning."

"Alaric would never take from your livestock without being invited to."

"Is that his name? Alaric."

"Yes." They'd reached the square and Cora was pleased to see that Alia's grandmother was right. In the daylight, the finer details of the monument were clear.

"What are you looking for?"

Cora ran her hands over the monument. "Something to help my friends."

"What happened to them?"

"A sickness came," Cora said, not wanting to scare the girl with stories of the Blight. "And they fell into a deep sleep. I'm searching for a magic that might be able to wake them."

"That's why you need the crystals?"

Cora nodded. She stopped examining the monument and turned to Alia, pulling the lodestone from her pocket. She let Alia hold it. "What do you know about the crystals?"

Alia shrugged. "We've never called anything a crystal. But my mother used to tell me a story before she died. I'm too old for it now."

"I'd like to hear it," Cora said.

Alia handed the crystal back. "My mother called them rock lights. She used to say that if you walked the mountains at night and lost your way, all you had to do was reach into the earth and pull out a rock light. She said the mountains hide their lights on the inside so the sun can't steal from them."

"I see," Cora said, massaging the sharp ache in her temple. She couldn't tell if she was merely thinking too hard or if the headache was worsening. Either way, Alia's description of the rock lights sounded exactly like a crystal deposit.

"Do you really think we have a bunch of crystals right here somewhere?"

"Don't you?" Cora asked.

Alia seemed to think about that for a second. Then she nodded. Cora remembered being that young, Nana Livi filling her head with tales about dragons and dragon riders. She'd been adamant about believing something everyone else was so quick to dismiss.

By the time Lenire found her, Alia had shown her to every monument hidden within the village and even a few in the woods. Cora had sent Alia on her way when her grandmother came looking, promising the girl that she would introduce her to Alaric and Yrsa properly later.

"Where have you been all day?" Lenire asked, shoving his way between the sticky pine needles.

"Gathering information," Cora said. "With no help from you, I might add."

"Let me guess, gathering information consisted of listening to nursery rhymes and skipping games."

"So what if it did?" Cora asked.

"We should be moving on. There's no deposit here. We're wasting our time."

Cora ignored him. First, she knew he was wrong. Second, there was nowhere to go until they found the deposit and the lodestone could sense the next direction. She neglected to tell him that last part however, instead pacing around a monument that had almost completely been grown over by the forest. "Don't these look similar to the carvings in the last village?"

"How can you tell? These things are crumbling," he said, pinching at a pile of rock dust. "I think you're trying to force a connection that doesn't exist."

"Why are you so difficult?" she asked, though he'd likely be less challenging to deal with if he knew everything she did about the crystals and the lodestone. Still, she wasn't ready to trust him, and his restlessness irked her. Not for the first time she wished it were Faron here with her instead. She missed his endless patience. "You might not be able to see it, but I can recognize the scraps of Tenegardian culture preserved in these stones and in the stories Alia told me today." Even if nobody else took them seriously anymore, Cora knew they had to follow the clues in the folklore.

"Okay, fine, they look like the carvings in the last village. What does that matter? There's still no crystal deposit."

"It must be hidden somewhere out of sight."

"And you don't think one of these villagers would have stumbled upon it at some point over the course of their lifetime?"

"I don't know," Cora said. All she knew was that the lodestone had pulled her here for a reason. She pressed her hand against the monument. "These relics are all that remain of the dragon riders of old. I wish I had an easier way to figure this out, but I don't. I have to work with what they left behind."

"Look, I know this lost history is important to you, to the Tenegardian dragon riders, but you can return for all that later. But as you've said, we need to find the Heart of Tenegard so we can destroy the Blight."

"You're calling it the Blight now?" Cora said with surprise. "I thought you said that was a stupid name?"

"It is! It's the most ridiculous name," he said impatiently. "But since you insist on calling it that …" He waved off the conversation about names. Apparently, Cora was rubbing off on him. "We need to get packed and get out of here."

"We can't leave yet," Cora said.

"Why not?"

"We just can't."

She stepped around the monument and he followed her. "You're going to have to help me understand here because all you're doing right now is wasting time playing in the woods."

She stopped, turning around to face him. "We can't go yet because I don't know which way to go."

Lenire's face folded into a frown. "What?"

"This," Cora said, producing the lodestone from her pocket, "is what I've been following."

"A rock?"

"A crystal." She pressed it into his hand. She could tell he was surprised by the weight. "Its glow shifts to tell us the way."

"It's not pointing anywhere."

"Because this was the last place it brought me. Until we find the deposit, it won't reset."

Lenire shoved the crystal back into her hand. "Why didn't you tell me this in the first place?"

"I hardly know you."

"We're supposed to be working together. How do we even know if this crystal is pointing us in the right direction?"

"That's how I found the last village."

"Well, there's no deposit here, so maybe the crystal stopped working."

"It's working fine," Cora said. A flash of pain shot across her forehead. She'd been troubled all afternoon by the growing headache. Earlier she'd imagined that she was thinking too hard about the location of this crystal deposit, but even Alaric wasn't feeling like himself and she'd urged him to get some more rest. Cora pressed at her head, willing the pain away.

"We've wasted another whole day here," Lenire said, still carrying on.

"Nothing is wasted."

"You're literally sitting here, listening to children recount bedtime stories, and every moment the Blight gets further away."

"Do you have a better idea for finding the way toward the Heart of Tenegard's magic? Because I don't. We have no idea where the Blight is right now," Cora retorted. "It could be holed up miles away from here."

"Or it could already be there, sucking Tenegard's magic dry."

"Can you just stop!" Cora snapped, pressing her thumbs into her temples. "Arguing with you isn't going to help me find the crystal deposits."

Lenire did stop, but instead of marching away in fury, he came closer. "Are you unwell?" he asked. "I could help you."

"I'm fine," she said, pulling back before he could reach her.

Lenire's eyes widened. "Fine," he said, letting his hands fall. He backed away.

"No, wait," Cora said. "I'm sorry. I didn't mean to yell at you. I'm just … short on sleep." It was a lie and Lenire didn't look convinced, but the last thing she needed was for Lenire to know that she and Alaric were both feeling poorly. It would give him another reason to complain about her incompetence.

"I really could help you."

"And I really am fine," she repeated. But even as she said it, her ears rang with a reverberation that reminded her of the sound that came from running a finger over the rim of a glass, and the constant low throb in her head worsened.

# CHAPTER 15

## CORA

P ain wrenched Cora from a dead sleep, and she woke suddenly, confused and grasping at her head. The headache she'd gone to bed with was worse now. Cora pressed the pads of her fingers into her flesh, trying desperately to pinpoint the source of the pain. If she could find it, perhaps she could massage the ache away. Rolling over, she sat up, but in the darkness her vision swam, each shadow clawing for permanence, and she jammed her eyes closed again.

As she waited for her head to stop spinning, the contents of her stomach moved uneasily. Cora pressed the back of her hand to her nose, taking a series of deep, calming breaths. But the focused breathing did little to help. With each passing moment, her headache grew worse, until she was hunched over the side of the bed, holding her head in her hands. It felt impossibly heavy, and there was a nause-ating vibration that rang somewhere deep in her mind. She could sense it in her teeth first, when she pressed her molars together. Then the vibration passed to the rest of her bones, and Cora felt like her entire body was singing.

It was a wholly unpleasant feeling, and she forced her eyes open. To her surprise, a familiar glow was radiating from her pack. The crystals were active again, like the other night when that mysterious voice had called out and greeted her.

"Hello?" she whispered, half expecting a voice to answer back. When nothing did, she reached into her bag for the two crystals that she'd taken from the hounds. The pain in her head exploded when her hand made contact with the crystals and she dropped them, the stones landing on the floor with a heavy *thud*. She pressed her palms into her eyes, where the pain was the worst, but it did not recede, instead pressing back, like sharp spikes attempting to force themselves through the backs of her eyes.

Cora hissed, sucking in a breath through her teeth. When she opened her eyes, the crystals oozed a familiar black mist that coiled like slime around her feet. "By the stars!" she whispered under her breath, stumbling free of the mist.

Her heart thudded in her chest as the Blight leaked across the floorboards of her room, exactly as it had looked when it had haunted her and Faron and Strida through the mountains.

As Cora recoiled from the sight, grasping at her hip for a sword that wasn't there, the mist twisted back on itself, coiling into something that looked like a rope. Then, just as Cora thought the mist had ceased, the rope began to shift and turn, tying itself into intricate knots. The knots began forming around the crystals, until they were pulsing masses, almost like twin black hearts. Cora edged around the crystals, diving back into her pack for the lodestone.

She gripped it, inspecting the hard edges. Whatever horror had infected the other two crystals didn't seem to have any sway on the lodestone. She dove for her sword next. It hung from the sheath on her belt that was currently strung over the back of the door. Armed now, Cora turned to face the infected crystals, clutching the lodestone in one hand and her sword in the other. Both her dragon magic and brute strength had been useless against the Blight in the past. She remembered the attacks in the mountains with sharp clarity—diving away from rebounding spells, feeling their Dragon Fire turned back on them, watching Faron be rendered unconscious. The hand clutching her sword grew sweaty.

It was a crystal like the lodestone that had shielded Cora from the Blight's attack at the school, but when the Blight seemed to be *coming* from the crystals she'd taken from the hounds, crystals that before had looked just like her own, she couldn't know if the lodestone would deter the Blight.

By the lodestone's dull crystal light, she watched those knots of pulsating darkness grow swiftly larger. Each knot seemed to generate another, stacking upon the last until recognizable forms began to emerge. First bone, then muscle, and with panicked horror, Cora realized what was happening.

The hounds they had slain days ago were reconstructing themselves around the crystals.

They were being reborn.

And even as it lacked an identifiable head, one of the hounds struck out at her, causing Cora to jump back. She shoved her bed across the floor, using it like a battering ram. But already the hounds had regained their strength, and she might as well have been forcing her bed up against a stone wall.

"Help!" Cora cried out, launching herself across the room as a gnarled black limb made a swipe for her. "Help!"

It was Lenire who answered the call, bursting through the door of her room, his clothes rumpled, the haze of sleep still clinging to his features as he clutched an alarmingly inadequate dagger. He stumbled back upon seeing the shifting masses of the hounds mid-regrowth and instantly he was wide awake, gaping at the sight. "What's going on?" he demanded. "What did you do?"

Cora wanted to lash out and tell him this wasn't her doing. Though she supposed at this exact moment it was. She was the one who'd carried the crystals around in secret for days. Cora shifted around the edge of her room, clinging to the wall to stay out of reach of the hounds. "I took the crystals from the hounds' bodies."

"What crystals?" he asked.

"There were two crystals in the remains you looked through. One from each creature."

"That strange glow?" he said, remembering.

She nodded. "I thought the crystals might be what gave them life. So I took them."

"And you didn't think to tell me?"

"Well, obviously not!" She yelped and ducked as her pack was flung across the room by a hound.

"So what is this? An experiment gone wrong?"

"I didn't do this!" Cora insisted. "I woke up. The crystals were glowing. A bunch of black mist poured out of them. And suddenly they were knotting themselves back together."

"Knots?" Lenire said, his brows drawing together.

"Yes, knots," Cora said.

Lenire shook his head. "How could you be so foolish?"

"I've never seen the crystals used like *this* before! How was I supposed to know the creatures could regenerate?"

"Never mind that now," Lenire said as an almost fully formed limb took a swipe at him. With each passing second, the hounds' bodies solidified as they gained control over their flexing limbs.

Lenire swiped at their mottled flesh with his dagger, but it did little against the growth. The two crystals had disappeared from sight, swallowed up inside the creatures. "We have to get out of here!" he cried.

A moment later, Cora yelped as the window shattered. It wasn't a hound's doing, though. Instead she spotted Yrsa, framed by the night. The dragon roared, having answered Lenire's silent call. Spotting the hounds, Yrsa ripped the frame of the window from the wall, raining glass and masonry down upon the street below.

One of the hounds began to take its first coordinated steps, and Lenire skirted around the figure, edging against the wall until he'd run right into Cora.

"Go!" he shouted. "The window!"

Cora didn't need to be told twice. She dove for her bed, scrambling over it and leaping through the hole in the wall onto Yrsa's back. Lenire was right behind her, the pair of them just barely managing to escape the building before the hounds had fully regenerated.

At the sound of the disturbance, villagers had emerged from their homes, torches and lanterns illuminating their confusion. As they spotted the hounds, however, their confusion turned to fear and they cried out, ushering children back into the safety of their homes. Using the rubble as a ladder, the hounds crawled from the inn, snapping and snarling at anyone close enough.

"We have to protect the people!" Lenire called, sliding from Yrsa's back. The instant he touched down, he dug through Yrsa's saddlebag for his sword. He grabbed it and ran off after the hounds before Cora had even had a chance to assess the situation.

She heaved her sword into her lap as she prepared to follow him to the ground, but before she'd left the safety of Yrsa's back, she was struck by a memory of her father. Remembering the headache that had preceded this event and the vibration that had heralded the creatures' rebirth, Cora thought of the time her father had run his finger over the rim of his wineglass, eliciting the same sort of curious ringing vibration. He'd told her that a glass made of crystal, when touched by the right sound, could shatter to pieces.

As a child, after her mother's death, she'd always been cautious around the glasses. Her mother didn't have many treasures, but she'd been gifted the two crystal glasses the day she married Cora's father. Worried she might inadvertently cause one to explode, Cora had always whispered whenever she was near the cabinet. Now she knew better, but she wondered if she might be able to use the same principle against the crystals inside the hounds.

It was Alaric's roar that brought Cora out of the memory, and she slid to the ground, hurrying to the stables as he burst from them. His tail curled around her out of protection, but Cora pointed down the torch-lit street, where the hounds were already wreaking havoc among the buildings.

Alaric lowered himself enough for Cora to grab onto the saddle, then he was off, running down the street, each footfall sending tremors through the village. People scattered across the street as Alaric passed, screams of terror lingering in the air. It was almost as if Cora could taste their fear. Young men and women with weapons appeared, but like the last village, their spears were no match for the hounds, and most fled to higher ground to watch the fight. When Alaric caught up with the hounds and Lenire, Cora slid from his back and laid her sword on the ground.

Alaric made a noise of surprise, nudging at her with his snout. When she didn't respond, he picked at the sword with his teeth, the sound of steel scraping across the cobbles, sending a shiver through her entire body.

Cora focused her attention on the lodestone, cradling it between her hands. She turned her head toward Alaric before gesturing back toward the crystal, hoping he would get the hint. She needed him to focus on her and not the battle. She needed him to bolster her magic with his own. Alaric gave a snort of approval and Cora glared at the hounds once more.

She guided her magic through the lodestone to give herself an extra boost of power. Then, she channeled the power into one of the hounds, hoping to snag on the crystal that had rebirthed the monster. To her surprise, the hound stumbled, emitting a high-pitched noise of distress. Alaric growled beside her, and Cora rubbed her ear against her shoulder. The sound echoed in both her ears, somehow both incredibly loud and oddly quiet at the same time. It was a strange noise that left both dragons shaking their heads.

"What is that?" Lenire cried, sticking a finger in his ear.

He dragged his sword behind him, having exhausted himself by hacking away at the other hound, revealing the other crystal.

"Channel your magic into the crystal inside the hound," Cora called.

"What?"

"Just do it!" she said. "Trust me. The crystal acts like a heart. That's what gives them life. Channel as much of your power as you can directly into the crystal. Maybe we can destroy them."

Trust was still in short supply between them, perhaps more so with the revelation that she'd been carrying the hounds' crystals, but Lenire did as she said, channeling his magic into the narrow point of the crystal. The other hound stumbled and whined, adding to the intensity of that high-pitched sound. The hounds turned in circles, heads to the ground, like they might be able to rub themselves free of the wretched noise. When it continued, they shook and whined and whimpered, but Cora didn't let up. With Alaric's help, she poured her magic into the crystal, into that tainted heart, imagining it shattering into dozens of pieces like a wineglass made of crystal.

Sweat began to pool along her forehead, running down the sides of her face and under the line of her jaw. It dripped off the tip of her chin where she gritted her teeth against that high-pitched keening sound. Every one of her muscles locked, shaking from the strain, but Cora did not let herself stop. The extra boost from the lodestone helped her magic match Lenire's strength, but even he was starting to wane, groaning as he tied intricate magical knots and forced them into the crystal heart.

Magic poured from her in what felt like endless streams, but soon the pitch of the sound changed, escalating into a piercing scream. Cora closed her eyes against the noise, both of her arms shaking, when suddenly there was a splintering crunch of sound. It was like dropping a plate upon the floor and watching it shatter. All at once the noise vanished and the hounds collapsed abruptly into nothingness. It wasn't like before when the hounds had left behind a shell of rotting flesh. This time, the evidence of their existence disappeared with them.

Cora let her arms fall loose at her sides.

Breath seeped from her in one great exhale.

The hounds were gone.

Alaric made a noise of comfort beside her, and she leaned into him. His air-cooled scales felt good against her clammy skin.

"We did it," she said, patting his side.

Alaric blinked at her once, lowering his head to the crystal still in her hand. "Safe?" he asked.

She nodded. The lodestone hadn't given her any indication to fear that a similar thing might happen to it. "I think so."

Cora looked over to where Lenire stumbled forward. He was caught by Yrsa, who held him up as he regained his footing. Expending that much magic had clearly left them both weak and dizzy.

"Are you okay?" he called over to her.

"Yes, I'm okay."

He glanced around in shock, which Cora understood. In a way, the moment, though hard won, almost felt incomplete. The hounds had disappeared with such suddenness that it was as if Lenire still expected them to leap down from a rooftop or appear at the end of a street, snarling for revenge.

Now that the fight was over, the villagers had begun to emerge from their hiding places, speaking in curious whispers. When children appeared on the streets, the victory felt real.

Lenire approached with Yrsa. "They're truly gone?"

"I think so," Cora said. Waiting a moment until she was steady on her feet, Cora inched forward, toward the space the hounds had occupied, looking for any sign of them. She knew better now, and if there was anything left, she would have the dragons destroy it with Dragon Fire. If that didn't work, they would carry the remains away to the great sea Lenire had crossed to get here and toss them into the depths.

Suddenly, Lenire knelt down beside her.

"Look!" He gathered a pile of glittering sand into his hands. The shimmer was similar to the glow of the crystals. "This is all that's left."

The sand sifted between his fingers in fits and starts before he opened his hands and released the grains to the breeze. Under the torchlight, Cora watched it disappear.

Lenire let out a heavy breath and sat back on the cobbled street. His collar was damp with sweat, his hands marred with the scuffs and blisters of battle. Cora could see where his palms had rubbed so hard against the hilt of his sword that the skin was left raw. She had no doubt that he would heal himself in time, but that wasn't the point.

Regardless of her decisions to keep the crystals a secret, Lenire hadn't hesitated to help her defeat the hounds again. It reminded her so starkly of Faron that Cora spared a moment for him in the quiet that followed their battle. She hoped he was faring well and that the healers kept his body strong for the moment she was able to wake his mind. Mostly, she let herself miss him. And Strida and Octavia. She missed teaching classes at the school and watching new dragon rider bonds take shape. It was the simple things she wanted now: a meal in the dining hall; an aimless dragon ride through the sky; even a lecture on the state of their finances from Emmett. These were the things she reminded herself of when she grew weary or when she questioned every step of their journey. These were the people she was fighting for. And she had to keep fighting if she wanted to see them all well again. Cora reached down and offered Lenire her hand.

Though she was still wary of him and his motives, he was slowly proving himself to be the dragon knight he claimed to be. Lenire took her hand and let Cora pull him to his feet.

"I'm sorry I didn't tell you about the crystals," she said as he stood before her. "When I took them, we'd only just met, and I wasn't sure that I could trust you."

There were still whispered voices that spoke of his treachery in the back of her mind, but tonight she owed him an apology and her gratitude.

"That was probably wise of you to be careful," Lenire admitted. "You didn't know me well at the time."

"I still don't," Cora said.

"No," he said. "Nor do I know you well. But hopefully that will change."

Cora nodded once and, unlike before when the dragons had encouraged them to team up, she now felt something like an alliance forming between them.

"I wonder where the fragments of the Blight have gone," Lenire said.

"The ones we saw swirling in the room?"

He nodded. "Perhaps they simply dissipate if the main bulk of it remains too far away to rejoin."

"Its hosts are gone," Cora reasoned. "Nothing left for it to reanimate. Maybe the fragments were destroyed along with everything else."

"One can only hope," Lenire said grimly. "We'll surely be in trouble if there are more of these creatures. Defeating these two took almost all of our strength."

The bubble of victory that had inflated Cora's chest quickly deflated. He was right. If they'd been faced with an army of hounds, there would've been no celebration tonight. As the reality of Lenire's words settled over her, a figure trudged through the dark. She squinted, lifting the lodestone higher, casting its dim light further.

"Alia?" she called as the young girl approached.

There was no answer. The girl moved as if her limbs had been encased in ice, each step stiff and stuttering. Her head lolled against her chest, her stringy hair tangled in front of her face. But none of that concerned Cora as much as the butcher knife Alia carried in her hand.

The girl's hand came up, poised to strike, and Cora screamed as Alia lunged for Lenire.

# CHAPTER 16
## CORA

"Stop!" Cora screeched at the top of her lungs. "Alia, no!"

Her words seemed to linger on the tip of her tongue, as if time had slowed down. Yrsa's wretched dragon cry echoed off the walls and tremors emanated from the earth beneath her feet as the dragon dashed for Lenire. It wasn't fast enough. So Cora did the only thing she could think of and threw herself at Lenire, hands colliding with his chest, shoving them both out of the way of Alia's blade.

Lenire hit the ground first, his head smacking hard against the earth. He let out a strangled cry as Cora bounced off him and rolled across the street.

"Cora," Lenire growled. "What in dragon's name is wrong with you?"

She couldn't respond at first, tasting nothing but sand and dirt on her tongue. The impact had forced the air from her lungs and her arms shook as she pushed herself to her feet, still gasping for breath.

But as Lenire rubbed at the back of his head, he finally spotted the girl and the knife. "Whoa!"

"Alia, stop this! There's nothing to fear anymore. The hounds are slain," Cora called. She was too late, though, and her eyes caught on the flash of silver that cut through the air near Lenire's head. With a startled yelp, he rolled out of the way, quickly scrambling back to his feet. His sword had been knocked from his hand when they fell, and he dove for it just as Alia struck out again, this time accompanied by an animalistic shriek.

Lenire snatched up his sword and ducked away from her next blow. He was quick on his feet despite the hit to his head, readying his sword in defense. Other villagers gathered around them, bringing torches and lanterns. The extra light flooded the street, and Cora finally got a good look at Alia.

She was as pale as starlight and her eyes were two blurred cavities, eerily vacant and devoid of any recognition as Cora continued to call her name.

"Stop! Stop!" A woman forced her way through the crowd and Cora recognized Alia's grandmother. She let out a strangled sob as she struggled forward. The crowd parted but hands held her back, preventing her from getting too close. "Please," she sobbed. "Don't hurt her. She's just a child."

Cora's own sword, still in her hand, fell limp by her side, even as Alia struck at her with the knife. Cora jumped back, watching the blade slice the air where she'd just been standing. Alia growled, the sound strange and unfamiliar, and struck out again. Cora dodged the attack but made no move to counter. She couldn't hurt this girl. This *child* who had shown her the ancient remains of their ancestors. Who had talked so freely with Cora about the lights that were said to be hidden within the mountains.

"She doesn't know what she's doing!" Alia's grandmother sobbed again. "Look at her ... something ... something is wrong!"

It was the only explanation. Her stiff limbs. Her vacant eyes. She was like a puppet, and someone was pulling the strings. It had to be connected to the mist. Cora thought back to the mountain venture with Strida and Faron. When the Blight had hounded them, it had taken on a mimicking shape and form, bearing an uncanny resemblance to members of their traveling party. "She's being controlled somehow," Cora called over to Lenire.

When there was no response, Cora glanced in Lenire's direction. He stumbled back from Alia like she was the most frightening foe he'd ever encountered. His brow was beaded with sweat and his hands shook so badly that he dropped his sword. It clattered as it struck hard stone, and Lenire flinched in response. He ducked down after it, never taking his eyes off Alia as he blindly grappled for the hilt. The longer he looked at her, the more his face distorted into a mask of genuine horror.

"Lenire?" Cora called. She hadn't known him long, but her immediate impression of him was that he was the type of dragon rider who immediately rushed into battle. The man before her acted as if he'd never held a sword in his life. "What is it?"

"The Blight's gotten inside of her," Lenire said, tapping his chest over his heart. "A piece of the Blight. It must have been freed from the hounds' broken crystals."

Cora looked back at Alia in shock. They'd wondered what had become of the Blight once the hounds were destroyed again, but she'd never imagined that it could embed itself into a human. A miniscule piece of the Blight couldn't hold such power over them, could it?

As if awoken by their conversation, Alia's blank face became darkly animated, her brows lifting and her lips stretching into an impossibly wide smile. Just when Cora thought her face might crack in two, Alia broke into peels of hideous laughter.

Lenire staggered back even farther, almost tripping over himself in his haste.

"Run, run away." Alia's voice was all wrong. She struck out in Lenire's direction, but Cora lifted her sword, fending off Alia's attack. The blade of her sword vibrated against the clash of metal. Alia was seemingly unbothered by Cora's interference, cackling at the look on Lenire's face.

In all her previous encounters with it, the Blight had never once been able to speak. This was something different. This was a mastery of the Blight that Cora had never encountered before.

"Lenire?" Alia taunted. "Don't you want to stay and talk? Haven't you missed our little chats?"

Lenire scrambled back through the crowd. It parted around him like he'd been infected by some contagious disease. He kept moving until he bumped into Yrsa's side, forcing him to stop and face Alia.

Yrsa growled, her long, serpentine body feathering out until she appeared to be twice her usual size. The show of force was in defense of Lenire, but even with every one of Yrsa's pearly teeth on display, Alia pursued him.

When Lenire began to climb up Yrsa's back, Alia cackled manically. "Are you a coward now as well as a thief?" she called. "Tell me, how does a thief fare among his peers? Do they welcome you with open arms? Do they still think they can trust you?"

Cora's feet stalled suddenly. She'd heard that strange, urbane, educated voice before. It had rung clean from the crystals and used the same words, fed her the same accusations. The voice that erupted from between Alia's lips wasn't hers at all.

"Who are you?" Cora demanded, jumping out in front of Alia. She held her sword up, the blade poised at the level of Alia's head. She did not mean harm against Alia; she only wanted to threaten whoever it was that had used the Blight to take control of her body. "What do you want with us?"

"I want nothing from *you*," the voice said through Alia. The girl shifted to look past Cora. "All I want is him."

"You would be wise to leave now," Cora warned. "Before anyone else gets hurt."

"You would stand between me and him?" Alia's expressions were just as foreign to the girl as her voice. The longer Cora looked upon the girl's features, the more she saw the stranger there, taunting them, teasing them.

"Let the girl go! She has nothing to do with this feud."

"I tried to warn you, Cora," the voice whispered. The sound trickled like a drip of water down her spine. "Lenire is dangerous. He cannot be left to roam your lands unchecked. You are aligning yourself with the wrong people."

"I am here to protect my people," Cora said. "And Alia is not a pawn to be used in your games."

"You're right. Of course, you're right," the voice said. "How foolish of me, picking on children." Suddenly, Alia's head snapped back and shrieks of cold laughter flooded out across the village. Then, all at once, she stopped. "If only this were a game."

Alia threw the knife. It embedded itself in Yrsa's leather saddle, close to Lenire's leg. Before either of them could react, Alia turned and fled through the village, the concerned pleas and cries of the villagers trailing after her.

"Please," Alia's grandmother said, stumbling forward on shaky feet. She grasped Cora's hand in her own. They were soft and wrinkled, reminding Cora of Nana Livi. "Please find her."

The old woman collapsed, and the crowd surged forward to gather her up.

Alaric made a noise of distress, inclining his long neck in the direction Alia disappeared. Cora turned. Over the heads of the villagers, she could see her own fear and horror reflected in Alaric's pearly black eyes. She was terrified for the girl. For a second she wondered if Alia's mind knew that her body was being controlled by the Blight. Did she have any sense of what was happening? Cora hoped not. She thought briefly of all the dragon riders at the school, still trapped by the sleeping sickness, trapped inside their own bodies. The Blight was a wretched thing. Cora's hand tightened around her sword. She was going to stop it.

The fire in her was lit, but as she darted forward, Lenire snagged her arm, pulling her to a hard stop. He'd slid from Yrsa's back to catch her, his eyes still wide with that frenzied fear. Cora's arm ached where it met her shoulder. "Let me go!" she demanded. "We have to go after the girl."

Lenire refused. "We have to get out of here while we have the chance!"

"What are you talking about? We're not leaving the village like this. We're not leaving Alia."

"It's no use," Lenire said.

"What do you mean it's no use?"

"Trust me, okay. We have to go. Now!"

A chill swept through her and Cora suddenly realized why Lenire had been so frightened before. It wasn't because a piece of the Blight had slithered into Alia and taken control of her. It was because he'd seen something like this before. And if he'd seen something like this, then he already knew how it would end.

"Can we save her?" Cora asked.

Lenire refused to answer, his head tilting back and forth like a top, his jaw slack.

Cora took him by the shoulders and gave him a hard shake. "Can we save her?" she shouted.

"I don't … I don't know."

Cora let him go. Defeat rattled inside her chest like a distant echo, beckoning her to lay down her sword before either of them were hurt. But Alaric growled in the torch-lit darkness, and Cora fought her own despair. "We brought this upon the village, Lenire. It's our fault."

"It's not … it wasn't … we didn't know," he stammered. "We couldn't have known."

Cora shook her head. He was wrong. They should have known better. She may have brought the crystals, but Lenire was being hunted. One way or another, that stranger would have found them.

"We can't abandon these people now," she whispered. And with that, she ripped her arm free of his grasp and turned to chase Alia through the village. "Alaric?" she cried.

He growled, calling to her in the dark.

Cora shoved her way past frightened villagers, jostling them with her shoulders. She'd barely reached Alaric and snagged the leather of the saddle before he was taking off. Cora flung herself into the seat as Alaric gave a great flap of his wings, dousing torchlights.

Alaric didn't fly very high, just enough to gain a view above the village rooftops. Before she could spot Alia, Yrsa rose into the sky, facing them.

"This is a bad idea," Lenire called.

"Then what are you doing here?"

Lenire's face was set in stone, like he was being marched off to his execution. He didn't say anything else, but he also didn't try to stop them. He remained at Alaric's flank as they scoured the village for the girl.

"There!" Alaric cried out.

The rest of his sentence was garbled growls to Cora, but she didn't need to understand anymore. She'd also spotted the girl.

Cora patted Alaric's scales with insistence, and he descended near the edge of the village, where the streets became the soft moss of the forest floor. It would be too difficult to spot Alia through the trees on dragonback, so Cora slid from the saddle and raced off into the woods. It was harder for the dragons to navigate, their large bodies snapping fallen logs and shearing entire branches from trunks.

Eventually Lenire caught up to her, his sword flickering in what little light they had. His eyes found Cora's once in the darkness, and she knew he still thought chasing after Alia was a mistake. Cora turned away then, spying the scraggly ends of Alia's hair whipping out behind her. Cora focused on the girl. That was their goal.

Whatever feelings Lenire harbored were his own.

They reached the edge of the woods with a suddenness that made Cora skid to a halt. She gasped for breath, scanning the steep drop that led to a stream. Splashing caught her attention, and she spotted Alia rushing through the water.

Cora set off down the hill.

"Cora, wait," Lenire said. "We don't know where she's leading us!"

Cora didn't listen. All she was concerned about was staying on her feet as the slick grass threatened to take her boots out from under her.

She hit the bottom and dashed across the stream. It was shallower than she'd expected, though filled with polished stones that made her wobble as she crossed.

On the other side of the stream, Cora summoned the last of her energy, racing off after Alia. She was headed to a spring at the foot of a large, craggy cliff.

"Alia," Cora cried out. "Stop!"

The girl did stop, but only for a second. She looked back at Cora and Lenire for a moment, that too-large grin on her face, then she dove into the spring. Smooth strokes took Alia toward the cliff where she climbed onto a rocky shelf before disappearing into the stone.

"What?" Cora said. She ran straight into the water after Alia. She waded through most of it, until it grew deep enough in the center that she had to swim. When she reached the rock shelf, it seemed as though Alia had disappeared into thin air, but as she ran her hands along the stone, she found a well-hidden split in the rock.

Cora managed to shuffle through the split. Lenire had more trouble, grunting as he scraped himself along the rocks. Inside, Cora had expected pure darkness, but as her eyes adjusted, she recognized a familiar glow. "The crystal deposit," she said, hurrying through the tunnel.

Once again Lenire caught her arm. "Not so fast."

"This is what we've been looking for," Cora said.

She tugged on his hand, pulling him around a bend in the passage. Sure enough, as they crested the turn, Cora was greeted with the most elaborate crystal deposit she'd ever seen. The cavern was enormous, the crystals on the roof so high up they twinkled like stars. Pools of water on the rocky ground reflected the glow of hundreds—maybe even thousands—of crystals that were embedded in the walls. They were even brighter than the ones in the last village.

Lenire's face was frozen in awe.

But Cora's amazement soon gave way to confusion. She felt the scrunch deepen between her eyes. "Why would the Blight lead us to the very thing we were seeking?"

Lenire opened his mouth, but nothing came out. Instead, the splash of footsteps caught their attention, and Cora turned just in time to see Alia collapse among a cluster of crystals.

Cora raced across the cavern to her side. As she approached, black mist bled from Alia's body. Cora clutched the lodestone in her hand, but instead of attempting to feed on her, the Blight's mist seemed to melt into the crystals around them.

Cora leaned over Alia's body. She was cold, her fingers like icicles, but her chest rose, and Cora let out a breath of relief. Beside her, the crystals, some of them as large as a person, ebbed with swirls of black smoke. And then, as the mist swirled, it formed the image of a man.

A face, weathered by age, frowned back at her. As suddenly as it had appeared, a dozen more appeared in mirror copy. In every crystal that the mist had touched, this face now looked back at her from each facet.

"Cora," it said. She startled, dropping Alia's hand and reaching for her sword. "After everything I've heard about you, I really thought you would have had more sense than this."

Behind her, Lenire breathed a name. "*Zirael.*"

The face twitched in amusement. "Why do you look so surprised, Lenire? Did you really think the Order wouldn't come after its stolen property?"

Cora got to her feet, turning in a circle, that wizened face everywhere she looked.

"It's much too late for the ragtag remnants of Tenegard's dragon riders to help you now," Zirael said. "You can try to run, like you did from Itharus, but know this, Lenire: we are coming."

And with that, the face melted into the smoke, and they were alone.

# CHAPTER 17
## OCTAVIA

O ctavia hated the sounds of the palace at night. It creaked and groaned and sometimes, if you perched at the top of one of the towers, it sounded as if the entire thing was sobbing. Without the daytime bustle of palace officials and staff to drown out its noises, the palace seemed to keep its own company, carrying on a myriad of conversations with itself. Even now, an errant breeze blew through the corridors and chambers, slamming shutters and making every curtain billow. Octavia froze as a shadow moved along the wall only to realize that it was her own cloak, fanning out behind her.

*You're jumpier than a mountain hare*, Raksha said.

*If those are the ones you eat for breakfast, I'd be jumpy too.*

*Why is your heart beating so fast?*

*I don't know what you're talking about.*

There was a beat of silence, a moment where her mind was quiet, and Octavia wondered if Raksha had finally rolled over and gone to sleep in her courtyard. But then a grumbling awareness sprang to life in her mind.

*Where are you?* Raksha demanded.

*In the palace, of course.*

*You know that's not what I'm asking.*

*I couldn't sleep,* Octavia said. *I decided to take a stroll.*

*You're lying,* Raksha insisted. *Where are you really going?*

*Nowhere important.*

*You're headed to Northwood's communication chamber, aren't you?*

Octavia grimaced. How had Raksha guessed so fast?

*There's a tremor of anticipation in your thoughts. It's only slightly stronger than your fear. What else could it be?*

Octavia hadn't told Raksha her plan tonight because she was worried that Raksha might try to talk her out of it. Sneaking around at night to use Northwood's communication anchors was probably a bad idea.

During the day, Octavia might be able to come up with another reason to use the anchors. Something that would keep suspicion at bay. But it would be difficult to convene with someone from Athelia during the day. At night, Octavia would be free to speak to whomever she wanted. The only problem was, if Octavia was discovered at night, holding council with an Athelian, then she would be branded a traitor. There would be no way to hide her misgivings and nothing she could do to reason with the council.

During the day she might have been able to stumble through an awkward apology. To pass it off as if she didn't really know how the anchors worked. She could tell Northwood or anyone who discovered her that she'd gotten confused. But under the cover of darkness, her deeds were her own. There was no confusion to fall back on nor ignorance to feign. At night, this venture was a methodical plan.

At night, she was conspiring.

Raksha grumbled in her head again. *I don't like this, Octavia.*

*I suspected you would say that, which is why I didn't bring it up.*

*What if someone catches you?*

*Then you better be ready for a quick getaway.*

*Be serious.*

*I am being serious!* Octavia stopped walking. *We can't keep waiting around. I need to know if Athelia can help the dragon riders. If not, we need to move our search somewhere else.*

*What good are you to the dragon riders if you are captured and named a traitor?*

*What good am I sitting in my room waiting for Northwood to see reason? I might be old and gray by the time that happens.*

Raksha couldn't deny the immovable wall they were up against in Northwood. That alone seemed to be worth risking her safety.

*Just promise me you will be careful.*

*I promise,* Octavia said. She'd brought a lantern with her but she'd yet to light the candle. She knew most of these corridors by heart, so she wouldn't risk being spotted by a guard just for an extra bit of light. Not yet, at least.

*If you run into trouble, let me know the second it happens. I will cause a distraction.*

*What are you going to do, bust down a wall?*

*If I have to.*

Octavia imagined it now. A crumbling crater of brick and glass punched through the side of the palace and Raksha's massive tail rearing up to strike again. Though Octavia knew they were joking to some degree, she also knew that Raksha wouldn't hesitate to do it for her. She would have preferred to have Raksha by her side tonight, but navigating a dragon through some of the more narrow chambers would be too conspicuous. If Octavia wanted to do this without getting caught, she had to go by herself.

A flash of warmth wrapped around the bond and settled over Octavia, heating her to her bones. It was Raksha's way of telling her she was still with her despite the distance. Smiling, Octavia quickened her pace.

She raced through the corridors, careful to duck into alcoves whenever she heard the jangle of chain mail. The guards patrolled the main floors in pairs, making regular rounds. When the latest pair of guards had vanished, Octavia stepped out from behind the statue she'd used as cover. Then, when even the muffled sounds of the guards' voices and the sharp echo of their boots had faded, Octavia ran, slipping into the familiar stairwell at the end of the hall.

Though it spiraled into complete darkness, Octavia merely pressed her hand to the wall for balance and counted her steps. When she reached the bottom, a chill caught her and she shivered. The lowest levels of the palace were always drafty, the walls slick with condensation. Octavia shuffled to the first dim torch left burning along the wall and lit her lantern's candle upon the lingering flame. Then she proceeded down the passageway. She counted the doorways, stopping at the one Northwood had shown her to the other day. Even under the close scrutiny of the candlelight, the door was almost invisible, blending in with the wall.

Octavia cracked the door and waited, listening for any kind of disturbance. When there was none, she poked her head inside. The room was empty, and she slid inside, relief flooding her as she placed her lantern near the sculpted arches that made up this particular anchor, and basked in the magical charge that filled the room. It was so thick, that if she stood still enough, Octavia suspected that she could simply float away on the currents of magic. She didn't have time for that now, though. Right now she had to make contact with Athelia. Preferably before anyone came looking for her.

Like last time, a ripple of sensation began in her arm, dripping down to her fingertips. Her own magic yearned for contact, and she released it, letting it chase the charge, hopefully all the way to Athelia. While she waited, pacing back and forth, Octavia tapped her fingers against her thigh, wondering what she would say if Athelia answered. She tried to imagine who it would be. Her greatest wish was to contact the Athelian senate. She envisioned a row of old, wizened men, with snowy white beards and beady eyes, wearing matching silk-sewn shawls. In her mind, they were certainly all older than Northwood, but each wore the same expression of impatience as they looked down upon her.

Octavia played with the soft hairs at the end of her braid. She didn't even notice how hard she was tugging until she felt the sharp pull against the back of her scalp. She flipped her braid over her shoulder. As she did, the archway nearest her began to vibrate and a grainy, ghostly image of a young woman took shape.

Octavia jumped back at first, then immediately straightened, years of etiquette catching up to her as she smoothed her hands over the lines of her dress.

"You're not our usual contact," the woman said. Her voice was sharp and clear, ringing like bells. Though she couldn't be much older than Octavia, she spoke with the authority of someone twice her age.

"No," Octavia said at once. "My name is Octavia. I sit on the Tene-gardian council. I wasn't certain my message had reached anyone, but I can say that I am relieved to have caught someone's attention. I had hoped to speak with a member of the Athelian senate."

"Octavia," the woman repeated. "There was once a princess in your palace by that name."

"And Tenegard was once ruled by a tyrannical king," she replied. "Things are different now."

The woman's eyes narrowed as she considered Octavia. Her dark hair, though curly, was cut short, the ends flaring just below her jaw. And her clothes, though a little stark for Octavia's tastes, exuded strength from the cut of every line and the drape of the exquisite cloth. Octavia could tell that this young woman would never let Northwood say one ill thing against her.

"My name is Serafine. I know you were part of the rebels who helped overthrow Onyx."

Octavia nodded.

"Then I will see what you have to say and consider whether to take the matter to my fellow senators."

"You're a senator?" Octavia said, surprise coloring her voice.

Raksha's thoughts cut into her mind, likely feeling the strong beat of emotion filtering around the bond. *Are you all right?*

*Yes,* Octavia said quickly. *I'm fine. Athelia has made contact.*

*Who is it?*

*A girl.*

Even Raksha was surprised to hear that. *A girl?*

*A young woman,* Octavia corrected. *Someone about my age.*

*And she can help us?*

*I don't know yet,* Octavia confessed. *But she claims to be a senator.*

Raksha's tone was impressed, if maybe even a little amused. *Sounds like you two already have a lot in common.*

*Perhaps,* Octavia said. *Though that doesn't necessarily mean she's going to help us.* Octavia tried to imagine the roles being reversed. If this young woman from Athelia had reached out to her, looking for aid from the council, Octavia would also be leery of the request.

"Is it so hard to believe I might be a senator?" Serafine was saying, pulling Octavia from her thoughts.

Octavia shrugged in apology. "It was only your age that surprised me."

"Are you yourself not a councilor?"

"Well, yes," Octavia said, frowning a bit. "Though most days I think everyone would prefer I wasn't. They do not take me as seriously as they would if I were perhaps ten years older."

"I would think a former princess would command more respect." Serafine's face remained smooth despite the grainy image, though Octavia thought the corner of her lips might have shifted. "Now tell me why you have defied your council to contact us."

"How did you know that?" Octavia said, her eyes narrowing in thought. She hadn't mentioned at all what she'd done to get here.

"It is the middle of the night. You are alone, sheathed in darkness and the light of a single lantern. I can only imagine that this meeting is held in secret because you have been forbidden to speak to us."

Octavia shivered at how accurate Serafine's assumption was.

"Am I wrong?" the woman asked.

"Not exactly," Octavia said. There was no use in trying to lie. She wanted Athelia's help. Lying to them from the start wasn't going to do anything to win their trust.

"Then ask what you have come to ask," Serafine said. "I would like to know what you deem so important."

Without any more hesitation, Octavia launched into a lengthy explanation about the dragon riders and the sleeping sickness. She didn't tell Serafine everything, keeping the school and the Blight out of it, but she told her enough to establish that there was a magical illness that the healers had been unable to cure.

"What do you think we could possibly do about this?" Serafine asked.

"I wondered," Octavia continued, "if your Athelian sorcerers had ever encountered something similar? And if so, if there was anything they could do to help us? We would be glad for their counsel in this matter."

Serafine's sharp chin jutted out. "Why should we trust the council of Tenegard or agree to aid them? Frankly, I'm surprised at this request considering the belligerence and obfuscation we've experienced from Tenegard these past months."

Octavia swallowed hard, resisting the urge to groan out loud. She didn't have to wonder who on the council might have provoked these harsh feelings in Serafine and the other senators. She sighed heavily. "In all honesty, Northwood wouldn't have been my first choice for an ambassador between our nations. I admit I am acting without his approval now, but I can assure you, he does not speak for everyone on the council."

*It was technically true*, she thought to herself. *Since he certainly doesn't speak for me or Raksha.*

"One good fruit does not ensure that the bunch is not sour," Serafine said. "I applaud your strength of character, but we know Northwood commands your armies. He holds more sway over the council than even you want to admit."

"You don't have to worry about Northwood or our armies."

"We are always worried," Serafine said.

Octavia knew the dragon riders, those that remained, would never let Tenegard go to war against Athelia. The problem was, there weren't as many healthy dragon riders left, and with the threat of Melusine and the Blight always looming, stopping a war was going to be difficult.

"Tenegard has proven to be unpredictable in the past."

Octavia didn't deny it. She couldn't make up for what had happened before. All she could do was try to barter better conditions for both their futures. "After everything I did to help overthrow Onyx, I'm not going to stand by and let anyone march down the same path to war and ruin the future for both our nations. When Onyx fell, I had a choice, rise up and lead in his absence, as the heir to the throne, or choose a better path forward. I chose the council. And at the time of its inception, I met with another Athelian senator. He made his wish for peace between our nations clear. I intend to honor that wish."

Serafine inclined her head. "All very pretty words, Octavia. Though I hear a *but* lingering in them."

"But ..." Octavia said. "If Athelia can help wake the sleeping dragon riders, proving their goodwill, it would help to bolster the argument against any further aggression. The council would have no choice but to agree."

For a long moment, Serafine simply stared at her. Octavia had the troubling sense that the young woman might laugh in her face. She was asking for Athelia to prove their goodwill when it was always Tenegard itching for war. But Octavia needed something bigger than Northwood's sway to convince the council that Athelia wanted peace.

They were both fighting the same bullheaded enemy here. North-wood's stubbornness. His greed. His hunger for battle. They needed to bring him down together. An alliance would serve them better than any feud ever could.

"What do you say?" Octavia asked, her hand automatically reaching for the end of her braid. She was more nervous now than she'd been sneaking down here. This moment might change everything about Tenegard's future. This moment could determine the fate of the dragon riders.

"I say," Serafine said diplomatically, "that you have made a strong argument on behalf of your people, Octavia. As such, I will take your request for aid to the senate and present it to them."

"Do you think they will help us?"

"I can't promise anything," Serafine said. "Except that they will consider the matter."

A noise, like a stone being kicked down an empty tunnel, sounded and Octavia looked over her shoulder, her eyes locked on the door for a moment. She turned back to the arch and quickly asked, "When can we speak again?"

Serafine considered her question as Octavia glanced to the door once more. She wanted to beg the senator to hurry. To answer faster. They might be interrupted at any second. "We will convene again at the same time tomorrow," Serafine said. "Then you will have our answer."

"Until tomorrow," Octavia sputtered, giving an awkward bow before ripping her magic free of the arch. The grainy image of Serafine disappeared and Octavia blew out the candle in the lantern, plunging the room into darkness. She sucked in a strangled breath. All of her plans depended on whether she heard voices or footsteps or the creak of the communication room door.

# CHAPTER 18

## CORA

Under the slanting light of the morning sun Cora pulled Alia's body through the final rocky crevice of the passage that led to the crystal deposit.

Free of the passage, Cora sank to the ground, cradling the unconscious girl's head in her lap, and she couldn't help but be reminded of Faron. When he'd fallen unconscious, sinking into the sleeping sickness like all the other riders, it had physically pained Cora to go near him. With Alia, that wasn't the case. Cora supposed it was different. Faron had been attacked, his magic siphoned, his bond weakened by the magical wounds the Blight left behind. Alia had only been a vessel. She'd had no magic for the creature to siphon. There were no leaking magical wounds for Cora to react to. Though with the new light of day upon her face, Alia was still as pale as the fog that lingered on the mountaintops. Her limbs were stiff and cold everywhere Cora touched, but most concerning was the frigid blue tint to her lips. Except for the soft breaths that rhythmically filled her chest, Cora would have thought Alia was dead.

With one final grunt, Lenire stumbled from the passageway, bearing scratches on the sides of his face and the tops of his knuckles from squeezing between the rock. Cora had never been more glad to be as small or as agile as she was.

"Are you okay?" she asked Lenire.

He rubbed the back of his hand across his cheek, sparing a moment to look at the blood smeared there. "Fine," he grunted. "We should get the girl back to the village. She should be with her family. And I should get their permission before I attempt to help her, just in case…" He trailed off, bending down to scoop Alia into his arms. He shifted her weight, until she was tucked against his chest.

"In case?" Cora asked. "Will she make it?"

"The fragments of the Blight seem to have left her body," he said, and Cora noted how careful he was not to make promises. "That is usually the most dangerous part. Not all are this fortunate."

Cora nodded, her fingertips still cold from where they'd held Alia.

Lenire looked up expectantly and Yrsa appeared as if called, sweeping down from a mountain ledge and splashing through into the spring. Alaric was right behind her. He made a noise of distress when he saw Cora, but she rubbed her hands along his scales, letting him know she was all right.

"Crystals?" he asked, or at least that's what it sounded like.

Cora was certain Yrsa had told Alaric whatever Lenire had telepathically shared while they were inside the cavern, but perhaps Lenire had been too occupied by the man in the reflections—the man he had called Zirael—to make much sense. Or perhaps Lenire and Yrsa were also keeping their secrets close to their chest.

Cora glanced over at Lenire as he helped Yrsa gather the girl carefully in her talons. Cora turned back to Alaric and nodded. "Lots of crystals."

Alaric let the underside of his snout bump her shoulder. It was clear that he hadn't liked being separated from her. Without their ability to communicate telepathically, being able to see each other was the only way to ensure the other was okay. Cora patted his scales once more, then climbed up into the saddle.

They followed Yrsa and Lenire at a distance as they flew over the forest that separated the village from the spring. When they touched down, Yrsa gently laid Alia's body on the road.

Cora slid from her saddle just as a wail of sorrow split the morning air. It was Alia'a grandmother. The woman raced toward Alia, but Cora caught her in her arms before she could reach the girl. "She's alive," Cora assured her. "She's still alive."

The woman was trembling all over and Cora could barely hold her up as they made their way closer.

As soon as they reached Alia, the woman sank to her knees, running her hands along the girl's forehead. "She's so cold."

Cora swallowed hard.

"Why won't she wake up?"

Cora didn't even know how to start explaining the Blight or that by slaying the hounds, they had inadvertently released a fragment of the creature into the village, and it had latched onto Alia, taking control of her body. It was all so ridiculous that Cora wouldn't have believed it had she not witnessed the event for herself.

Lenire saved her from having to answer. He touched the woman's shoulder. "I would like to try to help your granddaughter if I can," he said. "If you would allow me?"

The woman nodded, backing away.

"Do you need help?" Cora asked Lenire as he knelt by Alia's head.

"No," he whispered. "I've done this before."

His gaze was so steady and focused that Cora didn't ask him another thing, afraid she might somehow disturb the work he was about to do. She shuffled back into the gathering crowd, wrapping her arm around Alia's frightened grandmother.

She could provide little more than comfort in this matter, all eyes falling to Lenire and the healing magic that slipped from his hands. Lenire's arms moved in patterns, his hands dancing as if weaving invisible threads. Though maybe the threads were only invisible to non-Itharusian magic wielders. That would explain why he was so focused as he began making intricate looping and pulling motions, like he was tying more of those knots that he'd explained Itharusian magic was based on. Alia remained cold and still, like a corpse on the ground. Lenire's lips pursed, two deep lines forming between his eyes. He seemed to shake, though whether it was from the strain of his magic or his intense concentration, she couldn't be sure. The spells he cast were silent, and Cora wondered how he remembered such intricate magic. Her own magic came to her innately. It was based more on feeling, on the elements, and Cora could manipulate it to do things like pull fog across the sky or bend the earth. But to have to rely on her memory for such complicated knots? She didn't think she could do that.

With a sharp cry, Alia bolted upright, surprising both the villagers and Lenire. He stumbled back, his jaw still clenched from exertion. Cora's own heart was left racing as she stared at Alia.

"Child," her grandmother whispered. The pair hugged for a long moment, and it was clear to Cora that whatever remnants of the Blight that had taken control of the girl were gone. Alia's face and voice were once again her own, any traces of Zirael lost to Lenire's spellwork.

"Is this a dream?" Alia said, her thin arms shaking. "Am I dreaming now?"

"It is not a dream," Lenire spoke softly. Despite the low timber of his voice, Alia still jumped.

"But I remember it," she insisted. "I walked upon this road and the people cried out in fear." Alia lifted her hand, pointing at Cora. "Your sword. You lifted it as if to strike me." She clutched her head. "I must be dreaming. This can't be real."

"This is real," Cora said as Alia remained upon the ground, wrapped in her grandmother's arms. "You came in contact with a dangerous magic."

"I did?"

"You did," Lenire assured her. "But you fought it and survived."

Alia placed her hand over her heart, blinking through the memories as if wondering which were her own and which belonged to the Blight.

Cora knelt down beside the girl. "Alia, what else do you remember from last night?"

"Voices," she said at once.

"Voices?"

"And shadows. Like the ones you see in a nightmare."

Cora glanced at Lenire. Shadows sounded like the Blight.

"The shadows would pile together and then, if I squinted, I could see a woman."

"What did the woman look like?"

"She was young and beautiful, with long flowy hair," Alia said, touching her own for emphasis. "She wore skirts without shoes, which I thought was funny. But when I laughed she got angry. And when she spoke it didn't sound lovely the way I expected it to. Her voice boomed and her words made everything inside me tremble. It was like lying beneath a thundercloud. Then she told me to get up and I listened. She told me to go to the kitchen, where we kept the knives." Alia's voice grew stringy and fearful. "Everything she told me to do, I did. I didn't want to but I couldn't stop!"

"It's okay," Cora said, running her hand over Alia's head as the girl began to sob. "None of this was your fault, do you understand?"

Alia nodded but said nothing.

As Cora looked to Lenire, his face caught in shadow, the words Zirael had uttered to Lenire in the cavern played over and over in her head. *We are coming.*

*We.*

Cora had assumed Zirael spoke of others from Lenire's past. Perhaps members of the Order that Lenire had told her about. But now Cora couldn't help but think, judging by Alia's description of the shadowy woman, that Zirael had teamed up with Melusine.

Somehow their enemies had allied themselves, most likely drawn together by the Blight. And if they really had teamed up, Cora had no idea what they were capable of.

"I'd say a good rest is in order now," Lenire was saying as Cora's thoughts spiraled. She pulled from them just as Lenire helped Alia to her feet.

Though still trembling, Alia seemed steady, and with her grandmother's arm around her, she made her way back home. To Cora's surprise, it was Lenire who almost pitched over. Yrsa grumbled in concern, getting her snout under him before he hit the ground.

"Lenire?"

"I'm fine," he insisted, getting back to his feet.

"You're not," Cora said. Lenire must've expended considerable magical energy to wake Alia. For a moment, Cora wondered how close Alia had been to never waking again.

Lenire started off in the direction of Harlan's house, the man who had graciously taken them in when they'd first arrived at the village. Knowing that they'd left a gaping hole in the wall of the house where the hounds had spawned, Cora was eager to get back to repair what damage she could.

Lenire stumbled ahead, bumping into the wall of a homely cottage. He shoved himself upright, but in his exhaustion, he merely stumbled into the home on the other side of the narrow street. Cora surged forward, grabbing his arm, and slinging it over her shoulder.

"I'm fine," Lenire protested, trying to pull away.

"Yeah, you look it," Cora remarked.

Lenire tugged on his arm again, but Cora held it firmly. "I'm not letting go, so you might as well accept my help."

Growing quiet, or perhaps being bested by his own exhaustion, Lenire stopped arguing. As soon as they arrived on Harlan's doorstep, the man threw open the door.

"You're back!" he said, hurrying out to help Cora with Lenire.

Harlan was much bigger than she was, his shoulders broad and his forearms thick with strength. He dragged Lenire inside, getting him settled in a kitchen chair.

"You're in rough shape," Harlan said to Lenire as Cora hurried upstairs to take stock of the mess they'd left when Yrsa had ripped the window frame out to save them. In the light of day the damage was even worse than she'd expected.

Now Alaric sat in the street, looking in at Cora through the hole. Gathering what remained of her own strength after the long night, Cora dug her magic into the ruins, until it was all hot and malleable, fitting the mud and brick and earth back together. It wasn't pretty, but Cora was fairly certain it would hold against the mountain wind.

Cora returned downstairs, finding Lenire half slumped over a plate of potatoes and sausages.

"I repaired your wall the best I could," Cora said to Harlan. "I can't do anything about the glass, though. You'll need to have a new piece made to fit the window."

Harlan nodded in thanks. He didn't seem that bothered by it, and when Cora said as much he smiled. "It's not every day that you get to host two dragon riders. I suppose a little battle comes with the territory."

Cora still wished it wasn't so, but Harlan seemed to be rather pleased to have a story to tell.

"Here," he said, pouring Cora and Lenire each a tall glass of ale. "I think you both could use a drink."

He passed them each a glass, then hurried off outside to examine the new wall that had started to draw his neighbors' attention.

After a few hearty bites of breakfast and washing down most of his ale, Lenire looked remarkably better. Cora was glad for it.

"We need to talk," she said.

Lenire eyed her over the top of his glass. "We had a long night. Perhaps we should both get some—"

"Who is Zirael?"

Lenire frowned. "He's a high-ranking member of the sorcerous Order that began Itharus' war."

It was such a succinct and minimal reply that Cora knew there was more to the story. Before she could ask, his frown deepened, his eyes narrowing.

"But how is it that Zirael has come to know you?" As if his exhaustion had never existed, Lenire sat up in his chair, even leaning toward her with an accusatory stare. "He called you by your name in the cavern. How does he know your name?"

He'd known it the first time they'd spoken through the crystal, and as far as Cora was concerned, that was another reason to suspect that Zirael and Melusine were working together. "We've spoken before," she admitted.

Lenire dropped his fork. It clattered against his plate. He shoved his chair away from the table, taking a giant step back, looking at her as if she'd suddenly become the enemy. "How?" he asked. "When?"

"The night we first met. Zirael contacted me through the hounds' crystals. I didn't know who he was at the time. He never told me his name."

"What did he tell you?"

"He warned me to stay away from you. Said that you were a dangerous thief." Zirael had actually told her far more damaging things, but Cora didn't think accusing Lenire of being a murderer was going to foster the trust they needed right now in order to get to the bottom of this. "He told me about the disk you stole."

"That's what you were doing in my bag," Lenire said.

Cora flattened her lips. "I wanted to know if Zirael was telling me the truth."

Lenire rubbed at his eyes in frustration. "I had started to doubt myself and my magic. I thought maybe I'd tied the knotting spell wrong."

"You didn't," Cora said.

"And so you found what you were looking for?"

She nodded. "What is the disk for? Why does Zirael want it so badly?"

"The disk is one of three that were created and used by the Order in Itharus to summon the Blight. I *did* steal it from the Order. Zirael was right about that part. It was a quest Yrsa and I were lucky to survive."

"But why risk it?"

"The disks not only summon the Blight, but they have the ability to control it as well."

Cora's eyes widened.

"It's how the Order kept control during the civil war that plagued Itharus. No matter how we rose up, the disks gave the Order immense power. The one thing I learned after all these years of fighting was that no one should hold dominion over the Blight. It shouldn't even be here in the first place, but giving anyone access to a creature built for such raw destruction is putting the most dangerous weapon in the world into their hands."

For a moment Cora wondered if Melusine even realized the kind of monstrosity she had brought upon them. Her own experiences with the Blight had been terrible. It had taken people from her, left others caught in the sleeping sickness, but the way Lenire spoke, Cora knew that the Blight, left unchecked, could destroy more than the magic in Tenegard. It would destroy everything.

"When I realized what had happened, that the Order had lost control, and the Blight had fled here, I brought the disk to Tenegard in the hopes of using it to destroy the creature once and for all."

*He'd stolen it with good intentions,* Cora thought. If she herself had been in a similar situation, she would have done the same. Hadn't she, in fact? She had broken rules and defied laws in order to bring Onyx down.

Sometimes disobedience was the price of freedom.

Sometimes being branded a traitor and a thief was the cost of winning the war.

"I am not who Zirael claims I am," Lenire said quietly.

"No," Cora agreed. "You're not." She thought of Zirael's words again. *We are coming.* "But that doesn't mean he isn't still hunting you."

"I don't think he intends to stop," Lenire admitted. "Not until the disk is returned and I am dead. Yrsa and I have managed to evade him for a long time. But lately it seems that he's growing closer."

"I don't think he's working alone," Cora said.

Lenire's curious eyes found hers.

"Alia described a woman who sounds exactly like Melusine."

"The healer who you claimed controlled the Blight?"

Cora nodded. "Somehow it seems our enemies have united and are working together."

"Is that even possible?"

"I think so. Look at the construction of the hounds. I didn't see it before because I didn't know how Itharusian magic worked. I didn't even know there was such a place as Itharus. But they seemed to combine Itharusian knots to hold the flesh together, Melusine's power as a healer to grow that flesh, and the Tenegardian crystals to power the entire thing. It's a feat only made possible by combining more than one kind of magic."

"Itharusian, Tenegardian—"

"And Athelian," Cora said. "Melusine's healing abilities originate in our neighboring nation."

Now that she'd said it out loud, the hounds seemed less like fantastical beasts and more like a work of dedicated engineering.

"I wonder how many more hounds Melusine and Zirael have cooked up," Lenire said.

Cora took a sip of her ale. It slid like glue down her throat as she imagined an army of hounds standing between them and the mountains. She was suddenly aware of how much time they were wasting. "Hurry up," she told Lenire, wiping her mouth on her sleeve. "We have to get to the next crystal deposit before Melusine figures out another use for the Blight."

# CHAPTER 19
## CORA

Cora fastened her cloak around her as Lenire finished sharpening the blade of his dagger. After their night fighting hounds and chasing after Alia, she was eager to get back in the air, back in flight toward the source of Tenegard's magic. They had to reach the Heart of Tenegard before Melusine and Zirael did. But before they could head out, they had to return to the crystal deposit. Cora hadn't been paying attention to much besides Alia when they'd been in the cavern, so she hadn't even noticed that the lodestone hadn't picked up on the direction of the next crystal deposit. It was unusually light in her pocket, pointing nowhere but here.

Cora was about to suggest going back to the cavern when Lenire spoke.

"Are you ready?" he asked.

She nodded, feeling a sharp spike of pain across her forehead. She winced, catching her lip between her teeth in worry. The last time the pain in her head had spiked, the hounds had been about to regenerate. But those crystals were destroyed. She was battle-weary and exhausted, so it could easily be that, but she reached into her pocket anyway, pulling out the lodestone to examine it.

"We'll need to check in on the girl first."

"We don't have time," Cora said. Finding nothing of concern, she pocketed the lodestone again. "We've already stayed here longer than we should have."

"I want to make sure she's okay before we leave," he insisted, setting off. "Make sure there isn't anything else I can do."

As they walked, the villagers took note of them. Some nodded kindly, others were wary after last night, ushering their children inside. Cora couldn't blame them. Despite the fact that they'd slain the hounds and returned Alia, this remote mountain village had never faced a threat like the Blight. And with the arrival of her and Lenire, the village had seen nothing but trouble.

They reached a large wooden cabin with smoke spiraling from a stone chimney. Lenire knocked on the door. When it swung open, they were greeted by Alia's grandmother. She beckoned them inside. Other members of the village were crowded around a large kitchen table, nursing tea or broth, but Alia wasn't among them.

"We wanted to see the girl," Lenire said quietly to the woman. "Before we head off."

Alia's grandmother nodded, waving them down a hallway.

"We don't mean to wake her," Cora said.

The woman's wrinkled mouth folded into a line. "She's hardly slept since we brought her home. Poor thing. Just tossing and turning in fits."

Lenire nodded, walking straight into Alia's room and bending down by her bedside. Cora looked around as she entered, smiling at the childlike familiarity. There were treasures of every kind on the windowsill. Pretty bird feathers. Giant pine cones. Pieces of amethyst and jasper. Smooth rocks tumbled in the stream. And larger ones dug from the earth. Cora had once had a similar collection. Now it was probably gathering dust back in her father's house in Barcroft.

Whispers drew Cora closer to the bed, and she could see that Alia was wide awake despite the red that rimmed her eyes. Clearly, sleep had evaded her like her grandmother had said.

"What do you see?" Lenire was asking the girl.

"Terrible things," Alia said at once. "Flashes and snarls and a seeping darkness that crawls into every corner of my head. But the worst of it is a monstrous shadow. It starts small, but soon lashes out and covers everything. No matter where I hide, it finds me, leaking under the door like a rotten mist. And when I wake my heart is beating so hard that I think it might punch out of my chest." Alia made a fist and struck the air. "I don't think I will ever be able to sleep again."

Cora's own heart pounded at the description. She couldn't help but worry that the same horrific visions that plagued Alia's dreams also plagued Faron's. Perhaps he was suffering through an endless onslaught of Blight-tainted nightmares. Maybe all the unconscious dragon riders were. Cora wrapped her hand around the hilt of her sword, squeezing until her fist trembled. She had to beat Melusine to the heart. She had to stop the nightmares.

"You will sleep," Lenire promised, patting her head gently. "And you will dream without the darkness."

Tears filled Alia's eyes. "I don't think so."

"What if I promise to use a very special spell on your dreams? While you sleep it will fight back the darkness and the nightmares. And you will wake rested and well."

Alia nodded into her pillow.

"Close your eyes, then," Lenire instructed.

Alia did, peeking once to see Lenire's hands tie invisible strings above her head. And though there was a laziness to his movements that Cora hadn't seen before, Alia smiled and her breathing grew easy.

They left the room and Alia's grandmother closed the door gently. "These dreams," she began.

"Will fade with time," Lenire assured her. They moved quietly down the hall. "The terrors that plague her will become a thing of distant memory. But until then you should take precautions against her sleepwalking. The dreams can be vivid at times, and I wouldn't want her to accidentally hurt herself."

Alia's grandmother nodded and, to Cora's surprise, hugged them both. Cora didn't feel like they were deserving of this much gratitude, but she hugged the woman back, hoping that Alia would find peace.

When they were back on the street, Cora turned to Lenire. "Do you really have a spell for nightmares?" she asked.

Lenire shook his head. "I wish I did."

"You lied to her?" Cora was surprised and at the same time she'd suspected something was strange with his spellwork. Not that she really knew anything about how to tie magical Itharusian knots.

"It was for Alia's benefit, I assure you."

"How?"

"The mind is a powerful thing. I may not be able to fight off the nightmares for her, but if Alia believes that I have, that she is safe and protected, she might very well find the strength to combat the nightmares herself."

Cora nodded slowly. She supposed she would tell the same sort of lie if it brought Alia the sleep she so desperately needed. Her thoughts skipped back to Alia's dreams, the things that woke the girl in fits, focusing on the description of the Blight trapped in her mind. "Zirael has used the Blight to possess other people," Cora said aloud. "Hasn't he?"

Lenire had confirmed as much when he told her he'd seen this kind of possession before. And every interaction he had with Alia was tinged with the wisdom of experience.

He nodded in response to her statement. "We were lucky this time."

"What do you mean?"

"With Alia's possession, we were only faced with a Blight 'puppet' so to speak."

"What could be worse than that?"

"It was only the girl's body that was stolen, not her mind."

"How can you tell the difference?"

Lenire hummed softly, reluctant to talk about it. There seemed to be memories attached to this conversation that he didn't want to relive. But Cora thought this information important and pressed him further.

"Blight puppets are obvious. When the Blight has only managed to infiltrate the body, the body still belongs to the person. That's why Alia walked funny, why her movements were jerky."

"Why her voice and her face were not her own?" Cora asked. It was as if the Blight, as controlled by Melusine and Zirael, had been wearing a human suit.

Lenire nodded. "Most victims of that kind of a body possession can recover if the possession was not too lengthy."

"And the mind?" Cora wondered. At first, seeing Alia fall unconscious, Cora had immediately thought of the sick dragon riders. When Lenire had woken Alia, a seed of hope had blossomed in Cora's chest. Now, though, she was starting to understand that what happened to the dragon riders and what happened to Alia were very different things. The Blight hadn't possessed the dragon riders. It had fed off them.

"When the Blight manages to corrupt the mind, it becomes one with the person. It can hide behind the victim's true self for weeks, slip past defenses, attack unexpectedly. There is no coming back from that kind of possession," Lenire said softly. "Not as far as I have seen."

"But what—"

He cleared his throat, ending the conversation abruptly. "We should probably find the dragons and get going while we still have a good amount of light."

He charged ahead and Cora couldn't help but feel that Lenire had personal experience with this other kind of possession. Judging by the way he was acting, it must have been a pretty horrifying experience. Though curiosity bubbled inside her, Cora held off on asking him any more of those questions as she hurried to catch up with his long strides.

"We have to go back to the cavern," she said.

"What?" He shook his head. "No way. Zirael could know where we are. He could send more hounds. Let's get out of here and find your magical Tenegard heart."

Cora caught his arm, pulling him to a stop. She yanked the lodestone from her pocket. "We have to go back to the crystal deposit. The lodestone didn't reset while we were in there. I need it to know which way to fly. Remember?"

"What do you mean it didn't reset?" Lenire plucked the crystal from her hand, twisting in place like he was trying to find the position on a compass, and groaned. "Why didn't it reset?"

Cora snatched the crystal back. "I don't know. I wasn't exactly paying attention last night when we found the deposit. I was a bit preoccupied with Alia and Zirael and all that confusion."

"You're sure using the crystal is the only way for you to know which direction the Heart of Tenegard is in?"

"I'm positive," Cora said. "Do you want me to explain the role of the lodestone all over again? How it leads us to the next crystal deposit?"

"Wait." A line formed between his brows. "What are we even looking for? The Heart of Tenegard or crystal deposits?"

"I'm fairly certain the crystal deposits mark the way to the Heart of Tenegard. And I have no way of knowing how many deposits are between us and the heart."

"*Fairly* certain?"

"I am certain." She groaned. "We find the next deposit and we are that much closer to our goal. But we can't do that without going back to the cavern first."

Lenire huffed impatiently, running a hand over his face in frustration. "You could have told me this earlier."

Cora didn't argue, just stalked off in the direction of the crystal deposit. "Come on, Lenire. We're wasting time!"

The sight of so many glittering crystals in one place still took her breath away. Cora wished the passage into the cavern was large enough for Alaric to squeeze through so he could experience their beauty for himself. Without the full strength of their bond, Cora couldn't share the overwhelming sense of amazement that filled her, so he would have to take Yrsa's word for it. Because if Lenire still had trouble struggling through the passage, then there was no way a dragon was getting inside.

"Okay," Lenire said, looking around at all the crystals. "Where do we start?"

After the awe had faded, a gripping sense of dread filled Cora. Memories from last night returned and from the corner of her eye, she swore she saw a darting figure that looked like Alia. When she shook her head, pain flared to life in her temples. She hated Melusine and Zirael for tainting such a breathtaking site with ugly memories.

One day, when this was all over, Cora would return and claim it for the dragons once more, sharing its wonder with the people of Tenegard. But right now she was tired and her head throbbed, so she just wanted to let the lodestone activate and then move on from this place.

Cora pulled the crystal from her pocket again, holding it in her hands. She waited for something to happen. Anything, really. But nothing did. A frown tugged at her lips. With the last crystal deposit, the lodestone had reset itself, almost automatically. Now it sat in her hands as if waiting for something.

"What's wrong?" Lenire asked. He was crouched down next to a crystal, studying his reflection in the glowing facets.

"I'm not sure," Cora said. "It's not working."

"What exactly is it supposed to do?"

"Glow," Cora said, still waiting for the telltale weight to pull her in a new direction.

"Everything in here glows. Just pick another crystal."

"That's not how it worked before," Cora said. Though what did she really know about how the crystals worked? Using them in any capacity was still a new discovery. Until a few days ago she certainly didn't think they could power and turn chunks of rotting flesh into undead hounds.

Cora walked deeper into the cavern, watching her reflection bounce between the crystals, both large and small. The last reflection she'd seen here had been Zirael's. The image of his aged face was still imprinted on her mind.

"Maybe you need to use a spell," Lenire offered.

"Maybe," she muttered, growing impatient. She was the one who'd insisted they return to the cavern, and now the lodestone was acting up. Out of frustration, she clinked the lodestone against one of the crystals in this deposit, hoping it would trigger the direction to shift, but instead of glowing or growing heavy, Cora dropped the stone, crying out.

"What is it?" Lenire asked, immediately flocking to her side.

It felt as if a scalding hot blade had been driven through the center of her skull. She gasped, one eye closed against the remnant of the pain. Like before, when the hounds had been about to regrow, these crystals now gave off a similar ringing vibration that seemed to tug painfully at something in Cora's head.

Cora reached down to pick up the lodestone. It remained unchanged.

"What happened?"

"Nothing," she said but at the look on his face—the one that reminded her to stop withholding information—she admitted what had happened. What had *been* happening. "The ringing only started again when I touched the crystal," she said. "Until then the headache was a muted roar."

"Headache?" Lenire whispered.

Cora squinted against the pain, mostly in preparation for another sharp spike. This ringing headache had plagued her on and off, but whatever had just happened with these crystals had been the most painful of all.

Cora kept her arms carefully glued to her sides to avoid touching any more of the crystals. Before she could wonder if perhaps Lenire might have a healing spell that could help her, he'd jumped back at least a foot from her and drawn his sword.

"Lenire!" Cora exclaimed, looking around for some unseen enemy. "What are you doing?"

A roar thundered outside the cavern. It echoed through the passageway and exploded through the crystal deposit, rattling the walls. Cora couldn't tell if it was Yrsa or Alaric, but a sharp scratching noise followed, like dragon claws digging against rock.

"Stay back!" Lenire shouted at her as the crystals around them trembled.

"By the stars, Lenire, what are you doing?"

Lenire struck out with his sword as Cora tried to approach him. He didn't hit her, but it was close, and Cora's hand immediately went for her own sword. She didn't draw it, but she put more space between them. "What is wrong with you?"

"It's not me who's the problem." As he lifted his sword, leveling it at the center of her chest, his hand shook. "This is how it starts."

"How what starts?"

"The possession of the mind!" Lenire shouted at her. "The Blight's infiltration. It begins with a dull headache and ends with you committing untold destruction." As he said the words, he advanced toward her.

Cora scrambled out of the way. "Lenire, stop!"

"Zirael must have planted the seeds of it when he spoke to you through the crystal. Or maybe it's been there even longer than that. I have no way of knowing." His stance remained but his face grew impassive. "I'm sorry, but there's no other way. I have to kill you before it takes hold."

# CHAPTER 20

## OCTAVIA

There was no such thing as too much fresh air as far as Octavia was concerned, and she asked Raksha to make another loop of the city. After the scare she'd had in the communication chamber last night, which thankfully turned out to be nothing, Octavia wanted the breather. She let her hair out of its tight braid, and it blew unrestrained across her face, the blonde strands obscuring her vision as Raksha flapped her mighty wings, taking them even higher.

It wasn't often that she got out of the palace for something as trivial or purposeless as a ride around Kaerlin, but she'd taken the free morning to remind herself what it was to be a dragon rider. Raksha's powerful muscles surged beneath her, but even more than the intoxicating thrill of flight, Octavia could sense her joy. Dragons were built for the sky, but Raksha refused to leave the palace while Octavia was embroiled in council business, preferring to stick close in case she needed her. Usually Raksha would slip away before dawn to hunt, but she would be back before Octavia had even roused from sleep and would resume her vigilance.

It was nice to be together like this, away from the demands of the palace. Northwood had scheduled a council meeting this morning and for a split second, Octavia had worried that he'd discovered she'd been in the communication chamber last night speaking to Serafine. But then he'd canceled the meeting on account of some other business and her fear had dissipated. If Northwood had suspected her treason, he would have marched her before the council first thing.

"Never mind that," Raksha said, picking up the tone of her thoughts. "The two of us would have been arrested on sight."

"Why would you be arrested? You didn't have anything to do with it."

Raksha snorted. "We come as a pair, Octavia. I might not have been at your side last night, but I still very much knew what you were doing."

Octavia hummed.

"Besides, they would have to arrest me to prevent me from coming to free you."

"It seems like such a trivial thing to even be arrested over," Octavia said. "How can it be treason? It's not as if I am trading state secrets. I'm merely asking for aid. Shouldn't we be able to do that? Ask our neighbors for help?"

"There is much about human government that doesn't make sense to me. Their constant need to fight over petty things is one of them."

"Have dragons ever gone to war?" Octavia asked curiously. "For themselves, I mean. Not at the aid of a human."

"Not in my long memory," Raksha said. "Though I can only speak for those dragons in Tenegard."

Octavia thought of the dragon knight that Strida had mentioned when she'd visited. The one Cora had met. "Do you think there are a lot of lands with dragons?"

"I can't be certain. It feels like one of those blank spots left from Onyx's spell. But the world is vast. It isn't hard to believe that dragons would not have stretched their wings and made their homes across the lands." Raksha twisted higher, until they'd cruised right through the clouds and come up on top of them.

From there Octavia could see clear across Tenegard, and for a brief moment, she wondered what existed beyond their borders. Not just Athelia or this new land of Itharus that she'd learned the dragon knight hailed from, but even farther than that. Octavia grinned, running her hand over Raksha's scales. "Perhaps one day we will be able to find out."

"You think we will leave Tenegard?"

"Right now it seems like a distant dream, but I'd like to think that once we deal with Melusine and the Blight and the sleeping sickness, the dragon riders would want to set out, see what lands and people might exist beyond our borders. Maybe there would be other dragons, like you said. Maybe there would be people interested in becoming allies. We could open trade routes. Think of the things we could exchange. Magic. Medicine." Octavia trailed off. The council thought her foolish and idealistic in her youth. Northwood liked to claim that she had no idea what it was to run this country, but Octavia knew that wasn't true. She'd simply run it differently. Preferably without Northwood at the helm of the military.

"You are not foolish," Raksha said, picking up on Octavia's feelings through the bond.

"I know," she said. "I wish I was taken more seriously. That *you* were taken more seriously. I want nothing more than to help the dragon riders at the school and yet here we are, going to battle every council meeting just to talk Northwood down. His obsession with war is going to permanently scar our relationship with Athelia."

"Is that what the senator said?"

"Not in so many words. But Serafine and I both agreed that North-wood is probably not the best ambassador for our nations. They don't trust us the way one would hope. After what happened with Onyx, that's understandable, but Northwood is fueling the fires of mistrust. I don't know how the council can be so reckless, blindly letting him run around and destroy what remains of our relationship with Athelia."

They drifted through the clouds, descending slowly. Kaerlin came into view once more, the people skittering like bugs down on the streets. Bugs that Northwood would soon be responsible for squashing if he really was pushing more soldiers to the border.

"Maybe the other councilors don't know what we do. They see only what is presented to them in the council meetings. As far as I can tell, even the communication chamber seems to be a closely guarded secret."

Octavia sighed. "And I can't tell the council any of this because, one, I don't have clear proof of anything." Her understanding of what was really going on behind the scenes was supported by the whisperings of the people and her own gut instinct. "And, two, if I did say something, that would reveal I've been talking to Athelia myself."

Raksha's thoughts were complicated, but Octavia recognized them the way she recognized the tangle in her own mind. Everything was a mess. It felt like the sinking sands she'd once read about, the kind that swallowed travelers whole. Octavia felt like she'd stepped into a sinking pit and with every laborious step forward, she sank a little more. If she didn't make it across the pit before her head disappeared beneath the sand, she'd never get out. But at one end of the pit were the dragon riders swarmed by the Blight and at the other end was Northwood charging toward war. Octavia had no idea how to fight free of the quicksand, which left her well and truly stuck.

Surprise filtered down the bond and Octavia pulled herself from her own thoughts. "Is that a dragon?" she asked, spying the speck on the horizon that had captured Raksha's attention.

"Indeed."

"Strida?" she said at once. Work had once again torn them in two different directions and Octavia wanted to fix it. There was enough pulling on her at the moment, and she didn't want her strained relationship with Strida to be one more worry.

"It's not Strida," Raksha confirmed.

Disappointment filled her, replaced quickly by curiosity. "If not Strida, who else could it be?"

"The dragon and rider are unfamiliar to me, but the dragon says they come to hold counsel with you."

Concern and confusion battled in her mind. "Take us down," Octavia requested at once, and Raksha did exactly that, coasting between the palace towers and landing in the courtyard as the dragon and his rider drew ever closer.

Octavia slid from Raksha's back. A bout of nerves surged up from her gut as wretched thoughts spiraled through her mind. Had something happened at the school? Perhaps Melusine had returned and the Blight had attacked once again. Perhaps Strida was hurt. Or was it Faron? Had something happened to the riders trapped in the sleeping sickness?

Raksha sent her a wave of calming energy. Octavia settled herself, shoulders back, hands folded in front of her. She waited, every bit the assured princess. Then she remembered she was no longer a princess, that she'd rebelled against that title, and her hands dropped, smoothing the wrinkles from her tunic. She was dressed for riding not for royalty today, which was perhaps more fitting now that they were to entertain a dragon rider. She only wished she knew which piece of bad news he was here to deliver.

"I don't think they come with news of Strida or of the school," Raksha said.

Octavia raised a brow in question. "They want to hold counsel but it's not about the school?"

"The tone of the dragon's thoughts were more … political," Raksha explained.

"Political?"

"They haven't been sent on behalf of the dragon riders but on behalf of Emmett."

*Oh,* Octavia thought suddenly. With all the sneaking around and secret communications with Athelia, Octavia had almost forgotten about the request she'd made of Emmett days ago, when Northwood had first shown her the communication chamber. She had asked Emmett to find her someone in his line of work, someone loyal, who might help her gather the intelligence she was not capable of getting on her own. Her brows drew together.

"Is this the aide Emmett had suggested?" Raksha asked, her thoughts also tinged with confusion.

When Emmett had mentioned a man named *Jeth Arenson*, she'd been expecting a courtier or other palace aide. Instead he had sent her a dragon rider.

Octavia had chosen a room big enough to house two dragons. She'd obviously wanted to speak to the dragon rider away from the gossipy ears of the palace staff and other officials, but there weren't many private rooms that could accommodate two dragons and their riders. The council chamber would have worked well, but Octavia could only imagine who might be listening in the dark corners.

"I apologize for not being a better host," she said as soon as she'd closed the door behind the rider. He was a man in his fifties, with flecks of gray in his hair and in his beard. His dragon was jet black except for two streaks of silver that ran down the middle of her belly.

"This will suit our needs well," he said, unfazed by the old furniture or the dust that coiled in the beams of sunlight that cut through boarded-up windows. Whatever the room once was, it was clearly a storage chamber now, and Raksha walked from corner to corner, making sure they were truly alone.

The man had acknowledged Octavia in the courtyard, greeting her and Raksha by name, but the pleasantries had stopped there until they could find a safe place to speak. Satisfied that they were not going to be overhead, the man introduced himself.

"My name is Jeth Arenson," he said, holding out his hand for Octavia to shake. "And this is Zoya." The dragon dipped her head. "It is good to meet you."

"You're Jeth? You're not what I was expecting." Octavia blurted. She couldn't help herself. The dragon rider and Emmett's suggestion of an aide being the same person surprised her.

He laughed at the look on her face. "What were you expecting?"

"In all honesty, I'm not sure, but certainly not a dragon rider. When I asked Emmett who he might recommend, I expected it to be someone already here, in the palace."

"I have had a long and varied career," Jeth said. "I think you would be surprised to find that dragon riding is only my latest pursuit."

"Ah," she said. "So the capital is not unfamiliar to you?"

Jeth shook his head. He gestured to a table where old, embroidered chairs sat gathering cobwebs and fancy gold place settings were still set upon the table.

Octavia dusted her seat as best she could and sat across the table from Jeth. She had to move a tall, spiral-handled wine jug to see him better.

"I actually called Kaerlin home for many years," he continued.

"And you worked in the palace?" she asked.

"In a capacity, yes."

Octavia studied his face. The rough lines, the scars, the dark, inquisitive eyes. There was no recognition there. "I don't remember you," she said. Onyx had a myriad of officials at his disposal, but Octavia was good with faces. Even if she didn't know a name, she always knew the face.

"You wouldn't," he said. "If I was doing my job properly."

"Emmett said something similar to me," Octavia admitted. "The day I asked for a recommendation."

"And this recommendation," Jeth began. "Tell me what exactly you asked for."

"Did Emmett not tell you as much?"

"He did. But I want to hear your version and make sure we are both on the same page."

"I need an aide," she said at once.

"You must know upfront that paperwork is not one of my strengths. I was never much suited to life behind a desk."

"I don't think paperwork would be required for this role. In fact, it would be best if what we were to discuss was not written down at all."

"So it is information you are trading in?"

"Perhaps," Octavia said. It was strange to feel such kinship in another rider and yet be so wary of them at the same time. Jeth was a mystery and as much as she wanted to untangle that mystery, part of her thought it might be best to keep some of his shadow intact.

"And where might someone find the information you are looking for?" Jeth asked.

"Are you familiar with the border at all?" Octavia asked.

"Athelia," Jeth said, smiling. "I am very aware."

"Is that why Emmett recommended you to me?"

"Among other things," Jeth said. "As I've said, I had a career in the capital, long before you were born, providing the kind of *assistance* that I think you require."

"What did that entail?" Octavia asked.

"Smuggling, mostly."

Octavia felt her eyes widen.

"You have to remember, while Onyx was in power, any communication with Athelia was strictly forbidden and punished harshly. So I traded in information and secrets, smuggling messages across the border, and sometimes, even people."

"People?" she said, surprised.

"Those branded as traitors by Onyx. It was either execution or the Athelian wilderness. Most people opted for the latter." He smiled gently. "Why, you're not looking to run away to Athelia are you?"

"Are you calling me a traitor?" Octavia asked. Her tone was light, though her question was charged. If she was really meant to work with Jeth, she had to know she could trust him. And though he was a dragon rider now, something about him felt slippery, like if she pressed too hard, he would slide right from her hands.

"It is not my place to pass judgment," Jeth said. "In my experience, the most difficult part in doing what is right, is first having to do what is wrong."

His words settled over Octavia and for a moment she considered the magnitude of them. Everything that had led her to this moment had begun with a tiny revolt in her mind. The one that had told her to sit with an imprisoned dragon even though it had been forbidden.

She felt a burst of warmth filter down the bond and glanced over to Raksha. That revolt had marked the first day of her new life.

"What changed?" she asked Jeth, turning back to the table. He'd clearly left that life behind to pursue dragon riding.

He chuckled. "With Onyx's downfall, my services were less in demand, so I took my passions elsewhere. It may have been unconventional, but I have always strived to help my people in my own way. I may be a dragon rider now, but I still know the border well, perhaps more so since I became a dragon rider and could fly there, and have maintained many of the contacts I'd developed over the years."

"And was Emmett ever part of all this skullduggery?" Octavia asked. Clearly she didn't know the man half as well as she thought. When he'd aligned himself with the dragon-rider school, she'd started to worry that his loyalties shifted like the sails on a ship, but perhaps that had never been the case. Perhaps Emmett's moral compass had always been pointed in the right direction. As Jeth said, the path to doing what was right was often filled with wrong turns.

"As you've probably noticed, Emmett does much better behind a desk. Though he is very good at concealing his rather frightening competence."

"Yes," Octavia said. "I'm starting to see that. My initial impression of Emmett was that of someone hopelessly stuffy and bureaucratic."

Jeth lips twisted. It wasn't quite a smirk but close enough. "That impression is precisely correct … just not the complete picture. That's what intrigued me most about this assignment. If Emmett was reaching out, I knew it was something of importance."

Octavia tilted her head, studying those dark eyes again. She was hesitant to reveal that she was acting without the council's approval, but Jeth was clearly a very smart man, and it was the obvious conclusion he would come to even without her acknowledgment.

"When I first met Emmett, we did not get along. I thought his devotion to Councilor Northwood was unyielding and for that reason I had begun to see him as an adversary."

"Is it devotion you're looking for then?" Jeth asked.

Octavia leaned toward him. "You've built a life on lies and deceit, *Jeth Arenson*. But now you fly with dragons. All I want to know from you is where your true loyalties lie."

"You are nothing if not blunt," he said.

Octavia's mouth stretched into a thin line. "I cannot afford to be anything but direct. Lives are already at stake." Everyone she cared about was at risk, and though the dragon riders had their own battle, war would only make that harder. She needed to know what Northwood was doing.

She needed to know, and she needed to stop him.

The smile left Jeth's face and his teasing tone was gone. All at once Octavia saw the shrewdness of the man that had haunted the border for so many years, weighed down with nothing but secrets. "My allegiances should be plain," he said. "I ride with the dragons. My loyalties are to the dragon riders."

Octavia looked at Raksha and she nodded.

"You know," Jeth said, "in a world of lies and shifting allegiances, my dragon bond gave me an anchor for the first time in my life. One true thing to hold on to. This shared experience has made the dragons my family in a way I never expected."

Octavia tipped her head, regarding him with new eyes.

"I've never known anything like it," Jeth continued. "And I'd die before giving it up."

A familiar heat bloomed in Octavia's chest. "You know, Jeth, I think we're going to work well together." She understood what Jeth meant, because she too was willing to do whatever it took to protect her bond with Raksha.

# CHAPTER 21

## CORA

Cora ducked away from the end of Lenire's blade as it crashed down beside her. The metal slid against the wall of the cavern with a *tck, tck* sound that sent painful shivers through Cora's entire body. She didn't stop—couldn't—rolling out of the way and diving behind a small crystal cluster as Lenire whipped around, trying to take her head off.

"Lenire, stop!" she bellowed hoarsely.

"I can't!" he replied. "I told you. This is how it starts! When the Blight takes possession of your mind, one of the first manifestations is a lingering headache. Dull behind the eyes."

He struck out again and Cora pulled her own blade free, getting it above her head just as Lenire's sword came down upon her. Cora's forearms burned from the pressure as his weapon pressed against hers. He was trying to kill her, but using the adrenaline that surged through her body, she managed to throw him off. "I'm not possessed!" she growled.

Lenire stumbled back and Cora leapt to her feet. She was skilled with a sword. She'd been trained by Tamsin, had faced Onyx's shadow soldiers, but Lenire was a dragon knight, and she didn't really know what he was capable of.

Facing off, Lenire rolled his wrist, his sword slicing neatly through the air.

"You don't have to do this," Cora said.

"It's better this way. Trust me. If you knew what I knew, you would consider this a mercy. Don't fight me, Cora. I will make it quick. I won't let you suffer."

The walls trembled around them as Alaric and Yrsa roared outside the cavern. Cora watched a crystal break from the roof. It fell and embedded itself in the stone floor with a hard *thunk*. Lenire paid no attention, using the moment to lash out and strike.

Cora dodged, spinning out of the way. She turned to face him once more. "I don't want to hurt you."

Lenire didn't laugh at her, just clenched his jaw and struck out again.

When she dodged his next strike he growled. "You don't get it! You don't know the horrible things you will do under control of the Blight! It feeds on you. It *becomes* you."

Blood beat through her veins, the sound of his voice ringing in her head like the crystals. "What about Alia? You never considered killing her!"

Cora darted between a tall crystal deposit and his next strike missed her as well.

"This is different!" Lenire called. "If it was only a possession of the body, like the girl, there would be other options. I would be able to do more for you. But no one can stop an infiltration of the mind. You can't banish the Blight once it's seeped into your thoughts."

Cora stumbled as she ran. All she had to do was make it back to the entrance. If she could make it out, she could get to Alaric. And if she could get to Alaric and Yrsa, maybe she could talk some sense into Lenire. As she drew closer to the passageway, the ground trembled and she heard another strangled roar. Pebbles shifted upon the ground. More crystals loosened from their holds in the ceiling, threatening to fall.

She had no doubt it was Alaric on the other side of the passageway, clawing and clambering for a way in. Just as the passage was in sight, a dagger soared by her head, the blade slicing through the air before crashing and bouncing off the wall ahead of her. On instinct, she whipped around.

Lenire was close, but not close enough. Cora lifted her hand, summoning the magic that seemed to be pooling at the ends of her fingertips. Crumbled chunks of rock soared across the cavern, right for Lenire, forcing him to double back and take cover. When he leapt over a large boulder, Cora called a torrent of wind. This time it ripped Lenire's legs out from under him.

Lenire sprawled on his back, heaving as the air was forced from his lungs.

"I don't want to hurt you!" Cora repeated. She'd fought enemies before. She'd slain them. But Lenire wasn't her enemy, was he? She didn't want to *have* to kill him.

Suddenly he sat up, twisting his hands in the air before throwing something invisible at her. His knotted magic missed her, exploding against the wall, but a wave of rocks fell into the entrance, blocking her path except for a small gap at the top of the pile.

Cora surged up the fallen rocks, desperate to get to that gap before it was too late. "Alaric!" she screamed.

He roared back and the rocks beneath her shifted. Thunderous waves bellowed across the cavern as Alaric forced himself down the passageway. If they weren't careful the entire cavern was going to come crashing down on their heads.

Just as she got to the top of the rock pile, something latched around her ankle. It yanked and she slipped back down the rocks, smashing her chin on sharp stone. When she turned to look at her ankle, there was nothing there, but Lenire moved his arms like he was reeling in a rope, dragging Cora across the cavern. Her sword had dropped some-where in the rubble, her hands painfully empty.

Cora tried magic. Tried to sever the invisible string. But she couldn't get hold of it, and then Lenire was standing over her, sword clasped in both hands, ready to drive it down into her body. He said he'd be quick about it and in a flash she imagined the sword piercing her heart and the hot, red blood staining the crystal cave. She thought of Faron then, not unconscious on the cot, but grinning, his arms stretched out on dragonback as the wind ruffled his hair. She would never see him like that again—unburdened and happy and free. Now he would never wake. He would also never know how hard she'd tried to save him.

Cora closed her eyes and curled up, waiting for the sharp pain that was sure to follow, but suddenly the cavern exploded with sound. The ground rumbled and the crystals shook. Alaric had forced his way in, smashing through the rock wall that Lenire had created. Alaric wasted no time. He spread his wings and soared across the cavern, his talons poised to strike Lenire right through the chest.

Lenire shouted and threw himself out of the way, landing with a hard thump next to Cora. He groaned as he rolled over and Cora felt bad, but only for a second. Then she scrambled to her feet and dashed to Alaric's side. She'd never been so happy to see him. He took a mighty step forward, angling his body so that he stood between her and Lenire, and let out a hair-raising roar.

It was a sound Cora had never heard from him before, tinted with scratchy cries and sharp notes. There was a strangled fear in the echo as it reverberated around the cavern. Cora had to press her hands over her ears until the echo faded. Then she placed her hand on Alaric's side, silently reassuring him that she was safe.

Yrsa rushed to Lenire's side, roaring just as loudly, though she didn't lash out or strike at Alaric. Instead, she turned to Lenire, her chuffing noises sounding like pleas for peace. Lenire looked as if he wanted to duck past her and charge after Cora, but Yrsa's silent words must have reached him through the bond. The spell of panic that had claimed him before faded from his features.

Alaric's head snapped around to face her, his teeth still bared in warning, each one longer than a dagger and sharpened to an incredible point. They gleamed, reflecting the glow of the crystals, and Cora realized how menacing that image would be if she'd unknowingly stumbled upon Alaric like that in a cave. Even being a dragon rider, it would have made her pause.

His expression shifted, his growls becoming soft sounds as he beckoned her closer. "Okay?" he asked.

Cora nodded, leaning against him. "Thank you."

His eyes were narrowed in concern. "Blood," he said.

"What?" Cora looked down at herself, checking the folds of her tunic for any sign that she was injured. She looked back at him and shook her head. The headache still rang behind her eyes, a stark reminder of how this entire fight had started.

"Hurt," Alaric insisted. He bumped the side of her face softly with his snout and Cora felt a sharp jolt of pain shoot through her jaw.

Bringing her hand to her chin, she felt the sticky, tacky remains of congealing blood. She wiped her fingers on her tunic as she tried to remember how that had happened. Cora looked to the entrance of the cavern, which was now so wide beams of sunlight streamed through. The rocks Alaric had crashed through to get to her were scattered around the cave, lying in heaps, but Cora remembered sliding down them as Lenire had seized her with his magic. She must have smacked her chin harder than she thought. No wonder her head still ached.

"I'll be fine," she said.

Alaric snorted.

"I'm fine," she said again, pushing his snout away gently. Touching the wound had disturbed the clotting and a fresh drip of blood started. Cora held her sleeve against her face, putting pressure on it.

"Let me see."

Cora snapped around to look at Lenire. In all honesty, he'd been so quiet she thought he might have snuck off. But no, he stood there, next to Yrsa, his face wrinkled somewhere between concern and confusion, his sword still in his hand.

"I don't think so," Cora said.

"Let me see," he said again. "I can help you."

"And give you the chance to slit my throat? Thanks but I'd rather take my chances healing the old-fashioned way."

Lenire sighed at her obstinance, though Cora thought she had a very good reason to be difficult. Lenire had just tried to kill her. Instead of having a rational conversation, he'd pulled out his sword and looked at her like he expected her to lay down on the chopping block, neck exposed.

It was clear the burden he'd faced back in Itharus still haunted him. If her experience with Alia had been any indication, the Blight had done terrible things under the command of the Order, but that didn't change anything. If Lenire was willing to pull his sword out and run her through that easily, she couldn't trust him.

"I'm not going to hurt you," Lenire insisted. He took a step forward, retreating only when Alaric growled. "I can heal you. Please. It's my fault you're hurt. Let me do this and then we can—"

"Then we can do what?" Cora snapped. "Talk? Maybe that's what you should have done in the first place instead of pulling out your sword."

"You don't understand."

"No! I don't! And neither do you!"

"What?"

"Look, I know you saw some terrible things. That back in Itharus the Blight possessed people."

"Not just people, their minds," he insisted.

"Yes, their minds," Cora said, remembering Lenire's look of genuine horror the moment she'd mentioned her headache. "I'm sure that was awful to witness. But that's not what's happening to me."

"Cora, you don't know that."

"Dull behind the eyes," she said pointedly.

Lenire paused, confused, his response dying on his tongue.

"That's what you said to me before you tried to take my head off. You said it manifests as a lingering headache, dull behind the eyes. Mine is sharp and ringing, like a constant vibration humming in my head."

Cora saw the exact moment his confusion gave way to clarity, his eyes flickering over her face, processing her words.

"That ringing has spiked twice. Once here, when I touched the crystals, and again in my room the night the hounds respawned. Somehow, the crystals are causing my headache. I'm not possessed by the Blight."

"Cora—"

She plowed on, feeling like she had to get everything out before he could do something foolish again. "Think about it. The Blight possessed Alia. A random sleeping villager. If I was already possessed, if the Blight had already taken root in my mind, why would it bother with Alia when I was ready and waiting?"

Lenire had no answer to that, so Cora pressed her point.

"The crystals in this cave, all the crystals in fact, are linked directly to the source of Tenegard's magic. That's what I'm connected to, the crystals, not the Blight." Besides that, she'd had the lodestone in her possession for days now. It would have acted as protection against a direct attack from the Blight. "Ask Yrsa to confirm with Alaric if you don't believe me."

It took a moment, but Cora watched the silent conversation that occurred between Alaric and Yrsa and Lenire. At last, Lenire sheathed his sword. The sound stirred relief in Cora's gut. She'd finally convinced him that she wasn't possessed.

"But why would the crystals be causing you a headache?" he asked. "If they're a good thing … if they've protected you in the past, then why would they be causing you pain now?"

Cora looked around at the deposit. Crystal shards reflected everywhere. She thought of the hounds again, of slicing the crystals from their mutated bodies. She thought of the crystals turning to dust and the remnants of the Blight disappearing.

*Disappearing?*

It hadn't disappeared, though, had it? The Blight had just moved on to—

"They're infected," she said quietly as the realization dawned on her.

"What?" Lenire said.

"The ringing," Cora said. "I heard it from the crystals before the hounds ever respawned. But that must have been because they were still infected with the Blight. That's what allowed them to regrow. When we destroyed the hounds for the second time, the crystals were destroyed, releasing the Blight. Remember? We wondered what would happen to the remnants of the Blight."

"And it went and infected Alia," he said, still confused.

"Yes, but that wasn't all. The Blight feeds off magic. So when it left Alia's body, it must have been attracted to the crystal deposit and settled inside them." Zirael's grizzled face came to mind. She'd watched his reflection speak from dozens of these crystals. "That's how Zirael spoke to us! Through the crystals contaminated with the Blight."

The answers came to her faster than she could keep up with them. She'd been reacting to the contaminated crystals this whole time. The ringing headaches, they were warnings.

"So the Blight is still here," he said. "Lingering in all the crystals?"

"Maybe not all of them," Cora said.

"How do we check?"

Cora reached out to a small crystal, grimacing in anticipation. A sharp pain sparked across her forehead. She walked across the cavern, Lenire and the dragons on her heels. She touched another crystal and the same sharp pain dug at her head.

Lenire frowned at the look on her face. "It's this entire cluster, isn't it?"

"Any cluster that was close to where Alia collapsed," Cora said. "That's probably why the lodestone didn't work. If some of the deposit is infected with the Blight, it wouldn't be able to pick up on the direction of the next deposit." She didn't know what they should do now, with a crystal deposit that was tainted and festering … Cora gasped sharply, like she'd just been stabbed.

"What is it?" Lenire said. "Is it the pain again? We should get out of here."

Cora grabbed his hand, clutching it so hard he winced. "The Blight is lingering."

"Yes? We've established that."

Cora let him go and ran her fingers through her hair, tugging at the strands. "By the stars!"

"What?" Lenire demanded.

"It's lingering," Cora said again, louder. "It didn't just flee into the cave because it was attracted to the magic. It fled to the crystals so it could do exactly what it had been instructed to do!"

Lenire's mouth dropped open, but no words came out. She could see the glow of dozens of crystals reflected in his wide eyes as he made the connection. "Respawn," he finally managed to choke out.

Yrsa caught on first, then Alaric. They both made noises of concerned surprise, but the sounds faded to the background as Cora turned from them, gaping at all the tainted crystals, each one waiting to spawn into another hideous hound.

"There's dozens of tainted crystals in here," Lenire said. "That's dozens and dozens of hounds. Even if they don't all spawn that's still—"

"More than we could ever hope to defeat," Cora finished for him. Two hounds had taken all of their strength and magic to finally defeat. There was no way they could defeat a larger pack of them. She and Lenire didn't have enough magic. Especially with her dragon bond so fractured.

Cora heard Zirael's words echo inside her head again. *We are coming.*

This must have been what he meant.

# CHAPTER 22
## CORA

"How long do we have before the hounds spawn?" Lenire looked at her, his eyes squinting against the sun.

Cora gulped the fresh air outside the cavern, hoping some distance from the crystals would help ease the ringing pressure in her head. It didn't. Instead, she pushed through the pain and thought back on their travels. So much had happened she could have sworn she'd been gone from the school for weeks already, but the truth was it had been mere days. "About three-and-half maybe four days," she said. "Give or take. I'm not exactly sure. If there are rules when it comes to hounds spawning, I have no idea what they are."

"Should we pack up and leave?" Lenire said.

"Zirael told you they were coming. I think he meant *this*. But if we take off into the mountains and the hounds descend upon the village —" She couldn't force the words out.

"They'll have no one to protect them," Lenire finished the thought for her.

"Besides, without the lodestone's help, there's no way to easily get to the next crystal deposit." Cora could try to track the river manually again, using just her magic, but she already knew that could take weeks, months even. The lodestone had allowed them to cover an incredible amount of distance in a short amount of time. With a pack of hounds about to respawn, they didn't have time to mess around in the mountains.

"So we fight them?" he said uncertainly.

The dull ache in Cora's head intensified at the thought. "We could barely handle the two hounds that destroyed Harlan's place." She rubbed at her chin, then hissed and yanked her hand back. She'd forgotten about the wound there, and it started bleeding again.

"Let me heal that," Lenire said gently.

She regarded him for a moment, then nodded. She was pretty sure he wasn't going to kill her now. She'd made a strong distinction between her headache and a symptom of a Blight mind-possession, and he'd been convinced. That didn't completely erase the unease in her gut, however. She hadn't wholly trusted him before this, but now, she wasn't sure she ever could.

Cora sat against the mountainside and Lenire kneeled in front of her.

With his hand, he gently tilted her head back, then he began working and weaving those invisible knots. Surprised to feel the pressure on her skin, Cora moved to touch her chin.

"Don't," Lenire said, midway through what looked to be a complicated knot.

Cora put her hand down and let him continue. It was as if tiny threads had attached themselves to her skin, gently picking and pulling. It was so different to the wave of cold healer magic she'd become used to from Elaine or even Melusine. Cora thought back to the weeks she'd spent in the mountains tracking the river. Melusine had been by her side the entire time and had healed her after an attack from the Blight. Cora had been so grateful to her. So appreciative of her help. It had never even dawned on Cora at that moment that Melusine could intentionally hurt her, or her dearest friends.

She'd made the mistake of letting good deeds sway her before, but she knew better now. So although Lenire sat before her, seemingly apologetic for the role he'd played in her injury, she didn't fall for his kindness. She remained on guard. She needed to be ready should he ever pull his sword on her again.

Lenire caught her eye once, quickly looking away, and Cora wondered if he could tell what she was thinking. Maybe she wore a look of distrust on her face. If he suspected, he didn't let it deter him, he just finished his work with a few more magical knots.

When he was done, he sat back. Neither of them moved for a long while. There was nowhere to go. They didn't even speak. Yrsa tilted her head occasionally, and Cora suspected she was communicating with Lenire telepathically. The little ticks in Lenire's face gave it away: the clench of a jaw, the shudder of a muscle, the scrunch of his nose. Cora wished she could do the same and share her worry and fear and frustration with Alaric. Share her misery at this impossible situation. It was like every time she managed to get ahead, some terrible thing happened to shove her back five steps. Somewhere out there was the Heart of Tenegard, the one thing that might be able to wake the sleeping dragons and dragon riders, and yet Cora couldn't reach it.

She let her head fall back against the mountain, watching the sun reach its peak in the sky. Noon hour came and went. Lenire stood and began gathering firewood. He waded through the stream, Yrsa following closely, and trailed the edge of the woods for fallen branches. Cora's stomach grumbled.

Alaric curled up on the rocky shelf beside her, close enough that she could lean against him. "Okay?" he asked.

The word was as garbled as ever, and tears stung the corners of her eyes. She wanted to be able to talk to him. To *really* talk to him. He was her best friend. She could feel the breath come and go from his mighty chest. And yet, she'd never felt farther away from him. Cora swallowed hard, pushing down the heaviness that threatened to overwhelm her, and blinked away the unshed tears. "I'm okay," she said.

Lenire returned shortly after, dropping a stack of wood at her feet. "I figure we're going to be here a while. At least until we can figure out what to do about the crystals. Might as well be comfortable. Or as comfortable as we can be camped out by the deposit. I would go back to Harlan's, but I don't want to risk the villagers."

"We've put them through enough," Cora agreed. She reached out for a piece of wood, stacking the branches. "Plus, it's probably good that we stay close. Four days was only my best guess."

The muscle in Lenire's cheek twitched. Cora didn't say it, but they both knew what she meant. They should be here in case the hounds hatched sooner.

While Lenire got the fire going, Cora set out to hunt down something to eat. She wished Strida was here with her bow, but a trap would have to do. She used her magic to do a quick scan of the woods, then set up a trap using a combination of magic and string near the base of a tree with an active squirrel nest. She wandered away to wait, sitting by the tree line.

She watched Yrsa take to the sky, likely headed off to hunt for her own dinner. She slithered through the air, more like a snake than any dragon Cora had ever seen. Alaric remained behind with Lenire. The dragons wouldn't both leave now, whether it was to protect Cora and Lenire, or to protect Cora *from* Lenire, she wasn't sure.

Cora let her magic seep from her again, scanning the woods. She picked up a small, restless creature and she knew her trap had worked. Cora made quick work of dispatching the squirrel, carrying it back down to camp. Again, she missed Strida. She didn't relish having to clean the animal, though she would if she had to. Thankfully, Lenire reached for it as soon as she returned. Maybe he was still trying to make up for what had happened—what he had *almost* done—in the cavern. Or maybe he was hungry and eager to get something roasting on the fire. Either way, Cora didn't care. She let Lenire clean and gut the squirrel.

Yrsa returned from her hunt shortly after. Alaric hesitated to leave. Cora could tell by the way he kept looking back at her and she understood the feeling, loath to let him out of her sight. But eventually, Yrsa grumbled at him. It was a soft sound. A gentle sound. Whatever she said to Alaric must have been convincing enough because he dipped his head once and lifted into the sky with such speed Cora suspected he'd be back before the squirrel had even had time to roast. Plus, she knew he wouldn't stray far. He would stay close enough to hear her scream at any rate. Cora didn't need the bond to know that much.

Part of her thought she should be more fearful after what had happened, but now that they were out in the open instead of trapped inside the cavern, she was less concerned. Her magic wasn't very strong, but she could feel it pulsing at the ends of her fingers. Cora knew it was the lingering adrenaline, but she liked feeling powerful again, even if it wouldn't last forever.

"I'm sorry," Lenire sputtered suddenly, eyes downcast as he rotated the squirrel over the flames. "I let myself get carried away."

"I'm not sure that's the best description of what happened," she said.

"No," he agreed.

"If I didn't know better I'd have said you were the one who'd been possessed." There had been no reasoning with Lenire in the cavern. If Alaric had been even a second later, Cora had no doubt that Lenire would have driven his sword through her chest.

"Perhaps I *was* possessed," he said. "Fear can drive a person mad."

"I'm not going to say it's okay," Cora said. Forgiveness wasn't something she was ready to hand out just yet.

"I wouldn't expect you to." Lenire shook his head. "I should have noticed the contamination of the crystals right away."

"How would you?" Cora said. "Without the ringing, I wouldn't have even thought to question the deposit."

"Because this is exactly the kind of trick Zirael would try. And because we watched his face take shape in those crystals. I should have recognized that those remnants of the Blight remained. Instead I almost took that fear out on you, which is probably exactly what Zirael and the Blight would have wanted."

"And Melusine," Cora added. After the defeat at the school, Melusine probably wanted Cora dead. Or at least under control of the sleeping sickness like so many of the other dragon riders. "You said this was something Zirael would do. How do you know?"

"He's cunning and wicked and not opposed to tricks if they are a means to an end," Lenire drew his brows together. "Back home in Itharus, Zirael was one of the keepers of the Blight. One of its masters. He used the Blight to bring untold damage to my home city. When I stole the disk from him, he lost full control of the creature. He didn't just chase me to Tenegard to kill me. He's come to take back total control, which requires all three disks, even if it means working with Melusine. Without the Blight, I don't think he can return to Itharus."

"Why not?" Cora wondered.

"Civil war has bred anger in my people for years. Without the power of the Blight behind him, Zirael is just a man with a lot of enemies."

Cora nodded. "He must be desperate if he was willing to team up with Melusine. I spent weeks with her, trying to track down the Heart of Tenegard, before I knew what she was really after. She's tricky and calculating. I didn't see it, not at first, but she manipulates people to get what she wants. She's using Zirael as much as he's using her."

"How did she manipulate you?" Lenire asked. He turned the squirrel on the spit.

Cora listened to the crackle as grease from the meat dripped into the flames. "She pretended to be interested in Dragon Tongue. Then she revealed the Heart of Tenegard, the source of Tenegardian magic, as something that might be able to save the dragon riders. I was so desperate for answers that I believed she wanted to help us. I never suspected that she was the reason the Blight had attacked us." Cora prodded at the fire with a stick. "That's why my magic is so weak."

Lenire shifted and Cora saw the question in his eyes.

"While my team and I were in the mountains, trying to track down the Heart of Tenegard, Melusine invited the Blight to feed on our magic. We didn't know it at the time, but the continued exposure damaged our bonds with our dragons. It happened suddenly. One morning I woke up, and I could no longer reach out to Alaric through the bond. It was like a wall had been placed between us. It worsened, until I could only speak to him out loud, in simple words and phrases. Even now, if we talk too fast or in too much detail, it's all a mess."

"I didn't realize," Lenire said. "So the weakness in your magic is due to the—"

"Fractured bond," Cora finished for him. A small smile stretched across her lips. "Not from my lack of training."

An image of Lenire hovering above her, sword poised to fall, flashed through Cora's mind and her smile fell away. Once again her thoughts turned to Zirael's most troubling accusations. He'd told her Lenire was a thief, which turned out to be true. But he'd also said that Lenire was a traitor and a murderer. In all the information Cora had gathered about Lenire, she still hadn't accounted for those two accusations, and now with his little display in the cavern, she couldn't help but wonder. She supposed the accusations could have been fabricated completely, especially if what Lenire said was true, that Zirael would use any means necessary to get what he wanted. Even if she asked Lenire about the accusations outright, there was no way to know if he was telling the truth, and she hated to do anything that would cause their already fragile trust to further disintegrate.

Lenire pulled the squirrel from the flames, the meat broiled to an amber crisp. "I think it's done."

Cora cut herself a chunk of the rapidly cooling meat and they ate in silence. Alaric returned shortly after, curling up behind her. No matter how she tried to dismiss her thoughts, a seed of doubt remained. Lenire was still keeping secrets. Secrets that might get her killed.

Lenire wiped his mouth with his sleeve, turning to look at Yrsa with an expression that told Cora they were speaking privately. She settled against Alaric behind her, letting the warmth of his scales put her at ease.

When Lenire cleared his throat, Cora looked across the fire at him. "I think there might be a way that Yrsa and I can help restore your bond with Alaric."

"You can do that?" Cora perked up immediately. Alaric responded in a similar way, and Cora suspected Yrsa had told him the same thing.

"Now that I know your magic is weakened and why, I think I know how we can repair the bond and get you and Alaric back to full strength. The four of us together might have enough power to shatter the tainted crystals and destroy the contamination before the hounds can regenerate."

She wanted to tell him to do it, to do whatever it would take, but then reason took over. She needed to know more. "How do we fix the bond?"

Lenire dug into his pack and pulled out the disk Cora had only seen once before. "Using this."

"The disk that controls the Blight?"

He nodded. "The disks are tools that were originally made to create a magical connection with the creature. Though it has only been used with the Blight to my knowledge, in theory, the disk uses Itharusian knots to stitch two magical beings together. So if we can target your bond using the disk, perhaps we can stitch the two ends of your bond back together."

Cora imagined the bond like a string, one half from her, the other from Alaric. It had been frayed severely by the Blight, but if she could somehow tie a knot in the string with Lenire's help, maybe it would restore the connection.

"The only problem is," Lenire began, "you have to be the one to reweave the fabric of your dragon bond."

"I don't … I can't," Cora stammered.

"I'll help you," Lenire assured her. "We'll work together, and I'll use the disk to guide you through it. All you have to do is trust me enough to allow me to direct you."

Cora swallowed hard, her earlier concerns about him giving way to+++x blind hope. She still didn't know if Lenire was capable of murder, but right now she was willing to do anything to restore her bond with Alaric. If she and Alaric returned to their full power, it would only make dealing with the hounds easier. And if they managed to dispatch the hounds, they could return to hunting the Heart of Tenegard. Repairing their bond ultimately meant saving the dragon riders. It meant saving Faron. She nodded.

"One more thing," he said, his voice laced with warning. "With Zirael in Tenegard, using the disk will act as a psychic beacon, allowing him to pinpoint us from afar. He may even attempt to interfere."

"Will he be able to hurt us?" Cora wondered.

"Not directly," Lenire said. "But if he can make our intentions waiver for even a moment, it could disrupt the spell. And with magic so powerful, the consequences could be dire."

Cora looked to Alaric, thinking about all the things they could be risking. He closed his eyes and nodded once. Rebuilding her connection with her best friend was worth the risk.

"We'll do it," Cora said.

# CHAPTER 23

## OCTAVIA

A dark shadow passed across the window, blocking out what little starlight filtered through. Though her heart thumped in her chest, Octavia knew it was only Raksha, following her journey from outside.

*They're gone*, Raksha whispered in her mind, likely looking in through a window further down the corridor.

Octavia took a steadying breath before continuing, relieved to have confirmation that the guards had moved away. She'd departed for the communication chamber earlier than she'd intended to, which had clearly been a bad idea. The patrolling guards were in the middle of a shift change. If she stood still enough, she could hear the brush of metal armor echoing throughout the palace. She should have waited another half hour, but she was stuck now, halfway between her chambers and the communication chamber. She had two choices. Turn back and try again later in order to save face—no one would question her going to her rooms—though that would make her late for the meeting with Serafine. Or she could push on and hope she didn't come upon a lingering guard.

Usually, she could anticipate the movements of the guards with a measure of certainty. They kept to their familiar routines and traveled the same routes around the palace. And they always took the same amount of time to complete the loops of their patrols. But during shift change they were unpredictable. Were they dawdling? Chatting? Did they stop to polish a scuff from their boots?

*Quickly*, Raksha hissed. *The next corridor is clear.*

Octavia picked up her skirts and ran, the sound of her footfalls soft against the floor. She turned at the end of the hall to find it empty, just as Raksha had promised.

Only when she was halfway down it did she hear the voices.

Octavia froze.

*What is it?*

*Someone's coming!* Octavia reached for the first doorknob she could find and wrenched hard. Locked.

She tried another. And another.

One finally gave way and she stepped into the darkness.

Octavia closed the door and pressed her ear against it, listening for the familiar pitch of conversation. She had no idea what room she'd stepped into. A guard's bunk? A chambermaid's closet? One of Onyx's endless storerooms? She inhaled and covered her mouth suddenly, choking on dust. It smelled like old parchment, and she wondered if perhaps it was a private office or a library. Everything around her was cast in darkness, as pure and black as a moonless night. Her only bit of focus came from the strip of dull light peeking in beneath the door.

Octavia stared at it, watching and waiting.

*Are you okay?* Raksha asked, concern dripping down the bond.

*Yes*, Octavia replied. *I'm hiding in ... well, I'm not quite sure where I am at the moment.*

Suddenly, a light flickered beneath the door. Octavia felt for the door in front of her and her hand silently wrapped around the doorknob. She could feel her magic coiling and uncoiling inside her, on edge, ready to respond. She had no idea what she would do if someone outside tried to turn the knob. Melt the doorknob in place perhaps. Seize the lock. But then the light faded and Octavia relaxed.

*They are gone*, Raksha confirmed.

Octavia waited a breath, then another, before she popped the door open and poked her head out. Seeing no one, she hurried out of the room and down the hall. When she reached the spiral staircase that led to the bowels of the palace, Octavia looked over her shoulder and smiled at the darkened window where she knew Raksha was.

*If you need me, I will come immediately*, Raksha promised.

*I know.* Then Octavia fled, hurrying down the stairs and through the hall to that nondescript door that hid the communication device.

The instant she entered the room, the hairs on her neck stood up and Octavia could already feel her magic leaking out, attempting to make contact with Athelia. But despite her little run in with the guards, she was too early, which gave her time to worry about what sort of impression Northwood had been making on behalf of Tenegard.. Octavia was eager to rectify any misconceptions.

The people of Tenegard were relying on her to keep the peace between their nations. She wasn't about to let someone else stand in Onyx's place—especially not Northwood. She'd failed them as a member of the royal family, letting Onyx rule the way he did, but she intended to do better as a councilor. Octavia suspected she would carry the guilt of her ignorance for a long time. But Athelia might be the answer to everything. With this one conversation, she could possibly unite their nations and find a way to wake the dragon riders and their dragons.

Hopefully, the senate had agreed to help them, and this would be the last time she'd have to communicate with Athelia in secret. From here on, she'd tell Serafine to send communications directly to the council, and then she could pretend to be blissfully ignorant when they discussed it.

Then maybe she could sneak down here for other reasons. Octavia had already thought about using the communication room to reach out to Emmett again and request to speak to Strida. She missed her terribly, but they only seemed to dig a deeper trench whenever they were together.

*I'm not sure I like the idea of you sneaking around anymore than you already have*, Raksha cut in.

Risking Northwood's wrath was a foolish idea. Perhaps she should write to Strida instead. *Do you think Strida and I will always be this way?*

*Which way?*

*Distant. Unable to find peace in our relationship.*

*You found each other on the cusp of war, and now you are trying to grow together as your nation rebuilds and an enemy pursues the dragon riders. These aren't exactly the ideal conditions for a relationship to blossom.*

*No*, Octavia agreed. *They're not. But I feel as though we are always at odds. It's like we are fighting the same battle, the same enemy, but from different sides.*

*Sometimes the things we must do now only make sense for the sake of the future. But most cannot see the future, so they must trust that everything—*

The communication device crackled, and Octavia snapped out of her conversation with Raksha. It was the appointed time. She released enough magic to activate the communication device, letting Athelia know she was ready to talk, and then she waited for Serafine's image to take form in the massive arch before her. The image arrived, not all at once, but like grains of sand poured into cupped hands.

First Serafine's edges and angles appeared, her sharp chin and short haircut like the lines of stone that built the palace. She held herself stiff, her shoulders back, her hands folded before her.

"Good evening," Octavia said at once.

Serafine nodded in greeting. "Good evening. Or rather, good morning."

"I want to thank you again, for meeting with me at such an hour."

"Of course," Serafine said. "I understand your need to save face with your other councilors. But to the matter of our meeting, I will speak plainly."

"Please do," Octavia said, eager to hear what news there was. She could feel Raksha's curiosity hovering all around her, filtering through the bond. It lay against her like a film that she was itching to shake free. "What has the senate decided of Tenegard's request for aid?"

Serafine sighed. "I regret to inform you, Octavia, that the senate has decided not to offer the services of our healers or sorcerers."

A sinking pit opened in the middle of her chest, and Octavia clutched the front of her dress as if she might be able to fill the hole. Though she knew the senate might reject her proposal, she hadn't ever considered that they *actually* would. What could Athelia hope to gain by withholding aid? "But why?"

"The senate cannot offer aid to you when Tenegard increases their military activity upon our shared border. It seems almost a ploy, that with one hand you seek to distract us and with the other you are poised to strike."

Octavia was so shocked she could hardly form a response. She had heard the rumors of troops moving across the countryside from the people in the city, but none of it had been confirmed true. Had Northwood really lost his head and pushed for a battle that was not yet whispered about in the council chamber? "I don't know what you're talking about."

Serafine merely chuckled, the sound as sharp as her lifted jaw. "Sadly, I believe you. But unfortunately for you, Octavia, it seems someone is keeping you in the dark. You'll understand, of course, if this is the last time we speak. I cannot be seen contacting a member of your council, however good your intentions may be."

And with that, Serafine's grainy image faded to black.

*What has happened?* Raksha asked immediately, sensing Octavia's distress.

*Athelia has denied my request for aid.* Octavia's thoughts ran faster than she could as she slipped from the communication chamber and raced up the stairs, heedless of being caught. She didn't stop running until she'd reached her own chambers. The coals were dull in the hearth and she stoked them, watching the fire flame to life on new wood.

Raksha appeared at her window, the darkness of the night fading to blue behind her. *Octavia,* she said. *Don't do anything foolish.*

*Northwood is the one making a fool out of me. Out of all of us. Here I am attempting to help the dragon riders, the very force that Northwood will expect to ride to his aid should the occasion call for it, and yet he is doing everything in his power to make an enemy of Athelia.*

*You have to keep your head,* Raksha warned. *You cannot draw attention to yourself or to the conversations you've been having with Athelia. That is the very thing we were trying to avoid.*

But Raksha's words fell like water against the shore, beating against her and fleeing with the tide. Octavia's anger and frustration only smoldered like the coals in her hearth. What was happening? Had war broken out right under her nose? She was done sneaking around. If Northwood was bold enough to openly antagonize Athelia at the border without the council's approval, then it was time to call him out.

As soon as dawn broke, Octavia marched across the palace, her hands set in fists. She didn't bother to make an appointment or pause when Northwood's secretary babbled on about a private meeting. Instead, Octavia burst into his office, entering in the midst of his first meeting of the day.

"What is the meaning of this?" Northwood declared, rising from his seat. Several other council members stood at the intrusion, lowering themselves once they'd determined the threat was only Octavia. Most of them were councilors that Octavia recognized to be loyal to Northwood. "Octavia, I am in the middle of—"

"What is going on at the border?" she demanded.

"What?"

"Our border with Athelia. What's the military's intention there?"

Northwood shook his head. "I have no idea what you're talking about."

"I'm talking about you undermining the decisions of the council by making war inevitable with your military posturing!"

Northwood's look of shock was almost believable. "I don't know where you heard such things."

"Do you deny it?"

"Yes, of course I deny it," Northwood blustered.

"You're unbelievable." Octavia had to force herself not to shout. Only Raksha's voice, calling out through the bond, cooled her temper. "I want an explanation for the reports I've received of increased military activity at the border."

"Reports from whom?" Northwood demanded impatiently.

Octavia held her tongue.

"Somebody must be spreading misinformation to sow division."

Octavia looked around. Each of Northwood's colleagues watched her, some of them looking askance, others almost bored of the conversation. None of them suspected her words to be true, or if they did, they certainly didn't care.

Squeezing her fists so tight her hands shook, Octavia glared at Northwood. "I'm not letting this go," she said. Then she stormed from the meeting.

Octavia didn't stop until she'd reached the narrow hall of the palace where travelers often stayed. She'd been in this hall often, back when Strida stayed the night and they could actually enjoy a meal without arguing. She knocked on a door, hard, hearing the scrape of a chair across the floor. A moment later, the door swung open.

"Octavia," Jeth said. He was already up and dressed, a myriad of papers spread across his room. He'd only arrived yesterday but he already seemed to be hard at work. "You look troubled."

"What have you learned about the situation at the border?"

Jeth seemed startled, taken aback. "I thought perhaps I would take a more delicate approach first. You know, gather information. Talk to some of my contacts. It's probably a good idea, before I go sleuthing around the border."

"The time for that has passed. Gather whichever colleagues you need," she said, speaking fast, keeping her voice quiet, "and fly to the border. I need to know what's really going on. And I need to know *now*."

# CHAPTER 24

## CORA

Cora stared at the ice-like stone in Lenire's hands, her eyes getting lost in the dizzying Itharusian knots that covered its surface.

"Are you sure you're ready to do this?" Lenire held the magic disk out to her, and she shuddered.

The chill in her bones wasn't only from the mountain wind. It belonged to the hounds, festering to life inside that mountain and to the disk that might help her stop them. Since the moment Lenire had admitted that it might repair Cora's fractured bond with Alaric, the disk had haunted her thoughts to the point of insanity. She'd wanted to attempt using the disk immediately, but Lenire had insisted that they both needed some sleep before attempting such a complicated spell. After fighting off the hounds, rescuing Alia, and then fighting each other in the cavern, they'd both expended large amounts of energy and magic without properly recuperating. Sleep had evaded her, though. She'd spent all night tossing and turning, trying to imagine what it would be like to hear Alaric inside her head again. "If you ask me that one more time, I'll sew your mouth shut," she warned Lenire.

"If your sewing is as good as your sword skill, then maybe I'd believe you."

Her gaze flickered up to meet his. Cora saw the apology that was written in the fine lines that crinkled by his eyes. A twisting discomfort spun in her chest. What a strange situation they were in now. Yesterday he'd been prepared to kill her and this morning he might just be her salvation.

She still wasn't prepared to forgive him for what had almost happened, but if he helped her and Alaric repair their bond, she would owe him more than her forgiveness.

"I don't mean to make you nervous," he said softly.

"I'm not." Cora's voice wavered and gave her away. The corners of Lenire's mouth flickered, and Cora thought he might smile for the first time in their acquaintance. She'd begun to think that he didn't know how. "Fine. Of course I'm nervous. I think I was less concerned about facing Onyx and his shadow soldiers."

Alaric wasn't just her best friend, he was part of her, their souls intertwined since the day they'd met in the Therma Mountains. Standing here now, Cora knew she risked losing him completely. But the thought of having the bond restored, of being able to think and feel in tandem once more, filled her with a terrifying hope.

Perhaps even more terrifying was the thought that had wiggled its way into the darkest part of her mind. It had whispered to her all night. What if Lenire was lying and this entire scheme was a ploy to bind her magic and make her weak enough for him to defeat? The crazed look in his eyes inside the cavern was one she would remember forever. She had no way of knowing if Lenire had truly been convinced that the Blight had not claimed her mind. Separating herself from the crystals had lessened the headache, but camping so close, she still felt the occasional flare of pain across her temples. It was a constant reminder of the darkness that brewed inside the cavern.

Cora swallowed hard, playing her dark thoughts off as nerves.

"I have to confess," Lenire said. "I'm nervous too."

"You are?"

He nodded. "I've only tried this technique once before. I understand if you don't want to risk it."

Cora took a deep breath. She and Alaric were both in danger no matter what, whether that was from Lenire himself or from Zirael and Melusine and the hounds. "I have to give this a shot. If there's any chance it might work, even a small one, it's worth risking everything." If there was any hope of her finding the source of Tenegardian magic and the cure for the sleeping sickness, she had to restore her bond with Alaric. Faron's life, and the lives of all the other dragon riders afflicted with the sleeping sickness, depended on it. On her.

As if he'd been summoned, Alaric came and settled behind her in the field. Yrsa stopped next to Lenire, dipping her head, and nudging him in a way that Cora assumed was meant to provide comfort.

Lenire must have read a question in Cora's gaze because he said, "It's hard for me to admit to my limitations, knowing we're short on options, but I want to be worthy of your trust. I know I haven't given you much reason to trust me and that is working against us now, but I want this to work. And not just because I need help to defeat the hounds. I want you and Alaric to get back what you lost. Truly, I do."

Cora's mouth opened in surprise at Lenire's deliberate vulnerability. It was almost as rare as one of his smiles.

"I want that too," she told him, touched to hear his words. If trust was what it would take to repair her dragon bond, then she had no other choice. She would have to trust Lenire with this task. She was determined to.

"Good," he said, nodding in response to her. "I guess we should get started, then."

"How do we—" Her words dissolved as Lenire twisted his knotted magic around the disk. It responded immediately and those knots carved into its surface began to glow, swallowing up his magic. The disk pulsed, reminding her of the lodestone. As the glow became brighter and brighter, Cora squinted against the strength of the light. It was like looking directly into the sun. Even with her eyes closed, she could still see the image of the disk imprinted on her eyelids. The hairs on her arms lifted as magic crackled against her skin. She shot a glance at Lenire. His jaw was clenched tight, his teeth visible as the disk vibrated so hard in his hands Cora thought it might shatter between his palms.

"Lenire!" Cora stumbled back a step. She hit one of Alaric's claws, arms flailing, but he caught her, pressing his snout against the center of her back to keep her upright. His presence was steady. Whatever was happening, Yrsa had likely seen it before and forewarned Alaric.

"It's okay." The sharp line between Lenire's brows deepened, but his gaze was calm.

As suddenly as the disk began to glow, it darkened, as if the myriad of carved knots had swallowed the light whole. But then the light exploded out from the disk, and Cora yelped, watching it shoot across the field in every direction.

Cora's jaw dropped as the light settled like individual threads across the landscape. It was even more magnificent than her first glimpse of the cavern had been. Brilliant strings of magical light lingered all around them. They were woven together in formation, making up the trees and the rocks and the bubbling stream. Looking down at her hands, she noticed the threads twisted around her own body. It was like a living tapestry that existed in all things, and for the first time since meeting Lenire, she finally understood what it meant when he said Itharusian magic was based on knots.

Everything seemed to be based on knots.

It was a magic that was so foreign to Cora, and yet seeing it like this, it made absolute sense.

Cora looked from Lenire to Yrsa, noticing a bright, flowing thread of magic ebbing between them. It was their bond, she realized, in all its magnificence. Frightened now, Cora turned around slowly, looking for the magical current that connected her and Alaric. To her immediate relief, it was visible, but upon closer inspection, the contrast between her dragon bond and Lenire's was almost painful. While Lenire's thread pulsed with strength, Cora's was torn and ragged.

It looked like an overused climbing rope after the sharp edge of a cliff had sheared away at it until only a few lingering fibers remained. This was what Melusine and the Blight had done. Seeing it frayed between them made Cora's entire body stiffen.

Alaric made a whimpering sound, leaning down to worry over the last of the threads that held them together. Cora had always imagined the bond to be a solid thing. Something that could be repaired and rebuilt. This was almost worse. It was like she was waiting for someone to come and take a pair of shears to the remaining magical threads.

"Are you okay?" Lenire asked her.

She shook her head, feeling exposed. She knew it was a ridiculous thing to think. This was only a magical representation of her bond. But that didn't stop her from feeling the need to protect it. She wanted to wrap herself around the tattering threads and keep them from being harmed further.

"It's worse than I thought," she finally managed to say. "Seeing it like this it feels more … real." She turned around to look at Lenire. "If that makes sense?"

"It does," he said, approaching her and Alaric with the disk. "Are you ready?"

Before she could ask what she was supposed to be read for, he twisted the disk, sending coils of magic stretching from the disk toward Cora. She startled as they began to weave themselves into her hands, her palms growing impossibly warm.

"Cora!" Lenire must have seen the panic on her face. "Stay steady. You have to trust me."

Cora looked back at her bond and nodded. She took a deep breath and refocused, thinking only of the bond and how much she wanted to repair it. A wave of determination swept through her, and she settled, calm enough now to let the process continue.

The warmth in her palms moved, dripping into her wrists and then across her forearms. It twisted around her elbows and eventually reached her shoulders. As the magical threads moved with the heat, Cora realized she was no longer in charge of her arms. It was Lenire who had taken control of her and her magic, using her hands to retie and reweave the fraying threads of the bond.

Cora marveled at the way Lenire stretched new threads toward the ragged part of her bond, until a familiar voice spoke.

"I'm surprised you're letting yourself be walked into this trap so willingly." A translucent image of Zirael appeared and Cora's heart raced. Zirael's silhouette shimmered under the dull light that pressed through the mountain fog. His image moved against the magical tapestry, the threads of his shape clinging to the threads from the disk. He was both here and not here, just like when he'd used the crystals to taunt them in the cavern. "After everything you've learned, you still blindly follow Lenire, a puppet to his will. You must have more sense than that, Cora."

Lenire grimaced at his words and Cora felt it ripple through the threads that pulsed against her hands. "There's nothing Zirael can do to hurt us as long as we maintain our focus."

Cora nodded, her eyes darting away, then back toward Zirael's sneering figure.

"Don't listen to him," Lenire said. "He's just trying to scare you."

"Listen to your puppet master, Cora. I won't try to stop you. I'm actually quite content to sit back and watch. I'd like to see how well Lenire succeeds at possession."

His words rattled her, particularly his reference to possession, and Cora tensed, sending ripples of distress through the threads of the spell Lenire was working. She couldn't help but think of Alia's shambling, unnatural movements as the Blight clumsily controlled her limbs.

"Oh," Zirael taunted, "didn't you know that's what he was doing? Did Lenire not tell you that by letting him tie those threads to your hands, he was in control? That he could take possession of your entire body this way. And your dragon. That the longer you are connected, the more you are at his mercy?" He snickered darkly. "I can't say I'm surprised. Lenire hasn't been known to be all that trustworthy. Why would he tell you the truth?"

Cora's sharp intake of breath sent another ripple of distress through the threads, and they quivered, shaking free before they could reach the ragged part of her bond with Alaric.

Lenire ground his teeth. "Ignore him, Cora."

"Yes, you would like that, Lenire, wouldn't you?" Zirael said, amused. "You steal my things. Turn my people against me. And then you play the victim, the fool, the poor soul forced to flee his homeland."

Lenire cursed under his breath as another of the new threads snapped.

"I myself would like to know how he persuaded you to go along with this, Cora. Did he call it guidance, perhaps? Did he tell you that he would help lead you through this magic?"

Cora's focus slipped, and she glanced from Lenire, to the shadow of Zirael that was drawing closer.

"Look at me," Lenire told her. "Only at me."

"Jump, puppet," Zirael cackled. "That's exactly what he wants. Let him guide you. That's exactly how he talked his sister into it too."

Lenire almost dropped the disk, every thread of magic around them quivering. Cora could feel the threads he was controlling threaten to rebel.

"Lenire?" she whispered, but he was lost somewhere in a dark thought.

"He must have told you this story already?" Zirael said, pacing around them. "No?"

"Lenire?" she said again.

His jaw trembled.

"The disk's true use is control," Zirael continued. "I'm sure you've figured that out by now. And Lenire, the great dragon knight, weary from battle and trapped in a city on the verge of ruin, tried to use the disk to turn his sister into a weapon."

Lenire's entire body began to shake. The heat from the magical threads attached to Cora's hands threatened to scorch her. She pulled, the entire fabric of magic rippling dangerously.

"And when some heroic soul stepped in to mercy-kill the poor girl before Lenire succeeded, their reward was that Lenire killed them too. Unfortunately for you, Cora, there's no such hero to save you."

All Cora's fears resurfaced and the trust she'd so recklessly given Lenire faltered. She knew Zirael had to be lying, or at least twisting the facts. Right? It wasn't true. It couldn't be. Lenire wanted this for her. She'd seen the truth of it in his eyes. He wanted her to restore her bond. He'd set out to do good.

It was Zirael she needed to fear. He was the suspicious one that had linked up with Melusine and the Blight. He was the real enemy here.

And yet, Lenire's reactions to Zirael's accusations fueled her fear. There was some truth to what Zirael said. The threads around them shook unchecked.

"That's not how it happened," Lenire muttered but he couldn't even look at her. There was an edge of desperation and shame to his words that made the magic he controlled twist and buck.

He was hiding something. He was *always* hiding something.

She couldn't trust him.

She'd been a fool.

Cora felt the heat in her arms snuff out suddenly. She clenched her fists, tensing against the spell, instinctively pulling back. The strands of magic woven through her snapped like straining ropes, recoiling against their caster.

Recoiling against Lenire.

He cried out and Yrsa growled, the sound clearing the entire valley of birds.

Lenire managed to deflect some of the broken spell. He lashed out with one sharp strand of magic, smashing Zirael's ghostly projection and burning his shimmering image from the tapestry. But the rest of the strands whipped tightly around him, the disk fell, and he crumpled with a sharp cry of pain.

The tapestry of magic vanished all at once, leaving Lenire sprawled on the ground, blood blooming wherever the spell had struck.

"No." Cora rushed to his side, horrified. He was unconscious, but his words echoed in her head. *There's nothing Zirael can do to hurt us as long as we maintain our focus.*

She'd done this. She'd let herself be swayed by Zirael's words, and her doubt had wounded an ally. She failed herself and Alaric, Lenire and Yrsa, all the dragon riders who lay as unconscious as Lenire, and now they were more vulnerable than ever.

# CHAPTER 25

## CORA

No matter what Cora did, Lenire would not wake. She pressed her hands against his seeping wounds. He flinched beneath her touch and his wounds oozed right through his tunic, staining it bright red. She did the only thing she could think of and pressed even harder.

He moaned but did not rouse.

"Lenire," she said, shaking him. His body was limp, his features slack, and his arms flopped in the dirt as she attempted to wake him. "Lenire!" she said, louder. "C'mon, get up!"

There was no response.

And, *stars*! She was no healer. She didn't know the first thing about using magic to repair wounds like this. Back in Barcroft, when she was a young girl, she'd once watched an old woman sew a gash in a man's leg after he'd fallen from his horse. She'd used boiled thread and a fire-touched needle. The man had hissed through his teeth like a serpent.

It hadn't been very comfortable for him, but it had worked.

She would do the same. It couldn't be much different from regular sewing, which she could do. It just used ... skin instead of cloth. Cora swallowed the bile that bubbled at the back of her throat. They were in this mess because of her. Now she was going to have to fix it. First she needed to stop the bleeding. Then she could think about stitching him up.

But Lenire's blood seeped between her fingers, painting her knuckles red. "This isn't working," she growled. "I need ..."

Cora had no idea what she needed.

Yrsa made a bleating sound of distress, and Cora looked over her shoulder at the dragon. She couldn't understand Yrsa. She spoke too fast, her frantic rambling spilling from her in sharp growls and grumbles. Cora looked to Alaric for help. Yrsa was obviously trying to tell her something.

Alaric listened and attempted to translate Yrsa's panicky speech.

"Magic," he managed to huff out.

"Magic?" Cora frowned. "I don't know how to use my magic to heal him." She looked from Alaric to Yrsa. "Or I would, I swear!"

Alaric snorted in frustration. "Magic," he said again. This time he lifted his claw, and it snagged in one of the tears in Lenire's shirt that had been caused by the lashing coils of magic as the spell exploded outward. He dragged his claw gently down Lenire's side, tracing the path of the blood. "*Magic*."

It wasn't just blood Lenire was losing. That's what Yrsa had been trying to tell her. His wounds weren't only physical but magical. "He's losing magic too?"

Yrsa nodded. Cora couldn't be sure the dragon really understood her, but perhaps it was the look of defeat that had accompanied her words. This was all her fault. Lenire had warned her. He'd told her this could be dangerous. That if they didn't trust each other, that if she wavered, the outcome could be disastrous. Only she'd thought he'd meant for *her and Alaric*. She'd only worried that she could somehow damage her bond further, and had never once considered that things could go so badly for Lenire himself.

Cora readjusted her hands. They slipped in the sheen of blood and sweat that pooled in pockets beneath Lenire's tunic. "I tried to trust him," she said. "I really did. I thought I'd made up my mind about him. But I let doubt creep in when Zirael said all those things."

At the sound of Zirael's name, Yrsa growled.

Cora knew better than to let an enemy whisper doubt and suspicion into her ear, but when her faith in Lenire mattered the most, she'd failed. What if Melusine's betrayal had permanently damaged her instincts, making them overactive and a liability? Not only was she the reason that Zirael now had the upper hand, but the magic that was supposed to heal her bond had failed before he'd had a chance to complete the spell. Without Lenire and without a fully intact bond, she had no hope against the hounds.

A sliver of sun peaked from between the clouds, swallowed up again by the mountain fog. It would be getting dark soon. "Help me move him?" Cora asked.

Yrsa blinked at her, and Cora mimed picking him up. Yrsa understood immediately and gently scooped Lenire into her massive claws before sweeping across the field and back to the shelter of the mountain and the camp they'd made the previous night.

When Yrsa laid him down, Cora took the blanket from her pack and shredded it into small pieces with her knife. She pressed those pieces into Lenire's wounds, then covered them with a paste mixture of ash from the fire and water from the stream.

His wounds still seeped blood and magic, but at least she'd slowed the leak enough for her to get a fire started.

Something picked at her thoughts as she gathered the wood and had Alaric breathe the fire back to life. It was a tiny, slithering fear. One she was only now realizing.

She'd been so consumed and focused on the fight that would have to take place if the hounds managed to respawn, she'd never really stopped to consider what would happen *after*. What would happen if they failed? There was no way Cora could stand against a pack of hounds alone, even with Alaric at her side. And once the hounds disposed of her and Alaric, they'd know exactly where to find the next crystal deposit. They'd been absorbing the magic of the crystals this entire time and just like a lodestone, they'd be able to track it without a single obstacle in their way. That's exactly what Melusine was waiting for. She didn't need to go hiking blindly around the mountains. The hounds would do it for her.

Even if Cora managed to keep the villagers away from the hounds, avoiding a fight, that would leave the pack free to set off in search of the next deposit right away. Without an untainted lodestone, Cora had no way to get ahead of them. And if she couldn't get ahead of them, they would reach the Heart of Tenegard first, giving the Blight unfettered access. The Blight would consume and destroy Tenegard's magic, all while Cora chased after them.

Cora wrapped her arms around her torso as she felt a shiver travel up her spine. What had she done? Digging her fingers into her sides, she tried to shake off that sense of doom that was threatening to suffocate her. She was a pathetic excuse for a dragon rider. She didn't deserve the title. She hadn't managed to protect anyone. In fact, she'd made things worse.

As night fell, a chill settled around them, and Cora dragged Lenire as close to the fire as she dared. She changed the packings over his wounds once, washing the strips of cloth out in the stream, before leaving them on a rock to dry. She had no idea how long she was going to have to try to staunch the bleeding.

"I wish I'd paid more attention when I spent all those hours in the infirmary," she said, mostly to herself. Without Lenire to easily translate for her and the dragons, it had grown too quiet. "Not that it would help much now. I'm not a healer by nature. I never would have understood their magic."

Yrsa grumbled something, looking directly at Cora.

"Heal," Alaric said in response, attempting to share Yrsa's words.

"Heal?"

"*No*, heal." Alaric gestured to Yrsa with his snout.

"Yrsa can't heal? You mean … wait?" Cora frowned in thought. Lenire was a healer, but she'd thought that was a skill unique to him. Did all Itharusian dragons and their knights have the ability to heal?

"Magic," Alaric continued, gesturing to the blood stains on Lenire's shirt.

Cora nodded along. "The leaking magic?"

Alaric looked back to Yrsa.

"Yrsa can't heal because Lenire is leaking magic," Cora said, stringing the thoughts together. "She can't heal him because the magic is leaking. And Yrsa's magic … is connected to Lenire's magic because of the dragon bond."

Of course it was, the same way she and Alaric were connected—*had* been connected.

"Wait!" Cora said, getting to her feet. She paced and rambled, half at the dragons, half to herself. "You can't heal him because he's losing magic, so the magic you possess together isn't strong enough. But what if you had more magic?" Excitement bubbled up in Cora. "Alaric and I don't know a lick of healing magic, but we do know how to share our magic!"

She stopped, looking from Alaric to Yrsa, a smile splitting her face. Neither dragon did anything but look confused.

"Magic," Cora said again, gesturing to herself. She made a scooping motion, like she could gather the magic up from inside her, and mimed giving it to Yrsa.

Understanding, Alaric made a noise of agreement. Cora watched Yrsa's eyes widen as Alaric conveyed the plan.

Yrsa said something that Cora didn't understand, but judging by the dragon's tone, Cora imagined she said something like, *You would do that?*

Cora nodded. They only had limited reserves thanks to the fractured bond, but whatever they did have, they could share.

Yrsa growled something out loud to Alaric. The fact that she hadn't just shared it telepathically told Cora it was something of importance. A point that she wanted them both to understand.

Alaric turned to Cora. "Danger." He nudged at the sword that was sheathed on her hip and shook his head. She knew what Yrsa was saying then. Sharing their limited magic would leave them nearly defenseless until the magic had enough time to replenish itself. That could take days.

"I don't care," Cora said. "We have to try."

She put her hand on Yrsa, touching her translucent scales for the first time. They felt different from Alaric's, but the heavy sigh of relief was one she'd heard before. Yrsa closed her eyes and dipped her head. It was a thank-you.

Yrsa's concerns were valid, though as far as Cora was concerned, none of them stood much of a chance against the hounds. But with her unrepaired bond, if one pair had to defend their small group alone, Lenire and Yrsa were their best option. That wasn't the only reason she was willing to give up her magic, though. She also wanted to alleviate some of the guilt she carried at having underestimated Lenire. Zirael had done exactly what Lenire had said he would, messing with the spell and sowing doubt. Whatever the truth was, Cora had a role in botching this spell. She needed to make it right.

Glancing at Alaric, Cora prepared herself. She'd only learned to share her magic a few weeks ago in the mountains with Strida and Faron. Yrsa was a dragon from an entirely different country, but she figured the mechanics were about the same. She closed her eyes, imagining her magic like a physical thing. She gathered it up, feeling it pool in her fingertips. Her hands grew heavy, weighed down by her sides.

Then she imagined setting her magic free, moving it from her to Yrsa, and as the weight in her hands disappeared, Cora felt a sudden, unnamable loss and emptiness. There might be sparks left behind. Fragments of her magic left in her blood. But it wouldn't be enough to do anything. Not for a while. Cora opened her eyes, feeling a wave of dizziness sweep through her, and saw the surprise in Yrsa's own eyes.

"It worked," Cora said in relief.

Yrsa bent low, until her head was balanced against Lenire's chest. She closed her eyes and growled words that were too fast and complicated for Cora to understand. Then Yrsa scratched against the stone where Lenire lay. The sound of her claws against the rock sent terrible shivers ripping down Cora's spine. She grimaced and clasped her hands over her ears. As she watched Yrsa claw at the ground, she realized she was drawing knots, dragging the threads of healing across his body.

All at once, Lenire sat up, gasping like he'd just emerged from a great body of water. "What happened?" he asked as Yrsa nuzzled him. Lenire ran his hands down his tunic, feeling the holes ripped into the cloth. He poked his fingers through the holes, finding nothing but the gray remnants of the ash paste and newly-formed skin. "The spell?"

"Recoiled," Cora confirmed. "You were injured. Badly." She sank to the ground, a magical exhaustion overcoming her suddenly. Alaric reached for her, and she leaned against his snout as she settled on her knees. Despite the dizziness running circles in her head, she smiled.

"What's going on with you?" he questioned.

"Yrsa didn't have enough magic to heal you. We shared ours and she was able to revive you."

Lenire was quiet for a moment, his mouth open in disbelief. "You didn't have to do that."

"It was my fault," she said. "I let Zirael distract me. Let him plant doubt in my mind. He twisted the bonds of trust I was clinging to. And then everything went wrong."

"I don't blame you, Cora," he said. "Zirael would not have been a threat if I hadn't withheld information from you. I was worried how you would perceive it, and in doing so I gave Zirael ammunition to use against both of us. I played right into his hands." He sighed. "I should have been honest with you from the start. About everything. Including how the disk worked."

"Can it really be used to possess someone?"

Lenire shook his head. "You saw for yourself. The disk can be used to exert control, but not *full* control. Not unless it is over a mindless entity like the Blight. Your resistance broke the control I had over you."

Cora nodded. It really hadn't taken much resistance at all for her to destroy the threads that had controlled her hands. She'd let Zirael scare her into thinking Lenire could assume control of her entire body and mind.

"Only by wielding the Blight could the Order possess people against their will," Lenire explained. "And sometimes even without their knowledge."

"Tell me about your sister," Cora said softly. This was the secret Lenire had carried with him. The one that cut him the deepest. She wanted to understand. She *needed* to if they were going to move forward.

"I was tasked with stealing one of the three disks the Order used. We would have liked to have them all, but even one would give us an advantage." Lenire looked at the fire as he spoke. "When I returned successfully from my quest, I learned that although the distraction I provided had given my people time to throw up magical barriers against the Blight's next attack, my sister's mind had already been possessed. It had happened so slowly no one had noticed at first."

Cora wanted to ask her name. Ask if she was like Lenire. Had she fought by his side? Had she been a dragon knight as well? But she didn't want the memory to hurt any more than it already did, so she kept quiet.

"I was ordered to take my sister outside the city's defenses and kill her. I was duty bound to do so. We'd seen how much destruction a human possessed by the Blight could cause. We knew there was no saving her." Lenire's words grew tight. Each one struggled up his throat. "But I couldn't do it. I failed my greatest task. Instead I tried to use the disk to help her. To rid the Blight from her mind. And the friend that Zirael mentioned, the one who stepped in to do what I couldn't, was killed by the recoil of the broken spell."

Lenire's gaze was lost in the flames.

"I think I would have done exactly what you did," Cora said. She didn't have siblings, but she had her father, and there were other people in her life she loved like family. Strida. Octavia. Faron. If any of them had fallen victim to the Blight's possession, she would have tried to save them.

"I knew it was wrong to try. But I also knew I'd never forgive myself if I didn't do everything in my power to save her."

"And you did," Cora assured him. "I'm sure she knew that."

Lenire batted away a floating ember and finally looked at her. "It didn't end there, though," he said.

"What do you mean?"

"Using the disk on my sister to target the fragment of the Blight that had possessed her allowed the rest of the Blight to fixate on the stolen disk. It was still mostly controlled by the other two disks in the trio at that point. Somehow this allowed it to bypass the city's magical defenses, nearly destroying everything it touched before something drew it away—Melusine's call, I know now."

Cora tried to imagine the Blight loose in Kaerlin, free to feed and take what it pleased. "That must've been terrible."

"My punishment for my weakness was to pursue the Blight here. If I had slain my sister as I was supposed to, none of this would have happened. I didn't want to be responsible for her death, but I ended up losing her anyway. Along with a good friend and who knows how many civilians."

"Lenire, no one can blame you for not wanting to kill your sister. That was a horrendous order to have been given."

He shook his head. "I can't help thinking that my use of the disk was what ultimately enabled the Blight to break free of the Order. And if that's true, I'm the reason it followed Melusine's call to Tenegard. So if Tenegard's magic is lost, that will be my fault too."

Everything about Lenire made sense to Cora at that moment.

Zirael had called him a traitor and a murderer, but he'd left out the reasons *why*. With all the facts laid before her, she saw Lenire's stand-offish behavior in a new light. And those threads of trust that had been so shaky, started to solidify.

"Lenire," she said with all the certainty she could muster, "the only one to blame for the Blight's presence in Tenegard is Melusine. I can't speak to the rest of it, but if the Blight gets to the Heart of Tenegard, that's not your failing. It's mine."

"Cora, you don't have to—"

"I'm the one who confirmed the presence of the heart. I let Melusine manipulate me. I led her through the mountains, tracking the magic. I let her and the Blight hurt my friends. But I can't let that keep happening. I can still save Tenegard. I can still save the people I love, but I need your help to do it. We have to try again."

And with everything on the table now, all the secrets that scarred their hearts laid bare, she felt certain they could finally be able to work together to stop the Blight before it was too late.

# CHAPTER 26

## OCTAVIA

Though she longed to be doing something, anything, to stop Northwood, Octavia sat at her appointed seat in one of the lesser courtyards, serving on the small claims court, listening to citizens bicker about stolen tomatoes and wayward cattle. As yet another farm woman shouted accusations at her neighbor, Octavia wished she could focus on the real danger that threatened Tenegard: the sleeping sickness. But she and Raksha agreed that they needed to maintain appearances. She could not afford to shirk her duties and draw suspicion when she had openly defied Northwood and sent Jeth to fish for information about what Northwood was doing at the border.

Octavia's attention wavered, and her eyes drifted to the cloudless stretches of blue sky the courtyard granted a view of. What she wouldn't give to escape right now, flying off toward the sun. It was then that she noticed the distinctly dragon-shaped figure in the sky, approaching the palace.

Octavia stood as she watched the figure bob up and down. The dragon was clearly in distress. It careened suddenly to the left, then pulled to the right, losing altitude at an alarming rate. Raksha rose from the shadows to the alarm and awe of the gathered citizens.

*Who is it?* Octavia asked.

*Zoya and Jeth*, Raksha answered immediately. *They're in trouble.*

*They're back so soon?*

Panicked voices erupted around them as people spotted the struggling dragon. Fingers pointed and hands covered gasping mouths.

"You'll have to excuse us," Octavia said with urgency to the rest of the court. "There is an emergency we must attend to."

"What are you going to do?" a courtier asked.

"Clear the courtyard and call the healers." Octavia issued the order as she hauled herself onto Raksha's back. Nearly the instant she was settled, they were airborne. Raksha flapped hard, pulling them straight up and out of the courtyard.

*Faster,* Octavia urged, watching Zoya struggle for each flap. She felt the urgent push and pull of muscle beneath Raksha's scales as they climbed through the cloudless sky.

"Jeth!" Octavia shouted as soon as they were close enough. The rest of her questions died on her tongue as she realized how badly wounded he was. She could see the bruises upon his skin, like smashed blackberries in the daylight, and the trails of dried blood that strangled his neck. Then she spotted the tears in Zoya's wing, as if spears had been thrown and sliced through them like parchment.

Raksha turned sharply, flying alongside Zoya. She pressed against her, keeping the other dragon airborne. It was tricky and Octavia ground her teeth together as they fell, careening toward the palace faster than any of them would like.

They came to a rough stop in the same courtyard they'd left from, thankfully cleared of citizens, turning up stone walkways and crashing through statues and fountains.

"Princess!" one of the guards called out of habit.

"The healers!" Octavia beckoned, sliding down Raksha's side and scrambling up Zoya to steady the almost unconscious Jeth before he toppled to the ground headfirst. A flurry of people appeared by her side, gathering Jeth between them and carting him off to the infirmary.

Octavia felt Zoya groan beneath her, a pain-addle breath escaping her as she slumped to her side, forcing Octavia to leap from her back. And as Octavia looked from Zoya to Raksha, she had only one question: *Who or what had done this?*

The infirmary hadn't seen this much activity since the rebel leaders had declared war on Onyx, determined to overthrow the tyrant king. Octavia knew the cots that lined this chamber had once been filled with palace guards, young men and women forced to swear their allegiance to Onyx, some even under threat of death. Now it was mostly quiet, the healers usually left to sort the mundane ailments of councilors and palace officials.

There was a buzz of morbid excitement in the air as they hovered around Jeth, his bruised and bloodied body stark against the pale cream sheets. The eager hum increased even more when Octavia announced that there was a dragon in the courtyard that would need tending also.

"We do not know anything about healing dragons," one of the healers admitted.

"They are flesh wounds," Octavia snapped. "I imagine water and bandages work just the same to clean up the blood." There likely was no easy fix for the tears in her wings, but they could at least make Zoya comfortable.

Several young healers snatched up rolls of white gauze and metal basins, hurrying from the room with animated whispers. Octavia knew they were mostly glad for something to do, but it still irked her. Dragons were not novelties to be gawked at.

*Stay focused*, Raksha told her. She'd remained outside with Zoya.

"Can you help him?" Octavia asked the head healer.

He nodded once, then gave instruction to his apprentices. Palace staff flitted in and out of the room, some bringing supplies, and others merely hoping for a peek at the commotion. Octavia hovered at the end of Jeth's cot, watching healers staunch bleeds and magically knit his skin back together. Others rubbed sour smelling pastes onto the battered stretches of his skin. Jeth's knuckles were bloodied, his fingernails torn, telling Octavia that he'd fought back against his attacker.

When the door opened again, Northwood strode in with half the council. Apparently, news of Jeth's arrival had spread quickly.

"What is going on?" Bellamy asked. Her eyes were shadowed by dark brows, her confusion obvious. The old rebel leader looked to Octavia for answers. "Has there been news from the dragon-rider school? Have they been attacked again?"

This had nothing to do with the school. Octavia knew better. But she wasn't ready to admit to that in front of Northwood and his lackeys. "I haven't heard anything from the school, but let me take charge of the incident and I will find out."

Jeth murmured something about having news to share, his eyelids fluttering as the healers continued their work. When the healers parted, Jeth sat up suddenly, wide awake, pressing his hand against the pastes that dripped from his skin.

"Why make him repeat his story twice?" Northwood said smoothly. He took Jeth by the elbow and hauled him out of bed to a flurry of protests.

"What are you doing?" Octavia demanded.

"I must insist that the patient is not exhausted by questioning!" the head healer bellowed.

Northwood heard none of it, or if he did, he had no intention of stopping. "The quickest way to get to the bottom of this is to have the dragon rider tell his story to the whole council. We wouldn't want to make him have to repeat himself, would we?"

Jeth looked around, wide-eyed, perhaps searching for Octavia in the crowd, but she'd gotten waylaid behind a wall of arguing healers and council members. Before Octavia could get to him, Northwood had dragged him out the door.

"Northwood!" Octavia shouted, shoving her way through the crowd.

*What is going on?* Raksha asked, breaking through her frantic thoughts.

*Meet us in the council chamber. Hurry!*

There were more council members gathered in the hall and as Northwood announced an emergency meeting, they all filed toward the drafty council chamber. Raksha was last to arrive, slipping through the door and lurking in the shadows behind their chairs.

Northwood stood Jeth in the middle of the room. He wobbled there, but maintained his footing, keeping himself upright. He looked better than when he'd slumped over on Zoya's back, but Octavia still didn't think he should have been dragged through the palace.

"Go on," Northwood said. "You arrived on dragonback looking as if you've just escaped battle. You crashed into a courtyard, completely destroying it. And you say you have news. Tell us what news you speak of then, dragon rider. Who has done this to you?"

Jeth looked around the circle, his eyes lingering when they met Octavia's.

"What are you running from?" Northwood shouted. "I demand to know. Am I to arm the palace? Arm the streets? What is going on here?"

Octavia gave the briefest of head nods. There was no easy way out of this situation, and she didn't want Jeth to bring trouble upon himself by lying to Northwood. Whatever the consequences now, she would have to bear them.

"We were near the border," Jeth said. "Myself and a couple of colleagues. We'd been in such places before and we knew it could be dangerous. So we dressed the part, careful not to stand out to the Athelian troops that guarded the border. But we were ambushed by a handful of elite Athelian guards."

"You strayed too far onto their side," Northwood said.

Jeth shook his head. "But we didn't. That was the most curious part. As I've said, this was not my first time near the border. I knew where we would be safe. The guards grabbed us on the Tenegardian side of the border. One of us was killed immediately. Myself and my other colleague were taken."

"To Erelas?" Northwood asked.

Octavia recognized the name of the Athelian capital. Jeth shook his head. He stumbled but caught himself before anyone could rise from their seats. "No," he said. "We were taken to Melusine in a forest hideaway. She had set careful wards to alert her of any dragon riders in the area."

"Melusine," Octavia and Northwood seemed to say at once.

"She used cruel magic to extract the nature of our mission from us. It was eventually too much for my colleague. She didn't make it." Jeth's entire body seemed to slump. "I don't know how I managed to survive. Perhaps something to do with my dragon bond. Zoya was waiting helplessly nearby in the woods, and when she saw most of the guards marching away from the hideout, dispatched on a new mission, she came for me. We took advantage of the moment and made a daring escape. She was hurt in the attempt, but we flew straight here, as injured as we were, to relay the message. Melusine is working with Athelia." As soon as he'd finished speaking, Jeth collapsed.

Octavia hurried to his side, kneeling in the center of the room. "Call for the healers!" she said. "Hurry!"

The doors to the chamber swung open and panicked footfalls echoed across the room. Octavia sat back as two men appeared, taking Jeth by the arms and hoisting him to his feet. With their aid, Jeth stumbled to the door, and Octavia looked after them helplessly.

Northwood jumped from his chair as Jeth was escorted away. "There is no plainer evidence," he said, biding the others to listen to him. "The Athelians have shown their true colors, and we cannot allow their aggression to go unchecked. It is clear they are working with this *Melusine*, this enemy who has already attacked the dragon riders. I have asked before and now I bid you to see reason. Vote in favor of increasing our military presence at the border. A task which I have *not* ordered to be done yet," he said, looking directly at Octavia. "Contrary to the belief of some of those in this room."

"All in favor?" someone shouted loudly.

The responses came swiftly in support of Northwood and Octavia's heart thumped painfully against her ribs.

"It is not enough," someone shouted suddenly. "Adding soldiers to our border is the least of what we should be doing."

"Yes!" someone else agreed. "Tenegardians have been slain! A dragon rider was almost killed!"

As Octavia looked around, she realized that it wasn't only Northwood's usual supporters who were voicing their agreement. It was the old rebel leaders too.

"Athelia must answer for this," Northwood agreed.

*This meeting is getting out of control*, Raksha said.

*I know.*

*Northwood will rile the others into a frenzy.*

"Wait!" Octavia said, looking around the room. "Jeth's story suggests he might have been allowed to leave."

Northwood turned to her, both of them facing off in the middle of the room. "What are you talking about?"

"What if Melusine let him leave in the hopes that he would return to us with a story that would enrage Tenegard, hoping to bait us into open conflict with Athelia?"

"What purpose would that serve?"

"It would distract us from the real threat. The Blight!"

Some of the councilors murmured and waved off her theory. They'd not seen the power of the Blight. They hadn't stood in that dining hall watching Cora face off against the hideous shadow creature with the power to consume their magic. They had no concept of the kind of real damage it could do.

"Think about it," Octavia begged. "If Melusine could sense a dragon rider traveling across the countryside, wouldn't she be able to sense that Jeth was escaping right under her nose?"

"Perhaps you are the one trying to distract us!" a councilor shouted at her. "You're always asking us to keep the peace."

"I agree," Northwood said before she could respond. "The time for talking is over. It is time to take action against Athelia. They have struck us, so I propose we do the same."

"War?" Octavia breathed, knowing what the council was about to vote on.

"Open war!" Northwood shouted. "We declare our intentions. Make our stand. We have the numbers. We have the dragons!"

The councilors cheered, on their feet, bubbling with misplaced rage.

"We do not have the dragons!" Octavia said loudly, interrupting his fearmongering. "The sleeping sickness remains uncured. How can the dragon riders fly to your aid when our numbers are so depleted?"

"They will and they must!" Northwood said. "Now is the time that we rise up against our northern border. We must show Athelia that Tenegard is not to be trifled with!"

"You know what has happened at the school. What Melusine has done. Some of our strongest riders are still affected!"

Northwood narrowed his eyes. "The remaining dragon riders have sworn to protect Tenegard. They will fly on our behalf because there will be no other choice. Either they fly or Tenegardians die."

"Even if they wanted to, they cannot risk leaving the school at this time! Melusine and the Blight seek to destroy them, and you've done nothing to help. Offered no aid. No solutions to their problems."

"Says the Athelian sympathizer," Northwood declared, raising his arms to draw attention to himself. "We have a traitor in our midst, and it cannot be allowed! Athelia is the enemy here. Athelia has struck first. Killed *our* people!" Murmurs and cheers of agreement exploded around the room. "Do not let the murmurings of a fallen princess dissuade you from doing your duty! We must protect Tenegard."

Octavia felt like her head was spinning. This was all wrong. This … this wasn't how it was supposed to be. Northwood was looking at her, his mouth opening and closing, and when the wild conversations around her slowed, she finally heard what he was saying.

"Your regard for Athelia cannot be allowed to continue, not within these halls. We cannot let your misguided ideals poison this court against its own people," Northwood said, and the remaining councilors fell silent, looking at her as if she were some dirty thing pried from the soles of their feet. "You will be relieved of your council duties at once," Northwood continued. "And stripped of all your titles and powers."

"You can't do that!" Octavia said. Now more than ever the council needed her to be the voice of caution and reason. They needed her to remind them to stay their hands when Northwood was pressing them only to strike.

"I think you'll find with the evidence against you that we can."

"What evidence?"

Northwood sneered. "Who gave Jeth the mission to be at the border?"

Octavia swallowed hard.

"You didn't really think I would miss that fact, did you? Someone clearly sent him to the border in search of answers, and after you barged into my meeting the other morning, accusing me of stacking the border against Athelia, who else could have given Jeth such an order? How am I to lead Tenegard's military with you attempting to undermine me at every turn?"

"It was not my intention to—"

"To what? You are a child, Octavia. And children make foolish, reckless decisions that get people killed."

"And you have bullied this council into thinking war is the only answer!" Octavia said, both of her fists clenched.

"Sometimes it *is*," he shouted, his voice echoing around the room, his shoulders rising and falling from the effort.

"No," Octavia said, looking around for some sort of support. She glanced at the former rebel leaders. The ones who had once quietly risen up against Onyx, who had banded with Cora, turning the rebels from a tiny army to an army of dragon riders. They too had once been called traitors to the crown, to the nation of Tenegard. Where was their sense of duty now? Of justice?

"What's more," Northwood said. "You and your dragon—"

"Her name is Raksha," Octavia interrupted. She knew what was happening, standing before them, all eyes rimmed with accusation, and a darkness grew in her. It wasn't simply anger, but something else. Some ugly festering thing. "She is part of this council. You can say her *name*."

Northwood's lip curled in such a way that Octavia thought he might snarl at them both. He'd never approved of Raksha's place on the council. Never shown her one ounce of loyalty or respect. "You and your *dragon*," he said again, his voice barely above a whisper, "will leave here tonight. You are banished from the capital."

"You have no authority to banish us!"

"I have all the authority," Northwood hissed. "If you are caught within the walls of the capital, *princess*, you will be dealt with harshly. Do not take my words lightly."

He meant to threaten her, but Octavia would not be intimidated. She leaned into all the years of royal training and stood tall before him, spine fused with sword steel, her shoulders proud. She wouldn't give him the satisfaction of this moment. He was wrong for inciting war, and the other councilors were cowards for blindly following. She would not hang her head before any of them.

If she was banished, then so be it.

She'd never bowed before Northwood before, and she wasn't about to start now.

# CHAPTER 27
## CORA

If someone had told Cora to pick up her sword to defend herself, she wouldn't even be able to pull it from her sheath.

Lenire, on the other hand, was the picture of strength. "If you need to stop again to rest, we can. Or I can go on ahead and report back."

"I'm fine," Cora said, brushing aside Lenire's concern. Hours had passed since Yrsa had healed Lenire, waking him from his unconsciousness, and though he'd been restored to near perfect health, Cora had barely recovered.

In fact, after a fitful nap, she almost felt worse than when she'd initially shared her magic with Yrsa. She suspected the weakness had taken some time to set in, but she could feel it now deep in the hollows of her bones. Her muscles ached as if they'd been stretched to the extreme and laid flat against her skeleton, unable to recoil, leaving each of her limbs heavy and useless.

Her magic had become such an intrinsic part of her, Cora didn't recognize herself without it. How had she existed before Alaric, before becoming a dragon rider? It felt as if the entire world was pressing down on her, the weight of it threatening to crush the air from her lungs. Cora sighed and followed Lenire through a rocky portion of the stream, fighting for balance with every step.

Her toe caught on a rock and Cora fell forward, her hands and knees sinking beneath the stream's surface. The water was cold and refreshing. It felt good against her skin, hot from exertion, and Cora lifted a palmful to rub against her face.

Lenire appeared at her side, reaching down to haul her out of the water. Cora let him drag her up, worried she might not have the strength to do it herself. When she was upright, she perched against a tall, jagged rock that jutted out of the stream's edge, gripping it like a walking cane. Then she hunched over and clutched a stitch in her side.

The muscle cramps came frequently. Cora would be glad when her magic returned and this was all over.

"Perhaps it would have been easier on dragonback," Lenire said. He crouched down in front of her so he could look into her eyes. That way it was harder for her to evade his questions.

"We're almost there," Cora said. "No use now. Besides, it's better to survey the ground on foot. That way we know what we're working with."

He bit his bottom lip, worrying at the flesh. "Fine," he said. "But we're riding the dragons back."

Cora stretched to her full height, looking down the stream again. They'd been following it for more than a quarter of an hour, trying to determine the best place to face off against the hounds when they spawned. Since the disk had failed to repair Cora's magic, they'd resorted to their initial plan. They were going to have to fight.

And keeping the battle inside the cavern would put Cora and Lenire at a disadvantage. Once the crystals were consumed by hound flesh, it would be too dark inside the cavern to see the end of their swords, especially if the hounds hatched after the sun fell. Plus, inside the cavern, they only had one way in and out, giving them no exit strategy should the hounds cut them off from the entrance.

If they stayed too close to their current camp, the battle would take place too close to the village. If any of the hounds slipped past them or if any of the villagers presented a threat, the hounds would turn on them, putting a lot of innocent people in danger. Cora and Lenire had agreed that the safest thing to do was remove the villagers from the situation.

That way, if they fell in battle, hopefully the hounds would rush off into the mountains in search of the next crystal deposit, and not back to the sleeping families. To Alia who'd already faced enough because of them. Their best plan had been to follow the stream away from the cavern and the village, as far as they could go, looking for a place to do battle. Preferably a place with some higher ground.

"Cora," Lenire said as she fell again, sinking against the polished stones that lined the streambed. "We have to stop."

Cora dragged herself up the side of a rock, sitting on its ledge. "I can keep going. Just give me a second to catch my breath."

"Let me at least call Alaric. He can fly you the rest of the way."

"No," she insisted. "It looks like there's a clearing up ahead. It might work." She tried to look up at him, but her head was too heavy to move.

Lenire crossed his arms, his lips worrying between his teeth again. "What if I share some of my magic with you?" he asked.

Cora did manage to look up at him then. *Stars*, she didn't go through all of this just to pass their magic back and forth.

"I could even us out at least."

"No," Cora said, climbing shakily to her feet.

Lenire sighed, reaching for her elbow to steady her. "Don't be stubborn."

"It's not me being stubborn," she insisted. "We need at least one of us to stand a chance at holding out against the hounds. We don't have enough time for both of us to replenish our magic. It's better this way. Better that it's just me."

"You can barely stay on your feet. How do you hope to hold your sword?"

She didn't have an answer, or at least not one he'd like, so she ignored his question. "C'mon," she said, urging him along. "We're almost there."

The clearing was a craggy piece of ground that stretched up from the stream. They picked their way carefully around the many rocks that broke through the earth like rotting teeth. If Cora managed to regain any of her strength before the hounds broke free, she could imagine manipulating these rocks, pulling them from the ground to act as a wall, or maybe even a tunnel, that way she could control how many hounds broke through at once.

The slope was steep, and though Cora had to use her hands to pull herself up to the top, once she reached the flat expanse where the earth met the mountain, she thought it was perfect. The mountain was to their back, but there were ledges and cliffs where the dragons could perch, or where Cora and Lenire might escape if they got blocked in. "What do you think?"

Lenire had scrambled up the slope with more ease than she had, but even he breathed hard, assuring Cora that the hounds would also have to work for every inch.

"Well," he said. "It's certainly big enough. Shall I call the dragons and see what they think?"

Cora nodded. "And we have the high ground advantage."

Lenire looked up the cliff face as two large shadows circled overhead. Alaric set down in the clearing with them, sending a tremor up both Cora's legs. Yrsa clung to a sharp ledge, scrambling down the wall the way Cora had once seen a mountain goat do. She slithered, more serpentine than ever, from ledge to crevice, scoping out the positions of battle.

After a silent moment where it seemed as if Lenire and Yrsa were having a conversation, he nodded. "This seems like as good a place as any."

Lenire spoke not with the hopeful determination Cora would want from a dragon knight this close to a fight. Instead, he spoke with resigned acceptance. Perhaps the gravity of the situation had broken him, and he realized how this fight would likely end.

Yes, it was a good place to hold their ground, but it would also be a good place to die.

Cora tried to muster something positive to say, something that might instill a small amount of hope in him, but she couldn't think of anything no matter how hard she racked her brain. Her mind was a void, filled with nothing but exhaustion.

"We might even make it out of here," Lenire managed to say after a while.

"I'm less worried about us and more concerned about the Heart of Tenegard," she admitted. If she and Lenire both fell to the hounds, there would be no obstacle left between the hounds and the next deposit.

"You still think the crystals inside the hounds will act as lodestones?"

"I think they have been this entire time, we just didn't see it. The hounds remained in the village both times because we were there to engage them in a fight. If no one had stopped them, I imagine they would have run straight to the deposit, locked in on the next location, and had been long gone by now."

That's what the hounds had been designed for—finding the heart. Fighting was a secondary task, one required of them because Cora and Lenire stood between them and their goal.

"Maybe it was fate that we intercepted them."

"Or a curse," Cora muttered, because she knew that if she and Lenire didn't manage to fend off the hounds, those wretched creatures would reach the heart before any dragon rider could, and the fate of Tenegard would be sealed.

Lenire's brows met in the middle.

"Knowing what's at stake makes everything heavier," she said. Thoughts of Faron weighed her down. His survival meant everything to her.

"You don't have to bear it alone."

Cora smiled at him. Days ago, when Lenire dropped from the sky on the back of his strange dragon, she never imagined they would be standing here as allies now. Lenire was prepared to risk his life for them, and that deserved her gratitude. What had happened in the past would stay there. All that mattered now was what happened when those crystals hatched.

"Thank you, Lenire," Cora said. "Truly."

"You don't have to thank me," he said. "It's the least I can do."

"No, you could have left Tenegard to fend for itself against Zirael and the Blight."

"I thought about it," he admitted. "Trust me. I've thought of a dozen scenarios where Yrsa and I fly off into the sunset, leaving behind my knighthood and everything else."

"I've had those thoughts too," she said. "What matters is that you chose to stay."

He took in her words, nodding slowly. Perhaps he'd needed to be reminded that doubt did not make him a failure. Nor did his fear. "Come on," he said after a moment, offering her his arm. "Let's get you back to camp."

Lenire waved over Alaric and together they managed to help Cora climb up his back. Cora got herself seated, her muscles groaning but grateful not to have to walk back upstream. When she looked down at Lenire, he was still holding onto Alaric's saddle, a puzzled expression on his face.

"What is it?" she asked.

Lenire shook his head. "I was just thinking."

"About what?"

"How does the lodestone effect work exactly? I mean, what draws the crystals to each other?"

"Magic," Cora said without hesitation, thinking of the different, glowing deposits she'd encountered. "Their connection to the Heart of Tenegard acts as a pull—*like* calling to *like*, I presume." She frowned. "Why do you ask?"

"I just had a thought about how to stop the hounds."

Cora waited for him to continue, for him to connect the thoughts that were obviously plaguing him.

"Maybe there's a way to draw the hounds away from their target. If we could somehow create a decoy that radiates enough Tenegardian magic to distract them and plant it nearby ..." He trailed off. "It was just an idle thought, though. That would take more magic than either of us possess right now. Plus, even if we managed to distract the hounds, we'd still have to destroy them and that's already a problem that we're facing—"

Cora's mind raced at the possibilities. Perhaps Lenire was on to something. Destroying the hounds was going to be an immense amount of work. But if they distracted the hounds with a fabricated deposit, it would buy them time. The pieces of Blight that fueled these hounds would be drawn in by the magic, giving them no reason to rush off in search of the next deposit. Perhaps then they could pick the hounds off in smaller groups. Use the distraction to their advantage. "I think it could work."

Lenire's eyes went wide, and Cora slid down from Alaric's back to stand in front of him.

"I mean it," she said. "But there's one problem. Where could we get decoy crystals?" No sooner had the question left her lips, then the answer hit her.

"What are you talking about?" Lenire caught hold of both her shoulders to hold her steady. "Tell me what you're thinking."

"We need to find a store of magic. And I know just the place: the dragon-rider school," she said. "It has crystals. We took them from another deposit to help power the shield that we use to keep Melusine and the Blight out. But if they take the shield down, the dragon riders could bring those crystals from the school here. With their added support, there would be enough magic to fill the crystals and build the fake deposit. Then we use it to distract the hounds like you said, and destroy their crystal hearts."

It was the best plan they'd had so far. Cora hadn't wanted to involve the school or the other dragon riders before because she hadn't wanted to split their resources or leave the school defenseless, especially when the situation with the hounds seemed hopeless. Cora had been resolved to the fact that she would very likely die in these mountains. But Lenire's plan had lit a flame of hope inside her, and now it burned bright. They knew Melusine's focus was on the hounds and using them to track the crystal deposit to the heart. And if this was her focus now, then the dragon riders needed to do everything they could to stop her from reaching the Heart of Tenegard. They needed to protect their magic, even if it meant abandoning the school.

"Do you think they would come?"

"I'm certain of it."

"Do we have enough time?"

Cora nodded without really knowing the answer. "They'll fly hard."

The sun was setting and a mountain chill drifted down from the peaks, settling about their camp. Lenire stoked the fire, laying large branches across the hot coals. Cora pulled her traveling cloak tighter around her as she dug the communication anchors from her pack. A wave of guilt flared through her chest. She was supposed to have spoken to Strida every night, though with the chaos of the past few days, she'd forgotten to make contact.

It had been close to a week since they'd last spoken, and Strida was probably beside herself with worry. Cora looked up to see Alaric peering down at her, his midnight eyes twinkling with the reflection of the coals. She wished she could share her worries and fears and even the smallest, flickering flame of hope that now burned in her chest.

He lowered his head, close enough for her to reach up and run her hand over the small scales by his snout. They were warmed by the heat of his breath. He closed his dark eyes, leaning into the touch, reminding her that though he felt far away, lost in frayed strands of their bond, he was right beside her.

Emotion bubbled up from her chest and Cora swallowed it down. They could do this. It would work. It had to.

Cora climbed to her feet, anchors in hand.

"Good luck," Lenire said.

She lifted her hand as she walked off into the chilled darkness, far enough away to speak to Strida without Lenire overhearing. It wasn't that she didn't trust him to listen, it's that she didn't know what Strida's reaction would be. During their last conversation they'd both had reservations about Lenire.

She didn't want him to overhear that before she could update Strida. Not when they'd made so much progress as a team.

Cora stopped and shivered, lifting the anchor to speak into it. "Strida?" she whispered. "Are you there?"

No answer came.

"Strida?" Cora tried again. As the silence lingered, Cora thought the worst. While she'd been away in the mountains anything could have happened at the school. It wasn't like she'd done a good job of keeping track of things. "Strida!" Cora almost shouted, worry banging at her ribs.

"You're alive!" came Strida's answer. "I was starting to think we were going to have to send scouts after you. What happened to checking in every night? Do you remember making that vow? Because I sure do!"

Cora almost laughed at Strida's indignation. No matter her friend's tone, talking to her was a welcome relief. "It's good to hear your voice too and I'm sorry." She glanced over at Lenire. "A lot has happened since we last spoke." Cora launched into a recap of the last week, updating Strida on the hounds, Lenire, and Zirael's alliance with Melusine.

When she finished, alarm filled Strida's voice. "You want me to lower the shield? To leave the school unprotected? By the stars, Cora, are you even hearing yourself?"

"It's a risk," Cora agreed. "Every decision we make right now is fraught. But I think it's the right decision."

"Cora—"

"I know it's a lot to ask. And I wouldn't be doing it if I didn't think the dragon riders could help turn the tide of this fight. But the school isn't where Melusine's focus is right now. It's the Heart of Tenegard. And if we don't stop the hounds from reaching the heart, then we can pretty much say goodbye to dragon magic anyway."

There was a long pause and for a moment Cora worried they'd been disconnected somehow.

"Strida?"

"You're right," she answered. "Of course, you're right. We'll leave as soon as I've gathered the riders and the crystals."

# CHAPTER 28
## CORA

C ora's heart flipped over in her chest when the first dragon rider appeared in the sky, earlier than she'd expected. Alaric stirred in place, marching his feet with such excitement that Cora's knees almost gave out against the vibrations shooting through the rock ledge and up her legs.

"Who is it?" she asked, though she couldn't help but smile. With all the uncertainty they were facing, it was good to see another dragon rider. Part of her wished that Faron was among them, but another part of her was glad to know that he was far away, safe from the hounds.

Alaric puffed up, his wings fluttering at his sides.

"Mother!" was all Cora managed to understand between the string of grunts and growls that flowed from his mouth. She twisted around to face that dusky speck on the horizon line again.

"Raksha?"

What were Octavia and Raksha doing here? She was glad for their presence, of course, but Cora was surprised the pair had left the capital. Their responsibilities in Kaerlin didn't often allow them to leave.

*Then again*, Cora thought, Octavia and Raksha had come to their aid when the school had last needed her. This was no different. In her heart of hearts, Octavia was a dragon rider.

Cora placed her hand on Alaric's side, smiling up at him when he turned, wearing the kind of dragon grin that showed all his teeth. Lenire and Yrsa came to stand with them.

Together they watched as more dark specks appeared above the mountain peaks. With the sun behind them, the crystals in their saddlebags winked across the sky. Cora counted them off one by one.

"There's almost three dozen riders there," Lenire said.

"Thirty-five," Cora said matter-of-factly.

Lenire glanced over at her.

"I think every single ally counts in this kind of situation. We should be accurate."

He nodded in agreement. "Is this the bulk of your force?"

"Except for those who have not yet bonded or are too young for battle." Cora knew Strida wouldn't have let the youngest riders come, no matter how much they begged. "Plus, she needed to leave enough of the fighting force behind to protect the school." They'd taken the shield down, but Cora hadn't meant to leave it completely defenseless. "Or anyone still trapped in the sleeping sickness," she added without looking at him.

Cora's thoughts skittered to Faron. He would have been here with her if not for the Blight's attack. He would have fought by her side. For a moment, her hand itched for his, roughened from his time as a soldier and dragon rider, but always warm. Always *certain*.

"If our predictions are correct, the hounds will respawn tonight."

"I know," Cora said. It was already late afternoon. "We'll be ready."

"Will we?"

Cora summoned her strength and drew her sword, proving to them both that she was ready for the battle to come. She lifted her sword into the air, using it to wave down the approaching dragon riders.

The tiny specks in the sky took on distinct dragon shapes. Following on Raksha's heels, Cora spotted Strida and Emrys. They led the rest of the dragon riders who'd fallen into an arrow-tipped formation.

Cora and Lenire walked out to the clearing that stretched between the cavern entrance and the forest. The ground shook as the dragons landed, and Cora sheathed her sword.

Octavia slid off Raksha's back in an instant. She rushed to Cora, throwing her arms around her neck.

Cora hugged her back. "I didn't expect to see you here."

"Surprise," Octavia said, though when she pulled away, there was something melancholy about her smile.

Strida came up behind her. "We have a lot to talk about."

Cora nodded. "This is Lenire," she said, looking over her shoulder at him. "He's the dragon knight I told you about. From Itharus. And he's come to help us defeat the Blight.

"And that's your dragon?" Strida asked him, spotting Yrsa in the crowd.

"She's beautiful," Octavia tacked on.

"What news do you bring?" Cora asked Strida. Though she'd love to sit down and let everyone get acquainted, they didn't have time for that. They were working against a ticking clock, and the hour when the hounds would regenerate was drawing near. Plus, they had to make use of the sunlight while they could.

"It's about me and Raksha." Octavia sighed when Strida glanced her way. "There's been some developments in Kaerlin. We've been banished."

"From the council?" Cora said.

"And the city," Octavia said.

"And Northwood has declared war on Athelia," Strida cut in.

Cora's jaw dropped. "Wait … how? When did this happen?"

"A day ago."

"But why are we at war?" Cora asked.

Octavia grimaced at her but recounted a story of dead spies and the border and Melusine. "I can't be certain of anything, but my gut tells me Melusine wanted Jeth to make it back to Kaerlin to relay the news."

"You think she set this up? That she wants war between Athelia and Tenegard?"

"It would be a good distraction," Octavia reasoned. "While all eyes are on the border, she'll be free to attack—"

"The Heart of Tenegard," Cora finished for her. Octavia's instincts were strong. The border situation had likely been a trap and the council had fallen for it. And now the dragon riders' voice on the council had been silenced. What a mess.

Octavia clutched her arms to her chest. Her face was drawn and pale, her pink lips standing out against her flesh where her teeth worried them.

"Is there more?"

Octavia lifted her shoulder. "No, I just keep thinking about Jeth's colleagues. The Tenegardians that I sent to their deaths because I was desperate for answers."

Strida cleared her throat quietly. "Octavia."

"I should have just gone myself."

"And then Melusine might have killed you," Strida said.

"At least that would have been better than the guilt I now carry," Octavia said, touching the center of her chest. "They didn't deserve this."

Cora knew what it was like to have deaths weighing on her. She understood the guilt that came with being in charge, with making decisions that got people hurt. Or *worse*. Cora was intimately familiar with that tight, gnawing feeling. The only trouble was Cora didn't know which words would help soothe Octavia. She was still trying to forgive herself for what happened to Faron.

"No one deserves this," Strida said. "But you weren't the one who killed them. That was Melusine."

Octavia looked like she might be sick. "What do I do now? We have no advocates on the council. Northwood will run Tenegard into the ground fighting a war we are not prepared for right now."

She was distraught and Cora reached out to take her hand. Octavia had just lost the only home and role she'd ever known. It was a lot of change to handle in a short amount of time.

"Whatever you must do now," Lenire said, "just know that the dead are beyond your reach."

Cora was surprised to hear him speak so freely. From her earliest impressions, Lenire was standoffish, especially around new people, and yet here he was, sharing glimpses from his own past. Perhaps they really had moved to a place of trust.

Octavia looked at him, a small frown of confusion on her face.

"I, too, have faced exile for decisions I regret," he said. "So I know this well. You have to be the one to forgive yourself, because condemning yourself to carry this guilt forever will only hamper your ability to fight for the living."

Strida, who'd been hesitant to trust Lenire, especially after everything Cora had told her, said, "He's right."

"I don't know how I could possibly forgive myself," Octavia said.

"It is a lesson that I'm still learning to accept," Lenire offered. "But it's less lonely knowing that others struggle with it too."

"I feel lost," Octavia admitted. "Unmoored."

"You are not lost," Cora said reaching out to squeeze her arm. "You are a dragon rider, and you will always have a place with us."

"It seems," Lenire said to Octavia, "that you still have your real home. You just have to reconcile within yourself that you deserve it."

Octavia swiped at a tear that had gathered against her eyelashes. No other tears fell, but Cora could tell she'd been moved by Lenire's kindness. Even Strida seemed to be reevaluating Lenire as she looked from him to Yrsa, the line between her brows easing.

But then she cleared her throat. "I hate to break up this moment, but I think we have to set this conversation aside for now. We have an imminent enemy to face."

"You're right," Cora said. "Octavia, ask Raksha to have the dragons move the crystals downstream. Alaric and Yrsa will know where to stop." She waved Strida and Octavia toward the cavern.

"Where are we going?" Strida asked.

"Inside." Cora gestured with her chin. "I want to show you what we're up against."

"By the stars." That's all Strida said when Cora and Lenire showed them the crystal deposit, pulsing with regenerating, Blight-tainted crystals. It was amazement and fear all mixed into one. Octavia didn't say anything. She'd been even more shocked than Strida.

In fact, neither of them could form a single sentence until they approached the steep incline to the clearing where the dragons and dragon riders had gathered. "So each of those crystals is going to become a hound?" Strida asked.

"Most of them," Cora said. They couldn't be sure the Blight had infected every single one. But there were enough to create an army of hounds.

The sun was setting as they climbed the slope up to the clearing, casting a dark shadow over the piles of crystals that had been unpacked from saddlebags.

"I hate to say it," Strida said, "but we're outnumbered."

"Even with an entire fighting force," Cora said, picturing those who were still in the infirmary, "we would be outnumbered."

"As long as we're on the same page."

"The hounds' only vulnerability is the same crystal they will spawn from," Lenire said.

Octavia looked over with interest. "That's how we stop them?"

"Pouring a large amount of magic into the crystal will eventually shatter it," Cora said. "Killing the creature for good."

"But in the midst of battle, especially one where we are outnumbered, it might be best to disable the hounds first and destroy the crystals after," Lenire said.

"Okay," Strida said. "So how do we disable them?"

"Your dragon riders will need to attack with magic first. Once the crystal lights up, focus on separating it from the hound's body."

"Easy enough," Strida said, though her tone said this would be anything but easy.

"We should split our efforts," Cora said. "Octavia, since you have the strongest dragon bond, you and Raksha spread the word about how to fight the hounds. Strida, have the dragon riders place the crystals in the center of the clearing there." She pointed. "We need them arranged in a cluster formation similar to the one in the crystal deposit."

Octavia and Strida both hurried off to their respective tasks.

"You're good at this," Lenire said.

"What?" Cora asked as she went through her mental checklist. Once the crystals were arranged, all that would be left to do was fill them with magic. Hopefully, they had enough time before the hounds appeared.

"Leading."

"Oh," Cora said, surprised at how much that meant to her. She'd been away from the school for ages and didn't feel like much of a leader at the moment. And so much had happened while she was away, Octavia had been banished and war had been declared. "Thanks."

"I mean it. I'm sorry I ever doubted your skills and abilities."

"I'm sorry I originally told Strida you were suspicious."

Lenire laughed. Cora had never really heard him laugh like that before. "Is that why she keeps glaring at me?" he asked.

"Probably." She inclined her head. "C'mon. I still don't have much magic to give, so you're gonna have to help."

"Lead the way," Lenire said, following Cora toward the cluster the dragon riders had built.

"All right," Cora called loudly. "Just like at the school when we needed to power the shield, concentrate your magic on filling the cluster."

She walked around the cluster. Though she didn't have much magic to offer, she gave kind words to her dragon riders. The dragons all hovered on the outskirts of the clearing and Cora knew they were bolstering their riders' magic.

The crystals had a dull glow to them from the school's residual magic, but now that the dragon riders were pouring their magic into the cluster, it shone with a brilliance that Cora had never seen in any of the clusters so far.

Lenire dropped his hands when Cora reached his side of the cluster again. "This should attract every hound for miles."

"Good," Cora said. "Now we—"

A long, hideous howl sounded across the evening sky, and Cora whirled, her eyes drawn in the direction of the cavern.

Lenire came to stand beside her, staring into the dusky twilight. "It's starting."

"Everyone into position," Cora called, startling the dragon riders into action. "Up there," she said, pointing to a rocky ledge. "I want riders on the wall."

"You and you!" Strida yelled, gesturing to a pair of riders. They took off with their dragons, positioning themselves from above.

"The most experienced riders to the front," Cora said.

Strida picked through them, moving riders to the front, and pointing other riders to the back of the group. Mostly it was the younger riders with newer bonds that were pushed back. Though they would be eager to fight and to prove themselves, Cora knew they would have less control over their magic. And courage could only take them so far. They would need to follow the lead of the more experienced riders if they had any chance of succeeding.

"Add some riders on that ledge there," Cora said, pointing to another rocky shelf. "We can use the sky as an advantage if we have to."

"They're coming!" one of the riders shouted down from the cliff face. "They're headed right for us."

"It's working!" Lenire said. "They're taking the bait!"

There was no time to celebrate the success of their plan. The hounds could be heard in the distance and several of the dragon riders shivered in response. "Steady," she cautioned. Even though most of them couldn't hear her over the rising din. "We can't let them get away."

Cora yanked her sword free of its sheath, relieved she had the strength to do so, and stalked to the edge of the slope, watching the dark shadows approach at a run. Strida and Octavia stood to her one side. Lenire stood at the other.

"Ready?" he whispered to her.

Cora tightened her grip on her hilt. "Ready."

The hounds snarled and snapped, gunning for the fake crystal deposit that glowed with the brilliance of a thousand stars behind them. Their run was gangly and awkward, the beasts still learning the pattern of their misshapen feet.

Cora's heart throbbed so hard against her ribs that her pulse shuddered at the base of her throat. This was it. This was where they made their stand.

Behind her Alaric roared, his voice traveling clear across the valley and echoing between the mountains. The other dragons joined him, sending a shock wave of voices toward the hounds. The hairs on the back of Cora's neck stood up. If the hounds had been real creatures, they would have stopped in fear at the display of power, but they kept running, built for one goal only.

Cora readied herself to strike, lifting her sword in the air, but the hounds stopped suddenly, circling up.

"What's going on?" Strida asked, looking from one strangely formed hound to the next. "Why aren't they attacking."

"I don't know," Cora said. "I've never seen them behave like this." The hounds stamped and snarled and, at the center of the circle, a black fog began to bubble. It was like watching a kitchen pot boil over.

"They're summoning the Blight!" Lenire said. He turned to Cora, his face blank as he clutched Zirael's disk to his chest. "The hounds aren't conscious enough to make decisions."

Strida lowered her crossbow. "What does that mean?"

"This is something they've been ordered to do," Lenire said. "This is the work of Zirael and Mel—"

Lenire hadn't even finished uttering her name before the sky split open between the hounds, carving a window into the air, and the sorcerer herself stepped through.

"Oh *stars*," Strida said.

Melusine's hair was as wild and curly as ever, the bottoms of her skirts splattered with mud. Octavia's source must have been right about Melusine hiding out in the woods near the border. A look of shock crossed her face as she regarded Cora and the dragon riders. Her lips puckered as the shock quickly made way for frustration.

"Hello, Cora," Melusine finally said. "You do like to make yourself an inconvenience, don't you?"

Behind her, from the split in the sky, emerged an older man whose face Cora recognized: Zirael. The man's eyes lifted and immediately locked with Lenire's before a cruel grin formed on his face. But as his gaze drifted, darting from Cora to the numerous dragons and dragon riders, his smile fell away.

"You said we would be alone," Zirael hissed at Melusine. "Not facing a host of armed enemies!"

For a frantic second Cora wondered if the hounds were only meant to summon Melusine and Zirael upon locating the Heart of Tenegard. But before she could find her answer, Melusine waved her hands and the Blight struck out, ropey limbs of black fog slithering up the slope.

Strida caught Octavia by the arm and yanked her to the ground. Cora and Lenire dove out of the way, but those long tendrils didn't stop, instead lashing out at the closest dragon riders. The Blight's tendrils slithered into their mouths and noses, the way it had once done with Faron, but instead of collapsing, unconscious, the riders shifted jerkily, turning on their friends with raised weapons.

"Watch out!" Lenire called to a group of unsuspecting riders. "The Blight's in control."

Cora climbed to her feet, but Strida grabbed her hand before she could jump into the fray. Her eyes were panicked. "Melusine and the Blight weren't supposed to be here."

"I didn't know this would happen," Cora said.

"We were supposed to be fighting *hounds*."

Cora's entire body went cold. With all the crystals here, there was nothing left to protect the school. Melusine would see that now and she could use it against them. She could disappear with the Blight as quickly as she'd appeared.

Cora understood too late that they'd been tricked into abandoning their only defense. The school—Faron—was at risk, unless she could find a way to defeat Melusine and Zirael *and* the hounds.

# CHAPTER 29
## CORA

"Cora, watch out!" Lenire shouted as a sharp blade came down between her and Strida. Cora had just enough time to roll out of the way before the Blight-controlled dragon rider picked up his sword and tried to sever her arm.

"Oh, no you don't!" Strida kicked out with her feet, catching the dragon rider by the ankle, successfully knocking him down.

Cora snatched up his sword, but the blank, haunted look in his eyes didn't change. He merely lunged for her, both hands reaching for her throat.

Cora knocked him back with a small gust of wind. He charged at her again and she was forced to put more power into her spell, shoving him back until his dragon caught him by the back of the tunic, halting his approach.

"What do we do?" one of the riders shouted.

"Hold them off," Cora shouted to the group. "We need to relieve them of their weapons. They're not in their right minds and they'll strike to kill."

"And then what?"

"Trap them with magic if you have to. We have to get the Blight out of them somehow."

The clatter of steel accompanied her words, and Cora watched a pair of dragon riders take down one of their friends, subduing him against the ground. He fought against their hold on his wrists, snarling and snapping like the hounds. Another girl threw daggers and her dragon was forced to sweep her off her feet. Cora heard the *thunk* as her head hit the ground, hard, and she was knocked unconscious. This wasn't what she'd expected to happen, and it was torture watching dragon rider fight dragon rider. Melusine's dark cackle floated up from the base of the slope. She was *enjoying* this.

"Where are you going?" Octavia asked, grabbing Cora's wrist as she prepared to descend the slope to go after Melusine and Zirael.

"They can't control the Blight if they're dead," Cora said through her teeth just as one of the possessed dragon riders crashed into them, knocking them both to the ground. The girl was young and scrawny, but she got her hands around Octavia's cloak and twisted it hard around her neck, choking the air from her lungs.

Cora scrambled up and grabbed the girl from behind, taking hold of her hands, and prying her off Octavia. The girl screamed in frustration, flailing in Cora's arms, while Octavia rolled over, coughing and gasping.

Cora stumbled back, slipping on rock, and tumbling to the ground with the girl in her arms. When they landed Cora could feel the pebbles under her spine and despite the pain of her landing, an idea sparked to life. She tightened her hold on the possessed, struggling dragon rider in her arms and summoned her magic, letting it slither through the earth. She imagined dirt and rock parting and she rolled over suddenly, carrying the girl with her. A hole had formed, and Cora let the girl go, scrambling out of the hole as she used her magic to refill it, packing dirt and stone tightly around the girl's legs up to her thighs.

Cora let out a breath of relief as the girl screeched, her pale hands clawing at the ground around her. Her eyes were blank, recognizing only the command of the Blight, and her jerky arms dug at her legs, but Cora had used her magic to pack the girl tight. She was trapped.

"Nice trick," Octavia said, offering Cora a hand.

"Are you okay?"

She nodded, rubbing at the marks on her throat. "I will be."

As Cora rose to her feet, she looked around. They'd managed to subdue the possessed dragon riders. She turned to Melusine and Zirael once more, but it wasn't the sorcerers that held her attention, it was the hounds.

"*No*," she whispered, watching as those hideous beasts turned to the slope, one by one, eying the ascent. Melusine was done messing around. Now the real fight began. "They're coming!"

Cora backed away from the ledge, drawing her sword from her sheath just as the first hound flew over the ledge with its mangled paws poised to strike. Cora lashed out, slicing through the hound's limb, sending it skidding against the rock face. Cora heard a thunk and spotted the crystal buried in the hound's separated limb. The rest of it lay there, a reeking, unconscious mass.

More hounds ascended the slope, growling as they lunged and darted between the dragon riders. Some part of them were still distracted by the crystal formation, giving the dragon riders a split-second advantage.

Cora swung her sword, slicing through the air until her arms burned with the effort.

"There's too many!" Strida called. She was perched on a ledge, firing bolt after bolt from her crossbow.

Cora glanced up at her, then summoned her magic, attempting to wall off some of the hounds. But even as the energy coursed through her, the pebbles on the ground merely shook. She wasn't fully recovered and with her damaged dragon bond, she didn't have much to work with in the first place. She needed to be at full power. She needed her bond back.

Cora clenched her fist, glancing back up at Strida. "Cover me?"

"What are you going to do?"

"I'm going to try some last-ditch magic."

Strida's eyes narrowed in confusion, but she nodded, scurrying down from the ledge as she swapped her crossbow for a sword. "Good luck."

Cora smiled grimly. She would need all the luck she could get. She rushed off through the battle in search of Lenire. Except for maybe him, she was the strongest dragon rider here. If she could repair her bond with Alaric and reclaim her full power, they might stand a chance.

She skidded to a stop, coming face-to-face with a snarling hound. She ducked away from the crooked teeth that jutted out from its snapping jaws, but she was trapped by the wall of the mountain. Cora lifted her sword, preparing for an exhausting fight, but suddenly the hound was plucked from the ground by a pair of powerful jaws. It was Alaric.

He shook his head, swinging the hound back and forth before releasing the creature. It crashed up against the wall of the mountain.

Cora sighed heavily, but grinned at him in thanks. "Lenire?" she called.

Alaric looked at her, his dark eyes questioning, but then he lifted his head and pointed in the direction of a fierce battle. Cora spotted Yrsa first, her serpentine body slithering through the hounds, sweeping them away with sharp flicks of her tail.

Cora rushed off through the battle. "Lenire!"

He looked over briefly, then back to the hound he was fighting, slicing a chunk of flesh from its haunches. The creature was in pieces, and still it fought, fueled by nothing but the Blight-infused crystal.

As Cora approached, Yrsa swept the hound against the wall and the remaining flesh exploded from around the crystal. It fell to the ground in a pile of hound carcass.

"Are you hurt?" Lenire asked as she reached him.

"No, but we can't win like this."

He looked up, perhaps for the first time in a while, and saw the battle-field. The dragon riders were holding on, but they couldn't manage this pace forever. They would grow weak, tired. Exhaustion would make them sloppy. And the hounds could fight for years if they had to.

"We have to try to repair my bond again."

"What?" he said. "Now?"

"Yes, now. I need to be at full power. And maybe together we can stop Melusine and Zirael. It's the only way to halt the hounds."

"Okay," he said, sheathing his sword and pulling the disk from his pocket. He turned, speaking to Yrsa. "Do whatever you have to do to keep the hounds away from us. We've already had to deal with one rebounding spell."

"It won't happen again," Cora said. "I promise."

Lenire nodded. "I trust you."

"I trust you too." She was sweaty and exhausted and buzzing with adrenaline, but it was the most sincere she'd ever been with him. She hadn't trusted him before, not really, so the spell never stood a chance. But that was different now. Lenire was part of their team. He fought for Tenegard, which made him one of them, and Cora trusted him with her life.

Lenire infused the disk with magic, and Cora watched as those familiar threads shot out across the landscape, turning the battlefield into a woven tapestry. She looked for the thread that was most important to her, tracing the string from her, all the way to Alaric. The center was connected by a few frayed strands. It was now or never, she told herself.

Cora held out her hands to Lenire, offering them up freely this time. He knotted threads to her arms, starting at her shoulders, then her elbows and forearms, and finally knotting threads to her palms. Cora gave up control willingly this time, but even as she did, she didn't feel as if Lenire took what she offered. Maybe it was because she was actively working with him now. She moved her arms the way he directed, pulling new threads along her bond. Perhaps this is what he'd meant about guiding her. She had to be willing to be directed in order for it to work.

Around them, hounds and dragons roared, and she could hear the cries of the dragon riders.

"Stay focused," Lenire said, calling her attention back.

Her eyes returned to her bond, but she couldn't help but see the possessed dragon riders in her peripheral vision, still struggling where they'd been incapacitated.

"Wait," she said.

Lenire looked up at her and they both felt the spell wobble. It wasn't as frightening as before, because they were both still committed to the task, but Lenire still stared at her, his eyes wide.

"Let's untangle the dragon riders from the Blight first."

"Cora?"

"The longer the Blight is inside them, the worse it is, right? Plus, we could use the extra hands."

"All right," Lenire agreed.

Cora let him guide her, throwing knotted magic at the dark threads that claimed the dragon riders before ripping it free. One at a time they released the dragon riders from the Blight's control. She watched them stumble, shaking off the effects of the Blight's possession, regaining use of their limbs again. They hadn't been possessed long, not nearly as long as Alia, and thankfully none of them fell unconscious. Lenire must have been right. The longer a body was possessed, the more intense the response was upon being freed. Though not unconscious, the riders were slow. There wasn't much power in their strikes, but Cora was relieved to see them rejoin the fight.

Cora let her hands be guided back to her bond, and her heart fluttered. Already magic glowed in the new strands that she'd been weaving toward the damaged section. All she had to do was stretch the threads and knot the two halves together, reuniting the full strength of the bond. Cora did just that, watching as the magic flowed along the thread, brilliantly, blindingly. She almost couldn't look at it as she tied off the final knot.

And then, all at once, a massive wave of emotion crashed into her. It was so strong, filtering down the bond so quickly, that she was almost knocked off her feet.

*Alaric!* she shouted, calling his name in her mind as hard and as loud as she could. Every one of his emotions slithered down the bond toward her—surprise and relief and excitement.

*Cora?* he replied. *CORA!*

Cora almost choked on her next breath. She bit back the dry sob in her throat and blinked fiercely to hold onto the sudden onslaught of tears that threatened to spill down her cheeks. *You're back,* she said, looking across the battlefield toward him.

*I never left,* he replied. Then he threw back his massive head and let out an earth-trembling roar, shouting his happiness to the sky.

Their bond was restored to its full power and the fatigue that had been dragging her down for so long was gone. They were united once more. She held onto the moment for as long as she could, committing the feeling of their connection to memory, basking in the surge of magic that flowed between them. She wanted to jump and dance in celebration, but there would be time for that later. Right now, she needed to focus.

"Did it work?" Lenire asked.

"Yes," Cora said, swallowing down the emotion.

"You did it! " he said.

"*We* did it," she clarified, looking at him.

Lenire grinned at her, a full toothy smile.

"I think together we can get a hold of the Blight."

"I've never done that before," Lenire said.

"Up until a moment ago you had also never repaired a dragon bond."

"Right," he said. "Let's try."

Cora knew she wouldn't be much help in mastering the Blight with the disk, but at least she could lend her magic to help Lenire seize it, and then maybe he could wrestle the creature away from Melusine and Zirael. Together they inched around the base of the mountain wall, heading for the edge of the slope. All they had to do was lay eyes on the Blight.

"There," Cora whispered as she spotted the dark, swirling mass.

She studied the creature with Lenire and they could see where dark threads of magic twisted from Melusine to the Blight. "Do you think we can sever Melusine's threads?"

"No," Lenire said. "They're likely too strong. Reinforced with her own magic. I think we just have to attach our own and fight for control."

Cora nodded, summoning all the power and energy and magic she felt coursing inside her. The threads that Lenire had attached to her hands pulsed with glowing magic. "Ready?"

"Ready."

Lenire and Cora both flung their hands out and Cora envisioned Lenire's knotted spells sinking deep into the Blight's shadow. They latched on like hooks and Melusine's threads quivered in response.

"We did it," Cora said under her breath, astonished.

"Here," Lenire said, removing the thread from Cora's palm and hooking it into the ground. It was like an anchor point, straining against the pull of the Blight. "Give me your other hand."

Cora did and Lenire took that thread, anchoring it to the side of the mountain. Then he twisted his own spells over the threads, strengthening them with those intricate Itharusian knots.

"Go," he told her. "Help the others fight. I've got this."

Cora didn't need to be told twice. She turned on her heel and ran. *Alaric?*

*Over here!*

Alaric abandoned the hound he'd been snapping at and surged to her side. She threw her arms around his neck as far as they would go and for the briefest moment basked in the reunion. A strength unlike anything she'd ever felt before ebbed inside her, itching to spill out through her fingertips.

When they parted, Cora held her palms against his scales. "Let's take care of some hounds."

Alaric threw his head back, letting loose another roar that shuddered even the mountaintops. Cora turned back to the battlefield, to her friends, to her dragon riders, and let the pent-up magic spill from her. She directed its flow through the decoy crystal deposit, strengthening the magic even more, and directed a chilling blast of air at a group of hounds. They smashed against the mountain with such force they splattered, leaving their crystal hearts behind. Cora pulled a sharp spire of rock from the earth, impaling another hound. She lifted her sword and severed its head, digging the glowing crystal from its chest. Magic flowed from her as easily as her own breath did, and Cora didn't hold back. She tore the hounds to pieces and even flung the chunks down the slope, hoping they landed at the feet of their creator.

"Use the crystals!" Cora shouted. "Redirect your magic into their crystal hearts. It will shatter them for good!"

The ground beneath her feet began to tremble as the hound hearts vibrated with that shrill ringing sound. Cora wanted to clamp her hands over her ears but she didn't. Instead, she screamed, spilling more magic into the crystal hearts. They crackled as their surfaces split into a spiderweb of fissures and then with a wrenching screech, exploded.

Crystal dust flitted away on the wind and the dark fragments of the Blight scurried back to join the rest of it. Cora chased a remaining hound to the edge of the slope, using her magic to bury it in the earth. She cast a spell that revealed the hound's heart, then lifted her sword. She used the tip of it to dig out the heart, but stopped, watching the Blight roil below her. Lenire had left his position on the slope and was now engaged in battle with Melusine as he tried to wrest control of the Blight away from her.

Zirael had positioned himself behind a large boulder. He threw out a spell that just barely missed Lenire.

Cora charged down the slope to help him.

"Where are you going?" Octavia shouted after her.

"Keep that one alive if you can," Cora called over her shoulder as she pointed to the trapped hound. "Maybe we can learn something from it."

Then she turned and skidded down the slope, slipping and sliding on small stones as she raced to Lenire's side. Cora watched Zirael duck out of his hiding spot, his hands raised to throw a knotted spell her way, but a crossbow bolt struck the rock by his head, forcing him to retreat for a moment.

"Lenire, watch out!" Cora said, rushing through the stream where he stood. She threw up a shield wall just as Melusine released a twisting spell. The force of the spell shattered the shield, forcing Lenire back a few feet, though he remained upright. Cora skidded to a stop. In Lenire's hands the disk was burning up bit by bit, like an invisible flame ate away at the edges.

"It's Melusine's magic," he grunted. His hands were red and raw from fighting her.

Cora looked over her shoulder. The Blight swirled between them, its dark limbs lashing out only to be beaten back by Lenire's spells.

Through the shadow, Cora caught glimpses of Melusine. Her wild hair was blown back from her face, and Cora saw the rage written across her features. She'd never had to fight for control of the Blight before.

"What can I do?" Cora asked Lenire.

He gritted his teeth, the effort of fighting the Blight forcing him down on one knee. Water streamed around them. "The disk won't last much longer," he said. "Get to Melusine. If you can distract her, maybe I can tear the Blight away."

Cora nodded.

She rushed off and headed straight for Melusine. Zirael appeared in Cora's peripheral, and she threw up a shield just in case. Whatever spell he'd thrown crashed against it, sending sparks flying into the sky.

Another crossbow bolt zoomed by his head. This time Zirael caught it with a spell, and it crumpled to ash midair. Strida poked her head out from behind a rock. The dragon riders were making their way down the slope, covering Cora as she approached Melusine, sword raised.

Melusine lifted one hand, throwing out a spell that sent Cora stumbling backward. The other hand kept a firm hold on the Blight.

"Stay away!" Melusine roared at Cora, struggling to defend herself and hold Lenire off.

Zirael cast another spell, forcing Cora to crawl for cover. She crouched behind a rock, throwing out her own spell at Zirael. The dragon riders had amassed on the slope, using boulders as shields as they fired off magic and weapons. Zirael knocked them back, but it took a toll, forcing him to retreat to Melusine's side.

Cora took her chance, ducking as she dashed out of her hiding spot. She cast a shield in front of her as she approached Melusine.

The sorcerer lifted her hand in warning, and Cora had no doubt that whatever spell hit her next would be strong. Zirael fired a spell and it hit Cora's shield, making it shudder. Cora stopped.

"You have to know that allegiances with Zirael won't end well, Melusine!" she called. "Can't you see he's using you?"

Melusine sneered and cruelly said, "He can go ahead and try."

Suddenly Lenire gave a shout, as a spell swept across the valley. The force of the magical shock wave blew Cora off her feet. Then the sky cracked open, swallowing Melusine, the Blight and Zirael.

Cora stared up at the stars.

Melusine had gotten away. *Again.*

But Cora was alive.

They were all alive.

And the hounds were destroyed.

Strida and Octavia appeared in her hazy vision, blocking out the stars. They reached down and hauled Cora to her feet. She immediately stumbled toward Lenire, despite Strida's protest that she should take a minute to rest.

When she reached him, Lenire was still kneeling in the stream, water up to his waist and sweat dripping down his forehead. The disk, their best hope of controlling the Blight, their only way to repair broken dragon rider bonds, was just a crumple of ash in his charred palms. As Cora watched, Lenire dropped his hands into the cool water and the dusty remains floated away with the current.

# CHAPTER 30

## CORA

Nothing had changed in the ten days she'd been gone, yet Cora felt as if she were laying eyes on the dragon-rider school for the very first time. Without the shield shimmering over the school, it looked bleak. Worse. Defenseless.

They'd rushed back following the battle to ensure Melusine couldn't retaliate while the school was in a weakened state. Not only did Melusine still have control of the Blight, she also had Zirael. And Zirael's magic, like Lenire's, was different from anything they'd encountered before. Their shield wouldn't stand a chance against the Itharusian sorcerer unless Lenire added some defensive Itharusian knots to their original design.

"We need to get the shield back up," Cora said, the moment they landed. They'd brought back many of the crystals from the fake deposit that they'd created to lure in the hounds.

Strida dismounted and slid to the ground. "I'll take a group and start rebuilding the crystal border so we have something to power the shield with."

"I'll go help," Octavia said, looking more lost than Cora had ever seen her.

"Let me know the second it's done," Cora said to Strida. "I'll inform the healers that we're reconstructing the shield. We'll need them to stitch our magic in place with their own. Then I'll have Lenire add his Itharusian protections against Zirael's magic."

Strida raced off with Octavia and a group of battle-weary riders.

Lenire climbed down from Yrsa's back, unpacking the crystals that they'd transported.

Cora walked over to help him, lowering crystals to the ground. "You're sure you're up for this? It's a lot of magic to ask you to expend after what you've already been through."

"It's bigger than I imagined," he agreed, studying the area around the school. "But I want to help secure the shield."

Cora nodded gratefully. "I'm headed to the healers. Want the grand tour on the way?"

"Sure."

Cora led Lenire across the training field. Alaric and Yrsa took to the sky, patrolling the border while the shield was set up. There was a weightlessness to Alaric's thoughts. It had been that way since the moment he'd realized the bond had been repaired.

Cora didn't know how she was ever going to truly thank Lenire for what he'd done for them. She supposed there was no easy way. He'd repaired their bond. He'd battled the hounds. He'd even stood against Melusine.

Lenire might have been an Itharusian dragon knight, but as far as Cora was concerned, he was also a Tenegardian dragon rider, and she would welcome him on the school grounds for as long as he wanted to stay.

Cora pointed as they passed a row of buildings. "This is where we host classes."

"And what do new dragon riders learn?"

"Dragon Tongue. Aerial maneuvers. Battle strategy. We use the training field for the practical demonstrations."

"And who teaches them?"

"We do," she said, gesturing to herself. "I mean, those of us with the most experience. Strida. Octavia on occasion. Faron before he—"

"Was injured by the Blight?"

"Yeah."

"It's quite impressive considering how young this new generation of dragon riders is. I wish Itharus had been able to do more for you. That you didn't have to work so hard to rebuild."

"Speaking of rebuilding," Cora said as they hurried past the dining hall, "if you're hungry."

"What happened here?"

"This is where Melusine and the Blight first decided to visit us."

Cora led Lenire through the rest of the school, quickly introducing him to some of the administration staff and some of the other riders. She showed him the meeting hall and the dorms as they breezed by, and even found an empty faculty cabin where he could store his things.

Then they finally reached the infirmary.

Cora paused outside the doors.

Part of her didn't want to go inside. She didn't want to see the dragon riders that were slowly wasting away, trapped inside a spell she couldn't lift. And as much as she wanted to hold Faron's hand, part of her almost couldn't bear the thought of him, pale against the sheets of his cot.

"Is this where the sick riders reside?" Lenire asked.

Cora nodded. "There were so many that succumbed to the Blight's feeding that we had to temporarily relocate the infirmary to this dorm."

"Show me," he said quietly.

Cora looked over her shoulder. Lenire's features were cast in the shadow of the dorm, but she could make out the tight line of his mouth.

"I am a healer," he added. "Maybe there's something I could do to help."

"Maybe there is," she agreed, summoning hope from somewhere deep. Wasting no more time, Cora pushed through the doors, pausing as she was greeted by the sharp smells of vinegar and oils and lye. It covered the salty scent of sweat that covered the healers' brows as they toiled away, bending joints and moving muscles to prevent wasting and decay from setting in. Magic could only do so much to keep a body active.

Cora swallowed hard, trying not to frown as she regarded the perfectly positioned cots. Row upon row had been arranged, just as she left it, in pristine order, each bed made up. Each rider carefully positioned and draped with fresh linens.

It was like an army of the dead lying there until summoned.

For a moment, her head spun and she lifted the back of her hand to her mouth, worried she might be sick right there on the infirmary floor.

"Cora!" Faron's aunt Elaine quickly crossed the room and swept Cora into her arms. "You've returned." Elaine ran her hand over a scrape on Cora's cheek. "I knew you'd make it out okay. You always do."

Cora tried to smile but she couldn't. Not faced with the sleeping riders. "Strida and Octavia are preparing to raise the shield again. We'll need help from your healers."

"Of course," Elaine said, turning and waving down some of her colleagues. At her direction, they hurried out the door to join the dragon riders.

"How have things been here?" Cora asked. "Have you heard from my father?"

"The riders fare as well as can be expected. And your father sends his love. He wasn't happy to learn that you'd set off alone to the mountains again, but he was pleased to hear you'd found company."

Cora tried not to wince. Her father wouldn't be pleased to hear that she intended to set off for the mountains again the moment the school was secure. The Heart of Tenegard was still her biggest priority and their best chance of rousing the riders. Though they'd held Melusine and the hounds off for now, the win would only be temporary. The moment Melusine regrouped, she would resume her hunt for the source of all Tenegard's magic, so Cora still needed to beat her there. She turned to Lenire, beckoning him forward for a proper introduction. "This is Lenire. He's a healer from Itharus."

Elaine hummed softly. "I don't know that place." She gestured to a patient in one of the cots, seeming to have made a decision. "Would you?"

"Of course," Lenire said. "I'd be happy to take a look."

As Lenire was whisked away by Elaine and some of her healer colleagues, Cora made her way through the cots to the one she knew the best. She knelt down beside Faron, combing her fingers gently through his hair. It was soft and untangled. Someone had clearly been brushing it. Or maybe it was because he wasn't riding off through the sky on dragonback all the time, getting it messed up in the wind.

"I'm back," she whispered, picking up his hand. "For a moment, at least." She studied every one of his fingers, running her hand over the points and valleys of each knuckle. He was paler, his skin thinner somehow, or maybe it was that the sharp points of his body were more pronounced—the point of his chin, the cutting edge of his cheek-bones. She wanted to tell him everything. To whisper about the mountains and Lenire and Zirael and Melusine. She wanted to tell him about the crystal deposits and how much closer they were to finding the heart. Of course, without a new deposit to provide a direction, Cora was going to have to go back to manually tracking the river. She sighed, never more glad for her repaired dragon bond. Mostly, she just wanted to tell him how much she'd missed him. Footsteps echoed behind her, and she turned to find Lenire standing there.

"So this is Faron?"

"Faron, meet Lenire," Cora said. Part of her felt foolish for speaking to him as if he were actually awake and responding, though she also would have felt foolish speaking of him as if he weren't here.

To Lenire's credit, he didn't question the introduction, merely nodded. "It is good to know him."

"Any luck?" Cora asked, gently laying Faron's hand down on the cot.

"Not at the moment," Lenire said. "But Itharusian magic is intricate. I'm going to think on it for a while and try again later."

Cora tried to imagine how his complicated knots might help the riders and couldn't. Maybe that's why she had no business in the healing arts. Lenire reached down and Cora took his hand, letting him pull her to her feet.

They walked together to the door, and Cora couldn't help but wish that it was Faron escorting her through the building. That it had been Faron on this journey with her. She banished those thoughts as quickly as they appeared, feeling guilty and ungrateful. She was truly glad for Lenire's help. She just missed her partner. On the way to the door, they passed a window, one that looked out to the field of sleeping dragons. Lenire paused, his face falling more than it already had upon entering the infirmary. "You have a lot to fight for," he said.

"I do," she agreed.

"I apologize for making your journey so difficult."

Cora thought back to their first meeting. It seemed like months ago now. "We were both difficult. Besides, without you, Melusine and the hounds would have destroyed us."

"Without me and the disk, Melusine and the Blight might never have been an enemy of yours."

"I'm certain Melusine would have dug up another creature of doom if not the Blight." Cora was just happy that they'd walked away from this battle mostly unscathed. That's more than she could have hoped for after what happened in the mountains the last time.

"She does seem determined," Lenire said.

They passed through the door, back into the noon sun, and Cora caught her first glimmer of the new shield stretching over the school. She squinted at it. "We may have survived this battle, but there will be more to come."

"And now you have war with Athelia to think about."

Cora grimaced. "I can't put my energy anywhere else until Melusine and Zirael are stopped. If the heart is destroyed, there won't be any magic left to defend Tenegard with."

Lenire slowed by her side. "I know you're eager to get back to the mountains."

Cora bit her lip, refusing to voice the question on the tip of her tongue. Was he going to come with her? She couldn't ask that of him. Not after everything he'd suffered on her part, on behalf of Tenegard. Instead, she asked, "Know any good knots?"

Lenire's gaze followed the flickering glimmer of the shield. "I think I've got a couple spells that might work."

With that, he set off to help the dragon riders along the border of the school. Cora hurried back across the training field, meeting Strida as she supervised the positioning of more of the crystals.

"Octavia told me the good news," Strida said as Cora approached. "Well, I think Emrys tried to tell me first, but I didn't quite catch everything."

Cora frowned, confused.

"Your bond?" Strida said. "With Alaric."

"*Oh*," Cora said. "Yes. Lenire helped me repair it during the battle." Guilt suddenly twisted like a knife in her gut. "I'm sorry."

It was obvious Strida's bond was still suffering, and Cora felt terrible, especially knowing they'd had a way to repair it only yesterday. She wished she'd done more to protect that disk. That she'd somehow saved it during the battle. In the heat of the moment, she'd just been worried about surviving long enough to get to Melusine, but in hind-sight, she saw how vital that disk was. It had been the only tool that had worked so effectively against the Blight. There was a moment, during the battle, when Cora thought Lenire might actually be able to steal control of the creature. And if it hadn't been destroyed, Lenire might have been able to save the bond between Strida and Emrys in the same way. Her thoughts drifted to the two other disks Lenire had said existed. Perhaps one day, when this was all over, they might be able to retrieve one of those remaining disks from Itharus long enough to heal Strida's bond.

"Don't be sorry," Strida said. "I'm happy for you. Truly, I am. If any one of us needs to be at our full power, it's you. You're our leader. Cora." Strida took her hand and squeezed. "Emrys and I are getting along fine for now." Her eyes skittered to the infirmary and back. "And I am very aware that things could have turned out so much worse for us. Anyway, Emrys probably prefers the silence in his head as opposed to listening to my thoughts endlessly pine after Octavia or moodily stew about the capital."

Cora hummed, her own thoughts shifting to the capital once more. "We have a problem there."

"If you call *war* a problem."

"What do you call it?"

"A catastrophe."

A chuckle got stuck in Cora's throat. She didn't know if she wanted to laugh or cry. She really just wanted to lie down in her bed and sleep for days. Exhaustion hung from her limbs like a weighted blanket. "Can we deal with all the catastrophes tomorrow?"

"You're not going to get an argument from me," Strida said. The smirk Cora expected to curl across Strida's face never came. Instead, her lips parted and the words "*Oh, stars,*" spilled from them.

"What?" Cora asked. "What is it?" She twisted around sharply, then spotted a red-faced Emmett hurrying across the training field.

"He's running," Strida said. "Why is he running?"

Whatever the reason, it couldn't be good.

"Cora!" Emmett sputtered, doing his best not to double over as he gasped for breath. "Northwood!" He gestured back to the school in the direction of his office. "Would like to speak with you."

"Now?"

"It was less of a request and more of a demand," Emmett said.

Before Cora could respond, he whirled and rushed back across the training field. Cora glanced at Strida, then they both set off, chasing Emmett all the way back to his office.

"Councilor Northwood," Emmett barely managed to spit out as he sucked in another strangled breath. He gestured with his hand and Cora stepped toward the communication anchors, facing a grainy image of the man in question.

"I imagine Emmett has brought you up to speed?"

Cora glanced at Emmett and back. "I'm afraid I have just returned from a mission. There hasn't been time yet to debrief."

"How convenient," Northwood muttered. "You always seem to be occupied in those mountains of yours."

Cora's fingers twitched. "What can I do for you, Councilor Northwood?"

"I am reaching out to request your presence in the capital."

"For what reason?"

332

"There are things we must discuss. Things that should not be spoken about through such unprotected channels."

Cora could sense Strida and Emmett both stirring behind her. Thanks to Octavia, she knew Northwood meant to discuss his war with her. Meant to request the aid of the dragon riders in his fight against Athelia. More like demand.

"Very well," she said. "I will set out tomorrow as soon as I've made arrangements with the school."

"No," Northwood said. "You will set out today. Immediately."

"We have just returned—"

"And I have issued an order. You will report to Kaerlin post haste. Furthermore, given recent events involving spies within the capital and their clear tie to your liaison's professional network, Emmett needn't *ever* return to Kaerlin after his duplicity."

The grainy image disappeared.

"I can't believe you used to work for that guy," Strida muttered to Emmett.

He absorbed her comment stoically. Cora opened her mouth to say something, but Emmett simply lifted his hand to halt her concern. "I knew what I was doing and do not regret helping Octavia."

"Good," Strida said, turning to look directly at Cora. "Because you have bigger things to worry about right now."

"*We* have bigger things to worry about," Cora corrected her. "You're coming to the capital with me."

It was late when Cora and Strida arrived at the palace in Kaerlin—so late that it was almost morning again. Luckily, Strida was no stranger to the palace, and she led Cora through the halls toward the council chamber. There were very few staff members scurrying about at this time, so there was no one to greet them nor question their arrival. The few guards they did encounter let them pass unquestioned, so Cora imagined that they'd been told to expect dragon riders.

Cora could feel a bubbling of worry course down the dragon bond from Alaric as she and Strida moved through the palace. And though his concern set her on edge, the connection between them was strong, so powerful, in fact, that she could have cried out with joy.

"Should we knock?" Cora asked when Strida paused in front of a pair of closed doors.

"Why bother?" Strida pushed on the mighty doors without preamble, shoving her way inside.

"This is a private meeting!" a voice rang out.

It sounded like Northwood, but as Cora looked from one drawn face to the next, she couldn't be sure who had spoken. The council members were gray-faced with fatigue, clearly exhausted from a day poring over battle plans and logistics, though Cora had little pity for them. She was running on days of poor sleep and had not rested since the last hound fight.

The councilors parted and Northwood appeared, waving her further into the chamber. As they approached the circle of chairs, a large map was rolled up and dragged from the floor.

"We came as quickly as possible," Cora said, walking to the middle of the floor. Strida stood by her side. "Since there is urgent business you wish to discuss." Cora's eyes flickered briefly to Strida, waiting for some sort of silent acknowledgment.

Strida dipped her head, just a bit. It was hardly noticeable to the others, but for Cora, it was everything. It was Strida's grim acceptance of the plan they'd discussed during the long flight from the school to Kaerlin.

Now Cora needed to put it into action. "Let us hear what you have to say."

Northwood cleared his throat. "Cora Hart, leader of the dragon riders, we have called you here today to request your aid."

"My aid?"

"Tenegard is at war."

Cora tilted her head, feigning confusion. "Didn't we just finish a war?"

"And now another is brewing on our doorstep," Northwood said. "Athelia has—

"Athelia is our ally," Cora said. "The dragon riders will not move against them."

"Athelia is not our ally!" Northwood declared, rising from his chair. "They have struck first. They have moved against us."

"I cannot send dragon riders into Athelia. We will not kill innocent people for you."

"Athelia has already slaughtered our people! People you are sworn to protect."

"The dragon riders are here to defend Tenegard. We are not a weapon for you to deploy on a whim to fight an unjust war simply to make a name for yourself. I have already brought an end to one tyrant. I will not be responsible for creating another."

Northwood's chest heaved, his cheeks flashing pink, then red. Cora knew she'd just made herself an enemy of the council. Whispers began, first like a wave, and then like a crashing tide, stirring treachery in its wake.

"If that is all," Cora said, "then I think we are done here." She turned and walked away, the sound of a single tread of boots weighing heavy on her heart.

"She does not speak for us all!" Strida called loudly, drowning out the whispers.

Cora stopped. Even knowing it was coming, the words slashed against her. She turned around slowly. "Strida, don't do this."

Northwood looked between them, something like satisfaction in the way he eyed Strida. He settled himself in his chair. "The girl is right. You, Cora Hart, are as suspiciously soft on Athelia as your former council delegate had been." The councilors all whispered in agreement. "I'm sure Octavia has told you of her fate by now, hmm? Perhaps it is time you join her."

"Serve you or be banished, is that it?"

Northwood inclined his head. "We will have your answer now."

"My dragon riders will not fall at your feet."

"Some will serve," Strida said, assuring Northwood of her allegiance. She glared at Cora, putting on such a show that Cora almost believed it to be real. "If our leader is no longer fit to lead, then I will assume the spot on the council and speak on behalf of the *loyal* dragon riders."

"Very well," Northwood agreed immediately. "It shall be done. You are henceforth banished from the palace and the city of Kaerlin, Cora Hart. You no longer speak on behalf of the dragon riders when it comes to matters of this council or of Tenegard. Breaking any of these commandments will be considered treason."

Cora bristled, her heart thumping so hard against her chest she thought it might punch straight through her bones.

"You may leave, Cora Hart," Northwood said. "Return to your mountains. We have no need for you now."

# CHAPTER 31
## OCTAVIA

A loud thump startled Octavia from her sleep.

*Wake up, Octavia! Don't make me break down this door.*

She rolled over with such haste that she got caught in her sheets, dangling half off the bed. Only upside down did she realize that the thump had not been in her dreams but had actually been a bang upon her cabin door. It was Raksha on the other side, sweeping her tail against the wood.

*You're going to bring down the whole cabin on top of my head!* Octavia complained, righting herself on the bed and untangling her legs from the sheets. Sleep fog still stirred in her mind, and she considered simply flopping back down and pulling the sheets over her head.

*I thought I might have to in order to wake you.*

*I guess I should consider myself lucky that you refrained from knocking the door down.* Octavia stood, looking around the cabin for her tunic and boots. *What's going on?*

*Cora and Strida are almost here.*

*Already?* Octavia hadn't exactly expected them to hang around the capital, but their return was faster than she'd expected. They must've flown straight to the capital and straight back without stopping for rest. *What time is it?*

*Almost noon,* Raksha said. *Alaric reached out as soon as he was close enough to make a connection. They're not coming back to the school. Not yet, at least. They want to meet beyond the shield. Somewhere the other dragon riders won't see you all together.*

Octavia located her boots under the bed. She frowned. *I don't understand. Why don't they want to be seen together?*

*Alaric didn't elaborate. I only know it's important. They'll be here within a half hour. So hurry and get dressed.*

Octavia shoved her feet into her boots. Her riding attire required far less upkeep than the intricately beaded dresses she wore in the capital. She'd left most of them behind when she and Raksha had fled after their banishment. Part of it had been out of necessity. She wouldn't have put it past Northwood to arrest her for lingering too long in the palace. But it had also been the practical choice to leave those parts of herself behind. There would be no need for pretty dresses here at the school. Or, for that matter, ever again.

She'd been stripped of her titles and her positions. As far as Tenegard was concerned, she was nobody.

*You are not nobody,* Raksha insisted, nudging at the door. Her hot breath seeped under it. *You are a dragon rider, and no banishment can remove that title.*

Octavia pulled her tunic over her head and stuffed the bottom into her breeches. She threw open the door while she braided her hair out of her face. Raksha's head was so close to the door Octavia startled for a second, then smiled gently at her dragon. *I know that. I'm just being mopey. Don't listen to me.*

*I'm always listening,* Raksha said.

*Because you're nosy.*

*Because I'm worried about you.*

Octavia tied off the end of the braid and flipped her blonde hair over her shoulder. *I'm fine. Or at least I will be. Eventually. When I figure out just how I fit.* She was a dragon rider, of course. There was no questioning that. But Octavia could do more for the dragon riders than accompany Cora into battle. She could champion real change in Tenegard. She knew she could. She just had to be given the chance. And maybe wait until Northwood was booted off the council.

*All is not lost,* Raksha said. *You will figure out how you fit into this new world.*

*How do you know?*

*Because you are brilliant and unwavering in your dedication to the people of this land. This is one of many hurdles you will face, but Northwood will not be the one to ground you. Not when you have dragon wings to fly.* Raksha nuzzled her snout against Octavia. *We will figure it out together.*

*Together,* Octavia echoed in her thoughts, grateful for the endless wisdom Raksha shared with her. A burst of warmth filtered down the bond, then Raksha pulled away.

*Are you ready now?*

Octavia nodded, hurrying down the stairs from her cabin. *Where do they intend to meet us?*

*Far enough beyond the shield that dragon flight is warranted.*

340

*Won't that draw attention to us?* Octavia asked.

*I'll make a couple loops of the school. We'll say we're going hunting if anyone asks.*

*Okay.* Octavia tugged on the saddle straps that wrapped around Raksha's body, ensuring they were tight. But before she could haul herself up into the seat, Emmett walked around the corner.

"I didn't see you at breakfast," he called.

"Only getting up now. Raksha and I were actually heading out to do some hunting."

"Hmm," Emmett said, stopping as he reached them. "Most of the riders seem to be having a slow start to the morning."

"Can you blame them?" Octavia was exhausted herself, so she could imagine how the other riders felt. It had been a rushed flight out of Kaerlin upon being banished and then a hasty flight to the mountains to help Cora and Lenire with the hounds. They'd all fled back to the school immediately after the battle, worried Melusine might target it. Once Cora had been summoned to the capital, Octavia had spent the rest of the day helping the others secure the shield. By the time she'd fallen into bed it had been long after midnight. Octavia suspected most of the riders could have slept straight through this day and on to the next.

"I suppose not," Emmett said. "I was actually coming to find you to ask if you'd seen Cora? I'd heard that she and Strida had returned."

*Lie,* Raksha whispered in her mind. *Say nothing of your meeting. Whatever is going on, Emmett might not be privy to yet. Perhaps Cora will not wish him to know at all.*

"Returned?" Octavia said, keeping her voice even. "When? I haven't seen either of them yet."

"Oh," Emmett frowned. "My mistake. I must be getting ahead of myself."

Octavia sighed. Perhaps Emmett was feeling just as lost as she was. Before she'd flown to the capital, Cora had told Octavia what had happened when Northwood called through the communication anchor. Emmett had been banished from the capital the same as Octavia. She thought she should apologize. Somehow she felt responsible. If she hadn't asked Emmett for his help, neither of them would be here right now, but the truth was, she didn't regret it. She did what she had to do in the moment in order to get the answers she needed to protect the people of Tenegard. It may have backfired in her face, but her intentions had never been malicious. So, like Lenire had told her, she was going to have to find a way to live with the consequences of her actions. She was going to have to make peace with the Jeth situation and forgive herself for the deaths of his colleagues. Octavia hadn't swung the sword or dropped the ax. It was Melusine. It was *always* Melusine. She didn't exactly forgive herself yet, but knowing that she had been trying to do the right thing made it all a little more bearable. Besides, Cora told her that Emmett had said he didn't regret it either. So maybe they'd finally found some common ground.

"I'm sure they'll be back soon," Octavia offered.

Emmett lowered his head. It was brief and only a fraction of an inch, but it was still a sign of respect that Octavia would have received in the capital. "Enjoy your hunt."

She nodded, climbing up onto Raksha's back. "Enjoy your … liaising."

Emmett chuckled, then walked away.

*Let's get out of here,* Octavia said quickly. *Before anyone else asks about them.*

Raksha took a running start, then leapt into the sky and unfurled her mighty wings over the training field. She made a wide pass over the school, circling the border twice before passing through the shield and flying off over the woods that surrounded them. She kept low, skimming the tops of the trees with her claws. The green leaves shivered beneath her touch.

*There*, Raksha said, spotting a clearing up ahead.

Octavia spotted a flash of color between the trees, and when the leafy canopy split open, there they were: Strida and Emrys; Cora and Alaric.

Raksha pulled up short and Octavia gripped the saddle even tighter as they descended quickly. The landing was softer than she'd expected, the ground covered in thick moss. Octavia's feet sank into it as she slid from the saddle. "You're back!" she called.

"We're back," Strida muttered.

"What happened in Kaerlin?" She hurried over to join them on the giant boulder they'd settled on. Cora leaned against it, but Strida lay on her back, staring at the sky. "What's wrong?"

"What isn't wrong?" Strida lamented.

Octavia looked from Cora to her girlfriend and back.

"There have been some developments," Cora said. She didn't sound quite like herself.

Octavia climbed up on the boulder and sat between them. "Did Northwood ask for the dragon riders to support his war?"

"He did," Cora confirmed.

"And?"

"I refused."

"Good," Octavia said. "I warned him and the council that you would."

"Yeah," Strida said, sitting up on her elbows. "But then I defied Cora, told Northwood some of the dragon riders would stand with him, got myself elected to the council as the dragon rider representative and had Cora banished. All in all a productive trip."

"What?" Octavia said, certain Strida was simply being dramatic. Neither of them denied it, though. They both looked exhausted. "You can't be serious."

"We meant for it to happen," Cora said. "We planned for it beforehand."

"But why?" Octavia asked, confused.

"It needs to be this way," Cora said. "I thought about it all the way there, about simply refusing Northwood. That wouldn't really help us in the end. Without a dragon rider representative on the council, we would have no idea of the council's continued intentions for us or the school. We would also have no idea what was going on with his war planning. Melusine's clearly involved herself there, at the border, so we need to stay informed."

"The only way we can ensure that is with a representative," Strida said. She sat up fully, wrapping her arms around her knees.

"It couldn't be me," Cora said. "If I stood as the representative, the expectation would be that all the riders would follow. The only way to place a representative on the council now is to make Northwood believe there's a rift between us. That some of the riders might align with his thinking. It was the only way he would have accepted Strida."

Octavia nodded slowly, numb with shock. Listening to how everything played out almost made her sick. When Raksha had said they'd wanted to talk, she hadn't expected this reunion to be quite so grim.

344

But now Cora had been banished as well. Everything was falling apart so quickly.

"It was the right thing to do," Strida said, defending Cora's position. "We need eyes and ears in Kaerlin."

"Are you okay?" Octavia asked, glancing over at Cora. She was pale, the circles under her eyes baggy and purple. She looked shaken.

"I'm fine."

"No," Octavia said. "Something is bothering you."

"I know we orchestrated it." Cora scoffed to herself. "But it stung more than I was anticipating. Faking the rift. Being banished."

"You know I didn't mean any of it," Strida said, climbing down the boulder to sit by Cora's side. She wrapped her arm around Cora's shoulders and hugged her from the side. "I was only trying to get them to believe the ploy. The last thing I want to do is partake in Northwood's council and play nice."

"I know," Cora said. "I was mostly surprised at how quickly Northwood was willing to dispose of me and move on to you. That man has no loyalties."

"Whatever it takes to further his agenda. We knew that," Strida said.

Cora finally made eye contact with Octavia. "I can understand now how difficult it must have been to be banished. You've spent your whole life in Kaerlin. Those are your people."

The corner of Octavia's mouth flickered. "My people are also here." She reached for Cora's hand, and then Strida's. "You made the right decision. There needs to be someone there pushing back against the council's attempts to corral and subjugate the dragons."

Cora gave her a watery smile.

"But now what?" Octavia continued. "Where do you go from here?"

"I'm heading back to the mountains to continue the search for the Heart of Tenegard. Flying to Kaerlin was a detour I didn't plan on making, but now that the council has been dealt with and the school is secure, finding the heart is my goal. Even if I have to track the river inch by inch again, I have to beat Melusine to it."

"We still have to figure out what you're going to tell the school," Strida added. "We have to preserve the illusion of a rift between us so that I maintain a trusted place on the council."

Cora worried her bottom lip. "I think we should tell the truth to some people."

"Who?"

"Lenire," Cora said. "He's proven himself in the fight against Melusine. Maybe Elaine too. And a couple of the instructors."

Octavia hated to think of the division this would create within the school. Deceiving the other dragon riders, divvying them up ... "It feels like we're preparing to tear apart our family."

"I know," Cora said. "I'm not happy about it, but we need the council to believe that the rift exists."

"But will it cost us the riders' trust when the truth is finally revealed?"

"I think this is a cost we have to pay."

Octavia's eyes drifted to Raksha. The dragon hadn't said anything, hadn't even whispered in Octavia's mind, but as she dipped her large head, Octavia knew that Raksha agreed with Cora. Raksha knew how important it was for the dragons to have influence over the council. If this was the only way they could ensure that continued, then they would have to make the sacrifice.

Cora stood, striding out across the marshy field to Alaric.

Octavia shifted closer to Strida.

"You know this means we'll be apart," Strida said.

"I thought you'd gotten used to that?"

"You've been banished, Octavia. You can't pop by the palace for a visit." Strida picked up a pebble and tossed it into the field. "For me to play the part of collaborator, we won't be able to see each other for who knows how long."

Octavia hadn't really considered that. In truth they'd spent more time apart than they had together lately, and it had taken its toll on their relationship, but they'd weathered it. They were still weathering it. Infrequent visits were difficult, but she hadn't thought about what this rift would mean for them personally.

"Maybe you don't mind," Strida started to say.

"I mind," Octavia assured her. She tugged her close and pressed a soft kiss to her lips. "I do. But you heard Cora. This is what it costs us right now."

"You can come with me," Cora called from where she stood by Alaric. "Join the hunt for the Heart of Tenegard."

Octavia considered it for a moment, but she knew it wasn't the right place for her. There were other things she could do to help fix this mess. A tiny flutter of an idea had taken root in her mind the moment she'd been banished. She hadn't given it any real thought until now. It was so fresh she hadn't even shared it with Raksha. As she opened up that channel between them, letting her thoughts drift down the bond, Raksha looked up with interest, humming in the back of her throat.

"What?" Cora said, looking between Octavia and Raksha. "You have somewhere else to be?"

"It's not that I don't want to join you on your quest, Cora. I appreciate the offer. Really, I do. I think I might have a quest of my own to set out on." Octavia explained her dealings with Athelia and Serafine and how Northwood had been twisting that relationship even before the incident at the border.

"You think it would help?"

"I think I'm in the best position to try," Octavia said. "The council already thinks I'm sympathetic to Athelia. And I've already made contact with their senate. I think Raksha and I should cross the border and investigate the link between Athelia and Melusine's machinations. See what's really going on there."

"You'd be perfect for the role," Cora said. "But be careful. After what happened with Jeth…"

"Thanks," Octavia whispered. "I know."

Strida got to her feet. "I guess this is goodbye for all of us, then."

"For a while," Cora agreed. She hugged them both, then climbed onto Alaric's back and flew off to the school, leaving Strida and Octavia alone.

Strida took Octavia by the hand. "I'm not cut out for this. I don't know how to fill your shoes on the council."

"You'll do fine," Octavia assured her. "Try to keep a cool head where Northwood's concerned."

Strida snickered. "Right."

"And make sure you tell the council of my departure. It will only confirm to them that they've done the right thing in banishing me, but it will also help you ingratiate yourself to them. They will start to look at you as an ally."

Strida nodded, squeezing Octavia's hands. "Fly back with me?"

"I'll go as far as the outer limits of the city before I head for the border," Octavia said. "Wouldn't want to push my luck with Northwood or his army." He would suspect that she was seeking out allies against them, but in truth, she was determined to lay the groundwork necessary for peace.

# CHAPTER 32

## CORA

The rainbow glimmer of the shield wall welcomed Cora back to the school. With Lenire's added Itharusian magic, the color was even more vivid when caught by the sun, and if Alaric approached at just the right angle, she swore she could make out the knots.

It was beautiful.

There were no other dragons in the sky, but Cora did spot a few dragon riders scurrying across the training field, on their way to the dining hall for lunch. The only one waiting for her when she landed was Emmett. He stood alongside the training field, his hands folded behind his back, his steady gaze locked on her. As soon as she'd climbed down from Alaric's back, he strode to her side.

"How did it go?"

"How long have you been waiting here?" Cora asked him instead.

"I couldn't sleep," he admitted. "I tossed and turned all night, wondering what Northwood would do or say. The dragon riders have made enemies of themselves as of late."

Cora eyed him.

"Yes, yes," he said. "Myself included. I certainly haven't done us any favors. Northwood is more suspicious of our motivations than ever." He sighed. "Because of that I couldn't help feeling that you were walking, unprepared, into a trap."

"It wasn't a trap," Cora said. They moved into the shade of one of the buildings, and Cora stopped walking.

Emmett hummed under his breath. "Then what was it?"

"A discussion," Cora said.

"A discussion."

"Yes."

"And?"

"It went as well as could be expected." Considering the outcome she and Strida had planned for, she could even say that it was a roaring success. But she wasn't ready to disclose that to Emmett yet. She needed to take her time with him. He'd only recently been cut off from the council, and learning that he'd headed a spy network within the capital made Cora leery. On one hand, he'd obviously helped Octavia. The contacts he'd cultivated over the years might even prove advantageous inside Kaerlin. But if Emmett had woven this network right under Northwood's nose, what was to stop him from doing that to the dragon riders? Cora needed to be sure of him, and until she was, he would have to stay in the dark.

"I've worked in politics all my life. That was deliberately vague."

Cora ignored his prying. "I need you to gather up the dragon riders for a meeting."

"That sounds serious." Emmett laughed, but there was no humor in it. "We're not marching off to war, are we?"

Cora sighed. "We'll discuss it during the meeting."

Emmett glanced to the sky briefly. "I can't help but notice Strida's absence? Did she not come back with you?"

"Emmett," Cora said firmly. "The meeting?"

"Right, of course. I'll get right on it." He made a sweeping bow. "Expect the dragon riders in the meeting hall within the hour."

Then he turned on his heel and marched off to gather up the riders.

*Do you think I should have told him?* Cora asked Alaric as she watched Emmett turn around the next corner.

*I think you will when the time is right.*

*I don't want to do this. Lying feels like a betrayal.*

*It is,* Alaric said.

Cora's eyes widened as she turned to look at him.

*But it's a betrayal they'll be able to accept. Once they understand, they'll see you and Strida had no other choice. We need to protect the Heart of Tenegard, but we also need to protect the people of Tenegard. We can't do that if we are kept from the council. And letting Northwood run around with ultimate authority is dangerous. From everything my mother has told me of the council, it seems the others are hesitant to challenge him. Octavia was always the voice of reason.*

*And now Strida will have to be.*

Alaric lowered his head in agreement. *She will do a good job. But in order for her to do that job, we have to support her and that means we lie.*

Cora spied the swinging doors of the dining hall open. Out walked Elaine, accompanied by Lenire. *At least I don't have to lie to everyone.*

Cora hurried across the training field, slowing as she caught up with them.

"You're back!" Elaine said, pulling her into a hug. Cora would never tire of it—these hugs—though she did suspect that Elaine used them as a means of assessing her. Cora never felt the cold thrill of healer magic, but she didn't doubt that Elaine had other ways of judging her condition.

"I'm back."

"So quickly?" Elaine continued. "Did you stop to rest at all?" She pulled away, studying Cora's face. Her thumbs traced the dark circles under Cora's eyes, answering her own question.

"There wasn't time."

"A statement like that leads me to believe that you either bring good news," Lenire said, "or bad news."

Cora appreciated how easily he read between the lines. "I need to speak with you both. Privately, if you can spare the time." She knew Lenire had nothing calling his attention, but Elaine had an infirmary filled with sick riders.

"Of course," Elaine said. "The other healers can manage for a little while longer. The dining hall was almost empty," she added, gesturing over her shoulder.

Cora eyed the building but shook her head. The risk that someone might overhear them was too great. All she needed was one person to get a whisper of what really happened and then it would be all over the school. If the dragon riders didn't believe in the rift, it would eventually make its way to the capital, and Strida's cover would be blown. Strida had promised Northwood that some of the dragon riders would fly with her. That they would support his war. They never would if they knew the real truth. Cora needed to do everything she could to keep Strida safe, and that started with keeping this secret safe.

"Over here," Cora said instead, gesturing to a grove of trees. They walked past the tree line and into the shadow of long, skinny branches.

"Cora," Elaine said, concerned now. "What's going on?"

With a deep breath, Cora told them everything. She talked about plotting all the way to Kaerlin with Strida and convincing Northwood of the rift between the dragon riders. When she was finished, she closed her mouth, her lips pinched together uncomfortably.

Elaine blinked, taking in the shock of the news. Lenire absorbed everything quietly, his eyes trained on the ground, his hand massaging the line of his jaw. It didn't mean as much to him. These were problems of a country he didn't have any real ties to. But Cora appreciated being able to share the news all the same. It was a heavy secret to bear alone.

"I don't know if it was the best idea," she confessed. "But we had to do something drastic. Something that Northwood would believe."

"So Strida has gone back to the capital?" Elaine said.

Cora nodded. "And Octavia's gone to Athelia."

"Athelia?"

"The land you are now at war with," Lenire confirmed.

Cora sighed. "She's gone to gather information. She might have sources there, on the Athelian senate. If she can prove that Melusine and Athelia aren't working together, that the attack at the border wasn't instigated by Athelia, then maybe Strida will be able to talk the council out of war before there is any bloodshed."

"And if she proves the opposite?" Lenire said. "If she proves that Athelia is backing Melusine. Then what?"

"I guess there will be no stopping the war."

"How can you possibly keep up with the Blight and a war?" Elaine began. "The remaining riders are already being stretched so thin."

"I know," Cora said. And she was about to stretch them even further.

Cora's hands shook where they gripped the podium. She looked out at the assembled dragon riders, confusion arching their brows and lining their foreheads with deep wrinkles. She couldn't blame them. The last time she'd called them all together like this was to announce the mysterious sleeping sickness that had begun to infect the riders. That was back before they had any inclination of the Blight or Melusine. Back when Cora truly thought she was fighting an illness. At that time they'd barely been able to squeeze all the dragon riders and staff into the meeting hall. It had been packed so tightly Cora had to fight her way to the podium.

Now she stood before a scattered and depleted group. Her last call to action from this podium had been to unite the riders against the sleeping sickness. Today she called for division among them. She was asking them to choose a side when there were hardly enough of them to divide at all.

"What do you mean Strida has chosen war?" a young dragon rider called out, his forehead covered in a mop of bright red hair. He swept the fringes of his bangs from his eyes. "How could she betray us like this?"

"It is not a betrayal," Cora confirmed. "It was a choice." Conversations erupted between the riders. Cora rubbed her sweaty hands against her tunic, rolling them into fists to hide her nerves. "And now I am calling on you to make your own decision. You must choose today whether you will side with me and defy the council and their orders for war. Or if you will side with Strida and fight Athelia if Tenegard should ask it of you."

"What is the right choice?" a girl no older than twelve asked, her voice small and tentative. Her dragon bond must have been brand-new.

Cora's eyes flickered to Elaine and Lenire, standing at the back of the crowd. "It is not a decision that I can make for you," she said softly. "And I don't mean to sway you. Look deep in your hearts, speak to your dragons, and spend the afternoon considering carefully. The decision will come to you."

Murmurs of indecision swept through the room.

"I will ask," Cora said, "that those who choose to join me in the hunt for the Heart of Tenegard meet at the border alongside the training field at sundown. That is all. You are dismissed."

With that, Cora turned from the haunted stares, knowing full well that she'd sown the seeds of division among her dragon riders, and left the meeting hall. Under the afternoon sun, she felt like she could breathe again.

*You've done all you can*, Alaric said.

*Where are you?* Cora wondered, unable to see him.

*Waiting by the cabin. I don't know how long our next journey will be. So we should probably replace our stores and supplies.*

Cora smiled to herself. Alaric knew how guilty she felt right now, how torn she was, so he pulled her attention to the task at hand. She might live to regret this moment in the future, but right now she'd done what she had to do.

Cora made her way to her cabin. Alaric was curled up by the door. He'd dragged some extra furs from one of the storerooms for Cora to add to the saddlebags. She followed his lead and packed up the rest of her cabin, taking only the most important things. Blankets. Changes of clothes. An extra pair of boots. Her fingers brushed over the small wooden trinkets that Faron had carved for her. She would leave those here for when this was all over. Cora bundled everything together tightly and stuffed it in the saddlebags.

Next she and Alaric went to the dining hall and there they gathered up what dried preserves could be spared. Bread that would only last a few days. Thin slices of jerky would last longer. And a handful of berries. Cora packed it away carefully.

"I think we are almost ready," Alaric said. He wasn't looking at her but at the position of the sun as it fell slowly beyond the reach of the school, ducking down behind the trees.

"Almost," she agreed. "There is one more thing I have to do."

"Go on," Alaric said, pointing her toward the infirmary.

Cora ran all the way there and didn't stop until she was kneeling by Faron's bedside. Lately, it felt as if all she did was bid him goodbye.

"I don't know when I will be back," she admitted, taking his hand. "Though I intend to make this the last time. When I return to you next, it will be with a cure. And you will wake and wonder about all that has happened while you've been asleep." Cora brushed the hair from his forehead. "I will tell you the stories and we will laugh about it as we fly as far away as we dare. Maybe Lenire will even show us Itharus one day. I think you would like that."

Cora lifted Faron's hand and pressed one last kiss to his knuckles. He was still and silent and steady on his cot, but she had faith that one day he would open his eyes and smile at her again. Leaving him, Cora bid a silent farewell to the healers, letting them carry on with their tasks. As she headed outside, she felt a renewed sense of purpose. Everything she was doing was to save Tenegard. To save the dragon riders and the dragons. To save Faron.

She met Alaric in the middle of the training field and together they walked to the border, stopping at the very edge of the shield between a pair of crystals.

"What are you fretting over?"

Cora smiled despite herself, comforted by the renewed closeness of her bond with Alaric. It felt like forever since he'd been able to read the complicated emotions inside her, and even longer since he'd been able to verbalize them. "I'm worried no one will come," she admitted freely.

"They will come."

"But I'm also worried they will *all* come."

Alaric grumbled in agreement. "We can't leave Strida with no dragon riders under her command."

"Northwood wouldn't like that," Cora said. "But even more than that I'm afraid the riders who choose to follow me will judge me for creating this tension between them. For forcing them to choose."

"They will come because they believe in you, Cora."

"I hope so," she said, watching the sun sink a little farther beneath the trees. Then, one by one, riders and their dragons began to emerge, crossing the training field to join her, basked in the blush and gold of sunset.

Warmth swelled inside her. She had allies, though not as many as she might have hoped for. Strida needed them too, she reminded herself. She'd need support in Cora and Octavia's absence.

Cora glanced back across the training field, and to her surprise, she noticed Emmett, wrapped in traveling cloaks and carrying a bag, stuffed to the brim. He made his way slowly toward Cora. When he reached her, he stuck his nose in the air in that haughty way of his, though it carried none of the disdain it once had. "I figured I've effectively thrown my lot in with yours at this point. Might as well go all in."

"You didn't much like the mountains the first time around," Cora reminded him.

Emmett shrugged. "It's an acquired taste."

He joined the crowd that gathered around her.

A few final stragglers made their way across the field and Cora was pleased to recognize some of the instructors. Bringing up the rear was Lenire. He and Yrsa rounded out the group. Cora cut through the dragons and riders to reach him.

"I would understand if you wanted to pursue Zirael and the Blight on your own," she said. "You've already done more for us than I can ever repay. You don't owe us anything more."

"I left Itharus an outcast, with nothing but my mission to guide me. You've welcomed me here, as part of your team. Our fight is the same fight, Cora. Our enemies are the same enemies. So, for as long as I live and breathe as a dragon knight, I vow to see this mission through." He shared one of his rare smiles as the sun set and darkness overtook them. "For Itharus," he said, lifting his sword into the air. "For Tenegard!"

Cora pulled her own sword free, the steel of her blade striking his. "For Tenegard!"

# CHAPTER 33

## MELUSINE

The camp was set deep in the woods that grew along the border between Athelia and Tenegard. The canopy of trees was thick, but the area was lit with low-burning fires to keep wandering eyes from spying their lights in the dark. The night was pitch black, without a moon or even the stars to light her way, but Melusine passed easily between the hastily erected tents. She'd grown used to this path in the days since abandoning the battle at the dragon-rider school. The hot, glowing coals of the dinner fires turned the faces of easily bought men and women—thieves and mercenaries mostly—an angry shade of red. She'd learned early in her life that it never hurt to have some nameless muscle to do your bidding.

Melusine passed between old, weather-beaten tarps, unbothered by the amber-tinted stares of their owners. With the threat of the Blight, no one would so much as dare to raise a finger in her direction. She'd been quick to show them exactly what the Blight was capable of, and after poor Jeth and his colleagues paid them a visit, no one questioned if she was capable of such vicious ends.

Melusine pressed on. Her feet, left bare the way she liked, sank into the soft earth, the trail worn where she'd already walked dozens of times. She paused outside a tall tent, the only one that was properly furnished in the whole camp. She might currently be in hiding from the dragon riders, but she was certainly going to be comfortable.

She heard the snap of a gravelly voice inside and grimaced. Zirael had been in a terrible mood since returning from the mountains. He considered the battle forfeit, but Melusine knew that in reaching their end goal, it didn't matter how they got there, only that they did. If it meant she had to turn tail and flee every now and then, she would do it.

Survival was more important than standing against the dragon riders right now. If Zirael couldn't understand that, then perhaps he needed to find another sorceress to partner with. Melusine schooled her face into something neutral, then passed through the flap of the tent. A young man scurried out after leaving two bowls of steaming stew on the table. He accidentally nudged her in his haste, apologizing profusely, his head bowed, before fleeing into the night.

Zirael picked up his spoon and poked around in the bowl. He was not accustomed to a rough life hidden in the woods. Melusine knew he missed his fineries and his silk-threaded garments and his feather-soft pillows. His discomfort would almost make her smile but for the fact she had to listen to him gripe about these things every moment they were together.

Melusine crossed through the tent and sat opposite Zirael, picking up her spoon and biting into a tender chunk of meat. Squirrel most likely. The woods were full of them.

"Where have you been?" Zirael snapped. "I thought I might have to send a search party after you."

Melusine swallowed another bite before responding. "You know I am the most dangerous creature in these woods. I don't need fools traipsing after me in the dark."

"The fact that you think that is what's most concerning," Zirael muttered without looking at her.

Melusine felt a sharp stab of annoyance between her ribs. She did her best to keep it from flashing across her face.

"I have things to do," Zirael continued. "I don't have time to fret over your whereabouts whenever you disappear."

"I, too, have things to do. People to update," Melusine said, keeping her tone even. "You're just worried that I'm going to take the Blight and disappear. Leave you all alone here in the woods with only thieves and murderers for company."

Zirael abandoned his stew with a sour look. "That might be an improvement considering our current state of affairs."

"This wasn't my fault," Melusine said, tightening her grip on her spoon. "Those hounds were of both our makings. Neither of us knew they could be so easily misled."

Zirael leaned across the table. "You didn't tell me we would be walking into a swarm of dragon riders. If I'd known to expect that, I might have used different spells when creating the hounds."

"Well, maybe if you didn't go around taunting Lenire at every chance you had they might never have figured out how the hounds worked!" Melusine shot back.

"No." Zirael shook his head firmly, his face set in a fury of wrinkles. "This is because you continue to underestimate Cora. She's more resourceful than you give her credit for."

Melusine huffed. She'd been bested by Cora once and swore it would never happen again. But this time was different. This time Cora had joined forces with Zirael's enemy. So this was as much his fault as hers. "You didn't tell me Lenire also had a disk."

"What?" Zirael avoided her eyes.

"You said there were only two disks, one back in Itharus and the one which you have with you now." Melusine adjusted her gaze until Zirael was forced to look at her. "But Lenire had a third. So there were three in total."

"It wasn't important at the time."

"Wasn't important?" Melusine snapped. "Those disks control the Blight."

"Your point?"

Melusine's eyes narrowed. "I'm wondering why you didn't use your disk to help me when Lenire was attempting to wrestle the Blight away. Unless what you were really after this whole time was Lenire's disk, and you were worried about accidentally destroying it."

Zirael didn't respond.

"That's it, isn't it? You could care less about the boy. You wanted the disk he had."

"It's of little consequence now. The disk has been destroyed."

"I don't think—"

"You're fretting over nothing," Zirael insisted. "It's not as if a single oafish knight was ever going to be powerful enough to threaten our combined strength."

Heat bubbled in Meluine's chest. If she could have set his seat on fire just by looking at it, she would have. The heat gave way to doubt.

Given how restless and resistant the Blight had been since she wrested it away from Lenire, she'd started to wonder if the hold the remaining two disks had on the creature had weakened. Lenire's disk was designed as part of a trio. The fact that there were only two left might explain the added difficulty she'd had controlling the Blight once they'd returned from the mountains. Part of Melusine wondered if Zirael already knew that, like he seemed to know everything else. Would she lose control of the creature? *Could* she lose control? Would he try to steal it from her the way Lenire had? That worry settled deep in her mind, picking away at all her other thoughts until it was the only one left.

Zirael abandoned his dinner for his tea. "Besides, now that Lenire's disk is gone, it's not like he can try that trick again. Our plan is still on track. Letting yourself purposefully be seen with Athelian guards has spurred Tenegard into declaring war. A war that will play right into our hands."

"And what if the dragon riders don't take the bait?"

"Trust me. If there's anything I understand better than the Blight, it's a dragon rider. They have a sense of duty to the people. They will fly to Tenegard's aid. And they will fight. Then, while they're busy fighting a war of our design, they'll forget all about the Blight, as you call it, giving you and Serafine time to swoop in and establish yourselves as Athelia's heroes in the conflict."

"My sister wasn't happy about this latest setback."

"I'm sure she wasn't," Zirael said, running his finger over the rim of his cup. "But the goal remains the same. We find the Heart of Tene-gard, use the Blight to drain it of its magic, Tenegard is rendered powerless, and you and Serafine will be declared heroes, securing yourselves a nice, comfy position in Athelia."

"And then you take the Blight back," Melusine said.

Zirael nodded. "Then I get the creature."

It was all he really wanted in the end. Melusine knew that. And now she also knew that he'd probably been toying with her all along, hoping to get the third disk back from Lenire to ensure full control of the creature. She'd agreed to work with Zirael, thinking they were hunting down a common enemy who wanted to destroy the Blight. An enemy that could make her plans impossible if she wasn't careful.

Her skin prickled as Cora's warning surfaced in her memories. Zirael *had* been using her. The fact that the dragon rider had been right angered her even more. The only thing that saved Melusine was the fact Lenire's disk had been destroyed and he'd lost his leverage over the Blight. That was the only reason Zirael was still here now. He was forced to see this through to the end if he wanted to take the creature back without a fight.

And Melusine would give him a fight.

"Don't even think about double-crossing me," Zirael said. "I can see you plotting away over there."

He'd said it so casually, Melusine's eyes widened in surprise. She pulled herself from her own thoughts. "What?"

"I see the way you handle the Shagrukos. The way you speak to it, as if it were sentient. Don't get too attached and think about keeping it. Do you understand me?"

It was no secret that Melusine had been surprised, even a little unnerved by the harsher way Zirael had handled the Blight upon arriving in Tenegard. But she'd reminded herself, as she did again now, that the Blight was a means to an end. It was a tool. And she had to use it however she could to achieve her goal. She couldn't afford to get sentimental and start thinking of the creature as an actual living thing.

"I'm not attached," she muttered.

"Good." Zirael rose from his seat, leaning close enough that his words were uncomfortably warm against her skin. "Because you owe me a debt. Don't ever forget that I am the reason you've gotten this far."

Melusine turned away slightly. "You think too highly of yourself."

He sneered. "Without me you'd still be bumbling around the mountains, trying to figure out what to do next and whispering platitudes to your little pet like a lost child."

Melusine's fist curled and as Zirael left the table, she struck out in a flash of temper, flinging his empty cup after him. Then she sucked in a deep breath, settled her temper, and continued eating. Zirael was a fool if he thought to underestimate her. She was done being manipulated by him. And as she sat there, stewing over his words, she vowed never to let him seize control again.

# END OF DRAGON CRYSTALS
## RISE OF THE DRAGON RIDERS BOOK FIVE

*Dragon Tongue, December 28, 2022*

*Dragon Scales, January 25, 2023*

*Dragon Fire, February 22, 2023*

*Dragon Plague, June 28, 2023*

*Dragon Crystals, July 26, 2023*

*Dragon Wars, August 30, 2023*

PS: Keep reading for an exclusive extract from **Dragon Wars, Pack Dragon** and **The Dragon Tamer**.

# THANK YOU!

I hope you enjoyed **Dragon Crystals**. Please don't forget to leave a review.

Receive free books, exclusive excerpts and be kept up to date on all of my new releases, when you sign up to my mailing list at AvaRichardsonBooks.com/mailing-list.

# ABOUT AVA

Ava Richardson writes epic page-turning Young Adult Fantasy books with lovable characters and intricate worlds that are barely contained within your eReader.

She grew up on a steady diet of fantasy and science fiction books handed down from her two big brothers – and despite being dog-eared and missing pages, she loved escaping into the magical worlds that authors created. Her favorites were the ones about dragons, where they'd swoop, dive and soar through the skies of these enchanted lands.

*Stay in touch!* You can contact Ava on:

f facebook.com/AvaRichardsonBooks

a amazon.com/author/avarichardson

g goodreads.com/avarichardson

BB bookbub.com/authors/ava-richardson

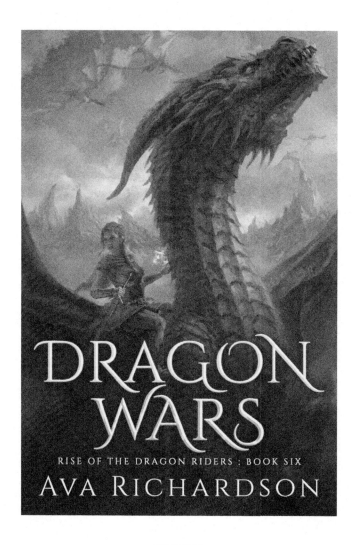

## BLURB

*The Blight must be stopped, no matter the cost...*

Cora and her bonded dragon Alaric have managed to slow the Blight, a sinister plague striking both dragons and their riders. But both the sickness, and the evil mages who control it, are still a threat to the Kingdom. If Melsuine seizes the magic in the Heart of Tenegard, there will be no stopping them.

With the help of the gruff Lenire and newly awakened Faron, Cora and Alaric harness one of Melsuine's own creations to reach the Heart of Tenegard before their enemies. But their success is short lived, when a new battle costs them dearly.

To end the Blight, Cora and Alaric must join all Tenegardian magic together, and cut to the core of the bond between dragons and their riders. To protect her Kingdom, Cora will pay any price.

But can she sacrifice the one thing she can't bear to lose?

**EXCERPT**

**Chapter One**
**Cora**

A sharp gust of frigid wind cut between the mountain shelves and Cora was almost hurled from her saddle.

*Hold on!*

The voice of her dragon, Alaric, broke through the din of thoughts inside her head. He spoke directly to her, using the telepathic connection they shared, and despite the wail of the wind that battered her chapped cheeks, his voice was clear and determined.

Another gale swept between the mountain peaks, threatening to blow Alaric off course, and Cora clung tighter to her saddle, desperate to stay in her seat. *Where did this storm come from?*

*We should get back to camp and warn them before the worst of it arrives,* Alaric said.

Sudden wintery storms were something Cora was still learning to contend with this far into the mountains. The weather was unpredictable, but at least she'd come better prepared this time. She pulled her hood up and squeezed the saddle harder, trying to generate some heat inside her gloves. Melusine, the sorcerer who was determined to use the Blight to destroy the source of all Tenegard's magic, was out there plotting, and Cora wasn't about to let a little cold snap deter her. She had to beat Melusine to the Heart of Tenegard if she had any hope of preserving the country's magic and waking her partner, Faron. Along with the rest of the dragon riders who'd fallen prey to the Blight-induced sleeping sickness, he still lingered in unconsciousness.

*We* will *beat her there,* Alaric assured her, reading the anxious tone of her thoughts. *But there is nothing we can do about this coming storm. Not even Melusine has mastery over the weather.*

Maybe if it was only Melusine they were fighting, Cora would be more certain of their success, but Melusine now had Zirael on her side —the wizened sorcerer who'd come to Tenegard to reclaim control of the Blight. One enemy was bad enough to deal with, but two powerful sorcerers and a mystical creature of destruction were pushing it, even for a group of dragon riders.

*We should turn back,* Alaric said, cutting into her thoughts again. As his words faded, a blast of cold air whipped past them. Alaric slowed dramatically, fighting against the current, and Cora's stomach dropped. She opened her mouth to scream but no words came out, just the howl of the wind as Alaric was forced into a dive.

He twisted between sharpened cliff peaks until he was able to unfurl his wings again. The moment he did, he pierced the side of a rocky cliff with his hooked claws. Cora bounced hard in her seat as she scrambled for purchase, digging her knees into the smooth scales of

Alaric's back. Her fingers were locked in place, curled around the edge of the saddle. She lurched forward, almost pressing her face against the midnight blue scales to avoid slipping and falling off into the dark canyon below. Alaric clung to the jagged peak, his massive wings fluttering and snapping like giant flags against the stone.

*Are you okay?* he asked.

*You were right. We should have turned back earlier.*

*We couldn't have known how bad it would get.*

*Let's drop to that clearing,* Cora said, pointing to a low-lying space between the cliffs. Alaric twisted his massive head around toward where she was pointing. *We've come this far. I think it's worth one more reading to confirm whether or not we should continue here tomorrow.*

*We* have *been making good progress in this direction.* He shifted against the peak carefully, his claws grabbing onto sharp ledges, sending handfuls of round stones skittering down the cliffs. Alaric had once promised to never let her fall. She didn't think she should test that promise now, so she clung even tighter as he maneuvered for take-off. In their current position, a poorly timed gale might force them back against the cliff and Cora would be crushed. She closed her eyes as a chilling gust snapped at her. Tiny ice crystals scratched against her exposed skin. Over the constant wail of the wind, she could hear the scuffing of Alaric's scales against the stone. She opened her eyes. The midnight blue shimmered against the dark gray granite.

*You trust me, right?*

Cora frowned at his tone. *Of course.*

*Then grab onto something.*

Alaric dove backward off the cliff face and the ground rushed up to meet them. For a long moment they were simply free-falling, then Alaric twisted midair, keeping his wings tight against his body to avoid shearing them against the spiked cliffs that jutted up around them. They plummeted through the sky, descending so quickly Cora could suddenly make out the terrain of the clearing below.

A bubble of nerves shot up from her stomach, colliding with the back of her throat so hard Cora thought she might be sick. But then Alaric unfurled his wings and they slowed, coasting over some tall, spindly pines before setting down in the midst of the clearing.

The moment they were on the ground, Cora slid from Alaric's back. Her legs felt like soup. With nothing of substance to hold her up, she plopped down on a rock to catch her breath.

"Are you all right?" Alaric asked out loud. The clearing was bordered by evergreens on both sides, creating a windscreen. Down here they were safe from the gathering storm, at least for a moment, and now that they weren't competing with the wailing mountain wind, they could hear each other easily.

Cora laughed and got to her feet. Her limbs were still shaky but the thrill of the flight had mostly worn off. "For a moment there I wasn't sure."

She removed one of her gloves and reached for him. Her fingers brushed the stubby scales of his snout, warmed by his heated breath. In his dark eyes she could see her own reflection. The wind had picked at her braid, leaving loose hairs sticking up in all directions. She tried to smooth them away with her other hand but only made it worse. "Come on," she said, inclining her head toward a patch of loose gravel. "Let's get to work."

Alaric followed her, his heavy tread making the small stones tremble. Cora knelt down, removed her other glove, and pressed her bare hands against the earth. She always got a better read without her gloves. As she let her magic seep into the ground, Alaric's energy burst through her. Their combined magic sunk deeper and deeper, crawling between dirt and stone, searching for a familiar pull from the river. After the last crystal deposit they'd found had been contaminated by the Blight and turned into an army of hounds, Cora had been forced to return to their old method of manually tracking the magical river back to the Heart of Tenegard.

It was slow-going and draining work, leaving her and Alaric exhausted by the end of each day, but at least their repaired bond made the task easier than it had been back when the Blight was feeding off their magical energy. She was grateful for her renewed connection with Alaric and the use of her full magical strength, especially now, but thinking of all the damage Melusine had caused still made her furious.

Cora channeled that fury and sunk her fingers into the dirt, pushing her magic farther and faster. She closed her eyes, sensing the path with her mind, searching for any sign of the river when it suddenly caught her like a hook around the waist. Her magic lurched into the swarm of energy and her glee at having successfully found the river was momentarily eclipsed by the strength of the magic that swarmed her. It was like trying to navigate the most dangerous of rapids. Cora's magic was dragged along, sinking into the uncontrollable torrent.

*Cora,* Alaric demanded. *Come back!*

The sound of his voice in her head was like an anchor point and she reached for it. Her magic twisted, spiraling around her as if it had been caught in a whirlpool. The force of the river had always been overwhelming, but she was certain lately that its strength was increasing.

*Cora!*

As if he'd grabbed her by the back of the tunic with his teeth, Cora felt Alaric's magic yank her from the river's grasp. The strength of their bond surged around her and Cora's eyes flew open. She was lying flat on her back, staring up at the looming mountain peaks and the darkening sky, the force of extricating herself from the river having knocked her off her feet.

A dark, pearly dragon eye came into view, blocking out the storm clouds.

"Looks like we found it," Alaric said, peering down at her.

Cora laughed. She couldn't help herself. She struggled to sit and Alaric propped her up using his tail. "It's getting stronger, right?" Cora asked. "It's not just my wishful thinking?"

"The signal from the river is becoming clearer," he agreed. "Plus the influence of the heart's magic is starting to show in the land."

Cora glanced around. He was right. For this far into the mountains, at this altitude, the clearing was unusually lush. The evergreens shielded green grass. Rich soil sprouted wildflowers from between rocky crevices. And a thick layer of earthy moss clung to the sides of great granite boulders.

"I'm trying not to get my hopes up, but I think we're getting close." Cora leaned back against Alaric's tail, letting herself relax for a moment. With every pause, every break, Cora was acutely aware of the fact their enemies were regrouping. It had been almost a fortnight since Melusine had fled their last battle. In that time, Cora had been banished from the capital for refusing to send the dragon riders to war with the neighboring nation of Athelia. Under Councilor Northwood's command, Tenegard was gearing up for battle—one that Cora was certain was unjust.

In order to maintain some control over the movement of the dragons, Cora and Strida had divided the remaining healthy dragon riders, forcing them to choose who they would fight for. Those who had chosen to stay allied with Northwood and the council stayed under Strida's leadership, dividing their time between the dragon rider school and the capital. The rest had followed Cora into the mountains.

"Our progress is heartening," Alaric agreed.

"Especially considering the anxious state of the dragon riders this morning." When Cora and Alaric had set out just before dawn, she'd sensed the tension brewing in camp. The hushed conversations. The cutting glares. Cora knew when someone was talking about her. Though she'd left the school with about twenty dragon rider pairs at her side—by their own choice—there was still a lot of discontentment to deal with.

"What are you worried about?"

"That the dragon riders who followed me are starting to regret their choice."

"Why would you think that?"

Cora's lips flattened into a thin line. "You really haven't noticed them all muttering to each other every time I walk by? They're impatient. They're starting to doubt me. My constant absence is only fueling the matter."

Alaric leaned down and nudged the top of her head gently with his snout. "A few of the dragon riders might grumble, but that's only natural, especially given what they've been through recently. Combine that with the stresses of training in a mountain camp and a little frustration is to be expected."

Cora hummed. It had been a stressful couple of weeks. They were constantly patrolling base camp for signs of attack, whether physical or magical, and keeping up with their training for the next inevitable confrontation with Melusine and the Blight. It was a lot to ask without any of the comforts of the school. Still, the weight of discontent was starting to get to her, and Cora wished she could risk communication with Strida or Octavia. There was a communication anchor in Alaric's saddle bag, but Cora had agreed only to use it if absolutely necessary in order to protect their schemes from being discovered. She couldn't upend everything just because she was overwhelmed. That didn't stop her from daydreaming that Faron might come flying over the mountain ridge, having miraculously woken from the sleeping sickness. She always regretted letting her mind wander in that direction. Though she missed him terribly, it hurt to have to drag herself back to reality.

"We should go," Alaric said. His snout turned to the sky, his nostrils flaring. "Snow is coming."

Cora shook off the chill of their flight by a dinner fire. No matter how far she and Alaric traveled, tracking the magic river, they always returned to base camp each night to regroup. They'd settled North of the last remote village where Cora and Lenire had tracked a crystal deposit and then subsequently fought Melusine and Zirael's hound creations with the help of the dragon riders. Cora didn't want to intrude on the village any longer, but the proximity meant the area was familiar.

"Cora?" a voice called as she flexed her fingers above the heat of the flames. She turned in time to see Emmett approaching. Once Northwood's lackey, the capital-liaison-turned-ally had accompanied Cora's group of riders to the mountains. Though he wasn't adept at dragon riding, Emmett had other *talents*.

Get your copy of ***Dragon Wars***
**Available August 30, 2023**
**(Available for Pre-Order Now!)**
**AvaRichardsonBooks.com**

## *Pack Dragon*

### BLURB

*An orphan searching for her future unlocks a destiny she never imagined...*

War has engulfed Destia, reaching even the remote country-side, where foundling Eva Thirsk lives. When army recruiters come to town, Eva sees a chance to find a place where she truly belongs—something she's never found on her adopted family's farm. She enlists, hoping for adventure...and perhaps a chance to learn what happened to her parents.

But when one of her missions goes disastrously wrong, a powerful enemy is accidentally freed. The Venistrare Warlock, sealed away eons ago to protect Destia, has been unleashed—and things begin to *change* for Eva.

Strange visions, an electric sense of energy, and an odd feeling of deep connection to Perrell, the pack dragon she's befriended... If she didn't know better, Eva would think she's somehow gained magic. Including the ability to bond to a dragon, but that's not possible at her age...is it?

As the war rages on, the stakes grow higher each day. Can Eva and Perrell figure out Eva's new powers in time—or will they be consumed by the fires of annihilation?

Get your copy of *Pack Dragon*
**Available September 27, 2023**
**(Available for Pre-Order Now!)**
**AvaRichardsonBooks.com**

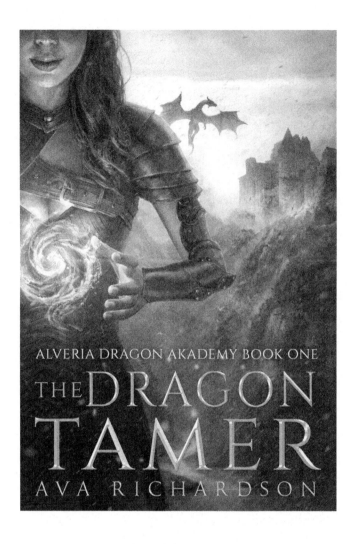

## BLURB

**The bond between humans and dragons has shattered…**

For centuries humans and dragons existed side by side, sharing a mystical bond. But no longer. After decades with no viable eggs, the survival of the Draconic species seems bleak. And the outlook for humans is little better, as rogue dragons raid and torment villages.

In the kingdom of Alveria, seventeen-year-old Kaelen Younger is an outsider, surviving off scraps at the bottom of society. It's a hard life, made even harder by her loyalty to the dragon crown. But when her dying mother reveals a terrifying secret from her past, Kaelen is thrust into a dangerous world, for which she is ill prepared.

Sent to the proving grounds for humans and dragons alike, Kaelen must reconcile both her mysterious past, and her new responsibilities as an Akademy tamer. But when she finds herself falling for a powerful dragon shifter, it will take everything she has to prepare for the danger they both face. The fate of the dragons she has sworn to serve rests in her hands.

Now Kaelen is no longer an outsider. She's the enemy…

Get your copy of **The Dragon Tamer** at
**AvaRichardsonBooks.com**

**EXCERPT**

**Chapter One**

Kaelen Younger cradled her basket under her arm as she skulked through the small, shaded market. She had to cradle it because it was full of eggs she needed to sell if she was going to buy the ingredients needed for her mother's medicine, and she had to skulk because she'd technically been banned from this particular market.

Ducking her head, she scoffed—quietly—as she wove between the vendors who were setting up shop. She was still upset about her banishment, especially since the incident that had caused it hadn't even been her fault. Accidentally break one guy's ankle, and suddenly the whole town turned against you. No one cared that she'd been stopping the jerk and his friends from pickpocketing a helpless old man, or that she'd technically done nothing more than give the boy a single light shove. He had gotten out of the incident scot-free—well, minus the broken ankle, which he'd more than deserved—while she'd been exiled to the lesser market.

Which was right next to the pigpens. In the mud. Where no customer with more than a few half-pennies in their pocket would venture. If she wanted to sell her eggs and herbs for enough money to buy the expensive, imported ingredients for the medicine her mother needed to live, she had no choice but to sneak back into the greater market.

Kaelan ducked her head and gritted her teeth, trying to concentrate on finding an unoccupied stall rather than thinking about her sick mother. Every time her thoughts ventured to the broken-down mountain cabin where Ma lay helpless in bed, Kaelan's stomach flopped over and her head went fuzzy with anxiety, and she'd need all her wits about her if she was going to get a prime price out of her goods. Not to mention avoid getting caught, which would mean the confiscation of every-thing she'd brought to sell.

She couldn't help the ugly and unwanted stir of resentment that always followed on the heels of her anxiety, though. The truth was, Kaelan was sixteen. She'd be an adult in a bare handful of years. She should be ramping up her studies as a healer-in-training, thinking about what she wanted to do with her life. Maybe even, if she was lucky, sneaking off to make out with some hot village boy in a broom closet. She shouldn't have to be here, risking her future and her repu-tation for the sake of selling a few eggs.

She shook off that last thought, ashamed, and shoved the resentment away. Ma needed her, and Kaelan would come through for her. And that was all there was to it.

She spotted a tiny stall in the very back of the market and darted towards it. It wasn't an ideal location, but it was right next to a vegetable vendor whose plump potatoes might bring a few extra customers their way. She made sure her ratty hood was pulled down far enough to hide her black hair and green eyes, and then she set her basket on the low table.

It was too early for the typical morning crowd to make their appearance yet, but she didn't have to wait long for the first trickle of potential customers. All she could see were two torsos, their heads cut off by the hood that draped over her eyes, but she could tell from the shiny buttons and fine leather that they were well-off. She pulled her hood back just a touch and worked up a charming smile which she'd practiced extensively that week since it never came naturally to her. "Good sires," she started off her sales pitch... but they'd already turned away, toward the vegetable vendor's stall.

Worry fizzed in her veins. It was still early in the morning, so she had plenty of time to make her sales, but every moment that passed heightened the risk of discovery. Maybe these customers could be swayed by a discount and she could get out of here quickly. "Good sires!" she called again, raising her voice this time and lifting her hood a little more so they could better see her hard-won charming smile.

The men—no, boys—turned away from their perusal of the potatoes and glanced at her. The worry in her veins turned to lead, freezing her in place. "You," she said, in a less-than-charming tone.

The boy in front—he was about her age—gave her an ugly smile, looking her up and down. His artfully tousled red hair bobbed with the motion. He swaggered back over to her stall and crossed his arms, probably trying to look tough, but the splint on his ankle ruined his pose.

"I thought I smelled a dragon-lover back here," he said, sneering. "I wonder, does the chieftain know you're in the greater market?"

*I may be a dragon-lover, but at least I'm not a pickpocket*, she wanted to reply, but didn't. The boys in town had taken to calling her that name—a slur for someone loyal to the dragon-blooded royal family— ever since her family had moved there. It didn't matter. It wasn't worth getting upset over. What she *did* have to worry about, though, was this jackass or his friend telling the village chieftain that she'd broken the terms of her banishment.

The vegetable vendor glanced over, giving Kaelan a long, suspicious look. The rest of the vendors were still preoccupied with setting up shop, but if this guy turned this into a confrontation, they'd all be on her like flies on a carcass, hoping for some juicy new gossip material. If she didn't convince the boy to move along quickly, her chances at a clean getaway would be shot.

Her mind skittered. What was his name? She couldn't recall it. All the guys were the same here, at least as far as she was concerned: a bunch of self-righteous jerks, bullies and proud of it. "Don't you have anything better to do than make trouble for me?" she tried, knowing it wouldn't work. "Surely I'm not worth wasting your time on."

The boy's ugly smile dropped. "Funny thing," he said. "Normally, I *would* have something better to do right now."

The other boy leaned forward, his sour breath wafting between them. "Knattleikr practice was supposed to be this morning," he said. "But thanks to your little stunt, Bekkr here is off the team till next season, and he was our captain. Which means the town's lost its chance at attending finals. You're now officially the least popular person in Gladsheim. So, if you ask me," he said, reaching out a finger and poking her arm hard, "making trouble for you *is* the best use of our morning."

Her heart sank, but before she could say anything in her own defense, Bekkr cut in.

"Actually," he said to his friend, "I think you do have something to do right now, don't you?"

The boy frowned, but then his eyes widened in understanding. He sent a leering smile at Kaelan before he trotted back toward the center of the market.

There was only one place he could be going—to tell the chieftain she was there. Hissing a curse under her breath, Kaelan snatched up her basket and wheeled for the side exit, but Bekkr caught her by the arm.

"Where do you think you're going, dragon-lover?"

Her temper flared and she yanked her arm away. "Stop calling me that!"

His eyes went mean and squinty, the way all her tormentors did when she lost her temper—because that was their goal. She huffed out a breath, frustrated with herself for taking the bait. She should know better by now.

"Why?" Bekkr taunted. "That's what you are, right? Well, let me tell you something, *dragon-lover*. You're not welcome here."

As if she hadn't figured that out on day one. Dragons and the dragon-blooded ruling class weren't popular in Gladsheim, nor were those loyal to them. The way these villagers looked at it, dragons used up the kingdom's resources and gave the common folk little in return. Kaelan had never agreed with that outlook, in part because she knew dragons provided many irreplaceable benefits to the kingdom. The other part of her feeling on the subject was, admittedly, due to her own fascination with the creatures.

She shook herself. She had to get out of the market before the chieftain had her goods seized. She tore herself free from Bekkr's grip and wheeled around to face the vegetable vendor. "I'll give you a thirty percent discount on these eggs and herbs," she said quickly, evading

Bekkr as he grabbed for her again. She kept her eyes on the vendor. Her offer of a discount would mean she'd only be able to afford broth for dinner again, but at least it would leave her enough to pay for the medical ingredients she needed. "You can sell them for much more than that and make a profit."

The woman squinted at her. "Don't need no eggs or herbs," she grunted, and then turned away as if Kaelan was invisible.

Kaelan groaned. What now? Should she try one or two more people in hopes of getting a sale here, or run before the chieftain arrived? Realistically, she knew she should run. It was the smart choice. She still had a chance at making a sale in the lesser market even if it made her next to nothing. But just as she turned to flee, Bekkr's hand snaked out and yanked her basket away. "Hey!" she shouted, trying to grab it back.

Bekkr smiled, holding the basket up out of her reach. Damn his tallness. "Say Queen Celede is a worm and I'll give it back."

Her blood boiled at the derogatory nickname for dragons. When the boys goaded her, it made her angry, but she was used to it. She'd be damned if she'd stand by and let him mock someone else, though—especially a descendant of the dragons she admired. "Queen Celede is a good ruler," she said staunchly. She had no idea if it was true, of course. She'd never been to Bellsor and never so much as seen the ruling family, but she was a loyalist at heart, and plus, at this point she was liable to disagree with anything this jackass said on general principle.

He raised an eyebrow, took one egg out of the basket and dropped it. She yelped and scrambled to catch it, but it hit the ground too quickly, splattering yolk all over the hem of her cloak. She fumed helplessly as he picked up another egg and held it aloft.

"One more chance," he said. "How about Prince Lasaro this time? Everyone knows he's not fit to rule, anyway. None of the royal brats are."

Her temper snapped. She took two jerky steps forward and shoved him, much harder this time than she had when she'd broken his ankle. He stumbled backward, that stupid grin slipping off his ugly face as he had to drop her basket and the egg to reach out and catch himself on a table.

She grabbed her basket and stood above him, raging. "You," she growled, "are *nothing*. All of you, including those other boys you hang out with, you're *nothing*. I don't even have to know Prince Lasaro to know he's twenty times the man you are. Now stay down before I break your other ankle."

She didn't dare look up, but she could sense everyone in a five-stall radius training their attention on her. Now that she'd made a scene and ruined all chances of escaping notice, she tucked the basket under her cloak in hopes of at least making a quick escape with her remaining goods intact. If she got out fast enough, and if there were already a few customers in the lesser market, she *might* still be able to sell her goods for maybe a third of their worth. If she was lucky.

She started to turn and nearly impaled herself on a dragon's skull.

Get your copy of *The Dragon Tamer* at
**AvaRichardsonBooks.com**

Printed in Great Britain
by Amazon